Larry Ivkovich's genre work has been published in over twenty online and print publications including Penumbra, Afterburn SF, Shelter of Daylight, SQ Magazine, Tower of Light Fantasy, Shoreline of Infinity, Beyond the Karlan Line, Star Quake1 , and Triangulation.

He has been a finalist in the L. Ron Hubbard's Writers of the Future contest and was the 2010 recipient of the CZP/Rannu Fund award for fiction.

Larry is a member of WorD and the Pittsburgh Mindful Writers Group East, two local writing and critique groups, as well as the statewide group Pennwriters.

T0118912

Kim Yoshima Adventures published through IFWG Publishing

The Sixth Precept (Book 1, The Spirit Winds Quartet)
Warriors of the Light (Book 2, The Spirit Winds Quartet)
Orcus Unchained (Book 3, The Spirit Winds Quartet)
The Return of the Luminous One (Book 4, and last, The Spirit Winds Quartet)

A Concerned Citizen (chap-ebook only)

The Return
of the
Luminous One

BY LARRY IVKOVICH

Orcus Unchained

All Rights Reserved

ISBN-13: 978-1-925956-26-9

Copyright ©2019 Larry Ivkovich

V1.0

Printed in Palatino Linotype and Last Ninja.

IFWG Publishing International
Melbourne

www.ifwpublishing.com

ACKNOWLEDGEMENT

At the ending of the Spirit Wind Quartet, I want to thank IFWG Publishing, especially Gerry Huntman, Grace Chan, and the great editors I've had during the last eight years. Their support, patience, help, and faith in my books has been deeply appreciated and valued. You all are the best!

Dedicated to Tim DeSantis, friend and fellow SF nerd.

This one's for you, Tim!

CAST OF CHARACTERS

PITTSBURGH, 2011:

Kim Yoshima—Former lieutenant/detective with the Pittsburgh Police. Inheritor of psychic powers who time-traveled back to medieval Japan to fulfill an ancient prophecy, in which she was referred to as "The Yomitsu" and "The Luminous One."

Wayne Brewster—IT analyst whose crime-fighting ambitions evolved during his adventure in medieval Japan with Kim. Possibly mind-linked to an alternate reality where super-heroes really exist.

Shioko Yoshima—aka the "Glorious Ko" from medieval Japan's Jade Court during the Veiled Years, and conqueror of the warlord Omori as a young girl at the Pavilion of Black Dragons in the Sixteenth century. As an adult, she lived in modern-day Pittsburgh with Kim.

Jackson Yamaguchi—aka the "Principal Advisor" for the Jade Court, and friend and mentor to Shioko. Member of the secret society, the Shuugouteki (Collective) in 2010 who worked to fight the warlord Omori's minions throughout five centuries.

David Amamoto—Shuugouteki head of security at Spirit Winds, Inc.

Bernadette Cameron—Shuugouteki security guard.

Jonas Thompkins—Maghi agent.

Andera Martouse—Maghi agent.

Xavier La Tan—Illustrious Master of the Totou.

Rebecca Parantala—Totou Inquisitor

Bobby Yoshima—Kim's nephew.

Ken Yoshima—Kim's brother.

Marjorie Yoshima—Kim's sister-in-law.

Joe Martin—Security head of Lazo Sibulovich's Old Books and Research Haven.

Osamu Ikehara—Aide to La Tan.

Mara Gellini—Shuugouteki counselor.

The Prime Breeder—Also called The Source of All Things. Female shadow-tracker forced to help create a race of her hybrid kind.

ODAWARA, Sixteenth Century:

Yoshima Mitsu—Presumed dead ancestor of Kim Yoshima.

Omori Kadanamora—Defeated and presumed dead tyrannical warlord of Odawara. Sworn enemy of the Yomitsu.

Hiroshi Yoshida—Chancellor of the Jade Court and former slave of Omori's Samurai freed by Wayne Brewster, aka the Ebon Warrior in feudal Odawara.

Midori Nakamura—Princess of the Jade Court and former Guardian of the Sleepers.

Zaronal—Last and leader of the Sleepers, mystical beings awakened after centuries to help fight against the warlord Omori alongside Kim and the others. A Warrior of the Light, revealed as rogue Maghi Amedio Zaronelli.

Eela/Martin Sakai—Omori's right-hand man and breeder of the shadow-trackers (also referred to as the Founder). Reputed to be a witch (majo), he was, in truth, a member of the Totou (a cabal allied against the Shuugouteki) and is from the future Pittsburgh of 2010.

Takeshi—Aide to Eela.

Izanami—Attendant to Shioko at the Jade Court, once the goddess of creation and death.

Agura the Hunter—Spectral hunter from the ambient-milieu.

VENICE, 2011:

Lazo Sibulovich—Retired police officer and close friend of Kim. Owner of a rare book store/research center.

Jenny Sibulovich—Acclaimed popular physicist/writer, and Lazo's wife.

Lenora Calabria—Resident of Venice and self-proclaimed Monster Hunter.

Edmondo Vincherra—Aide to Lenora.

Lydia Carpensco—Aide to Lenora.

Estansa Milaar—Lamia/Vampire and Grand Mistress of the Maghi in Venice, Italy.

Marceeka—Bat-like humanoid and servant of the Maghi.

Daiyu—Chinese sorceress and aide to Lenora.

Roberto—First Lord of the Maghi and servant of Estansa.

Bella–Servant of the Maghi.

ArcNight—Masked vigilante/super hero from an alternate reality trapped in our world.

Antonio Calabria—Lenora's son.

VENICE, Fifteenth Century:

Lorenzo Portera—Scholar and inventor. Friend of Daiyu.

Papstesel—Chimeric creature of the Mystic Realm.

JAPAN, Early Twentieth Century:

Yoshima Ayako Mitsu—Grandmother of Kim Yoshima. Keeper of the Shuugouteki's Sacred Artifact and bearer of the title, "She-Who-Comes-Before."

Pascal Lukungu—Congolese ancestor of Jackson Yamaguchi and revered member of the Shuugouteki.

THE YOKAI (both Light and Dark):

Damara, the jorōgumo/Spider Demon—Mythological creature of an alternate reality where such beings actually exist. Pulled into our world by a disruption in spacetime.

Amanozako—Winged, hybrid goddess creature also trapped in our world by the same spacetime rift.

Komainu—Guardian lion-dog.

Hiroshi—wolf Ōkami.

Trell, the Kirin—Unicorn-like creature, parts deer, unicorn, horse, and ox. Able to call forth lightning and heal injuries. A Warrior of the Light.

Azure Seiryuu—Guardian Spirit Dragon. A Warrior of the Light.

Jaraal, the bakeneko—Cat being/shapeshifter and a Warrior of the Light. Also trapped in our world.

Renta'Mur—Karura soldier/Sensitive, servant of Azure Seiryuu.

Susanoo—God of Sea and Storms.

CASTLE DE GROOT, 2011:

Parker—Reincarnated soul of Omori Kadanamora.

Mr. Tammelou—Aide to Parker.

T'sai the Huntress—Kim lookalike who is an alternate incarnation of Agura the Hunter.

Dwayyo—Appalachian folk monster displaced by the Spirit Winds.

Peter Gurkovsky—Team Leader, Shuugouteki DragonEye Hunter-Squad

Steven Kikuchi—Team Second, Shuugouteki DragonEye Hunter-Squad

KINGDOM OF THE KONGO, Late Nineteenth Century:

Kutumba Coulibaly—Shuugouteki Seer.

DARTHAM CITY:

Ronald Angrini, aka FireDragon—Comic-book hero of ArcNight's world. Has the ability to turn into a fire-breathing dragon.

Kim Yoshima—Alternate version of Kim in ArcNight's world. In this universe, a writer and poet.

THE VOID:

a'Kasha, the Archive

GROUPS/ ORGANIZATIONS/ ALTERNATE DIMENSIONAL REALMS:

Shuugouteki (Collective)—Secret centuries-old society dedicated to fighting the Totou in order to preserve the timelines and keep Japanese history intact.

Totou (Cabal)—Secret centuries-old society dedicated to usurping the timelines in order to pervert Japanese history and gain uncontrolled power.

The Guardian Spirit Convocation—A military group made up of the avian humanoid karura who serve the Azure Seiryuu.

Ambient-Milieu—Mental dreamlike universe inhabited by numinous entities both living and dead. Also called the Dreamspace.

The Dark Demesne—More an altered state than a physical existence, one of evil, cruelty, and twisted desire.

Mystic Realm—Ancient Venetian world of mythological creatures.

Aizenev—Alternate-Reality version of Venice, once home to the Maghi.

The Sanctuary Conclave—Home to the Sanctuary Elders, guardians and administrators of the ambient-milieu.

The Akashic Records—Interdimensional time-spanning repository of all knowledge throughout the multiverse.

Shadow Clans—Precursors to the Maghi.

PART ONE: CHRONONAUT

Time traveling isn't all it's cracked up to be. Or will be. Or won't.

Or hasn't been. Or never was.

Kim Yoshima

PROLOGUE

The Archive

A vortex, a maelstrom of cosmic proportions, a'Kasha churns with unlimited power, Its spectral surf crashing onto intergalactic shores. Intertwined throughout space and time, It thrashes and shudders in a clash of opposing primal forces. Ancient, unknowable, It strives to unleash Itself throughout the ages and branches of the multiverse, to keep Itself in check within the nexus of existence in order for the Balances to be maintained. Its powerful duality, formed during the Great Beginning, wars constantly. To contain Itself and the annals of knowledge and history, It absorbs and stores of all times and places. To unleash Itself to share that knowledge, to advise, to cajole. To contain Itself. To unleash itself. Over and over infinitely.

Arcs of blue lightning, temporal energy, surges and convulses like enormous, flailing tentacles. Streamers of coronal flares explode, erupt, cascading outward. Across the multitudes of stars, galaxies, nebulae, dimensional and temporal rifts, a'Kasha spews winds of turbulent energy, only to rein them back into Its numinous, whirling heart.

Until...

a'Kasha senses a great awakening. Its awareness sparks exponentially. An event of elemental importance transpires on an insignificant world, in a time and place seemingly inconsequential. An entity, an indigene of that backwater planet, reaches out to a'Kasha, unaware it has done so.

Great power resides in the indigene, more than even the entity Itself suspects. A Warrior of the Light. But such a warrior! The indigene and others of its kind know of a'Kasha but call It by another name.

The Void.

The Warrior struggles to correct the universal Balance of her world as a Dark power arises in opposition. Another indigene, a Warlord of great power, whose actions threaten to upset the multiverse. A conflict as old as time. Yet, a'Kasha senses this situation is different, somehow manipulated in favor of the Dark and its Warlord servant. How can that manipulation have occurred? How could a'Kasha not have anticipated this before this moment? It wonders. Somehow, the eternally-maintaining mystical forces of the cosmos have been distorted. Corrupted. Perverted.

Curiosity, a heretofore unknown concept, overwhelms a'Kasha. Plus a desire to correct this unnatural imbalance burgeons within It. And so a'Kasha finally breaks Its spectral bindings and ages-old precepts...

And becomes involved.

Shuugouteki Enclave

Soyo Province, Kingdom of Kongo

1863

With a loud gasp, Kutumba Coulibaly exited the Farseeing trance, his body trembling. The Shuugouteki seer's heart raced, his mouth dry, his head throbbing beneath graying, corn-rowed hair. His sleeveless robe clung wetly to his thin, brown-skinned frame, drenched in sweat.

What had he just divined? He had thought to look ahead to discern the immediate future of his master, the Honorable Pascal Lukungu. Instead, Kutumba had glimpsed a power, a hidden force outside his comprehension. A vast realm, a...repository of wisdom, lore, and knowledge.

a'Kasha? The Void? Strange designations, ones that filled Kutumba with confusion and perhaps a little fear. How had he envisioned such a wonder? And these indigenes a'Kasha sensed? The Warlord and the Warrior? Who could they be? For, surely, the "backwater planet" mentioned must be Earth!

Did his master know of this? The Honorable Pascal Lukungu had talked of the Spirit Winds, the temporal displacement tremors, and their time and space-spanning capabilities. But, from what Kutumba had farseen and intuited, this Void controlled those immense powers with an intelligence.

It possessed life. Of a kind.

Candlelight and the sweet scent of incense surrounded the seer within the meditation hut. Constructed simply of wood, plaster, and thatch, the hut possessed one window and a single door, both closed and latched on the inside. Kutumba rubbed his eyes. Through the wooden slats in the window blind, Mount Nabemba rose in the distance above the Nzere River. Smoke from the Shuugouteki enclave's communal cooking fire spiraled into the clear, blue sky.

Kutumba slowly rose from his sitting position on the reed mat. His knee joints cracked, aching from the time sitting cross-legged during his self-imposed trance. He must hurry and inform his master. The Honorable Pascal Lukungu must know of this Void phenomenon!

But to contact Master Lukungu would be difficult. He had left on a great journey two weeks ago to meet with the Shuugouteki Elders in the island-nation of Japan. Master Lukungu had to explain how the Collective must first locate what Lukungu referred to as the Sacred Artifact. Once found, several copies of the book written by one Samuel Kim must be printed. It was crucial to distribute those copies detailing the teachings of the mysterious Asian philosopher Yira in order for the Collective to conduct a search for the esteemed personage known as She-Who-Comes-Before.

The book, The Five Precepts to Enlightenment. The writings which would put future events in motion, allowing the great hero, the Yomitsu, to be brought forth into the world.

How will they even know where to look for the book, let alone make copies? Kutumba wondered for the thousandth time. He and Lukungu had talked of this at length more than once after his master had arrived from the future at the enclave by the Spirit Winds. Yet, Lukungu had reassured him, the events concerning the book had already happened, and so must not be too difficult to arrange. Strange words indeed. And yet Lukungu's expression belied his outward confidence. Nothing, it seemed, would be easy in this endeavor. Including Kutumba contacting his master.

Kutumba looked at the possessions his master Lukungu had left behind. Spread in front of the seer and used to assist in his farseeing, an object stood out among the coins, handkerchief, and comb owned by his master.

His master's cell phone. Kutumba marveled at the communication device, unable to function in this past time. He blinked. What was this? A small circle of light shimmered in the device's small screen, blinking like a wayward star. It expanded, lighting up the hut's interior with a soft blue radiance. Overcoming the candlelight, lambent streamers wove within and about themselves to knit a glowing blue nimbus. Taller and wider than a person, it pulsed and shimmered above the floor. Shards of luminance winked in and out, forming and rearranging like one of the new kaleidoscope instruments Kutumba had seen.

A voice intoned from within the strange nimbus, its words filling the meditation hut. <<Kutumba Coulibaly.>> the voice said, vaguely female-sounding and seeming to intone from the very air itself. <<You're needed.>>

Kutumba stared. The voice called him by name! His knees weakened, buckling. Before he collapsed in fear and astonishment, a tendril of light reached out from the nimbus and encompassed him. A comforting warmth flowed through him, calming and strengthening.

"Who…who are you?" he asked, enthralled.

The voice replied, softly yet clear. <<I'm an Elder of the Sanctuary Council. Those numinous beings who monitor the ambient-milieu and other levels of the multiverse. I'm here because of the fragmenting of the timelines and the disquiet of the Archive. These are matters we must correct. Solutions for this have been put off far too long. Like in any bureaucracy, unfortunately.>>

The Archive? Does this Elder mean the Void? And the ambient-milieu? More strange words! Yet, he asked the most important question first. "What…what does that have to do with me? You said you need me? How can such a powerful being as yourself need someone like me?"

<<You're part of one of those solutions, Kutumba Coulibaly. You'll help to write the book. The Sacred Artifact.>>

"I?" Kutumba's pulse raced. Was he still farseeing in some way? This was more like a dream, confusing, strange, of a nature he couldn't interpret.

The nimbus roiled, its shape churning. <<Yes. It's your destiny.>> A pause. <<I've always wanted to say that.>>

Was the Elder making a joke? "But how? The book was written long ago by a man named Samuel Kim, not I."

The nimbus shimmered, evoking a chortling sound. Did the Elder now laugh at him? What kind of numinous being was this? <<No.>> the voice said. <<The Five Precepts to Enlightenment hasn't yet been written and yet it has. Such are the temporal paradoxes of the multiverse. Confusing and utterly irritating. Yet there's always a beginning and you must be part of one such beginning. You and another will both be Samuel Kim. And a third will be the philosopher Yira.>>

Despite the calming influence exerted on him, Kutumba's mind reeled with bewilderment. "I still do not understand."

<<You and one other lucky person will both be Samuel Kim with a

third taking the part of Yira. Try to keep up.>>

"Two of us? Who is the second and the third you speak of? How... how can this be done? Did not Samuel Kim and Yira truly exist?"

<<All will be revealed in time. As for the how of it, leave that to me. I'll return periodically during this process to check in. But you must travel to a level of the ambient-milieu to begin the work. I'll transport you there. You'll need to be ready to leave tonight. You know, get out of town by sundown, that kind of thing.>>

"Travel to the ambient-milieu? And what will I tell my master and those I attend to here?"

<<Relax and don't worry about any of that. Pascal Lukungu will have other matters to contend with for a while. He won't return here for some time. The members of your enclave will be assured all will be well in your absence.>>

"This strange portent I have envisioned. This Void..."

<<The matter of the Archive is out of your hands. Don't worry about that. It'll be attended to as well. In time.>>

Kutumba felt as light as a feather. The Void truly was this Archive? "May...may I take my acolytes with me?"

<<You sure do ask a lot of questions!>>

Kutumba bowed. He didn't want to offend this being! "For...forgive me..."

<<Just kidding. No, your acolytes must stay here. All will be provided for you and the others, although you may want to bring some writing materials of your own. Maybe some incense, that kind of New Agey thing. Most importantly, say nothing of my presence in this matter. It could piss a lot of people off. >>

Piss off. "You have a most interesting way of speaking," Kutumba said, a smile forming.

<<It's a gift. Will you accept this responsibility I put before you?>>

Of course! "I will, noble Elder. Thank you for putting your faith in me."

<<Don't thank me yet. None of this stuff ever runs smoothly, believe me. And, unfortunately, we can't pay you for your services, though we do have a health plan of sorts. I can't believe I'm about to say this, but the fact you're doing something to benefit all of humankind and beyond should be reward enough.>>

"Yes, Yes! I agree."

Afterwards, Kutumba walked outside into bright morning sunlight. Moabi trees, palms, and high grasses surrounded the Shuugouteki Kongo enclave and its village. A warm breeze whispered over him. His attention focused on the huts, outbuildings, and the central square, that had been his home for many years. He was barely aware of his two acolytes as they gathered around him.

"Wise One," Emeka said. "We heard voices and saw a strange light. Who were you talking to?"

A strange being with a distinctive voice, he thought. One with a sense of humor perhaps. "Emeka, Imamu," he said to the young man and woman. "I will explain later. In the meantime, fetch ink, quills, and paper. A great quantity of each. I will need your help to prepare for a journey."

"As you wish, Wise One," Imamu said with a puzzled frown. "For what purpose?"

"I must go away for a while." Kutumba smiled. "There is a book, a very important one, which needs to be written."

Venice, Italy

Luprio Sestieri

C.E. 1457

Lorenzo Portero reveled in his newfound ability to read the Chinese language. The fact his friend, and self-confessed sorceress, Daiyu of the East, had magically bestowed that ability on him, further added to his rapt enjoyment and sense of wonder. Not only a Maghi, Daiyu was descended from the Dragon's Conclave, a group of powerful mages and adepts from the far-off eastern realm of China.

How extraordinary! Never in his logical, reasoning, scientific life did he ever think he would find himself in the midst of such miraculous, mystical wonder.

Daiyu's "hidey-hole," as she described it, was marvelous! The underground chamber which served as the sorceress' secret refuge lay beneath an abandoned chapel only a short walk from Lorenzo's own humble abode. He had passed the chapel many, many times, and never suspected what lay hidden beneath. But, then again, invisible and unapproachable warding spells conjured by Daiyu concealed this location from all but a select few.

Lorenzo felt honored to be one of those few. Especially since his life would soon be cut short by a fatal illness. He thanked the Divine for this gift of new knowledge allowed him near the end. A simple hip-length brown tunic and white woolen trousers garbed his short, still-portly figure, though the illness strove to strip the meat from his bones. Long white hair fell from a balding pate past his shoulders. His brown eyes, despite the constant pain he struggled to hide, twinkled at the sights around him.

Four floating glass orbs, the size of a human head, illuminated the long rectangular chamber. Petrified wood pilings bordered the richly carpeted floor. Lorenzo marveled that the pilings, which served as part of the upper foundation helping to keep Venezia afloat, functioned as walls. Bulging floor-to-ceiling bookshelves, Daiyu's library, lined one of those walls. Many of the tomes had been saved and preserved secretly by the sorceress from even the powerful First Lords of the Maghi.

A couch and chair were placed against the opposite wall. An archway opened into a small comfort-niche. Lorenzo sat at a desk upon which sat a small globe, candles, and a large, faceted crystal inset into a bloodstone base, its purpose, he suspected, more than decorative. A pleasing aroma of basil drifted throughout the chamber. A tray of fruit, cheese, bread, and a bottle of wine had been set out invitingly.

Which Lorenzo had yet to partake of. He had become too immersed in his reading, which he discovered, he now could execute incredibly fast. Again, no doubt, because of his friend's magic. He had been able to peruse several books and scrolls quickly and expertly. Daiyu had asked him to study whatever subjects he could find on the idea of "mind control." What he found could be useful to her, she had told him, especially since she had experienced the phenomenon of being controlled by another's thoughts herself.

His sorceress friend had gone to a gathering of the Maghi assembly, she a reluctant and rebellious member of that insidious group. Lorenzo desired very much to find the answer for her before she returned. He hoped she had encountered no danger. If the Maghi discovered Daiyu now worked against their evil machinations, her life would be forfeit.

He wished there was some way to know if she was safe. He had been so absorbed in his studies he had momentarily forgotten her. As he shifted his position in the chair, he accidentally brushed his fingers against the bloodstone base of the crystal. A slight humming emanated from it. The crystal lit up with a blue radiance. Lorenzo watched in astonishment as an image formed in its faceted surface.

Daiyu appeared therein, still garbed in her black Maghi robe and cowl. She entered a small canal aboard a strange vessel, rain falling over all but that vessel. A boat, constructed entirely of shells and glittering gemstones, surrounded by a thin aura of light, transported her as if under its own power to the edge of the canal. None of the few passersby paid any notice to Daiyu and her magical craft (for what else could it be?). The sorceress disembarked and the boat simply…vanished.

Ah, how wondrous! Lorenzo thought, a great relief washing over him. This must mean she has returned from the assembly meeting safely and will be here soon. What type of boat was that?

Before Lorenzo could take a breath, Daiyu walked through the door.

"Daiyu!" Lorenzo exclaimed. "I am glad you are safe."

"Lorenzo, my friend," she said, throwing back the hood of her cloak. Rainwater dripped onto the floor. Daiyu's green eyes flashed in the candlelight. "It has happened again. I was taken over by that same presence. But now I know who, what, that presence was, though not how the act was accomplished. We have much to discuss. How have you fared in your reading?"

"I believe I understand a little, though I fear I cannot be of more help. But this mind-control has happened to you because of your ability to work magic, no? This power of yours allows you to breach the confines of time itself, to reach out to touch or to be touched by the mind of another, who also possesses a similar type of magic."

"That could explain it, though it was an act performed without my knowing."

"You said you knew who this possessing presence was."

"Yes." Daiyu gave Lorenzo a strange look, as if she, herself, didn't believe what she was about to say. "The one who possessed me was myself, from a future time."

Lorenzo's mouth dropped. He had not expected that revelation. "Truly?" He chuckled and shook his head. "I must confess, Daiyu, despite discovering magic is real, it still seems so incredible."

"But now, with your confirmation as to how this mind contact might occur, it must be real." A questioning look shadowed her face. "You have activated the Divining Globe?"

"This?" Lorenzo looked back at the glowing orb. "Not purposely, I assure you. It reveals you sailing back here in a wondrous boat."

"From a short while ago, yes, that is true. A craft presented to me from one like myself, a renegade against his own kind. A papstesel of the Mystic Realm."

"A papstesel. A legendary beast. More astonishing happenings! But, look, what is this?"

Daiyu came to his side and both watched other images form in the crystal's depths. A whirlpool of blue light spun within. Lorenzo gazed into the crystal, fascinated.

The light spoke.

<<Lorenzo Portero.>> a woman's voice resounded from within the crystal. Daiyu gasped.

Which somewhat unnerved Lorenzo. "I…yes, I am he."

<<And Daiyu of the Dragon's Conclave.>>

"Yes, my Lord." As powerful as his friend was, Lorenzo detected a hint of awe in Daiyu's voice. She placed a hand on his shoulder and squeezed. Without thinking, he reached up and covered her hand with his suddenly trembling one.

Gyrating within the small glass sphere, the light enlarged right before Lorenzo's eyes, encompassing an entire wall of the chamber.

The light continued to speak. <<I'm a Sanctuary Elder, Master Portero, of the ambient-milieu.>>

"Sanctuary Elder? Ambient-milieu?"

<<Yes. Daiyu knows of us.>>

"I'm sorry, Lorenzo," Daiyu said. "There's much I haven't told you."

<<I'm not here to harm either of you.>> the Elder continued. <<But you're needed, Master Portero.>>

"Needed? Whatever for?"

<<To assist in the writing of a book.>>

"A book?" Lorenzo leaned back in the chair. This was very strange indeed.

"What kind of book, my Lord?" Daiyu asked.

<<One that will change everything. I know, I know, pretty corny, huh? We Elders have to say things like that to sound dramatic. It's in the manual.>>

"I... I beg your pardon?" Lorenzo said. What odd words!

"It's all right, Lorenzo," Daiyu said. A smile curled her lips. "It appears you have a more important role to play in this tableau than I thought."

<<Very true.>> the Elder continued. <<Now, two things. I'm not really a Lord, at least I haven't gotten used to that title yet. More a Lady.>>

"My Lady," Daiyu said. "And the second thing?"

<<Lorenzo Portero, before you begin this task, we've got to get you back in shape.>>

"In shape?" It seemed his only responses to this being were questions!

<<Can't have you being sick, can we? Consider this, as I indicated to your co-writing partner, part of our health plan.>>

An undulating tentacle of light reached out from the nimbus and enveloped Lorenzo. He gasped as a comforting warmth flowed through him. A healing warmth. After a moment, he looked up at Daiyu and began to laugh.

PAST IMPERFECT

To reach the Inner Self, we must walk our own path.

The Sixth Precept

FIRST INTERVAL

Odawara, Japan

C.E. 1912

Ah, the old one is here.

The Hunter manifested into a wide and spacious room within a private medical clinic. The spectral spoor of his quarry's essence had led him here—a human era of the early Twentieth Century. A single window, with the curtains pulled back, allowed sunlight to brighten the room's clean and organized interior. A ceiling fan slowly turned above the wooden floor. Mokuhanga block prints hung from the walls. A faint smell of incense wafted through the air and small ikebana flower arrangements were situated throughout.

The bed was empty. The patient now dozed in a nearby chair, dressed in a dark suit. The Hunter studied the old gentleman, the elder's suitcase and silver-tipped cane lying at his feet. Despite his illness, his will is still strong, the Hunter thought. He desires to leave this place. And so he shall.

The Hunter cocked his head. What is this? The empty space in front of the old gentleman shimmered, gathering together to form a human shape. A woman of the mortal world. And more. Dressed like a warrior in bamboo-and-leather armor, she stood facing the Hunter.

"Yomitsu," the Hunter said softly, hiding his surprise at the appearance of the famed Warrior of the Light. "And so we meet."

Appearing startled herself, the woman stepped back. "You...you see me?"

"Indeed. I have that ability." He regarded her with a coolly appraising gaze. "You are often discussed within the ambient-milieu. I am honored. I wonder, though, how it is you inhabit the phase-shifting stream. Your strength and abilities are well known, but to phase-shift is extraordinary."

The Yomitsu recovered quickly from her surprise. "Phase-shifting stream? So that's what I've been experiencing rather than the usual temporal displacement tremors?"

Experiencing? So, she does not control her shifting. "Of a sort. Phase-shifting is an offshoot of the tremors but is able to be manipulated by those within the stream. And those who can manipulate it are of the highest power." The Hunter smiled. "Except in certain situations."

"Like what I'm going through now. So that really does mean someone else is pulling the strings. Sending me off on these trips into the past? The Dark Demesne?"

Agura started in surprise. "The Dark Demesne? I know nothing of that."

"Above your pay grade, is it?" The Yomitsu shook her head. "Who are you and why are you here?"

The Hunter held back a rebuke at the insolence, even though it was given by such a prominent entity. He had no time for petty protocol and certainly none for explanations. Yet her mention of the Dark Demesne troubled him. "I am Agura. I have been charged to find this honorable elder seated here."

"So you've found him." The Yomitsu studied the old gentleman. A strange look came over her face. Her manner changed. "Now...now what?"

"I regret I have little time to converse. The elder has a journey to make and I must escort him to his destination. Perhaps we will meet again." The Hunter placed his hand on the old gentleman's shoulder, leaned down, and whispered in his ear.

―――――――――

Ambient-Milieu

Sanctuary Elders Stronghold

Agura the Hunter stood before the Sanctuary Conclave. His white eyes unblinking, he kept his tall, black-robed body completely at attention. Despite his own immense power, he knew his place in the midst of the Sanctuary Elders, those who patrolled and supervised the many levels of the ambient-milieu and the multiverse.

Those he served.

He put the memory of his meeting the Yomitsu from his mind. He'd thought it had been a chance encounter, despite her ignorance of the phase-shifting stream. Now, he wasn't so sure because of her mentioning the Dark Demesne. That level of the ambient-milieu was not easily accessed, permission rarely given. Odd indeed. He would consider it later, after he'd made his report to the Elders.

The Stronghold's domed Conclave chamber roof arched high overhead. Fragments of colored luminance lanced through slotted windows. Around the sides of the oval room, light-orbs shed more uniform radiance. Runic designs flashed serpentine over the walls, their blue and silver hues flickering and shining.

Six of the seven Conclave members hovered over a jeweled, mosaic floor, their amorphous forms pulsing. Four of the entities had only just joined the Conclave, Agura knew, replacing others in a recent hierarchical adjustment. The balance of power and its accompanying change in some of the Elders' governing principles had shifted. One such change had been the ending of the ages-long conflict between the Elders and Azure Seiryuu, the Guardian Spirit Dragon, and her Guardian Spirit Convocation of karura soldiers.

A wise move in Agura's opinion. Such a cold war had proven too distracting and counter-productive and had gone on for too long, though he would never venture such an opinion to those he served. Though, now that changes had occurred within the Conclave, the Elders might be more amenable to differing points of view.

There was also the attack on the milieu by the shade of the daimyo Omori Kadanamora. Some of the milieu's levels had been overrun and annexed by the powerful spirit-avatar of the ancient warlord. Until a legendary Warrior of the Light had repulsed the attacker on the milieu's Plain of Becoming. Agura knew this incident had contributed to the modifications enacted by the Conclave.

Still, he wondered about the missing seventh Elder, one of the newly appointed ones. Why wasn't it here?

<<Report.>> The command emanated from nowhere and everywhere. <<We have a quorum despite our comrade's absence.>>

"My Lords." Agura bowed deeply, his long, white, braided hair falling about his wide shoulders, his long-nailed hands clasped in front of him. His normally whispery voice carried loudly within the Conclave chamber's acoustics. "My mission has been completed. The resurrected goddess Izanami-no-Mikoto obeyed the Conclave's order. Adhering to the request of the human, the Glorious Ko, Izanami has evoked the Spell of Unknowing to disallow any knowledge of the Jade Court's existence in history until the correct time period. In this way, future events will unfold as they should."

<<And her punishment for breaking her spectral imprisonment?>>

"She has been informed of her banishment to the houjin city of

Odawara during the shrouded reign, the Veiled Years, of the Jade Court."

<<She did not oppose this?>>

Why would she? Agura thought. Izanami, once the goddess of creation and death, had herself died giving birth. But her spirit had re-coalesced after her death, becoming strong enough to allow her to regain her goddess powers and to escape her earthly tomb at Mount Hiba on the Nipponese islands. Forsaking her past and adopting a human persona, she found refuge as the Glorious Ko's attendant and Regent at Odawara Castle. She'd hidden well, even foiling Agura's search for her for many years until he finally tracked her down. Initially, with the previous Elder regime in power, Izanami would have had to leave Odawara and return to the Plain of Heaven, leaving her second life behind. Now she could stay in Odawara with those houjin she had come to love.

"No, Lords, she did not oppose this."

<<Well done.>> The Elders' aspects whirled and shimmered. Even with Agura's acute senses, the Hunter had to concentrate to keep them completely in his sight. <<And what of this arrangement of yours with Izanami. Tell us.>>

Ah, Agura knew he couldn't hide that from those he served, not that he would. He bowed again. "Forgive me, my Lords, but in return for the great and dangerous lengths Izanami and Ko enacted to protect the future, I agreed to help find one of their comrades. The Principal Adviser of the Jade Court known as Jackson Yamaguchi, he who had become ectopic, displaced within the timelines."

There had been another reason he decided to locate the Principal Advisor, one Agura wouldn't share. The Hunter intuited Izanami and Ko had become more than just a ruler and her servant. He had loved once and been loved in return. It had been a very, very long time ago, yet he recognized the signs of such affection. He had to admit, sensing the women's closeness had helped him to make his decision to find the Principal Advisor. A moment of weakness on his part? Perhaps, but he didn't regret it. Agura steeled himself for a rebuke from the Elders, at the very least.

<<We approve.>> The Elders announced. <<Now we have another task for you.>>

Agura relaxed, somewhat surprised. Yet, what more did they require of him? "Yes, Lords?"

Two figures approached from the side of the chamber, concealed until now. Agura arched a white eyebrow in surprise. One was a karura, garbed in protective leather armor, avian features commingling with those of the human. A set of golden wings lay folded at her back. Yes, definitely a female, Agura observed.

The second was also a woman, but of the human Nipponese race, a houjin. Tall, with long dark hair, she stood barefoot and dressed in simple sashed, cotton trousers, and short jacket. She radiated a certain power, one that belied her common appearance. Interesting, Agura thought, appraising her more closely.

Both took places near the Hunter, bowing to the Elders. The Elders spoke, <<Agura, this is Lanta'Gen, the Guardian Spirit Convocation's Aerie Leader.>> The karura turned and bowed to Agura who returned the courtesy. She remained in subtle, constant motion, feathers quivering, arms and legs shifting position. But her golden eyes gazed steadily at Agura.

<<And this is Yoshima Mitsu, guardian of the milieu level The Sea's Blissful Garden.>>

Ah yes, but she is more than that, Agura thought, bowing to the woman, once called the Luminous One. Yoshima Mitsu had started certain spectral events in motion long ago as a mortal, events whose effects still lingered, still influenced. It had been she who protected the ambient-milieu by destroying the shade of Omori Kadanamora. She too, affixed the Hunter with strong, dark eyes.

The Elders continued. <<Now that we have settled our differences with Seiryuu, her convocation has made a request of us which includes Yoshima Mitsu. We have agreed to this request in return for their assistance in stabilizing the Archive a'Kasha.>>

Ah, a common problem has brought the Conclave and the Convocation together then. Agura had been informed of a'Kasha's mysterious break and independent thought, its actions causing rippling effects throughout time and space. Could this explain the absence of the seventh Elder? Possibly, possibly, but not entirely. Agura wondered if there was more to the missing Elder.

<<You will assist Yoshima Mitsu and Lanta'Gen.>>

"As you wish, my Lords. What is the nature of this assistance?"

The karura stepped forward and spoke first, her beak-like mouth forming the words carefully, her voice rich, melodic. "Noble Agura, our mistress Seiryuu is lost to us and one of our soldiers, Renta'Mur, who had gone to find her in the earthly realm, is now also missing. We humbly request your assistance in locating them. But, I fear there is more."

The woman, Yoshima Mitsu, took up the explanation. "Noble Agura, a powerful demon has been foolishly summoned. Even now, he attempts to breach the already-weakened Veil Between Worlds."

"Who is this demon?"

"A creature purported to be of the mythos of the mortal land of Italy, known as Orcus. But I believe he is not the true Orcus, that is, not the Orcus of Italy, but a demon from a Place Apart."

Agura's eyes narrowed. A Place Apart. That of an alternate reality.

"However, this creature, even as a secondary demon, poses a threat just as great. At this point, he is contained within an interdimensional Zone of Concealment between the earthly realm of Venice, Italy, and the secondary realm of the Maghi city of Aizenev. I believe this Zone of Concealment has been created to straddle both worlds by magical means in order to conceal a faction of the Maghi and serve as a base for their machinations. I have been able to glean some of this information, and deduce more, from my spirit-bond with the one known as the Yomitsu, who was present at the demon's manifestation. Do you know of her?"

"Or course." How ironic! Agura once more recalled conversing with the powerful, multiverse-spanning, protector of history, and Warrior of the Light. This female standing proudly in front of him possessed more than an ancestral spirit-bond with the Yomitsu, he remembered. Yoshima Mitsu was, in fact, the previous incarnation of the mortal Kim Yoshima, the Yomitsu. Impressive. And humbling.

Before Agura could speak of his meeting the Yomitsu, the Luminous One continued, "I communed with the Yomitsu a short time ago within the Blissful Garden to explain the weapons she now possesses to fight this Orcus. I then sent her back to the simulacrum of Venice created within the Zone of Concealment to confront the demon. At least that is what I intended."

Agura listened, his interest growing. He cocked his head. "And so?"

For the first time, the Luminous One paused, her expression darkening. "And so, she has vanished, not returning to where I transported her. I cannot sense or contact her anywhere. Our spirit-bond has been severed. Though I am not completely certain, I do sense a'Kasha may be manipulating, in part, the Yomitsu's journey."

Ah, within the phase-shifting stream. Yes, possibly. Agura glanced at Lanta'Gen, who stared intently at Yoshima Mitsu. "So then," he said, returning his attention to the other woman. "For what reason do you suspect a'Kasha has for this manipulation?"

"I do not know however my greater concern is this—I also sense another presence, another force, warring with a'Kasha's hold upon the Yomitsu. Hence her disappearance."

Agura turned toward the Elders. "My Lords, is this presence the Honorable Yoshima Mitsu describes apparent to you?"

<<No. We sense a'Kasha's hand in this but that is all.>>

"Your spirit-bond," Agura said, once more addressing the Luminous One. "The spectral connection you have with the Yomitsu is strong enough to allow you to feel some of what she feels."

"I believe that is true, yes." The Luminous One surprised Agura by showing a trace of uncertainty upon her face. "Noble Agura, I know it is much to ask but, as well as tracking Seiryuu and Renta'Mur, can you locate the Yomitsu as well?"

Agura blinked. It wasn't often he was taken by surprise. "I already have."

The Luminous One started. "How so?"

<<Indeed. Explain.>> The Elders roiled, their forms darkening. So, even the all-knowing Elders expressed surprise at his revelation.

"I encountered the Yomitsu in the phase-shifting stream upon locating the Principal Advisor. I know not how she came to be there nor did I know then you sought her."

"Ah, so!" Yoshima Mitsu clapped her hands. "Then she survives."

"Yes, but she claimed she had no control of her movements within the phase-shifting stream."

<<a'Kasha has done this.>>

"I suspect now that is so, Lords. For the most part."

"Can you find her again?" Yoshima Mitsu asked.

Agura pondered that question. As a Hunter, he had been endowed with certain abilities, some extremely powerful. "There is a way, a method I have employed before when so required. With the Elders' permission, I can retrace my own temporal spoor to that exact moment, time, and place, and manipulate the phase-shifting to experience the encounter again. But I can also alter some of what transpires. This will allow me to alert the Yomitsu to your concern and attempt to find out what has happened to her and possibly to the Azure Seiryuu and her karura soldier. Now that you and the Honorable Lanta'Gen have supplied me with these facts, I have a sense the three entities may be connected."

"As do we," Lanta'Gen said.

Agura turned to the Elders. "My Lords, will you allow me to manipulate the phase-shifting stream and alter my encounter with the Yomitsu?"

<<We will.>>

"Then you will help us?" asked the Luminous One.

Agura had been assigned many difficult tasks by the Elders over

27

the millennia. But this one might prove to be the most stimulating, if not maddening. Three entities to track and locate. He wasn't the only spectral hunter available to the Elders. He ventured another question.

"Will I be acting alone in this endeavor, Lords?"

<<Yes. We do not wish to incur undue curiosity and attention in this action. It is still too soon after our truce and the other Hunters are involved in various assigned tasks. We rely on your superior talents to complete this hunt successfully.>>

Well, Agura always enjoyed a challenge and, really, what choice did he have? The Elders had already decreed it and he was a Hunter after all. Hunting was what he did best. "I agree to the task," he said with a bow. "Thank you for your trust in me."

He turned to Yoshima Mitsu and Lanta'Gen. "Honored Ones. I am at your service."

CHAPTER 1

The ouroboros is an ancient symbol common in many
cultures, a symbol which the Totou readily adopted.
The circular depiction of a dragon or snake swallowing its own tail
may represent the idea of eternal renewal, of constant re-creation.
Or, as our Eminent Lord undoubtedly desired, returning to settle an
old score.

Xavier La Tan, Late Illustrious Master of the Totou

"You know of this Orcus then?"

"A demon of the under-realm. Yes."

"A demon. I thought he was the demon."

Enigmatic as always, Yoshima Mitsu continued unabated. "You possess a powerful weapon to fight this creature. That is why I am here with you, to explain it, and to give you another protective talisman."

The amulet Kim Yoshima wore warmed against her neck and chest. She touched it. "This? The... the cornicello?"

"Just so. And these sora gemstones, the source of the karura's strength, will augment the amulet's power. Though you are not karura, you will be able to utilize their energy."

Mitsu held her hand out. Within her palm rested three small but dazzling gems. Each the size of a marble, they blazed red, green, and yellow. Kim thought of the pouch hanging from the karura Renta'Mur's belt where he must have kept the gems.

She took the stones from Mitsu and closed her fingers over them tightly. "Now you must go," Mitsu said. "May the sun goddess Amaterasu protect you."

Kim knew better than to ask any more questions. Mystery, confusion, and self-discovery frustratingly abounded in this ethereal realm. Still... "But, Mitsu-san. How do these stones work? Renta'Mur told me he was a Sensitive, attuned to the power of the sora stones. I'm not any of that and, Hell, how does the cornicello work for that matter? Can't you or the karura come back with me? You said you'd explain. I'll need help!"

"Help awaits you. Trust in this, Kim-san. As always, your path unfolds as it must."

"Easy for you to sa..." And then Kim felt herself yanked like a yo-yo on a string and she was gone.

29

And made a left instead of a right...

Ambient-Milieu

A force of dark power reached for her. She cried out, her voice smothered by the rushing stream of energy propelling her through this numinous realm. A vicious, desperate entity, clawing and hungry, tried to intercept her, to tear her away from the cosmic path she traversed.

An entity that felt oddly and terrifyingly familiar.

Odawara, Japan

1520 C.E.

The blanketing luminosity dissipated; a glowing radiance faded before Kim's blurred vision. The now familiar roaring in her ears subsided, the sense of unreality fading. She leaned back against something cool and solid, taking deep breaths. That was a rough one, she thought. A wisp of a memory faded from her mind, a sense of great fear and danger sparked then vanished. Somehow, this trip through the Void had been a little different, more intense, if that was even possible. She shook her head, disoriented, but just for a moment. It didn't matter how difficult the journey had been, as long as she had returned to face off against the Orcus demon. She had to help Zaronelli and Jenny!

Except for one thing.

She blinked, starting in surprise. This wasn't Venice, that is, the false Venice Edmondo Vincherra had described as a "Zone of Concealment." Kim didn't stand in the rubble of the destroyed alternate City of Masks. Instead, she faced a narrow, muddy alleyway, bordered on each side by small, wooden thatch-roofed huts (one of which she leaned against). The alley ended in a circle of wooden shanties, garbage baskets, privy sheds, and boarded up lean-tos. A dead-end littered with trash.

An alleyway. Part of a slum? A depressed area of the city called the Gettoo in feudal Odawara. How did Kim know that? Shioko, she thought. She described the Odawaran Gettoo where she had first been taken by the displacement tremors. This must be it! Have I gone back in time again?

She automatically checked herself for any injuries. What in heaven? She no longer wore the jeans, T-shirt and sneakers she'd donned since reviving in Lenora Calabria's apartment in Venice. A type of samurai armor now covered her body. Kim had been outfitted in a flexible, lightweight bamboo-and-leather armored uniform, boots, and gloves. Thin links of chainmail lined the uniform. She touched her hair, done up in a topknot. A small cloth pouch was tied to her waist, along with a sheathed kaiken dagger, one of the preferred weapons of the onna-bugeisha, a group of feudal Japanese female warriors Kim had read about.

A good weapon to have, Kim thought. Thanks, Mitsu, though I hope I don't have to use it. Her new look and protective gear had to have been provided by her ancestor, from the ambient-milieu. Kim allowed herself a soft laugh. Whatever worked. At least the armor fit her perfectly. Of course, Mitsu and I are the same size.

She pondered again, why had she been sent to this blighted area? This ghetto, instead of the false Venice? Kim shook her head. She, or a mental avatar of herself, had just been with her ancestor/incarnation Yoshima Mitsu in the ambient-milieu through what Mitsu called their "spirit-bond." Mitsu had presented her with three of the sora gemstones, a source of the warrior karuras' power. Those, along with the cornicello amulet Kim still wore, given to her by the courageous and selfless Lydia Carpenscu, could be used to fight back against the Orcus demon.

Kim still gripped the gemstones in her fist, not exactly sure how to use them. The amulet remained a mystery as well. Frustratingly, most of the help given her from such magical sources were never fully explained. Their purposes always had to be discovered on her own, it seemed.

But Orcus rampaged back in a different Venice, a simulacrum where Jenny Sibulovich and a long-missing Wayne Brewster were trapped. Where the sorcerer Amedio Zaronelli lay mortally wounded. Where Edmondo Vincherra had been killed helping her. Wasn't Mitsu supposed to return Kim there so she could stop Orcus?

She needed to find her friends!

Not another multiverse screw up! Kim thought angrily. She placed the gemstones in the waist pouch, realizing her firearm had gone missing, the Luger lost somewhere along the way. To balance that loss, Kim no longer felt tired. The aches and pains from Orcus' attack didn't bother her. Which was a good thing, and her revived energy was possibly another gift from Mitsu.

The sound of voices and approaching footsteps caught her attention. Two figures walked toward the end of the alley. A woman came into view. She looked to be a peasant but, even at first glance, that appraisal seemed not to be entirely true. A small girl, a child really, dirty, barefoot, dressed in rags, her long hair unwashed, walked behind the older woman.

Kim gasped. Shioko! Shioko as Kim had found her in the North Side warehouse last year where Kim had fought the male shadow-tracker. Shioko, as the One Child, had been transported from feudal Japan by the temporal displacement tremors from this spot just like she'd told Kim.

And the woman with her was Yoshima Mitsu. Alive in the past mortal world as a shirabyoshi, an artist/entertainer, now disguised as a laborer. Both women walked past Kim as if she didn't exist.

They can't see me, Kim realized. Or sense my presence.

Kim reeled for a moment. She thought herself long past being shocked by the twisty, magical courses her life had taken. Those were almost second nature to her now. Yet, a chill ran up her back upon seeing her past incarnation and the young Shioko. The only other time she had glimpsed Mitsu in the flesh outside of the ambient-milieu had been after the shirabyoshi had been killed. Kim had taken on her identity in order to confront Omori Kadanamora at the Pavilion of Black Dragons at Odawara Castle to prevent the skewing of the timelines.

Why was Kim here at this moment in time, in Odawara, Japan. Again?

She watched, transfixed, as Mitsu knelt in the mud and spoke to a tearful Shioko, telling her she would be sending the child away forever to safety. To the future, to one who would care for and protect her. Kim's chest swelled, her breath catching. Shioko's future savior was Kim herself. The older woman rose and walked back the way she had come. But then, she stopped at the sound of Shioko's choking sobs. Mitsu turned, ran back, and embraced the child.

"Please, Mitsu-san, please..." The girl clung to Mitsu, crying pitifully. "Why can't you come with me? You will be in danger too if you stay!"

"I cannot come with you," Mitsu said, her voice breaking. "It is not the will of the kami. My Dreamspace visions saw only you escaping, and only fleetingly at best. And I cannot stop it. It is what must be, no matter what. I can only help in this small way, as whatever happens is already written." Mitsu released Shioko and backed up. "Goodbye, Shioko-chan," she whispered. "I love you."

This is it, Kim thought, caught up in this past drama, forgetting her own sense of urgency. This is where the tremor whisks Shioko to the future.

But something felt wrong. Kim's esper abilities had evolved to where she could sometimes sense the Spirit Winds approach and also guide them to their destination. She had done so when directing Shioko from Pittsburgh back to this era. Now, she sensed nothing. Was it because of her present state of invisibility or whatever she consisted of at the moment? Or was it something else?

Abruptly, the sora gemstones through the waist-pouch, and the cornicello amulet, radiated a pulsing heat. As if in...warning?

Could the temporal displacement tremors be off course? Kim watched Mitsu turn away from Shioko, a momentary confused look transfiguring her features. She didn't detect the tremor either, though she had seen it arriving here in what she had called her Dreamspace visions, those images from out of the ambient-milieu Mitsu could foresee.

Acting solely by guesswork or instinct, Kim projected a beam of esper energy at her ancestor, her past incarnation. It resolved successfully in Mitsu's neural realm, igniting within her Dreamspace.

The women's energies merged. Kim gasped at the sensation, the expansion of both their minds feeling like a jolt of caffeine. Like a beacon, their minds reached out and took hold of the wayward Spirit Winds with a powerful mental tether. Kim felt the tremors as if they possessed substance, a form, as they latched onto her and Mitsu's combined energy. For the first time, Kim observed the Spirit Winds from outside their imprisoning influence. They appeared as serpentine whips of blue temporal lightning, fixed into a single column of unimaginable, blazing power.

Yet Kim felt no resistance from that power as she and Mitsu pulled the tremors toward the Gettoo.

"Mitsu-san!" At the sound of Shioko's last, wrenching cry, the temporal displacement tremor arrived to scoop up its small, young passenger. The ground spun out from Kim, and, once more, she faded away.

Zone of Concealment

C.E. May 2, 2011

Kim stood shakily on broken concrete, the air filled with dust and the stench of burning wood. Covering her nose, she waved away ragged flakes of ash, falling like dark snow. Images of the young Shioko and Yoshima Mitsu in the Odawara alley replayed themselves in her mind. I helped them, Kim marveled. I worked with Mitsu to get Shioko to the future.

"I am Orcus. But you may know me as the devil. Satan. Iblis. Beelzebub. Apophis. Superna. The list of what I have been called throughout the ages is endless."

Kim whirled. Once again she stood before the smiling Orcus demon in what Edmondo Vincherra had described as a crossroads of space and time, a Zone of Concealment created to resemble Venice, where the Maghi basically hid in plain sight. Now that realm had been devastated, as if struck by an earthquake. Zaronelli had described it as "An incitement of dark magic. Of ancient demonic powers." Orcus' violent entry through the dimensional barrier had reduced much of this Venice to rubble. The demon devoured Kim with his gaze, his stunningly handsome figure surrounded by a glowing red aura.

I'm back! Right at the moment I left! Kim thought.

Orcus' smile changed then, contorting into a wide maw full of black needle teeth. The blue eyes turned reptilian, its head, the blond-hair and flawless features became skull-like. "You," it said, its voice harsh and grating, like fingernails scratching a chalkboard. Orcus had expanded, standing over eight feet tall now. In his true demon guise, he seemed even larger, towering over Kim like a hideous wraith. "Have you followed me here, then? I ask you once more, who are you?"

Anger burned within Kim at what this monster had done. Injuring Amedio Zaronelli, killing Edmondo. Edmondo had died from Orcus' attack while bravely leading her and Zaronelli into this strange concealment zone. Still, Kim paused, studying the creature. What did it mean asking her if she'd followed it? Asking her once more who she was? The demon seemed to think they'd met before.

"I have no idea what you're talking about." Well, now that she thought about it, maybe they had met. Who really knew at this point? Plus, Kim really didn't care anymore. "And you don't scare me one bit."

"Well, then," Orcus said. "I'll have to remedy that."

The demon reached out with a clawed hand. Dazzling red streamers erupted from its fingertips. Kim stood her ground, forming a deflective psi-bubble around herself. The radiant blasts curved around the mental shield, exploding harmlessly behind her. She dropped the bubble and let her anger take over, reaching deeply into her neural realm. Her esper energy amplified, her body shot through with increased strength. A pressure built up at the base of her spine and rose upward, culminating in a bright lambent explosion within her mind.

A psi-stun erupted, stronger than Kim had ever produced. Flaring tracers shot from her fingertips and flashed from her eyes like lightning.

Molded into a blazing blue arc, it struck Orcus in the chest. Once before she'd felled a giant oni in the same way. Unlike then, this was personal.

The monster howled and stumbled backwards. Surprise twisted his monstrous features as he dropped to his knees. The creature struggled for breath as it spoke, "What is this? How…have you come by this power?"

Taking advantage of Orcus' confusion, Kim struck again. Using her telekinesis, she lifted and flung a large chunk of debris at the demon. It struck Orcus in the head, causing him to lurch sideways. Kim hit him again with a second psi-stun, and, though weaker than the first, still knocked the demon over onto his back.

"This is for Edmondo!" Kim screamed, fully energized, her psi-powers exploding, fueled by rage and determination. Mentally grabbing a still-standing wall of a damaged building, Kim pulled the brick remnant over and onto the downed Orcus. It buried the demon beneath shattered and smoking rubble.

Kim stood, hands clenched at her sides, trembling, breathing hard, dust and ash whirling around her. For the first time in a long time, blood leaked from her nose. Her head pounded. She had exerted a lot of her power and energy. Too much...

She wobbled, her legs unsteady. Ah shit, she thought, feeling light-headed. She tried to self-rejuvenate with her telekinesis but much of her strength had been sapped. She wiped her nose with the sleeve of her uniform.

Yomitsu.

A voice in her head. Zaronelli.

CHAPTER 2

Fallen warriors of ages past are not ephemeral.
Their spirit, their loyalty, their courage, live on forever.

Takeo, Sohei Warrior Monk

Aokigahara, the Sea of Trees
Honshu Island, Japan
C.E. 1390, Nanboku-Cho Period

Zaronal the mahoutsukai shouted in defiance. The sorcerer fought against the murkiness shrouding his mind, the powerful magic launched against him and his followers. The sounds of battle surrounded him, the war cries of his samurai and the brave people of Odawara who had joined them, the roaring and screaming of the spectral enemies attacking them, the smell of blood. Despite their courage, he and his followers fought defensively, losing ground.

Here, in Aokigahara, the haunted Sea of Trees, an army of monsters had been unleashed. Forces of the Left Hand Path had marshalled in a bid for ultimate conquest of the Nipponese Islands. A horde of giant oni and kijo had arisen in the Sea of Trees. Both ogres and ogresses had been made even more powerful by the ghost of a malignant magician, his yūrei spirit escaping from the after-realm and channeling the phantom energy emanating from nearby Mt. Fuji and from the mysterious Sea of Trees itself.

Zaronal's own magic resurged, desperately pushing back the formidable dark forces directed against him and his followers. His invisible foe retreated, allowing Zaronal to center himself and regroup his warriors. The samurai rallied, battling against the yokai set against them. The ogres and ogresses, in spite of their great size and strength, fell back. The power of Zaronal's sorcery swelled like a great wave.

37

A hissing sound, a deadly perturbation in the air, reached his ears. Despite his protective armor, Zaronal sidestepped from another attack. An arrow shot past him and imbedded itself in the tree behind him.

At that moment, everything changed. The world dimmed, became shrouded in a misty ambiance. He no longer stood on the battlefield.

A displacement spell, Zaronal thought. I've been transported to another plane of existence.

A man strode through the mist toward Zaronal. Like the mahout-sukai, he carried a longbow in one hand, a quiver of arrows slung over his back. Like Zaronal, he gripped a katana in his other hand. No armor covered his tall, muscled frame though, only a tunic, trousers, and sandals. Arrogant and confident in his approach, he halted a few strides away.

The magician Hamamoto Iwao. Or rather his yūrei, his ghost.

"You're finished, Dark One," Zaronal said. "Pull back your yokai or they'll all perish. Return to Yomi, the after-realm, the World of Darkness, where you belong."

A smirk spread over Hamamoto's scarred face. He dropped his quiver and bow and unsheathed his katana. Positioning himself in a guarded stance, he held the weapon with both hands before him, pointed at a slight angle toward his feet. Tendrils of mist curled about his ankles like serpents.

"You and I, sorcerer," Hamamoto said, his voice barely above a whisper. "We'll settle this now. Winner take all. I will never go back to yomi. In this place Between, I'm as corporeal as you. No magic, just the skill of the blade will decide our fates."

With an ear-splitting cry, the magician raised his sword and charged. Zaronal rushed forward to meet him, his own katana held high. Both swords met with a resounding crash, sparks igniting from their silvered surfaces.

A throbbing vibration shot down Zaronal's arms as the two weapons clashed. Zaronal stumbled backward from the force of the blow, and barely parried Hamamoto's next strike. The sorcerer's vision blurred, his reflexes slowed. Of course, the magician had lied, bespelling this place to weaken Zaronal. Hamamoto Iwao meant to win at any cost in his bid to resurrect himself from the dead and control the Nipponese Islands.

Seeing an opening, Zaronal lunged toward his opponent. Hamamoto dodged the blow and swung his katana, striking Zaronal on the back of his head. Zaronal's protective helm flew off and he fell to his knees. His head burst with pain, his ears rang. He looked up. "You have no honor!" Zaronal cried hoarsely to Hamamoto. "Coward! Filthy dung-eater!"

Hamamoto laughed. "And you? You hide behind that armor, pretend you're someone you're not. Where's the honor in that? Oh, yes, I know who you are, First Lord of the Maghi. Once I'm done with you, I'll absorb your foreign, barbarian magic and nothing will be able to stop me." The yūrei stepped closer and raised his katana for the killing strike.

Close enough! Zaronal thought and raised his right hand. Hamamoto wasn't the only one who could be deceptive. At Zaronal's magical command, the cornicello ring encircling his finger flashed to life in a corona of orange light. The horn-shaped gemstone, worn as protection against the Evil Eye, was more than just an Italian superstition. Especially when employed by an expert wielder of magic.

Hamamoto cried out and stumbled backwards, his longsword flying from his grip. At that moment, a flash of blurring motion, dark and fast, burst from the mist and struck the magician. It dragged Hamamoto back into the enclosing fog. The magician's screams echoed, becoming fainter until fading away to nothing.

Zaronal stood, the ring crumbling away from his finger into dust, its magic spent. He blinked and sucked in his breath. The hairs on the back of his neck tingled. Three ethereal figures stood before him, their limbs and heads moving sinuously, their torsos shimmering like reflections in a smoky pool. Though he'd hoped the "barbarian" magic of the ring would be useful, he hadn't expected it to lead guardians of the after-realm to their escaped prisoner.

For surely, that's what the aspect of these beings had to be.

One of them raised its translucent hand as if acknowledging Zaronal's inadvertent assistance. And then they were gone.

In a heartbeat, Zaronal found himself back on the killing plain of the Sea of Trees. Even though the magician had been defeated, the tide of battle had once again turned against the samurai. Zaronal took a defensive stance as an oni charged him.

With a grim smile, he met the beast's attack.

Dreamspace

A deafening wave of sound.

An explosion of light, shards of emerald, azure, motes of silver and gold.

He stood on a small, rocky island in the middle of a vast lake. A giant red tori gate towered above him, its crosshatching lintels casting a long shadow onto the surface of the calm blue water. Far off on either side, jagged, snow-capped mountains circled the lake, a meadow of tall grasses sprawling between.

He watched calmly as a pinpoint of light flashed above the lake at eye-level a few yards away. The light grew, expanded into what he could only describe as a portal. A window to other times and places. Other worlds.

Images of events-to-come flashed by within that glittering expanse. The Spirit Winds. The Prophecy of the One Child. The rise to power of the Eminent Lord. The sohei warrior monks. Shadow-trackers. The disruption of space and time.

A girl-child, threatened by the edict of the Eminent Lord commanding all such children to be killed. The arrival of the Spirit Winds to save that child. Her guardian, her elder sister sacrificing all for her.

And, there! A young black man lying injured in a teahouse in Odawara, wearing the clothes of a far-future era. A girl, the teahouse proprietress, tending him. He smiled. He knew her, or, more precisely, he would know her and serve her. Someday.

A second image replaced the first. An awakening. The correct ritual performed, the exact incantation recited. All enacted by the same young proprietress, she who was the Guardian of the Sleepers. Of him.

Finally, a more mature woman, a warrior, appeared. Felling a giant oni by her "gift of the mind." Rallying the people of Odawara to free themselves from their oppressors. The Yomitsu.

The Luminous One.

He heard an intake of breath at his side. Turning, he beheld another standing beside him, watching those same events. She, too, a woman, much like the Luminous One but dressed in the garb of an entertainer. The girl-child's elder sister. A shirabyoshi.

She turned and returned his gaze.

Aokigahara, the Sea of Trees

Honshu Island, Japan

C.E. 1390, Nanboku-Cho Period

So, he thought. That's how it will be. How it must be.

Zaronal breathed heavily, the battle finally over. Even the hot, smoke-filled breeze felt good on his sweaty face. He knelt on one knee, his rainbow-hued armor, soot-blackened, scratched and dented, his katana blood-stained, his breath rattling in his throat. His great bow lay broken at his side, but as a practitioner of the Way of the Arrow, he had exacted brutal justice against his attackers before his beloved weapon had been destroyed.

The battle with the dark yokai had left the sorcerer and his warriors sorely weakened. Though they had been the victors, their lifeforces had been sapped by the deadly spirits' powerful magic. Only eleven of the twenty samurai Zaronal led had survived the battle. Those survivors lay exhausted or dying on the rocky killing field beneath the shadow of Mt. Fuji, their armor covered in blood and gore. Smoke rose from the thick haunted forest behind them, clouding the afternoon sky and the sight of the sea beyond. The blackened bodies of the yokai lay scattered on the scorched, hardened lava that formed the island's surface here. The stench from their dissipating dark souls rose into the air.

With Zaronal helping to drive the yūrei magician back into yomi, the World of Darkness, Hamamoto's minions had lost their bloodthirsty zeal. Zaronal and his warriors stopped their attack and defeated them, But at a great cost.

There's only one thing I can do to save these brave men, Zaronal thought, appraising his wounded warriors. Only one thing he knew, as a mahoutsukai, the word for sorcerer in this exotic, foreign land…only one thing he was still strong enough to accomplish. For he knew they'd be needed again. They had won this battle today, but more would be fought. The enemy, those of the Left Hand Path, would return.

He had seen it in a vision.

"Lord Zaronal!" A follower of Zaronal's samurai rushed to his side. Nakamura Fuyumi, a resident of Odawara, wore her own style of leather and bamboo armor, holding a broken sword in one gloved hand. Zaronal picked up and donned his helm, the horned helmet and stylized mask completely covering his head and face. He'd never revealed his true nature, his European heritage, to these people. He was not Nipponese, but he gladly served the inhabitants of this land, having come to admire and respect them.

"Ah, Fuyumi-san, I rejoice you survived."

"You've saved us all, Lord Zaronal." Fuyumi knelt beside him, her face full of concern. "You are truly the Demon Queller."

The Demon Queller, a legendary being, a Radiant One and Warrior of the Light. He balked at such a designation. He wasn't worthy. Too many had died today. "I and my samurai couldn't have succeeded without you and your people's courage, Fuyumi-san. We are all demon quellers this day." Several of the villagers of the fortress city of Odawara had joined Zaronal's "army," willing to help in the battle against the yokai. Many had died as a result.

Fuyumi blinked back tears. "You're hurt. Your men are hurt."

"That doesn't matter now." Zaronal took a deep breath. What he was about to ask was no simple request. "I have a great boon to ask of you."

"Anything, Lord."

"My warriors and I will die unless I give them time to heal. A very long time. Despite Hamamoto Iwao's defeat, his magic was very powerful. We must sleep to dispel the effects of the black conjuring he used against us today, the magical sickness pervading our bodies. It has to be a sleep of generations. You and your family and your descendants must conceal us and look after us until we are well and needed again. Do you understand?"

Fuyumi looked stricken. "No, Lord, I do not. What of the warriors' families, their wives and children? And of my own family? What will I tell them?"

"My men, like myself, have no family, no loved ones. We're all ronin, unattached, serving no masters. It's one reason we gave so much of ourselves in this battle."

"Oh, Lord Zaronal."

"Listen to me, Fuyumi-san. I've just had a vision. It came to me after the heat of battle. It's a vision of far-seeing into a future time. A savior known as the Luminous One will one day come to the Nipponese Islands in a time of great upheaval, when the forces of the Left Hand Path will rise again and be even more powerful than before. The advent of a dark-skinned man from another time and place will precede the Luminous One, a herald of her impending arrival. You must pass this knowledge on to your descendants so they'll recognize the signs and be ready to awaken us."

"But how will we transport you back to Odawara in your wounded conditions? And how will we awaken you?"

"We must be hidden here in Aokigahara first, to be transported by boat back to Odawara at some later time. There's a cave in the foothills of Mt. Fuji where we can begin our sleep. I'm not yet completely spent. I can use my remaining power to convey myself and my samurai to this cave." Zaronal bowed his head. "I don't ask this of you lightly, Fuyumi-san. You and your people have already suffered so much. If you accept, you and those who come after you will have the burden of a great responsibility to fulfill. One which you may never see completed."

Fuyumi smiled, a great resolve radiating from her. "Of course. I'll do as you ask, Lord. I, my family, and the people of Odawara will not fail you."

Zaronal smiled. "One day I'll see you again in the Plain of Heaven."

"And I'll rejoice at our reunion."

"Thank you, my friend."

Zone of Concealment

C.E. May 2, 2011

Jackson Yamaguchi had been the herald foreseen, the dark-skinned man who had met with Midori Nakamura in the Odawara teahouse so long ago. Then the Yomitsu herself, Kim Yoshima, just as envisioned, came after, brought by the Spirit Winds from a future era.

This era.

Midori, soon to be the princess of the Jade Court, had, at that time, been the current Guardian of the Sleepers, a duty passed down from her ancestor, Fuyumi. Many years after the battle with the magician and his minions at the Sea of Trees, the Sleepers had been recovered from Honshu Island. From there they'd been taken to the Teahouse of the Five Flying Storks in Odawara, then run by Nakamura Fuyumi. Hidden in the chambers beneath the teahouse, the Sleepers slept their magical slumber.

Another life. Another time and place. Another persona for the former mahoutsukai.

Exiled Maghi First Lord Amedio Zaronelli heard the sounds of combat, of destruction, of the eternal battle between the Light and the Dark he knew so well. He lowered his concealment veil amid the debris surrounding him. In his weakened state, his mind opened, memories long buried flared to life. Once he lived life as Zaronal the Sleeper, banished as a rogue Maghi to feudal Japan by the Primi Signori, his fellow First Lords of the Maghi

Yet he had found a purpose in that Land of the East, forming a samurai band to fight against the Left Hand Path, only to bespell his followers in order to save them. The Sleepers became legend, awakened when they were needed once again. To help the Yomitsu. To pledge their loyalty and protect the Glorious Ko, the One Child of the prophecy. Until only he remained, steadfast to the end.

And now it appeared his own time as the Demon Queller wouldn't be over any time soon. Demon Queller was an honorific only a few had called him, but it was the name he'd felt was the closest to his true self.

Despite everything, it was his first life as a Maghi which haunted him. In an ancient Venice, the Solomon's Raptor named Marceeka and the lamia Estansa Milaar weren't the only ones he'd had a history with. Daiyu, the Chinese sorceress. Zaronelli had loved her once though she never knew it. He, with all his power and confidence, had been afraid to reveal his feelings to her. If only he had, he may have prevented her murder by the First Lords! He had tried to help her but it was too late. He'd waited too long. And so, he'd been alone all of his long life. Even as the leader of the Sleepers, he'd remained apart, content to stay back, coming close enough only to advise, strengthen, encourage, and then withdraw again.

The same with the Glorious Ko, the young ruler of Odawara he had resolved to keep safe. Even she had never seen his true face. He had never allowed anyone to peer beneath the samurai armor. Indeed, the internal armor he'd constructed around his soul had been the most resistant of all.

Fool!

His breathing quickened as he watched the Yomitsu bravely fight against the Orcus demon. Saw her defeat him with the last bit of her strength. Zaronelli knew what he had to do to help. What he must do. In this separate zone in the fabric of time and space, this false Venice, the Maghi concealed itself from the umana, the humans of the mortal realm. Here was a place where the First Lords and their servants could renew their powers and keep their more powerful enemies at bay. This place between Venice and Aizenev was surrounded by its own concealment veil; one larger and stronger than what Zaronelli could create. He had had trouble breaching that barrier. If not for Edmondo Vincherra unknowingly helping him, Zaronelli would have failed to gain access. Even Orcus had not been able to weaken the barrier.

But here, within the shimmering curtain hiding this place, Zaronelli could find a way out, a way which would require much of the strength and magic he had left. One aspect of the barrier led to the moral realm of the true Venice, another to Aizenev, the dying city, which had been home to the Maghi, rotting and decaying in another time and place.

Zaronelli called forth his magic, and gently probed the barrier, directing his thoughts toward the real Venice. The barrier held...pulsed... There! A weak spot. His thoughts slipped through! Beyond stood his comrade, a Warrior of the Light he had fought with, one who, with two others, had saved him from an everlasting slumber. He touched the bakeneko Jaraal's mind.

Gritting his teeth against the pain, sweat enveloping him, he turned his weakening powers to the Yomitsu, spreading his magical net over her.

Zaronelli, the Yomitsu thought-replied to his mental hail. *You're... you're supposed to be healing.*

Follow my thoughts, Yomitsu. You must come to me.

CHAPTER 3

Kim's mental powers transmuted into something else entirely from what she's described. She was able to form her thoughts into weapons she named psi-stuns, protective barriers she called psi-shields or bubbles. She claims to have actually sent Shioko through time, her story convincingly backed up by Wayne Brewster and Jackson Yamaguchi and an adult Shioko Yoshima herself. That's powerful stuff.

Even though the CT scans show no damage or alteration to Kim's brain, symptoms of PTSD are present, and it's no wonder.

The Shuugouteki are greatly concerned about her well-being. As am I.

Report on patient Kim Yoshima to acting
Shuugouteki Director Cheng

Mara Gellini, Counselor
C.E. January 2011

Zone of Concealment

C.E. 2011

Kim turned, her head throbbing, her strength weakened by the attack on Orcus. She slowly picked her way to where Zaronelli had hidden in the remains of a fallen building. There, the wounded Amedio Zaronelli had secreted himself within a magical concealment veil. Using his regenerative powers, he had begun to heal his injuries caused by Orcus' violent entry into this pocket of reality. The air shimmered among fallen mortar, exposing the sorcerer. He beckoned to Kim.

"I thought you were sleeping, your metabolism slowed," Kim said, kneeling in front of him. Zaronelli's dark complexion had paled, but the terrible wound in his side looked better. At least the bleeding had stopped, his trousers and tunic stained with now-dried blood.

"Difficult to sleep with so much noise," Zaronelli replied straight-faced, his voice weak. "Ah, I see you have changed your clothing. Quite becoming." He attempted a smile.

"Zaronelli..."

"Listen to me, please... Kim." Zaronelli's features twisted as he spoke, sweat covered his forehead. "I have pierced the barrier surrounding the Zone of Concealment. Without awaits my comrade Jaraal. He's in Venice with others of the Radiant Way."

"Oh, Amedio, that's wonderful!"

"Hopefully, they can be here quickly and get through the Veil. Orcus, this incarnation of him, will not be subdued for long. I can help you heal and regain your strength. You must prevail at all costs until Jaraal and the others arrive."

Kim shook her head. "No! You can't afford to expend any more of your power before you're completely healed yourself. I don't need to be psychic to know that! I sure as hell will need your help but not like this."

Ignoring Kim, Zaronelli grasped her wrist. A jolt like an electric shock shot through Kim. Her body shuddered as Zaronelli's healing magic coursed through her body, her mind. She slumped forward, supporting herself with one hand to keep from falling over, the other still held by Zaronelli's iron grip. Kim felt strong again. Renewed. "Zaronelli," she said, looking up. "Amedio, you didn't have to do that."

"But I have." Zaronelli lay visibly weakened even more but he grasped Kim's wrist tightly. "Go," he whispered, his voice ragged and hoarse. He released his grip and, with what Kim thought must be his last reservoir of strength, renewed the concealment veil around him.

"Thank you, my friend. I'll be back for you."

She rose and walked to where Edmondo Vincherra's lifeless body lay. Carefully, Kim used her telekinesis to lift pieces of brick and mortar to gently cover the corpse. She wasn't about to let anything defile this brave man's body.

A thunderous explosion threw Kim off-balance. She turned, and ducked, throwing her arms up over her head. The shattered wall which had buried Orcus heaved upward. Bricks, wood, stone, and metal scattered. Orcus rose out of a billowing cloud of dust, screaming in rage.

The cornicello amulet radiated an intense heat against Kim's chest. The sora gemstones pulsed. Kim felt their energy penetrate her waist-pouch. Zaronelli had instilled more than just renewed strength in Kim.

He had given her knowledge.

"All right, you son-of-a-bitch!" Kim shouted at the demon. "Now I'm really pissed!"

With one hand Kim pulled the sora gemstones from her waist-pouch, removed the cornicello amulet with the other, and ran toward Orcus. The demon kicked what was left of his imprisoning debris aside and strode forward to meet her. His terrible eyes flashed, his claws once more shimmered with deadly energy.

Kim stopped and screamed, a cry of defiance, of resistance, of... NO MORE!

Holding both sets of jewelry out in front of her, she directed a wide-beamed psi-stun through the gemstones and amulet. With an explosion of light and heat, the air in front of her ignited as if afire. The combined might of her own power, Zaronelli's knowledge, and the sora and cornicello's magic, formed a stabbing beam of concentrated energy. It lashed out and enveloped Orcus.

Before Kim could do more, her own unleashed fury engulfed her.

North Side, Pittsburgh PA

2010 C.E.

Not again. Not now!

Kim ran a hand over her face, knowing the Spirit Winds had once more transported her. The sora gemstones and cornicello necklace fell away from her grip. Both pieces of jewelry had turned black, as if burned out from within. "Thank you, Lydia and Mitsu," she whispered.

She gulped air and rubbed her hands together. Even with her gloves' protection, both of her palms tingled and itched from the jewelry's power. Had it been enough to stop Orcus? She was certain she'd, at least, hurt the bastard. But why was she taken away before she knew for sure? Why was she kept bouncing around like this?

Where in Heaven have I been dumped now?

Then she knew.

She knelt on the floor of what appeared to be a warehouse. Fractured moonlight lit up the interior through grimy windows and a broken roof skylight. The North Side warehouse. Where she'd fought...where she'd first...

She jumped at the sound of gunshots. Standing up, she looked out a dirty, cracked window. It was dark outside; Kim intuited it being close to midnight. Another alley, illuminated by a glowing trash fire, stretched between contemporary brick buildings to a dimly lit street. Just beyond the warehouse, a woman struggled against an attacker. It was she who'd fired the gun at her attacker.

Kim pressed her hands against the window, suspecting what she'd see but still shocked. The woman's attacker was a shadow-tracker! The human-animal hybrid, dressed in a black, form-fitting jumpsuit, attempted to assault, to kill, the woman.

The woman was her! Kim watched herself fighting the shadow-tracker. Just like it had happened more than a year ago near Lazo's Old Books and Research Haven on Pittsburgh's North Side. Once more, as if in a dream, Kim viewed the events of the past play out.

In the alley, Past-Kim screamed and stumbled backwards after shooting at and missing the shadow-tracker. She fell onto the pavement, her gun clattering across the alley. The creature crouched on all fours, his muscles tensed as he readied to pounce. He grinned at her like a deformed circus clown.

Past-Kim kicked at the thing's face, the upper part wrapped in a piece of ragged black cloth (where one of the gang-bangers the shadow-tracker attacked earlier had shot and grazed the hybrid's temple). Past-Kim's tennis shoe clipped the creature on his wound. The shadow-tracker howled in pain and backed off, holding his head. Past-Kim scrambled to her feet.

Inside the warehouse, Kim remembered her right shoulder burned like fire where the creature had slashed it with his claws. She could once again picture and feel the hot blood coursing down her arm.

The shadow-tracker retreated, climbing up one of the sides of a building like a spider. So that's how he seemed to vanish from the alley, Kim thought. I didn't know they could do that then.

Past-Kim had scooped up her weapon and ran toward the warehouse. She shot out the lock of the building's rear door. Goddess, Kim thought. I was so afraid!

Past-Kim kicked open the door and rushed into the warehouse. She glanced briefly in Kim's direction and ran past. She, I, can't see me either, Kim thought absurdly. Like Mitsu and Shioko.

Moments later, the shadow-tracker returned and followed, also unaware of Kim's presence. Lean and feral-looking, the human-animal hybrid sniffed the air and loped into the interior of the building. His yellow dog eyes narrowed, he licked his lips, running his tongue over sharp, pointed teeth. He hunted the Yomitsu, the Great Enemy of the Totou, the cabal obsessed throughout the centuries with finding and killing her. To stop Kim, as the Eminent Lord's "Great Enemy," from traveling into the past.

Past-Kim stood against a tall stack of wooden crates, pressing a hand to the shoulder wound caused by the shadow-tracker. The pain, the confusion, the fear. It's okay, Kim thought, as if to reassure herself. I sensed the shadow-tracker as he tried to surprise me. It's okay.

The shadow-tracker had crept behind the crates, silently climbing to the top of the pile. All right, Kim thought. This is where my emerging esper-sense envisions his attack and warned me. But what's she, what am I, waiting for? Past-Kim seemed distracted, oblivious. The shadow-tracker crouched at the top of the crates, preparing to jump.

Damn it, Yoshima! Kim shouted in her mind. She visualized the creature's attack as she had remembered it, shooting it out in a tight esper-beam toward her past self. There! Kim detected the latent esper abilities that lay within her past-self's mind, the power she'd always possessed but never realized. They lay there as if asleep. Like a mental slap-to-the-side-of-her-head, Kim's energy struck her past-self's power and brought it to life. Look up!

The other Kim jerked as if struck a physical blow. "Aaagghhhh!" she screamed and brought her gun up, firing directly above her as the shadow-tracker jumped. "Eat this, you freak!"

The creature twisted in mid-air, falling mortally wounded. Kim turned away, knowing what would happen next. The beast would speak to Past-Kim before it vanished, taken by a temporal displacement tremor. Via the same tremor, Shioko would appear from the past here in the warehouse, where Past-Kim would find her later. Lazo Sibulovich and the police would take Kim and Shioko to the hospital.

It was me, Kim marveled. I helped ignite my own psychic abilities.

She placed a shaky hand against her chest where the cornicello amulet had rested. Kim calmed her thoughts and concentrated about what she'd done. In both instances, here and in the Odawara Gettoo, she'd added her own esper power to her past-self to help make the events in those two time periods transpire.

What in heaven?

She remembered Jaraal the shapeshifting bakeneko, saying the Spirit Winds took some of those it transported to where they were needed the most. As if the tremors were guided by an intelligence and weren't random at all.

An intelligence.

As if on cue, Kim slipped away.

And zigged instead of zagged...

Ambient-Milieu

It came at her again. A malevolent entity, a sentience full of blood lust, insane with murderous rage. The intensity of those emotions lashed out, seeking purchase, hungering to grasp her essence and destroy it.

Utterly.

The Dark Demesne

Kim stood on a vast, dry, wasteland. Bare earth spread cracked and barren as far as she could see in any direction. No mountains loomed in the heat-shimmering distance. No trees, bushes, animal life of any kind. No sounds, not even the buzzing of insects. A blazing red sun burned overhead. The thick, close air smelled of sulfur.

This…is…different.

Suddenly dizzy and nauseous, Kim knelt on one knee, placing a hand palm-down on the ground to steady herself. Head lowered, she took deep breaths, despite the thick, close air. Even through her glove, the ground felt odd to the touch. Her head swam. The energy boost she'd received from Zaronelli had apparently been depleted.

But it had done its job, enabling Kim to strike at Orcus. But would Zaronelli still be able to fully heal? Kim slapped her hand against the ground, fighting back tears at the thought of the selfless sorcerer. And for Edmondo, who'd given his life to help her.

She couldn't let their sacrifices be for nothing.

Kim took another breath. Ever since she'd figured out how to modify her telekinetics to adapt to certain situations, she'd been able to revive herself by directing that energy inward rather than sending it out. It hadn't worked earlier in the Venice simulacrum because she'd been weakened in the battle with the demon. But now, anger and determination sparked her telekinesis' replenishing ability. The energy coursed through her body to calm her stomach and ease the headache. At least temporarily. Kim wondered again about the controlling mechanisms of the multiverse. Mitsu had said to Shioko that everything was already written.

Which means no matter what I do, it doesn't matter! Kim thought. I don't, I won't, I can't believe that!

She stood up and studied her surroundings. The landscape had changed in just the last few moments. Behind her, jagged, rocky peaks thrust into the sky. Silhouetted against the blush-colored horizon, the mountains resembled skeletal, grasping hands. Clouds scudded swiftly over them, their own roiling shapes dark and foreboding.

Geysers of flame erupted in the distance, columns of fire shooting upward like a group of hellish Old Faithfuls. The red sun beat down on Kim. *What is this place? It looks like an image of Hell.*

A spark of memory formed. Kim remembered Wayne telling her about the first time he'd encountered the Jorōgumo, the Spider-Demon. The creature bragged to Wayne she came from a place called the "Dark Demesne." *Was that where Kim was now?*

She glanced to her right. Where only a heartbeat ago had spread dry, empty ground, several figures stood yards away. From this distance, they appeared as checkered silhouettes, dark yet somewhat recognizable. Each one stood or knelt on a separate stone dais, chains shackling them to the platform from around their necks, ankles, and wrists. Both male and female, some of the figures were human.

Others were not.

Now, what's this? Other dimensional refugees? Kim wondered.

Before she could form her esper-sight to look more closely, the figures fluctuated, dimming, blinking out of sight. Others popped up further in the distance, then they too dissipated like smoke on the wind.

Except for one. A man-like figure, dark and with a strange, non-human aspect, it appeared unmoving, silent. Like the others, yet unlike the others, he remained.

Kim sent her esper-sight winging toward the figure, its aspect growing in her mind's eye. Like a camera mounted on a drone, her psychic vision gave Kim a kind of panoramic view, then zeroed in on the figure. At least six-feet tall, the man, an almost femininely beautiful man, stood upright on his own stone dais. Large, taut chain links also encircled his wrists, ankles, and the front and back of his neck, shackling his muscular body to the dais. Curly blond hair topped a fair-skinned, blue-eyed face. Thin, red veins spiderwebbed his broad-shouldered, barrel-chested torso, and thick legs and arms. He wore a white, Egyptian-style kilt, similar to what the Orcus demon in the false Venice had worn.

That demon, in its human form, looked very much like this chained figure.

Is this a statue of the one I encountered? Or is it real? she wondered, jumping to a conclusion that didn't seem at all speculative anymore. *A second Orcus?* In her meeting with Yoshima Mitsu, Mitsu had referred to the Orcus Kim had fought as "a demon from the underworld," rather than the demon, Satan himself.

Kim walked toward the figure. *What else should she do?* She had to find out why she'd been sent here and how she could get back and those reasons might coincide with whatever here and this were. She reached the front of the dais, staring up at the godlike figure. For an absurd moment, she thought of all the old jokes about what men wore, if anything, under their kilts.

Kim walked around the dais, inspecting, studying the captive. This close, she could see the red veins pulsing beneath the white skin. Not a statue then. She circled back to face the man again. When she looked up, the figure's eyes sparked, lit up with an inner fire. The eyelids flickered, the dazzling blue orbs looking directly at Kim. "You've come," the being hissed, its mouth opening to reveal long, black, needle-like teeth. "At last."

Before Kim's eyes, the creature changed, metamorphosing. Its body shrunk, falling in upon itself. Its face...

Omori Kadanamora stood shackled to the dais. A close-cropped, dark beard covered the lines, crags and scars of his battle-worn face. His unbound hair fell to his shoulders. His black, unblinking eyes burned with anger and fanatical desire. His bare chest heaved, the hands below his shackled wrists clenched. "I told you once, Ghost," he said, his voice hoarse, guttural. "It's not yet over. I will come back again, and again, and again."

Kim screamed and stumbled away from the dais. She felt another invisible tugging, almost like two opposing forces vying for her. One wanted her here, the other somewhere else. That other won as an encompassing luminance took hold of her again and whisked her away.

CHAPTER 4

The phrase "Once Upon a Time" loses all meaning in the
multiverse. And gains so much more.

Dr. Lilith Cardazio
Dreams and the Unmapped Territories of the Mental Universe

Strip District, Pittsburgh PA

2010 C.E.

Kim shook as if awakening from a nightmare. The chained creature,
the Orcus thing.

It was Omori! But it couldn't be.

Was she dreaming again? Kim had experienced lucid dream-states
before, when asleep or unconscious. She remembered Omori Kadanamora
as the monstrous winged serpent Uwibami on Mt. Hokata, the devastation
of the town of Otsuchi from the Fukishima Daiichi Nuclear Power
Station disaster where she'd met Susanoo the Japanese Storm God
who had initiated the earthquake and tsunami, seeing through Aimi
Yamaguchi's eyes in feudal Odawara, and being driven by a pack of
shadow-trackers to the sea's edge to be confronted by yet another
version of the Eminent Lord, the water dragon Mizuchi.

Now this.

Shioko had once accused Kim of being too negatively affected by
those dreams, of being obsessed with them to the exclusion of all else.
Had Shioko been right? Is that what was happening to Kim? Again?

No, no. Some force had come after her as she transported. But
Omori Kadanamora? Kim barked out a laugh. How many times do we
have to kill that bastard? She forced herself to calm down. There had to
be another explanation. She remembered the sensation of being pulled
in two different directions, as if being fought over. One of those forces
must have been the Orcus-Omori thing. But what was the other? She
took a deep breath and looked around.

The Horowitz Box Factory. Kim jerked in surprise again. She crouched in
an office doorway of the then-abandoned structure of 2010, rehabbed into

an upscale apartment complex the following year. Like she remembered, the huge building arched over her, dirty and cavernous. Graffiti covered the walls; trash, broken glass and dust lay thick throughout; a smell of disuse and decay surrounded her. She smiled grimly at the memories, once more feeling as though she'd been swallowed up in the belly of some dark and insidious beast. The walls and ceilings glowed dully with the temporal power unleashed by the Totou. But she sensed that power fading, dissipating, which told her she'd arrived shortly after the Totou had fled, their time-manipulating equipment destroyed, their centuries-old mission and purpose shattered.

That means I must be here with my past-self again. But for what purpose?

A noise from across the wide, rubbish-littered floor snapped her to attention. She rose and made her way to a stairway on the opposite side of the empty office. There it was again. A woman crying. It had come from the top of the stairs, on the floor above. Except for that sound, the building was eerily quiet.

Kim started up the steps, scanning ahead with her esper-sight. And jerked as if slapped. Her esper-sight slammed into an invisible obstruction, dissolving from her mind's eye. She tried the sight again. Nothing, and then, as she reached the upper floor, Kim experienced a heaviness, a blocking, slowing her movements. She pushed through whatever the hindering…membrane…was just as a heavily face-painted woman emerged from the shadows ahead of her. Kim stopped, surprised. The woman looked like something out of a Kurosawa movie, as if she'd walked out of feudal Odawara straight into the warehouse. Her hair done up in an elaborate topknot, she wore a diaphanous, red kimono and carried a large, intricately illustrated paper folding fan in a long-nailed hand. Her dark eyes regarded Kim as she waved her fan.

"Yomitsu," the woman said in a soft, silky voice, casually fanning herself. "We finally meet although you watched me die, did you not?"

She can see me. Plus… Kim squinted. That's no paper fan. "What do you mean I watched you die?" Kim almost smiled at that odd comment. "Who are you?"

The woman hissed, her face suddenly flickering. Another face overlay it, grotesque, insect-like. No, not an insect. A spider. Once more human-seeming, the woman said, "How is your friend, Wayne Brewster? I should thank him really. If not for him I would never have gone looking for you and become this nebulous being."

"What?"

"Sarcasm, you see. I have a score to settle with Brewster. And you too, Yomitsu. And that fucking komainu!"

The komainu? I watched her die? As odd and unrelated as those aspects were, Kim remembered a connection. Wayne and a…a spider? Her eyes widened.

"I see you have figured it out."

"Jorōgumo, a Spider-Demon."

"Yes." The woman smiled, rows of needle teeth glinting in the light. "But you may address me as Damara."

"Goddess!" Kim spat. "Can't any of you damn yokai stay dead?"

Damara yelled something unintelligible and launched herself at Kim. She swung what Kim had recognized as a metal tessen war fan at Kim's head. Kim ducked away from the razor-sharp steel edges. The spider-demon whirled back around, her robe flowing around her like waves, her free hand now holding a deadly shuriken. She flung the throwing-star at Kim. Kim tried to form a psi-bubble but...

Nothing happened. Crying out in surprise, Kim barely sidestepped away from the shuriken, its serrated edges tearing one of her leather sleeves as it spun out of sight behind her.

"Where are you vaunted powers now, Yomitsu?" Damara sneered. "You have none here in my domain."

The yokai charged again. Hell with this! Kim thought. She sidestepped Damara's rush and instinctively slammed a fist into her ribs, realizing too late the punch would have no effect. Wayne had told her how powerful the jorōgumo was and Kim had seen her in her giant spider persona fighting Jackson's komainu guardian. But, incredibly, Damara grunted and stumbled sideways.

"Your powers on the fritz too, are they?" Emboldened, Kim stepped up the offensive. Angling her body, she delivered a side-kick to Damara's stomach. The spider-demon fell back against the wall but backhanded her fan in a swinging arc at Kim. Kim lunged away from the deadly swipe then stepped forward. As Damara pushed herself from the wall, Kim thrust and twisted a punch to the yokai's face.

Damara's head snapped back, her legs buckling. Kim took hold of the woman's wrist and dug her fingers down hard. The yokai cried out, released the fan, and dropped to her knees.

Apparently, even celestial beings have pressure points, Kim thought. Good to know. "How did you get here?" Kim demanded. She stood, keeping her hold tightly on Damara's wrist. "What is this place? Why the hell are you still alive?"

Damara hissed in reply, her face once more shading into that of a spider, then back to human. Kim got a hunch; once more a spark of knowledge blossomed in her mind. "You can only do so much in this form or place, is that it? You can't become your spider-self because you're exerting too much power to create this little reality bubble, right?"

"Curse you, Yomitsu! My anima is trapped in a nether-realm. Only when I sensed you was I able to latch onto your esper wake as you traveled through the temporal slipstream."

"Esper wake, huh. So that was you who tried to attack me during transit."

"Yes! When you landed here, I was able to create this 'bubble' as you call it, which mutes your abilities."

"How could you do that? I doubt you possessed such powers even when you were alive!"

"I am alive! And I've grown in power and strength despite my banishment. The Veils Between Worlds have weakened and others have added their power to mine. I... I..."

Before Kim could react, parts of Damara's body began to change, becoming gauzy, almost transparent. Her carefully applied face paint began to slowly melt and run down her forehead and cheeks like multi-colored tears. She sparked like dying embers and vanished. Kim stared at her empty hands. The yokai always dissolved into dust after dying in the human world, but since Kim hadn't inflicted a mortal wound on Damara, who was technically already dead...

This "domain" of hers, she mused, backing up. The rules must be different here. But where is this nether world she mentioned? A type of limbo? And why could she manifest here, so close to the original displacement tremor anomaly? She looked at the empty spot on the floor. And what did she mean by "others" augmenting her power?

And threw her hands up. Damn! More and more questions. She needed answers!

Something she had considered once before came back to her. The box factory had once been the Nexus Point of the temporal displacement tremors, the reason the Totou had built their laboratory in this place in an attempt to harness the Spirit Winds' time-traveling power. The temporal anomaly had been the most prevalent at that time here. Like a vertical cold spot in a haunted house, this was where everything had originated.

Yet, afterward, it had all changed. Kim realized a new Nexus Point for the Spirit Winds had never really been pinpointed, yet the temporal displacement tremors continued. She'd assumed they were mostly random and uncontrolled all this time. Now they always seemed to focus...on her.

Just as her ancestor Yoshima Mitsu had been a center of temporal activity as the Luminous One before being killed, had Kim become the new Nexus Point for the displacement tremors? Did she have that kind of influence? It could explain at least some of the recent past, even landing here with Damara in spectral tow, giving the jorōgumo a chance to attack her.

Then again, it hadn't just been Mitsu who had been the Luminous One, had it? It had been her too, Kim Yoshima, impersonating Mitsu in the distant past in order to defeat the Eminent Lord.

A murmur of voices drifted up from the stairwell.

She knew at once who the voices belonged to. Kim put her hands out at the top of the steps, but the thick, unseen membrane was gone, as if vanishing along with Damara. Immediately, Kim's powers returned, rushing back like a sudden storm. Yes, she thought, taking a deep breath. That's better.

She hurried down the stairs. There, to the side of a long hallway, a door stood ajar, looking as if it had been blown open by an explosion. Kim ran into the room, filled with types of equipment and computers, some of it gutted or damaged. The Totou laboratory, partially destroyed by the rampaging dragon inadvertently pulled from its universe into the box factory. Kim had guessed correctly. This time period was just after the defeat of the Totou, the Collective.

In the middle of the room, Wayne Brewster and the eight-year old Shioko stood with Kim's past-self.

Her breath stopped upon seeing Wayne. In Kim's recent mental communication with Jenny, her friend had said Wayne had been with her in the Maghi warren back in the Venice simulacrum. Without thinking, Kim had asked her, "Which one?"

Could her Wayne have returned from ArcNight's world? ArcNight had speculated both men had exchanged places in their respective realities through a displacement tremor. She was certain if ArcNight had found Jenny, he probably wouldn't have introduced himself as Wayne. But, if her Wayne Brewster had come back, had ArcNight returned to his own reality? Could both exist together in the same plane of existence? Or was that just some comic book trope? And how the hell would anyone know anyway?

She cleared her mind of the convoluted possibilities and watched, knowing she couldn't be seen. She held her breath as Wayne and Shioko tried to convince Past-Kim to send Shioko back to feudal Odawara by using her esper powers to summon the Spirit Winds. Kim had been reluctant to do that; afraid of losing Shioko, not even sure she could perform such an act.

Knowing what she did now, Kim was certain she really didn't have the power to direct the tremors by herself then, even with Yoshima Mitsu adding her own strength to hers from the ambient-milieu. That had to be why Kim was here now, to help, to combine her own power to that of Past-Kim and Mitsu.

"You have to send me back, Oneesan," Shioko said.

"It's dangerous, honey," Past-Kim said. "Yes, I'll be there with you too but..."

"Kim, it's already happened," Brewster said. "I don't think you have a choice, not if the outcome is to be the same, not if you and Shioko and I are to be here, in this moment, right now."

"And how do I do that?" Kim asked, her voice breaking. "Just wave my magic time-travel wand? And if I can, why don't I just go back to a time before Omori becomes a daimyo and stop him then? Why do we have to go through all this?"

Good question, Kim thought. I'm still wondering about that!

Brewster shook his head. "I don't know. But you must because, again, that's what happened. On some level, the knowledge of directing the tremors is there because you've already done it. Shioko came back to Odawara Castle and defeated the Eminent Lord Omori Kadanamora as prophesized. You just have to dig deep to access the how-of-it. Somehow, this is the way things are supposed to happen. We had to experience all of this in order for history to play out correctly."

The old pre-destination angle again, Kim thought. Wayne was right about that then, but I just can't believe we have no choice in all of this! Wayne said the knowledge I used had been there and, basically, I just had to access it. Was it because I'd inherited those powers from Yoshima Mitsu or is it more than that? Where's all this information coming from?

Past-Kim knelt in front of Shioko. "Damn it!" She held the girl at arm's length. "You're too young for such a responsibility. It's not right. You're just..."

Shioko shook her head. "I want to help! I want to make everything right. That evil man Omori made me afraid all this time. He made me hide and, while I hid, he hurt my friends and did bad, bad things. Please, Oneesan, let me help."

"All right," Past-Kim whispered. "I'll try."

It was so surreal for her to watch this! Kim blinked back tears, remembering the anguish and confusion of sending the brave little girl through time. Even though, in minutes, the adult Shioko accompanied by Jackson Yamaguchi would walk through that side door.

Jackson. Just for a moment, the face of her lost friend formed in Kim's mind. Ah, Jackson, she thought, saddened. What happened to you? Where did the Spirit Winds take you?

And where were the displacement tremors now? Once again, Kim felt no approaching tremor, sensed Past-Kim and the spirit of Yoshima Mitsu having difficulty. Like she had done in the Gettoo alley and in the North Side warehouse, Kim added her own powers to the psychic mix.

The blinding white light arrived.

And Kim took another detour.

CHAPTER 5

The concept of the multiverse and its many aspects has been debated for years. Alternate realities, quantum universes, parallel worlds and dimensions, infinite number of individuals and their exact doubles. I doubt the argument will ever end. Unless, of course, you include temporal displacement tremors, which ignore all the rules. Not to mention time travel and the Void.

Of course, this book is fiction, remember? Don't believe everything you read.

Jenny Sibulovich, popular physics and fiction writer
Afterward: The Kairos Effect

Dartham City

Specific Location and Time Unknown

Kim stumbled into the wet alleyway, gasping and holding her right side. A biting rain stung the cuts on her face and arms. The ringing in her ears caused by her attacker's punches made her head spin. Bastard, bastard, Kim thought, gritting her teeth against the pain and dizziness. Got to get away.

Behind her, her pursuer's footfalls slapped against the wet pavement, moving closer. Her unseen attacker had surprised her as she walked home from the grocery store. Through desperation and sheer force-of-will, she had managed to escape, but not before the maniac had roughed her up and caused her to drop her bag of groceries.

Kim cursed herself for leaving her cell phone at home. She just walked to the Giant Eagle, just a couple of blocks; she wouldn't be gone long, just a few minutes.

Stupid, stupid! You know what this neighborhood's like! Where the hell is ArcNight or Crimson Osprey when you need them?

The lone street-light cast her slim, jean and T-shirt clad body in dancing shadows against the alley walls. Her short dark hair plastered wetly against her head. Despite the cleansing downpour, the smell of garbage and cat spray hit her like a slap in the face. She slipped in something soft.

In her panic-driven retreat, she'd run in the opposite direction from where she lived. If she could make it to Uptown's main street, she'd be safe. There'd be bars open where she could find refuge, get help. She could call the police from there.

Pain shot through her right side. The son-of-a-bitch had punched her there repeatedly, probably bruising a rib. Kim tasted blood in her mouth from her swollen lips. The flesh around her left eye began to swell.

Damn it, damn it! I don't even have my pepper spray. Pounding footsteps echoed behind her. A strong grip encircled her neck and yanked. Kim fell to her back, crying in pain. Her attacker stood over her, holding a long, wicked-looking knife at his side. Slowly, he raised the blade and pointed it at Kim. A sudden lightning flash revealed the man fully. He looked like a refugee from a costume party. Wearing a black mask, top hat, gloves and a pink tuxedo, the cartoonish figure grinned through a wide mouth set in a pale, thin face. The Bespeller! The meta-villain's eyes flashed with a maddened hunger and lust that jolted her to her soul.

"Hey, sweetie," he said in a husky, quivering voice. "Let's finish what we started, shall we?"

"Get away from me!" Kim cried. "ArcNight's on his way here right now."

The Bespeller cackled. "Sure he is. You know as well as I he's been missing for days. No sign of him anywhere. Poor Crimson Osprey's had to pick up the slack fighting Orcus and even she won't get here in time to help you."

"Why me?" Kim raised herself to a sitting position. "Why are you after me?"

The Bespeller grinned, spinning the knife in his hand. "Mmm, I've been checking you out. I doubt you'll be missed. I don't think anyone cares about a mousey little loner like you."

"I care, punk."

The errant whisper seemed to come out of thin air. A shimmering silhouette rose up behind Kim's attacker like an apparition. Broad in the shoulders and taller than the Bespeller by at least a foot, the strange figure stood wavering in the rain.

The Bespeller whipped around as the figure swung a fist at his head, once, twice. The villain's head snapped back, his top hat and knife flying. He went down hard and didn't move again.

Kim hyperventilated, her heart seemed about to burst out of her chest. She tried to push herself away from the apparition but couldn't, as if she were frozen to the wet asphalt.

"It's okay, it's okay." Her rescuer knelt down in front of her, placing a surprisingly gentle hand on her arm. "I know you." The words flowed over her with a calming strength. "You're Kim Yoshima, yet you're not." For a moment, the rain, lightning and thunder seemed to stop. As the figure moved closer, its face became revealed.

"Who...who are you?" Kim asked, not recognizing her handsome savior. "What do you mean... I'm Kim, but I'm not?"

"My name's Brewster," he said. "Wayne Brewster. Let's get you to an ER."

Kim sighed suddenly as her head swam; her arms grew heavy. Through an encroaching darkness, she drifted away.

Wayne's alive! Kim thought, exultant. His "you're Kim, but you're not" reference confirmed it. Like an out-of-body experience, she, or her essence or astral form, her spirit-avatar, floated above the alley, looking down. Rain fell around her, through this amorphous vessel she'd become, somehow separate from her physical self. Which was where? Still in the grip of the Spirit Winds?

Below her lay the other Kim Yoshima, one whose mind Kim had inhabited, if only for those few minutes. The experience reminded her of Daiyu taking over the mind of her own centuries-ago-past-self in Venice. But that had really been Daiyu in her early life as a Maghi, not an alternate doppelganger in a parallel universe. Kim had joined Daiyu on that mental time-traveling adventure. On the Lido, where a secret meeting by the Maghi had been held, Kim hitched a ride in the mind and body of another Maghi sorceress. With Daiyu's help, of course.

But this... Did someone help her now in this journey? Kim lived a short time as another, different Kim Yoshima, tried to escape her vicious, costumed attacker. Once the other Kim passed out, Kim exited the alternate's mind, hovering above the alley. Wayne, her Wayne, knelt beside the second Kim, lifting her in his strong arms. The unconscious attacker, the Bespeller, lay still.

The Bespeller. Many times Kim's eleven-year old nephew Bobby had related the comic book adventures of ArcNight, the Dark Avenger of Dartham City, to her. Kim always listened patiently, interested, unlike Bobby's parents. She knew how excited Bobby became in telling those colorful tales since no-one else besides Kim really cared. The Bespeller was one of ArcNight's evil adversaries. The other Kim had thought of ArcNight and another hero called the Crimson Osprey. She also mentioned Orcus.

This was Dartham, ArcNight's milieu, a parallel universe where super heroes and villains really existed. This is where Wayne had been transported by the displacement tremors from Spirit Winds, Inc. Wayne was alive, yes, but could he get back to his and Kim's world?

Damn it, Wayne! she cried mentally. Come home.

Just before Kim faded from this alternate plane, she saw a huge wolf appear at the alley entrance.

Odawara, Japan

C.E. 1542

Kim heard the cries first, the screams, the shouts of rage, metallic ringing of swords against shield, the thrum of arrows released from their bows. Sounds of a great battle cascaded around her. Kim caught her breath, leaning back against a stone wall within an empty circular stone room, like a turret of a fortress. She ran to an open window.

It is a castle, she thought. Outside, through a smoky haze, the ramparts of a huge fortress rose around her. Beyond, a broad lowland stretched to the horizon. Mountains, hills, and a series of plateaus served as a stark backdrop. A river snaked blue-green in the distance. The Kanto Plain, Kim thought. Odawara Castle. She looked below. I'm here when we stormed Odawara-Jo.

On the main ground-level bailey below, amidst ruined gardens and broken fountains and sculpture, blood flowed and men screamed in terror and agony. A cadre of stylized-armored samurai struck at Omori's defenses, crumbling them with supernormal prowess. The Sleepers, Kim thought. She remembered Jackson's description of the battle. Though not yet in the castle, Jackson related what Midori had told him afterwards. Midori herself had to be below, leading the Sleepers and fighting alongside them. There! Kim saw the courageous young girl, regrouping her "troops."

But, as the remaining defending samurai fled back into the castle, leaving their dead and dying comrades, six of Omori's warrior monks appeared on the second-level balustrade overlooking the bailey. Nocking their bows, the sohei rained arrows down upon Midori and her Sleepers. One of the Sleepers pulled Midori to his side and both crouched behind his shield as a storm of arrows fell on them from above.

That has to be Zaronal, Kim thought. This is where Midori and the Sleepers break through into the castle to join Hiroshi and his group who are already inside. In the meantime, Kim, as her past-self dressed like her ancestor, would soon fight Omori Kadanamora at the top of Odawara-Jo, in the Pavilion of Black Dragons.

How strange, she thought for the thousandth time. How very strange.

The sohei archers continued their assault, their arrows pinning down Midori and the Sleepers. That's not right, Kim thought. She focused her telekinesis on the newly-nocked arrows and as the six deadly projectiles were loosed, she grabbed onto them and sent the arrows wildly off-course, curving into the air, and whistling back toward the warrior-monks. The sohei scattered, crying out.

Midori and the Sleepers rose and charged the bailey door. And abruptly stopped. The door was locked, blocked. Something prevented even the Sleepers' strength and Zaronal's magic from breaking through. That had never been mentioned in the telling. So...

That's another cue for me, Kim thought. She ran through an open doorway and pounded down a set of circular stone stairs. She marshaled her esper-sight to scout ahead. And stopped dead at the bottom of the stairs, the space opening up into the torch-lit, sparsely furnished bailey antechamber.

Nothing. Kim tried again. What in heaven? She could form her esper-sight but, like the Sleepers at the door, couldn't push forward with it. The same as when she'd fought Damara in the box factory. But Kim felt no opposing barrier here. Something else negated her powers.

Before she could get suitably confused, an intake of multiple breaths, a soft whispering of hard-soled feet against stone, diverted Kim's attention. She turned as a wooden doorway opened on the far side of the antechamber. Three armed figures stood looking out of an adjoining room. Behind them, a soft orange glow flickered. A slight acrid stench hung in the air, wafting out into the antechamber.

The figures' bodies were covered alternately with armor plates and chain mail over black robes. Winged vests overlaid their shoulders while balloon breeches billowed around their knees, revealing armored shin guards glinting in the light. Wooden clogs covered their feet. A long, flowing turban/scarf swathed their faces and necks.

Each held a spear-length weapon, a naginata, clenched in their hands. A gleaming curved blade sprouted from the end of each weapon, connected to a long, black and bronze lacquered handle.

Sohei. Warrior monks. But... These three were different, taller, their eyes of a Western nature. Something was definitely off here. The orange glow, her esper-sight...

"Who the hell is this?" one of the sohei exclaimed. In English!

English? Kim gaped, momentarily too surprised to move. Not only could they see her, they spoke English!

As one, the sohei riveted their attention on Kim, stepping into the antechamber. Outside, the thuds of the Sleepers' fists and weapons on the door continued as the samurai tried to break through. The frustrated cries of Midori echoed along with the blows.

"How long will the energy field hold them?" one of the monks asked.

"Long enough for us to get the hell out of here. This looks bad for both Kadanamora and Sakai."

Sakai? Martin Sakai aka Eela! Kim reeled. These three knew Eela by his real name. And the energy field. The orange light, possibly from some device in the other room. "Who are you?" Kim asked. "What's going on?"

"You speak English?"

"As do you. Who the hell are you?" A sudden light clicked in Kim's mind. "You're Totou, aren't you? Some of their scientists caught up in that final displacement tremor from the box factory."

"Hell, she's from the future. Like us. Got to be."

"More than that, she's probably Shuugouteki."

She readied a psi-stun. She had to get that energy field down to allow the Sleepers inside. Nothing. Again, like her esper-sight, nothing. Kim tried to control her anger. She felt deprived again, as if one of her senses had been stolen from her. It had to be that device, that energy field also neutralizing her powers somehow. How did these three construct it? Or did it come with them from the future?

The sohei or scientists or whatever they were positioned their naginatas and assumed an offensive stance. Kim tried to send her thoughts into the monks' minds. A third time, nothing happened. She placed her hand on the handle of her kaiken dagger.

"Please, listen to me. I'll help you get out of here if you turn off that device of yours."

"She's lying!" one retorted.

"Listen, don't you want to return home?"

"You can do that? For what, to get us arrested? Executed?"

"No..."

With a shout, the speaker rushed Kim, readying his naginata for what he no doubt hoped would be an easy death blow. Shit! Kim sidestepped the sohei's charge and kicked out with her left foot, catching her attacker in the ribs. He crashed against a large table, grunting as he fell to the floor.

Kim leaped away as a second naginata flew past her. The fallen monk had regained his feet; his two comrades joined him, facing Kim. She pulled her dagger and crouched. She had depended on her psi powers too much and for too long. She wasn't sure she could defend herself against the threesome without those powers. Even if they weren't real sohei they'd had plenty of time in this era to train and learn how to fight.

She flung the dagger, giving it some spin. The kaiken blade spiraled away from her in a wide arc, momentarily getting all three sohei's attention. As they moved away from the whirling blade, Kim turned and picked up the thrown naginata behind her and, swinging it at her leftmost opponent, hit him in his shoulder and knocked him off-balance. She ran into the side room. In the middle of the small chamber a large, rectangular metal cabinet sat. Lights on its surface blinked and flickered. The hum of machinery emanated from its interior, the orange glow surrounding it. Wasting no time in wondering how those three had constructed and powered this thing, Kim rammed the device with the naginata's blade. Once…twice.

"Screw this!" one of the sohei cried. "Let's get out of here!"

Gritting her teeth, Kim raised the weapon over her head with both hands and brought it down in a hammer blow. The light fizzled and died.

The antechamber door burst inward with a crash. Kim ducked down behind the broken cabinet. If the sohei could see her, Midori and the Sleepers probably could too. She watched the young girl and the samurai rush inside and vanish deeper into the castle. The sohei were nowhere to be seen.

Kim let out a breath. And smiled. Her powers had also returned. Still, she got taken by surprise.

"Who are you? I know you are there."

Kim jumped. One of the Sleepers stood at the room's doorway. His armor bloodied and dented, he, nevertheless, looked imposing and quite formidable. "I'm on your side, Honorable Samurai," Kim said, stepping out from behind the box, her hands held palms outward in front of her.

"Onna-bugeisha?"

"Not exactly." She decided to take a guess. "Zaronal? Is that you?"

The Sleeper raised his sword, pointing its blade at Kim. "How do you know me? We have never met though you do seem familiar."

Kim smiled. "But we will. Someday, we'll be comrades-in-arms."

He pointed the blade at the damaged box. "You damaged this device?"

Kim nodded. "Do you know what it is?"

"I have heard tales of such a thing. It was what kept us blocked from entering. I thank you for your assistance. Here, I believe this is yours." The Sleeper tossed Kim's kaiken dagger to her. He half-turned his head, as if listening. "I must go. I look forward to seeing you again. As you say, someday."

"And you will. I promise."

As Zaronal the Sleeper turned and exited, so did Kim.

CHAPTER 6

They say the Devil is in the details. But sometimes, he's standing right in front of you.

Kim Yoshima

The Dark Demesne

"**U**gh!" Kim jarred to a halt. She balanced on hands and knees, her head down, breathing hard. Blinking the stars from her eyes, she tried to catch another fleeting thread of memory.

The spider-demon. The battle of Odawara-Jo. Wayne in Dartham City.

Like in the flipping pages of a book, written in no particular order, Kim had traveled into the past, into an alternate reality, into a…nether-realm.

And now…

She'd landed on rough, dry ground. A seared plain of hot, hard-packed earth stretched away into infinity. She pushed up to a kneeling position. She'd been here before, in this Dark Demesne. In the heat-wavering distance, the Orcus-thing stood upright in his captive stance. Behind it, other imprisoned, wavering figures dotted the arid, bleached landscape.

No, Kim thought, zeroing in on the Orcus-thing. Not Orcus. Omori Kadanamora.

No, that wasn't right either. At least she hoped it wasn't. She'd rather face the devil himself.

She rose to her feet. Too fast. Dizzy, she put her hands to her head. The heat, the thick air. She felt exhausted. What kept her going? She needed to eat, to sleep. Groggy, her stomach roiling, she rubbed her temples, and once again tried her inward telekinetics. It fizzled, her head throbbing in the attempt. Then it kicked in, belatedly energizing and settling her as well as cooling her off within her armor, at least somewhat. But for how long this time? And how long could she keep this up anyway? It wasn't as if she had an unlimited power supply. Did she? Even after all this time, she wasn't sure of the limits of her abilities. They seemed to change all the time.

She blew out a frustrated breath, rolling her shoulders and neck and stretching her arms over her head. She bent over and touched her palms to the warm ground, staying in that position for a few seconds. It felt good to stretch, to know she was still flexible and strong enough to continue, at least for now.

She reconsidered: First I'm back in the warehouse with the spider-demon and the past-me and the shadow-tracker and then I'm in Dartham City with Wayne and, hell, me again! Another me. An alternate Kim like what happened with Wayne and ArcNight. And what was that wolf in the alley anyway? Then I'm in feudal Japan with Zaronal. And now I'm here again.

One thing at a time, Yoshima! she chided herself. Concentrate on the present, on the now.

She once more walked toward the shackled Omori figure. Maybe she could get some answers there. This time she wouldn't let the sight of the Eminent Lord shock or distract her. She had to find out what this was all about. The warlord's flickering body resolved as Kim got closer

"You have returned," Omori Kadanamora spoke as Kim stood before him. His voice sounded hoarse, his throat dry. He smiled and Kim braced for the sight of hideous monster teeth, but only yellowed human molars flashed back at her.

"What are you really?" she asked, not wanting to waste any time. "You're not Omori. You can't be!"

Another smile. "Still a doubter after all you have experienced? I'm surprised."

"Not half as much as I am. Explain. What the hell are you?" Anger sizzled inside Kim. "Are you Orcus or Omori? How can you be here, wherever here is?"

The man's flesh rippled. Orcus' red veins had gone, replaced by blue blood vessels pulsing visibly under the skin. Sunlight glinted off his chains. He glared at Kim. "Hmmm, well, it seems, in my current position, I must answer your questions."

"I'm waiting."

Omori nodded. "You are indeed as strong and determined as described. Oh, yes, even here, I and the other exiles have heard the stories circulating throughout the ambient-milieu of the great Yomitsu. Then again, having fought against you myself, I should not be surprised."

"Exiles? You mean the others here?"

"Yes. We are all exiles here in the Dark Demesne."

So that's what this is, which explains nothing.

"Of course," Omori continued. "I have only encountered you physically three times, and then only briefly. At the Pavilion of Black Dragons when you disguised yourself as the Ghost of your predecessor, in my Parker incarnation both at the box factory parking lot and in your apartment abode."

He knows all that! Is it really him? Kim covered her shock. "When Parker and Sakai tried to kill me, Joe Martin, and Shioko."

"Just so."

Maybe not. "You're forgetting about when you, as Parker, hid in Shioko's mind. And the dreams I've had."

"I did say 'physically', did I not? I haven't forgotten Uwibami and Mizuchi. Or how you brutalized me in the girl's mind." Omori grinned. "Perhaps you have forgotten something though, yes?"

"I wager you're going to tell me regardless."

"It was I in my Parker-incarnation that day outside the box factory who first indicated you were a borderline telepath, a wielder of many esper or psi powers, some of a very high caliber. And then, again, wasting away in the girl Shioko's mental realm, I revealed to you the Totou's ultimate plan and their history with your ancestor, your past incarnation."

Damn! It is him! Kim gritted her teeth, tamping down a rising fear. "I... I remember. In the box factory parking lot, I entered Parker's mind, then found you inside his neural realm. Because Parker was your reincarnation." That was the first time she'd encountered the warlord, reverting to his true form within the milieu. "You appeared as a dragon, naturally. That seems to be your favorite alternate identity. Like your sigil, the ouroboros."

"Indeed. And you drove me and the Parker-incarnation off, instinctively bringing your fledgling powers to bear. Impressive."

"So, what, you want to have a reunion? Get to know each other better? Stop screwing around, damn it! I believe you. You're Omori or yet another mental remnant of him."

For a moment, Omori's eyes flashed. Anger? Hatred? Kim felt a little satisfaction at that. Anything that got under Omori's skin was fine with her. The warlord was right. Unencumbered by chains, she had a certain advantage here, which emboldened her. Whatever worked. She pressed it.

"It was you who sent the spider-demon after me. To kill me."

Omori looked honestly puzzled. "Spider-demon? I know not what you speak of. Unfortunately, you're no use to me dead. At least not yet. Why would I kill you?"

"I felt you in the phase-shifting stream. Twice. You wanted my blood."

"It was not I, I assure you."

So that really was Damara using some rejuvenated power of hers. Kim shivered. How many other entities could gain access to the phase-shifting stream? Especially if what Damara said about "esper wakes" and "Veils Between Worlds" being weakened were correct. "All right, never mind. What do you want?"

Still, he hesitated, baiting her. "Why do you think you dreamed of me?"

"Enough!"

"I must convince you. Do you remember this?"

Kim blinked in surprise. Despite his captivity, Omori's spirit-avatar still retained some of the spectral power he'd attained in the ambient-milieu. He'd have to, she guessed, to have intercepted and pulled her here, for she was pretty certain now that's what happened. As she suspected, he was the opposing force latching onto her as she transported. Then again, opposing to what other force? Damara? She stepped back in surprise as an image became superimposed over the stark landscape surrounding her and the chained daimyo.

She stood in a field of waist-high wheat. A rolling meadow of amber grain stretched to the horizon, broken up into jigsaw patterns by a series of small vernal pools. The largest, a lake-sized body of water, glistened mirror-like in front of her. Blue sky, almost cloudless, formed an endless roof over her head

---

Parker's mind. Like before, the landscape appeared as Kim remembered that day a year ago. A year? It seemed like a century. "What is this? Tell me!"

Omori laughed, his face twisting into a sneer. "Don't you know, Ghost? Surely you recognize this place."

"Why are you doing this? You fucking spectral beings need to stop talking in circles all the time and get to the fucking point!"

"Such unseemly language!" Omori chortled. "Very well, I shall get to the...fucking point.

S he felt a surge of power as a hidden fire ignited inside her. From somewhere deep in her mind, something clicked. Whether spurred on by her rising anger and fear or the powerful mental environment she found herself in, it coiled deep inside her.

Without even thinking, Kim aimed that rising force straight at the one who called himself the Eminent Lord.

The flames around her and Omori leaped and wavered as if blown by a giant gust of wind. The Eminent Lord started in surprise, his samurai façade withering as he shielded his face with his hands.

Omori's features twisted into an animal's rage. A dragon once again, the beast reared its massive body to its full height, wings unfurled, anger and madness flashing in its red eyes. The mythical creature opened its jaws and arched forward, shooting its fiery breath straight at Kim. Stop! Kim shouted into the mental slipstream. She raised her hand as if to ward off the approaching flame and felt the power enveloping her whirl her around in an ever-tightening grasp.

Just then, just before she dematerialized from Parker's neural landscape, she saw a figure in the distance, watching.

A fter Kim had forced back the Omori-Dragon and Parker himself, Parker had escaped from the parking lot, staggering, Kim remembered, as if drunk. She'd thought at the time he'd simply been weakened by her mental attack. Now she knew, it was something more.

It came to her, somehow crystallizing in her mind. That source of knowledge again.

"The dragon fire," she said to Omori. "The dragon fire created some kind of backdoor in my mind, an entry point for you to use, to exploit. Yes? Is that it? In the process, it drained Parker."

"Indeed. But, as you can see, I am not exactly welcome here. This level of the Demesne is reserved for those who, shall we say, have committed certain crimes against the ambient-milieu."

"So you've been here since Yoshima Mitsu cut your ugly head off?"

"Yes, curse her!"

Kim ran her hands over her head. "But you've still been able to reach into my mind, cause me to dream about you." She turned away, her head throbbing. Her stomach roiled. She bent over and threw up. Even now, encased in a mental spirit-avatar, she could still be so sickened. She wanted to scream, to lash out. Instead, she wiped her mouth and faced Omori again. "You've been linked to me since then! You slimy parasite!"

"Indeed. However, this is a special level of the Dark Demesne. In a hidden recess connected to the minds of all entities, there exists a secret place of darkness, of fear, of predation, what many refer to as the 'lizard brain'. That's where my entry-point to you was obtained. In your lizard brain, where you might never notice it."

"But you've been held a prisoner here in the Demesne, haven't you? You've been trapped, unable to work any influence on me, except for the dreams."

For the first time, Omori lost control. He scowled, pulling at his chains. "Yes, damn you! Like the girl-child Shioko, your…very nature, your disgusting decency and wretched morality, even through your mind's darkest realm, has deterred me and kept me a prisoner."

Kim took a step toward the dais. "Until now. Now you're able to reach out to me, interrupt my journey." Like Damara. "Through my lizard brain. Why? What's changed? Tell me!"

"a'Kasha," Omori said softly "a'Kasha has changed."

"a'Kasha? Who the hell…?"

And then, right before Kim slipped away, she remembered seeing something in that mental flashback inside Parker's mind, something she hadn't remembered before…

Just then, just before she dematerialized from Parker's neural landscape, she saw a figure in the distance, watching.

CHAPTER 7

That Which Will be Taken, Must First be Given.

Lao Tzu
Tao Te Ching

A Place Between

Who the hell's a'Kasha? The figure I glimpsed in Parker's mind? Why hadn't I remembered seeing it before?

"Oh, damn!"

Kim descended. Or shot upwards.

Or traveled sideways.

At the very least, her speed-of-thought journey had slowed, infinitesimally but enough for her to realize she'd been forced out of her true path again (though it wasn't really her path of choice but of whatever power or powers at work here). And this environment was very, very different.

Anger, a thirst for revenge, a mad desire to lash out, buffeted Kim like an icy gale. It was the same sensations she'd felt before but stronger here, more assured. Not Omori, or his spirit-avatar, but Damara.

The jorōgumo.

Omori denied essentially recruiting Damara to kill Kim through the attack at the warehouse and the two times during Kim's astral transit. Still, it had been Omori who'd sidetracked Kim to his own captive location. Kim felt certain she hadn't been hijacked to this place by the original force (whatever that was…a'Kasha?) that first started her on this journey.

So, the spider-demon had to be the likely candidate.

Kim found her conscious mind cocooned in a similar type of spirit-avatar as when she'd sighted Wayne in Dartham City All her senses were engaged, unencumbered by anything physical. Kim blinked her virtual "eyes" at the flashes of segmented white light that appeared at the blue-black "horizon." Tendrils of undulating mist, of glowing sparks of multi-hued energy, coiled and reached out.

Now and then, a burst of blossoming silver radiance appeared in the virtual distance. Snaking arcs of fiery iridescence flashed between columns of ragged blue-and-red stalagmite formations. Carefully (for, she realized, she had some control here) she maneuvered among the craggy pillars and cubed constructions of this alien place.

She suddenly rocked back and forth as if by a physical blow. Large shadowy shapes darted past her like schools of giant fish. Arcs of smoky web-like "clouds" glimmered and spiraled overhead, temporal lightning launching from their underbellies. Ahead of her (behind?) Kim made out a roiling line of darkness approaching.

Kim didn't wait. She urged her spirit-avatar toward the oncoming darkness. In its smoldering midst, a shape had begun to form.

Kim closed in, watching the shape become…a woman. Naked, curled in a fetal position, a Japanese woman raised her dark-haired head to stare at Kim from black-as-night eyes.

Yomitsu, the spider-demon said, uncurling, stretching her limbs as she floated. My wrist still hurts, you bitch.

Damara. So this is that little "nether-world" of yours, is it? Nice. I love what you've done to the place. Where are your clothes? You'll catch your death here if you don't bundle up.

You were never described as flippant, Damara said. Or jaded, shall we say. Do not become too overconfident, Yomitsu. Many a great warrior has allowed hubris to be their undoing.

You mean like you? How is it you're here? The komainu killed you. I watched you shrivel up and turn to dust.

I told you, I have help. The others have found me. They empower…

At that moment, Damara writhed as if in pain. A bright sphere of light emblazoned around her. Fiery tentacles spiraled around her, tightening and holding her fast. No! She cried, struggling, trying to fight back. Not now! Not when she's within reach. Can't you see her? Can't you? Let me have her. It is my right!

Kim blasted backwards as if from a released coiled spring. The spider-demon winked out of existence.

As did Kim.

Dartham City

Location and Date Unknown

Kim yelped as she appeared in midair a few feet above the ground. Hitting a detritus-strewn length of concrete, she rolled as best she could to soften her landing. Thankfully, the bamboo-and-leather armor of her new outfit helped to cushion her fall as well.

"Oof!" She lay on her back, surprised she hadn't cracked her head open on the hard surface. Just for a moment, she wanted to close her eyes and sleep. Just for a moment. When was the last time she'd slept? Or gone to the freaking bathroom? Everything ran together, time, space, faces, events both mundane and extraordinary, all the adventures, the dangers, the threats, the excitement.

The deaths.

Kim cried out as a car sailed through the air over her supine body, as if in slow motion. Awareness and normal time returned as the air suddenly exploded with sound. Ear-splitting detonations, metal rending, concrete crashing, people screaming. She scrabbled to her knees, crouching behind a section of upheaved pavement.

She'd ended up in what looked like a war zone in the middle of a large city. Buildings ablaze and damaged, cars and busses overturned, streets reduced to rubble, crowds racing in panic. Gunshots sounded as two policemen fired at something hidden from Kim's view behind a column of smoke. She sent her esper-sight ahead, expecting to see, hell, Godzilla!

Orcus.

Orcus rampaging through the street in his true guise of a demon. She'd ended up in Dartham City again, this time physically. This is what the Bespeller had meant by Crimson Osprey fighting Orcus.

Whatever the case, as in the Venice simulacrum, this demon was causing some damage. Foregoing his supernatural powers, he generated simple brute force to pick up another car and fling it at the two cops.

Kim reacted, sending out and creating a psi-bubble around the police officers. The car slammed into the mental shield and bounced off. The cops stood, astonished, giving Kim time to lower the bubble and transmit a message into the men's' minds. Run! Get the hell away! Not that they needed to be reminded, but the men took off, gaining cover between two still-standing buildings. They looked back as if trying to spot the person who had warned them. One used his shoulder radio to report, hopefully call for backup.

A sudden quiet settled over the carnage as Orcus stopped his onslaught, no doubt wondering how the officers had eluded him. Bodies lay in the rubble, casualties of the monstrous attack. Once again, rage built within Kim at the horrible sight. She felt sick with anger and disgust. This has got to stop, she thought. Why can't I make it stop?

She communicated with the cops again. Please, don't reveal yourselves. Kim didn't know what to do but she didn't want any more people hurt. Stay put.

A low moan diverted her attention.

She scurried to her left. There, crumpled within the doorway of an apartment building, lay an injured woman. Kim rushed to her side. Slim, dressed in torn and stained jeans and sweater, the woman looked of Asian descent, short dark hair. Kim gasped, moving back away from the woman in shock. It was her! This woman was Kim herself.

But, it wasn't. It was her alternate self she'd seen being rescued by Wayne from the Bespeller.

"Kim!"

She turned at the sound of that familiar voice. Wayne Brewster stood a few yards away with another man, a short, dumpy older guy dressed in rumpled clothes. The man grabbed Brewster's arm. "Go!" he cried. "I'll distract Orcus."

The man turned and clenching his fists and closing his eyes, shimmered, morphed, his body rapidly changing. A small dragon, about the size of a horse, stood in his place. It leaped into the air, wings spread, and flew toward Orcus.

No!" Wayne shouted. "FireDragon, wait! Damn it."

Wayne turned and ran toward Kim. A huge wolf-like creature loped at his side, appearing through the settling dust like a ghost. It was the animal she'd glimpsed before in the alley. "Wayne!" she cried, moving to meet him.

Wayne ran right past her, oblivious. Of course. He couldn't see or hear her. He had called out to her injured doppelganger.

The wolf, on the other hand, stopped dead in front of Kim. The black-furred beast's green eyes flashed, its ears cocked forward, its nose in full sniffing mode. It looked directly at Kim.

An Ōkami, for Heaven's sake! It knows I'm here. Instinctively Kim readied for an attack, but it looked like the Ōkami was with Wayne. Was this one of the yokai from the Spirit Winds encounter? Had to be!

Time seemed to slow down again for Kim. Orcus stood across the ruined street, swatting at the dragon who buzzed around him like a fly. The two policemen remained where they were. The Ōkami wagged its tail.

"Where's ArcNight?" the woman said behind Kim. "Where's he gone?"

Kim turned and watched as Brewster got the woman into a sitting position. "He should be here," she added, leaning her head against Wayne's shoulder. "He's the only one who can help us. He...he's battled Orcus before. We need him. I need him."

"He'll get here," Wayne answered, though Kim thought he didn't seem convinced at his own words. "I know it. Now be careful, Kim. Let me help you."

The woman pulled back, staring at Wayne in confusion. "This is the second time you've helped me. Are you following me? Who are you?"

"Come on. I've got to get you out of here." Wayne helped the woman to her feet and looked at the Ōkami. "Hiroshi," he said. "What's the matter?"

Hiroshi. The Ōkami chuffed softly in Kim's direction, turned, and loped after Wayne.

ArcNight. Orcus. FireDragon. Crimson Osprey. Kim reeled, remembered something Bobby had told her about his favorite comic book super hero. One of ArcNight's recurring villains was a demon called Orcus! Why hadn't she remembered that before? And FireDragon was another super-hero from the same comic book universe.

True to his storyline, FireDragon belched a column of flame at Orcus. Orcus bellowed, stepping back from the fire. He backhanded FireDragon, his meaty fist striking the dragon in the head. FireDragon arched backwards and spiraled to the ground, wings gone limp. Just stunned, Kim hoped. Please. Just stunned.

Orcus turned his reptile gaze to look directly at Kim. Like the Ōkami, the demon suddenly sensed her presence. "Who are you?" it hissed. "You're not of this place."

Is this what he meant in the fake Venice? Kim thought. Asking if I'd followed him?

Venice.

I can stop it! Kim thought. I can keep Orcus from traveling to the Zone of Concealment. I can stop him from killing Edmondo and injuring Amedio. That's got to be why I'm here. I can... "Ugh!"

Kim writhed as a powerful force took hold of her. The phase-shifting stream. "No! No!" she cried. Kim fought back this time, surrounding herself with a psi-bubble. "You won't take me this time! Not now!" She fought against the force of the tremor, pushing back with every ounce of esper power she could summon. She concentrated it into the bubble, denying, rejecting the lassoing capability of the phase-shifting stream. Not now! Not when she could stop Orcus here.

Kim's mental shield crumbled. She cried out, her arms outstretched as she got sucked up into the stream.

PRIMARY COLORS

Comic Books have been referred to as modern mythology.
But, like most myths and legends, they spring from a basis in fact.
At least in some universes.

Wayne Brewster

SECOND INTERVAL

Dartham City

Location and Time Unknown

I'm in Dartham, Wayne Brewster thought incredulously. ArcNight's city. ArcNight's world.

The Void. The mystical domain in which the temporal displacement tremors originated, working their seemingly random and indiscriminate mayhem. Wayne hadn't been thrown back into the past at all but into a different reality, an alternate dimension, a place where fantasy, where his dreams, actually existed.

Manifesting into the realm of imagination, of super-beings.

Huddling on a rain-swept rooftop of some fantastic skyscraper, Brewster stared out into the moonlit night, his mind a blur. A sound, like metal scraping against rock, whirled him around. A shadow slinked ghost-like from the far end of the roof and loped into the light.

A huge, black-furred wolf.

Ōkami.

It's him, Brewster thought with an intake of breath. The one I fought at Spirit Winds.

The Japanese mythological wolf growled, his black pelt rain-soaked, but his expression alive and alert. He paused and cocked his head, seeming to recognize the human before him. Through bared teeth came short, sharp chuffing sounds. He shook his head and looked again with those shining green eyes.

I guess I'm not the only one lost. I wonder who he exchanged places with? As the moon itself seemed to grin down on his astonishment, Wayne Brewster knelt in front of the waiting

Ōkami.

And held out his hand.

They slept side-by-side that night, curled up together on the rooftop, both exhausted, confused, and a little afraid. Their combined body heat kept them warm despite the rain.

———————

The next morning, the Ōkami nudged Brewster awake, the wolf's eyes bright and insistent. Softly growling and shaking his head, the wolf urged Brewster to action. Bright warm sunlight illuminated the rooftop. Brewster guessed it must be the spring or summer season here. Relishing the warmth after last night's cold rain, he stood and stretched, his body aching, his mouth dry, his clothes damp.

He stopped and surveyed a brilliantly lit city sprawling around him. It was a fantastic, glittering metropolis, a place conceived from a dreamscape, from a wondrous imagination.

From a comic book.

Gothic and art nouveau architectural styles abounded, skyscrapers and low-slung domed edifices. Giant stylized sculptures of men and women and animals looked down from their rooftop perches onto a buzzing hive of rushing vehicles and throngs of people. In the distance an airship docked at an aerial mooring tower, sharing the space with a small descending shuttlecraft. The sounds of a bustling modern yet retro-style Gotham filled the air.

Wow, Brewster thought, speechless. He looked down at his wet, rumpled clothes. Love to take a shower, he sniffed, wondering what to do next.

The Ōkami decided for both of them. He chuffed repeatedly, moving away and then coming back to Brewster's side. His nostrils flared repeatedly. He wants me to follow him, he thought, ridiculously reminded of Lassie. "All right, boy," Brewster said.

The wolf trotted to the rooftop access door. Brewster found it unlocked and opened it. The Ōkami ran down the steps ahead of him. Does he sense or smell something? Brewster wondered. Surely something more urgent than food. With that thought, his stomach growled. Later, he thought. I've got no choice but to trust my new… sidekick.

They made it to the first-floor stairwell unhindered, the entrance door before them. Brewster knelt in front of the wolf. "Now what, boy? You're not exactly inconspicuous."

The Ōkami's fur suddenly flickered, rustling as if blown by the wind. The wolf became semitransparent, fluctuating as if his body suddenly absorbed all light. Essentially invisible.

Brewster sat back on his heels, smiling. "Nice," he said. "I'm glad you didn't do that at Spirit Winds! Well…" He stood up and opened the door. "After you."

They walked out of the stairwell onto the first floor, a large lobby with a bored-looking security guard checking his cell phone at his desk. The man didn't even look up as Brewster strode across the marble floor. *I guess cell phones are just as distracting in this world as in mine*, he mused.

Brewster found a men's room and refreshed and cleaned himself up a little. He still had his own phone and his wallet. A scratching at the door reminded him the Ōkami was in a hurry. Brewster took a quick drink from the water fountain, then he and his invisible companion walked out, again unchallenged, into the street.

The warm morning sun revealed a busy mercantile district, presumably in the heart of Dartham. Brewster momentarily forgot his misgivings, the sights, sounds and smells enveloping him in a pleasant haze. He allowed himself a brief moment of self-indulgence, opening his mind to the buzz of activity around him. This area reminded him somewhat of the Strip District in Pittsburgh.

Passersby didn't even give him a second glance. None noticed the cloaked Ōkami at all. The wolf pressed against his thigh, interrupting his reverie, and directed him down the street to their right.

He stopped at a newspaper vending machine. The headline on the current edition blared "ARCNIGHT MISSING!" Fishing some change out of his pocket, Brewster bought a copy and, noticing an outdoor café a couple of storefronts down the street, immediately went there. He pulled up a chair at one of the empty tables and sat down. With the Ōkami lying under the table at his feet, Brewster ordered a large coffee, a couple of bagels, and began to read the paper.

Interesting, he thought. Apparently, some witnesses, including two police officers, reported seeing ArcNight patrolling the city rooftops as he does every night and then just…vanishing. That was two nights ago.

A nudge against his thigh. "Okay, boy," he whispered to the impatient wolf. *I wish he could talk!* After finishing his coffee and slipping one of the bagels to the Ōkami, Brewster paid his tab, and, with the wolf again prodding him, resumed walking down the street.

He felt a little better now with some caffeine in his system and a little food in his stomach. He focused just on the Ōkami, allowing the wolf his lead. After a few moments, they made another right down a smaller side street away from the gentrified mercantile district into a more blue-collar neighborhood. The Ōkami stopped at the entrance to what appeared to be a soup kitchen. Again, the wolf nudged Brewster, indicating they needed to go inside.

Brewster entered. The well-furnished and clean interior sported a number of tables and chairs with a cafeteria-style counter. Only a handful of men and women sat eating and drinking One man slept at a table, his head down on his folded arms. Two of the staff behind the counter smiled at Brewster, one asking him if he wanted something to eat and drink.

Brewster watched the wolf trot to a far corner of the room. "Not right now, thanks," he said.

"Have a seat, then," the worker said. "Stay as long as you like."

Hmmm, he thought. I must look like I need help. Well, I guess I do. The Ōkami had gone to a single table in a corner of the room. Brewster joined him and frowned. Was this what the wolf was so impatient about?

The shrunken little man who sat alone there looked tired and old, though somehow Brewster sensed he was much younger. His dull, gray eyes blossomed to life when he saw Brewster standing in front of him. He smiled witheringly beneath a balding pate, his gnarled hands gripping a cup of coffee. "Have you come to take me home?" he asked hopefully.

"Home?" Brewster asked.

The man shook his head, the jowls on his neck quivering. "Yes. Home. Away from here. Can I…can work with you again, ArcNight?"

He thinks I'm ArcNight. He recognizes that character even without the cape, suit, and cowl. Brewster sat down across from the man.

The man smiled, looking down to Brewster's right. "Who's your friend here? You never had him before."

"You…you can see him?"

"Sure. He looks like a nice dog. What's his name?"

Name? Good question. "That's…" A thought occurred to him, an impulse. "Hiroshi. His name's Hiroshi. What's yours?"

The man looked at Wayne with watery eyes, his lips trembling. "Ronald Angrini."

"Do I know you?"

"Of course you do! I'm FireDragon! Don't you recognize me, Arc-Night? I know I don't look like I used to but, you know, I fought crime with the best of them. Including you."

FireDragon. During Brewster's research into the comic books field, he'd read about FireDragon, a short-lived comic book that had recently suspended publication. In Brewster's reality. FireDragon had been paired up with ArcNight in a few issues in order to generate more interest and sales.

Which hadn't worked. Could the cancellation of FireDragon's comic in Brewster's world caused this kind of ripple effect to happen to the man here in this alternate world?

"You said you'd help me," Angrini, FireDragon, continued. "But then you just disappeared. Where were you?"

"Long story. Listen..." Hiroshi butted his head into Brewster's hip. Once. Twice.

"Okay, FireDragon, it looks to be more than just me helping you. My friend here's intimating it's me who needs your help."

FireDragon's eyes became wild, desperation shining from them. "Yes, yes, take me with you!" he pleaded, grasping Brewster's arm. "I can help you! Whatever you're going to do, I can help you!"

"It could be dangerous. You might get hurt."

"Look at me! I've already been hurt! But I'm FireDragon! A super hero! I can turn into a dragon, for chriminy's sake! Fire breathing and everything!"

"Okay," Brewster said. "But it's complicated and I'm not sure even where to start. Let me tell you my story."

Hiroshi suddenly became visible, his hackles raised. He turned toward the front of the kitchen, growling.

An explosion rocked the street outside. A figure appeared through a writhing cloud of smoke. Monstrous. Not human.

Brewster stood up, turning toward the kitchen staff. "Is there a back door here?"

"Yes. What's happening?"

"Get everyone out the back way. Now!"

"It's him," FireDragon said, pointing to the hideous creature roaring in the street. "It's Orcus."

CHAPTER 8

Without knowledge, we are helpless.
Without a way to convey such knowledge, we are lost.

Lorenzo Portero, Fifteenth-Century Venetian Scholar and Inventor

Zone of Concealment

Maghi Warren

C. E. May 2, 2011

Kim! I'm here!
Jenny! Goddess, are you all right?
Yes, I think so.
Keep concentrating. I'll follow your neural signature.
You're here? In Venice?
Yes, long story. On my way.
Be careful! There are sorcerers here, dark magic, believe it or not.
The Maghi.
Yes! A temporal aftershock occurred but it became conflicted with the Maghi's magic and caused a massive upheaval and a lot of damage. I'm surprised I survived.
Okay. Just hang on!
I will but, Kim, Wayne's here!
Which one? Never mind, I'm coming.

Jenny Sibulovich breathed deeply with the effort it took to mentally communicate with Kim. It was so…so strange! Yet exhilarating. Wonderful! It had worked! She and Kim had made contact and her friend was coming for her.

Kim said "which one." What did she mean by that? Kim's mental transmission abruptly ended before Jenny could ask her that question. Now, she was too exhausted to contact Kim again. She'd been through Hell, almost literally.

Jenny leaned against one of the still-standing walls of Estansa Milaar's now wrecked Maghi warren. Covered in dust, her shoulder and hip still smarted from where she'd been thrown to the floor from the Summoning Chamber platform. She gratefully accepted the supporting arm of a popped-out-of-nowhere Wayne Brewster. Like her, his clothes were rumpled and dirty. Soot streaked his handsome face, dried blood arched above one eye.

He helped her to sit down on the remains of a stone column. With his wolf-like Ōkami "sidekick," Hiroshi, standing at his side, he knelt in front of Jenny. The large animal eyed Jenny curiously with no threat evident in his piercing, intelligent eyes.

"Jenny, are you all right?" Brewster asked. "What happened to your neck?"

Jenny placed her hand on the now scabbed-over bite wounds inflicted by Estansa Milaar. She shuddered at the touch, of the memory, of that foul creature biting her! "I'm okay," she said. "I'm glad you're here. In more ways than one."

"Me too, believe me."

"I... I just..." Jenny smiled, shaking her head. "Spoke, I guess, is as good a term as any, with Kim, a minute ago. She contacted me, psychically, that is. Well, you know how that works. She's able to not only transmit her thoughts to us but enable us to receive them and transmit back. She found my neural signature and contacted me. She's here, in this false Venice."

"Thank God," Wayne said, relief evident in his brown eyes. "I didn't know what happened to Kim or any of you, for that matter. I guess you could say I've been out of the loop for a while. But we'll talk about that later. What about you and Kim?"

"Kim's on her way here now. At least that's what she communicated to me. I told her you're with me."

"Good. Can you tell me what happened here?" Wayne asked, indicating the mess around them. "Kim and I knew you'd been abducted but that's as far as it went."

Jenny attempted a smile as she began her tale. Any part of what had happened to her would be difficult to tell in just a few words. So, she began after being abducted, moving quickly to the lamia, the vampire Milaar's attempted use of her as a conduit for the temporal displacement tremors. Bitten by the Maghi's Grand Mistress, Jenny thought she had lost all control of her thoughts and actions, forced to help aid Estansa's sick and seemingly impossible plan to essentially open a wormhole to Hell.

She described the red, pulsing orb of light hovering in the Summoning Chamber. Milaar explained it was a gateway portal to the Maghi's original realm, called Aizenev. Once Jenny helped pinpoint the displacement tremors, her scientific knowledge augmented by the Maghi's magic, the portal's energy would be redirected to link up with the tremors in order to bring Orcus to this world. Without Kim being part of the magical mix as originally intended, Milaar fell back on basically a Plan B.

But in Jenny's mind, an image had formed as she lay on the Summoning Chamber platform—the powerful force known as the Void. She'd managed to connect with it in some mental fashion. Was it because of some hidden, untapped strength of her own? She wasn't entirely sure that had been the case, yet the sensation was truly powerful. And with it came a knowledge, an understanding, of sorts.

"My god," Wayne said. "Does that imply you have some sort of psychic powers too?"

Jenny shook her head. "I don't think so, although Lazo and I share a type of intuitive connection. I think someone or, dare I say it, something, helped me. Added their considerable power to me. I just don't remember exactly who or what that was." She told him how, after the explosion or whatever powerful event had destroyed the chamber and most of the warren, she'd witnessed an injured Estansa Milaar being taken through what remained of the gateway portal by two Maghi sorcerers, vanishing into whatever lay on the other side.

"Back to this Aizenev you mentioned?"

"Possibly." She sighed as Wayne gently took hold of her arm. She looked up at the man, her friend and Kim's lover, who had apparently arrived just in the nick-of-time. "Thanks. I'm just tired. But, Wayne, I saw the Void."

"The Void. The source of the temporal displacement tremors. Yes, so you said."

Jenny looked away, knowing how crazy her next words would sound. "It's alive, Wayne. It possesses a sentience, not like ours, but alien and extremely powerful."

"Then that means none of what's happened to us has been random. Is that what you think?"

"I do. We've been directed, manipulated. At least to an extent."

"Damn."

"But not without problems. It seems other empyrean forces can interfere with the Spirit Winds, can interrupt the flow of the tremors, changing direction and destinations, making them erratic. It's as if the intelligence, the binding force that keeps the Void contained, has weakened, aged, or been breached."

"Yes, that's what Kim thought about our accidentally being sent to feudal Japan. Somehow the tremors had been misdirected by the Totou scientists' interference." A thoughtful look came over him. "There could be another reason. Maybe the Void has decided to cut loose on its own, so to speak."

"Yeah, well, who knows?" Jenny shook her head. "All of this goes against the science I've been taught and learned and experienced." She felt weak again, momentarily woozy.

"Hey, Jenny…"

"I'm okay. I'm okay."

At that moment, Hiroshi growled and loped off down the rubble-strewn corridor. His large, muscular body moved fluidly, running to a set of broken, but still intact, ascending stone steps. A single barely functioning torch flickered in its wall sconce as Hiroshi mounted the stairway and rushed upward.

Leaning on Wayne, Jenny and he followed the black-furred Ōkami. "Where'd you get him?" Jenny asked.

"Long story," Wayne replied.

"Can't wait to hear it."

Wayne smiled as he supported Jenny. The upper level stairwell was damaged but passable. Jenny and Wayne climbed over some rubble, coughing from the still-swirling dust. They emerged on an upper floor, strewn with debris. To their right lay two bodies, prostrate and unmoving in the wreckage.

"Maghi," Jenny whispered, recognizing the torn remnants of the sorcerers' robes.

"Looks like their magic couldn't help them at the end," Wayne said. "There's Hiroshi."

Hiroshi stood at what remained of a window, a huge hole in the wall that faced out onto the streets of this simulacrum of Venice. The Ōkami's hackles rose, a low growl emanating from his throat. Jenny and Wayne joined him and followed his pointed gaze. The building which housed Estansa's warren was no ordinary edifice, Jenny knew, just as this Venice was no ordinary city.

At least what was left of it. The devastated remains of the city spread out below her, a hidden realm located somewhere between separate quantum realities. The sky had turned purple, black clouds churning, lightning flashing. My god, she thought in awe. Did I help cause this?

On the wrecked courtyard outside, a horde of creatures, of every size and description, walked, scuttled, and slithered onto the cracked tiles. Monstrous, alien, nightmarish, they all seemed directed, organized. Two of the creatures standing at the front looked as if they were the leaders of this fantastic, chimeric throng. One was a giant animal, part dog, part lion. "Huh! It looks like Jackson's komainu statue," Wayne said softly.

"Yes," Jenny said. "Down to the torn ear."

Beside the komainu stood a very tall feline/reptilian being. Stubs of what once must have been wings fluttered at its broad, scaled back. "I recognize that one," Wayne said. "We fought against her and the other yokai at Spirit Winds, Inc. She held the komainu statue in her arms when we all made peace and joined forces at the end."

"Yokai? Wow. What happened while Lazo and I were away?"

"That's part of the same long story."

"They're all facing in one direction," Jenny said, pointing to the strange group. "As if waiting for something."

Hiroshi growled again, his fangs bared. His ridged back came up past Jenny's waist; his left flank touched her thigh. A shiver, a trembling, ran from his body into hers. But not of fear, but of anger and anticipation.

A grotesque figure limped from the smoky shadows at the far edge of the courtyard. Taller even than the cat-lizard leader, it confronted the group of creatures. A large, white head with the face of a fanged skull, gleamed out of serpent eyes. Long, ropey arms sprouted from a tattered tunic-clad, broad-chested body. A weak red glow surrounded the creature. There appeared to be blood staining the creature's chest and scorch marks spotting its legs.

"My god," Jenny breathed. "What is it?" She put a hand on the wall to steady herself. She felt nauseous. "Is that Orcus?"

Wayne looked down at the Ōkami. "Hiroshi," he said. "Is that him?"

Hiroshi stood on his hind legs, placing his front paws on the edge of the window, his nose twitching. He growled, his whole body taut.

"Yes," Wayne said softly. "It's Orcus."

Jenny slumped forward, deflated. "God help me. Despite Milaar being gone and all of this destruction, I didn't stop the Maghi after all."

"No, I think you may have," Wayne said. "But not like you or whatever helped you were supposed to. Or maybe it did. That monster out there is a demon, all right. But not the devil of this reality."

Jenny looked at him with a frown. "How do you know? How does Hiroshi?"

Now it was Wayne's turn to sigh. "Because we fought him in Arc-Night's world, which is where the displacement tremors took us. He calls himself Orcus all right, but he's one of ArcNight's bad guys, a super-villain, if you will. I doubt he's the devil of our world but a devil nevertheless. Hiroshi got a good whiff of him and I wager even different demons have different scents."

"Are you sure?"

"Hiroshi's sure. And that's proof enough. Hey, you okay?"

"I'm not certain." Jenny held back a laugh. "Let me see if I understand. You were in a…a comic book world, and you fought that thing?"

Wayne smiled. "Yeah, I know it sounds bizarre, but what hasn't been in all of this? That's what happened. But 'fought' is a relative term. With no weapons, Hiroshi and I did a lot of running and ducking and yelling at people to take cover. We did have help though, a hero named FireDragon, and I hope he's still alive and uninjured. If not for being pulled back here, who knows how we might have ended up. So, thank you for that."

Jenny looked back at the creature. Her stomach calmed and her head cleared. "So you inflicted that wound on his chest? His leg? The burns?"

"Not me. He wasn't hurt at all the last I saw him." A faraway look came into his eyes. "I wonder…"

"Kim," Jenny said with a smile.

"That's who my money's on." Wayne took hold of Jenny's arms. "Whatever you did, Jenny, it must have worked to an extent. The displacement tremor brought Hiroshi and me back into our world, but also grabbed ArcNight's Orcus, at least as far as we know. As I said, that guy out there's a demon, but he's not the Maghi's demon. And he's hurt. That might play out in our favor."

Jenny gaped, speechless. She didn't know whether to laugh or cry. "Then we did succeed in stopping Orcus! The real devil."

"We?"

"Yes! As I said, something helped me. Somehow I know it! I just know it."

"We've got to get out of here then," Wayne said. "We've got to get to Kim."

"No, wait." Jenny knew this was a chance to finally escape this nightmare, but something bothered her, something nagged at her, something unfinished. "There's still someone here who poses a danger to us."

Brewster frowned. "Who? I doubt many survived this."

"I did."

He smiled. "You've got me there. Who are you talking about?"

"Bella, the woman who abducted me. I didn't see her in the

Summoning Chamber after the explosion. Yes, she could have been buried by the collapsing walls, but I don't think Bella's dead. She's a pretty powerful sorceress despite her seeming subservience to the lamia."

"And you think she may be up to something? A Plan B of her own maybe?"

"I don't know why I think so, but yes."

Hiroshi nudged Brewster's thigh with his great head. "Well, Hiroshi agrees," Brewster said. "So, all right, let's go. Where do think she'd be?"

Jenny shook her head. "No, I don't want to endanger you two."

Brewster folded his arms over his chest. "Have you forgotten I'm a super hero? And Hiroshi is my sidekick? Danger is our middle name. We're not leaving you on your own, in any case, Jenny."

Jenny laughed. "All right," she said, a great relief washing over her. "Let's see if we can contact Kim first and let her know what we're doing."

"You contact her."

"Not you?"

Wayne nodded, his lips turned down in a slight frown. "Not yet. Let's just say there are some other things Kim and I need to talk about first and I'd rather do that face-to-face."

"All right," Jenny said, a sudden sadness momentarily taking hold at Wayne's words. She knew he and Kim had been growing apart, though she was certain they still both loved each other. Now, after all this, who could say how those feelings had changed? That wasn't the case with her and Lazo! She had to get back to her husband and their life together. She closed her eyes and concentrated. "Nothing," Jenny said after a few moments. "Not even a busy signal." She smiled. "I'll try again later."

"Too bad there's no mental voice mail," Wayne added.

"Wayne, about Bella. Milaar told me my mind was a laboratory, that I could use it to pinpoint and redirect the displacement tremors. But…"

Brewster stood ramrod straight, his attention on Jenny. But Jenny wondered if, like his wolf-like sidekick, his own meta-senses were monitoring any other sounds, both inside and out in the courtyard. "But what?" he asked.

"Milaar said she needed both me and Kim to make it work, me because of my scientific knowledge, and Kim because of her psychic connection to the tremors. Without Kim, they tried to use me as a conduit for their magic to try and accomplish the same thing."

"You think there really is a lab here?"

"Yes. And I have this strong feeling that's where Bella went."

"Providing, of course, both Bella and the lab survived."

"Right. I'm wondering if it's in the underground level where the Summoning Chamber was." With Jenny taking the lead, she, Wayne, and Hiroshi descended the stairs back to the first floor of what remained of the Maghi warren. Jenny stopped and turned to her companions. "Plus there's something else. I'm remembering something I sensed when I encountered the Void. It's like a delayed memory but I recall it now and think I know what the Void is."

Brewster focused his full attention on her. Even Hiroshi had turned and eyed Jenny with interest.

"Have you ever heard of the Akashic Records?" she asked.

CHAPTER 9

The realm of the Myriad Things offers many comforts.
But nothing can replace the inner strength of the spirit.

Samuel Kim

The Teachings of Yira ~ The Five Precepts to Enlightenment

Venice, Italy

Cannaregio District

C.E. May 2, 2011

"**D**aiyu! What's happened to her?"

ArcNight watched as what had to be the winged karura warrior Kim Yoshima had described as an "unexpected ally" lay the unconscious Daiyu on the alley floor. The avian-humanoid had dropped from the sky, carrying Daiyu in his muscular arms, literally "out of the blue."

"This one you call Daiyu is injured but she lives." Surprisingly, the karura spoke in English, its words pitched and warbling. It appraised ArcNight, probably wondering who or what this costumed, cowled figure before him was. "I detected another ally of the Yomitsu and brought Daiyu here. You are that ally, yes?"

"Yes, but who are you?"

The small, feathered crest on the top of the karura's head flared upward. It turned burning avian eyes toward the young girl huddled behind ArcNight. Uh oh. ArcNight stepped between Marceeka's human persona and the karura. The three faced each other in an alleyway in Venice, just outside of what ArcNight had perceived as an invisible courtyard, separated by a magical, protective barrier. "You," the karura said to the girl in a sibilant whisper. "You are a creature of the Dark Demesne. You are the one I fought at the canal and then again when you tried to kill the Yomitsu's comrade."

The girl, naked beneath ArcNight's heat-webbed cape, stared wide-eyed at the leather and bamboo-armored avian humanoid. Her right arm, inked in tattoos, rose as if she meant to protect herself. Beneath a crop of short, blond hair, her gaunt features screwed up in fear. Quite different than the bat-like, flying Maghi servant who had attacked

ArcNight, Lazo Sibulovich, Lenora Calabria, and her son, Antonio. "The feathered one…" the girl whispered in Italian, half in fear, it seemed to ArcNight, and half in awe.

"She's no danger to anyone now," ArcNight said to the karura. "Let me check Daiyu…"

The karura rushed forward. It barreled into ArcNight, knocking him aside. Grunting more in surprise than pain, ArcNight bent his knees and launched himself at the karura. The bird-man loomed over Marceeka, its taloned hands poised to strike the girl.

ArcNight slammed into the warrior and pushed him across the alley. A shrill cry escaped the beak-like mouth of the creature as it shoved back against its attacker. It grasped ArcNight under his arms and lifted him off the pavement. It whirled and threw ArcNight into the opposite wall.

ArcNight struck the stone surface and slid down to the alley floor. His armored suit cushioned most of the impact but, as he got to his feet, the karura came at him again. ArcNight barely ducked under the creature's flashing talons. The thing was fast! He delivered three quick, hard punches to the karura's midsection and leaped away from those deadly claws. ArcNight had seen the mangled results of the karura's deadly attack at Lenora Calabria's apartment building against the Maghi. He quickly backstepped away from those slashing weapons. He assumed a defensive posture. The karura stood in front of him, wings still extended, talons glinting. Its eyes flashed.

"Stop!" Marceeka cried. "Please, stop!"

"Listen to me," ArcNight said to the karura. "I'm on your side, and this girl is not your enemy. I'm an ally of the Yomitsu, remember?"

"You are strong, quick. You fight well." The karura seemed to reassess the situation. Its ruffled feathers smoothed, its wings slowly furled. "Apologies. It has been a frustrating mission. Please explain."

ArcNight pointed behind the winged being to the veiled, shimmering curtain of light his cowl's vision enhancement webbing had revealed. "Marceeka may be able to help us get through this barrier into that camouflaged campo. I'm pretty sure that's where the Yomitsu's friends are. They may be in danger."

Like an owl, the karura swiveled its head almost completely around, scanning the barrier with its own, undoubtedly, superior eyesight. "Indeed," it said. "A hidden dimensional realm lies beyond."

"How badly injured is Daiyu?" ArcNight asked. "Please let me look at her."

The avian being gestured toward the sorceress. ArcNight knelt at

Daiyu's side, feeling for a pulse. As the karura had said, she lived but seemed comatose. "What happened?" ArcNight asked.

The karura studied ArcNight, its feathered face twitching, its head cocking first to one side then to the other. "I am not completely certain. Daiyu had fallen, as if weakened, though no other entity was present. A lingering, an afterspell, of spent energy surrounded her, suggesting she may have engaged in some great battle, possibly against a magical adversary. I carried her here, intervening before the dark creature you protect arrived and could inflict more harm. It seemed enraged, as if it knew Daiyu's opponent and sought revenge."

"Yes!" Marceeka cried. "She fought Roberto and destroyed him. I'm glad he's dead! Roberto controlled me, forced me to kill."

ArcNight pondered the girl's outburst. He wondered if the beast side of her felt differently as the karura had suggested. ArcNight felt pity and anger for the cruel way the girl had been forced to live. He vowed to help her and turned back to the karura. "Thank you for rescuing Daiyu," he said. "And for helping us at the Grand Canal. I know you're a karura but what else are you?"

"I am Renta'Mur of the Guardian Spirit Convocation. Not a 'what' but a male of my kind."

ArcNight nodded. "Sorry, Renta'Mur. I, uh, meant no disrespect."

Renta'Mur continued. "I am a Sensitive of my kind, given the task of searching for my mistress, the Azure Seiryuu, I found and agreed to assist Kim Yoshima and her comrades. And so, I flew to Daiyu's aid, opposing this dark creature you now protect."

If ArcNight remembered his Asian mythology correctly, the Azure Seiryuu was the Guardian Spirit Dragon of the East, a powerful deity. And if Renta'Mur served her, he would also be no one to mess with, as he had just discovered. He was pretty sure the karura would have whipped his ass had their struggle continued. There weren't many opponents he could say that about. Still, ArcNight needed Marceeka. "Does she look like a creature to you now?" he replied, pointing to the girl. "I'm telling you she can help me and Kim Yoshima, maybe even you and your mistress."

Renta'Mur raised his head, his eyes closing. "This is unfortunate," he said. He turned to ArcNight. "The essence trail of my mistress, the Azure Seiryuu, has been blocked from me by an unknown source. Nevertheless, I must find her and will escort her here. She possesses the ability to help this one you call Daiyu." He reached a taloned hand into the pouch fastened to his waist and took something out. He held it out to Brewster.

A brilliant blue gemstone. "Take this," Renta'Mur said. "It is a sora gemstone, possessing great power. I, as a Sensitive, am attuned to that power. It is possible, as an ally of the Yomitsu, you too can use the stone to defend yourself and the others."

ArcNight took the offered gem. Even through his gloves, the warmth of the stone was evident.

"Will that suffice?" Not waiting for a reply, the karura spread his wings and leaped into the air.

"Hey, wait! How do I use this?" Even for ArcNight, the situation had started getting more and more complicated. Characters were jumping out of the woodwork, magic of all types proliferating as if the cosmos' controlling mechanisms had all gone to hell. Still, Renta'Mur evidently possessed some power of his own, one they could use on their side. If this mistress of his could help Daiyu, then the sooner the karura located her and led her back here, the better.

He took a last look at the gem, placed it in one of his belt-pouch's compartments and turned toward the girl. Kneeling, he produced his collapsible micro-fiber street clothes from the pouch. "Put these on," he said in Italian, unrolling and expanding his sneakers, jeans and T-shirt. "They may be a little big on you but at least they're something."

"Why are you doing this?" she asked as she took the clothes with shaking hands. "Protecting me after what I've done?"

"As I told Renta'Mur, you can help us." ArcNight paused for a moment. It was more than that. The girl before him was a lost soul, possessed by a power and will not her own. None of what she'd done had been her fault, he was certain. "And, maybe, I can help you in return."

"Grazie. Tha…thank you." Marceeka blinked back sudden tears. ArcNight took his cape from her and turned away to give her some privacy. He draped the cape over Daiyu, examining her again. The sorceress' breathing seemed regular, but her eyelids fluttered, her face pale.

His smart phone buzzed.

"Hey, hero!" Lazo Sibulovich's voice chimed loudly as ArcNight picked up. "What the hell's going on?"

ArcNight checked the GPS on his forearm control panel. "Follow my cell's signal, Sibulovich," he said, pressing the panel's tracking button. "And get here as fast as you can. We may have something finally going our way."

Cannaregio District

Strada Nouva

"It is gone."

David Amamoto stopped and regarded his shape-shifting companion. "What's gone?" he asked Jaraal, the bakeneko. It had been close to half an hour since he and the three members of his unusual "team" had been whisked to Venice, Italy by Azure Seiryuu, the mythological guardian spirit dragon. They had walked a short distance south from St. Mark's Square through a small city garden, the Giardnetti Reali, according to an identifying sign, the Grand Canal glistening beyond in the sunlight. A few more minutes brought them to the Strada Nouva, Venice's main boulevard. Surrounded by bustling crowds, bordered on both sides by shops, osterie, and assorted other restaurants and bars, Jaraal put a hand to his forehead and abruptly halted.

Behind the bakeneko, a shop window displayed dozens of hand-crafted masks. David suppressed a shudder as the masks seemed to stare at him through their empty eye-holes. He wondered if other tourists felt the same unease at the display. Venetians and tourists walked by, none giving the group a second glance, no doubt due in part to Seiryuu's mystical influence. Jaraal removed his sunglasses and, his face framed within his sweatshirt's hood, turned his own mask-like gaze to David, then to Seiryuu herself. "Splendid One. The Maghi mistress' essence I gleaned from Jonas Thompkins' blood is gone. I no longer sense it."

"How so?" Seiryuu asked. She, like David and the rest, wore simple human clothes in her human persona to avoid undue attention. But even with the long skirt, blouse, jacket, and sun hat, Seiryuu's aspect differed. She was, after all, a goddess.

"It is as if the Maghi mistress is being blocked in some manner."

"I bet Estansa's split," Jonas Thompkins said. Wearing cargo pants and T-shirt, a small backpack slung over his shoulders, Thompkins fidgeted, as if, David reasoned, still trying to get used to being one of the "good guys."

"You mentioned the Maghi told you about a different pocket of reality," David said, remembering what Thompkins had told them. "You think this Estansa's there?"

"Maybe. There're these uh, gateways to two Venices. They're located in this other place. They called it, like, a…a…"

"Alternate dimension," David finished.

"No, somethin' else."

"Zone of Concealment," Seiryuu said. "An encircling realm existing between two different worlds. One created by magical means."

"Yeah! That." Thompkins spoke to all of them, but his eyes centered on Seiryuu. The goddess had mended his broken back, the injury received in the battle with the yokai leader, a chimeric cat-lizard creature. As a result, Thompkins had severed ties with Estansa Milaar and pledged his loyalty to Seiryuu. At least, David thought, for the moment. "The one gateway from that zone leads here, the other to another, different Venice. That Venice has got a different name too, I can't remember what. The Maghi used to rule there. Now they just hide and hang out. I bet that's where Estansa went. Maybe your soldier dude too."

"Karura," Seiryuu said with a smile.

"Right! Maybe's he's there too."

Unless they're dead, David thought, frowning.

Seiryuu looked thoughtful. "Maybe that is why I cannot sense Renta'Mur. If he or the others were dead, our perception of that lifeless state would be evident, no matter what. Another power prevents me from contacting my karura."

David nodded, irritated he'd let his thoughts reveal themselves. He kept forgetting he was with real, honest-to-god, magical, celestial beings.

"What could that power be, Splendid One?" Jaraal asked.

"Unknown, as yet."

Abruptly, Jaraal jerked, his eyes widening.

"What is it?" David asked.

"Splendid One," Jaraal said to Seiryuu.

Seiryuu looked stricken. She turned toward David and Thompkins. "An ally, a comrade, has fallen," she said softly. "

"And a friend," Jaraal added.

"Who?" David asked, concerned, suddenly afraid. "Not Yoshima?"

"No," Jaraal said. "Another. Zaronal."

"The Demon Queller," Seiryuu added. "He is not dead but sorely wounded."

"Ah, I'm sorry," David remembered the Sleeper from the battle waged at Spirit Winds, Inc., though he'd never heard him referred to as the Demon Queller.

"But he has performed an important service," the bakeneko explained. "He has revealed to us, and pierced, a clouding barrier surrounding a place between realms to show where the Yomitsu is. This could be the

Zone of Concealment spoken of. If so, we may find the Maghi mistress there also."

"Damn," David said. "I'd like to shake that guy's hand."

What was that? David turned to his left. There'd been a movement flitting in his peripheral vision. Not any of the passersby. It had been furtive, as if whatever made that movement tried to do so in secret. As if it didn't want David and his comrades to know it was there.

"What's up, dude?" Thompkins asked.

David looked at his companions who, in turn, returned their own puzzled looks. He frowned. "Jaraal? Seiryuu? Didn't any of you notice that? Thompkins?"

Seiryuu lightly touched his arm. "You saw something? Something we could not?"

"I... I don't know. How could I?"

The goddess looked beyond David, scanning the crowded street. "I sense nothing or no one untoward."

David looked back. There it was again! A figure, blurry and indistinct, but in the shape of a human. It stood right in the middle of the street and then whisked away into the crowd. David pointed. "Seiryuu, it was right there! A shadowy figure. It moves really fast."

The goddess nodded. "You are the only true human among us," she said. "Perhaps this thing you see can only fully nullify the senses of non-mortal beings. I know of such."

"But why don't the other humans here see it?"

"Unknown."

"You sure you ain't tripping, man?" Thompkins added with no trace of humor.

"No, no, I did see something human-like, darting around like it's following us."

Jaraal sniffed the air. "I sense nothing either but, if what you say is true, Splendid One, then this entity may also be the one blocking you from the karura." He turned to David. "Also, perhaps your sensitivity to this being is the influence of your grand-sire, David-san."

David frowned. "My grandfather? How do you mean?"

Jaraal's feline features, which David once feared, became almost human as he smiled. "I said to you once your grand-sire's blood and noble purpose runs through you very strongly. He instilled in you the knowledge and lore from the tales of his homeland, did he not?"

David nodded. "Yes." As well as the stories of his grandparents' imprisonment in an American detention camp during World War II. Both sets of tales had left strong impressions with David. The ancient

Japanese legends and the unjust, irrational racial fears ignited by war.

"Then this creature could be attracted to your unique human makeup, you and your family's history.

"Yeah," Thompkins said with a grin. "In other words, dude, you the man."

Seiryuu smiled at David. "You see, David-san? This is why we needed you to accompany us."

"But I'm the one who attracted that thing!"

"And now you will help to repel it."

David forced a smile in return. How could he not with Seiryuu giving him that beatific look? Lucky me, he thought.

CHAPTER 10

We served as best we could. Now, only time and
history will be our judge.

Fuyumi Nakamura, First Guardian of the Sleepers

Zone of Concealment

Maghi Warren

2011 C.E.

"The Akashic Records?" Wayne said. "Yes, Kim mentioned it to me. You know she's got books on a lot of different arcane subjects. Some kind of Ancient Astronauts theory, isn't it?"

"Well, in part," Jenny replied. "Certain esoteric religions like theosophy first came up with this idea of a compendium of all knowledge: past, present, and future. It's supposed to be an archive, a repository located in another plane of existence. It can be accessed by people with a higher level of consciousness. Some accounts posit geniuses like Einstein, Darwin, and Mendeleev were able to tap into it, without knowing they did so, through dreams or fugue states, sometimes head injuries, to form their theories, ideas, and creations."

"Well, your intellect would certainly fall into that category and explain why you were able to reach out to the Void."

"I suppose so and I think Kim might be able to do that, too. In any case, I knew what to do when laid out on the Summoning Altar."

"You're saying you were able to access the Akashic Records?"

"I don't know for sure, but how would I have gotten that knowledge otherwise, as if out of thin air? Not exactly scientific but it certainly fits in with most of the other things we've experienced."

"So you think Bella's in the lab trying to recreate the experiment, as it were? To latch onto the real Orcus? How can she do that without you? By also accessing the Akashic Records?"

"Don't know, but we need to find her to be sure." Jenny let out an angry breath. "Plus, I've got a score to settle with that bitch."

Brewster nodded approvingly. "Do you have any idea where the lab's located?"

"Maybe…"

Hiroshi suddenly growled, his hackles raised.

"Perhaps I can help you, signora, yes?" a voice from the shadows said in broken English. Bella limped out into the muted light, a revolver clutched in one claw-like hand, the other holding onto her cane. "Control your beast, signore, or I'll shoot the signora."

Barely concealing his anger, Brewster calmed a snarling Hiroshi. Jenny took a step toward the woman. "You need a gun for that?" she said. "What about your precious magic?"

"Silence!"

"You look pretty good despite being involved in a cosmic explosion." Jenny's own anger ignited at the person who'd started this whole nightmare for her and Lazo.

Bella glared, her good eye wide and flashing. "I have my ways, which are none of your concern."

"Which took all your strength to escape that conflagration, I'll wager. Now you're recharging, right? Waiting to get stronger. That's the reason for the gun."

"You will come with me," Bella hissed. "Or I'll kill your friends right here."

"We better do as she says, Jenny," Brewster said. "She's bound to get lucky and shoot one of us before we take her down."

"No," Bella said. "Only the signora will accompany me. You, signore, and your beast, will come no further or I'll shoot Signora Sibulovich anyway, wound her. It's true she's no good to me dead, but you and your beast are another matter."

"Go," Jenny said. "Find Kim and Lazo." She touched a finger to her temple, hoping Brewster would guess what she meant, that she'd keep in mental contact with Kim, if she could.

Brewster fixed a steely gaze onto the sorceress. "All right, but know this…Bella. If anything happens to Jenny, you'll have more than Hiroshi to contend with."

Bella spat on the floor. Brewster laughed and said to Jenny, "I'll be back. Take care." He embraced her, surprising Jenny. But then she felt him slip something into one of her jean pockets.

"Enough!" Bella shouted. "Go!" Brewster winked at Jenny and led a growling Hiroshi away.

Jenny turned toward the sorceress. She wasn't about to cower in fear before any of these Maghi anymore. She'd fainted at the sight of Estansa Milaar revealing her vampiric nature while eating a lit cigarette, had resisted Milaar and her followers but, though outnumbered, had been afraid to really fight back. Until the man Edmondo Vincherra had approached her in secret, bravely resisting the lamia's control and offering Jenny his help, giving her hope. What had happened to him?

Then Jenny had touched the Void. She felt stronger since that moment, more determined than ever. She'd bide her time with Bella, let the sorceress take her to the lab and then, when Bella's guard fell, do what she must to stop her.

"All right, Bella. Where to?"

J enny was right.
The laboratory was located on the same lower level as the Summoning Chamber, but on the opposite side of that floor. Unlike the paganistic Summoning Chamber, the lab had been constructed in a surprisingly modern fashion. A roomful of computers, monitors, servers and other assorted electronic equipment greeted her astonished sight. Lights blinked, internals hummed. The room's walls and ceiling were a stark white, the raised flooring modern, the lighting bright and contemporary. Air-conditioning goose-pimpled Jenny's arms, the climate-controlled environment obvious. It looked and felt nothing at all like the rest of Estansa's warren.

"How was none of this damaged?" she blurted out. "Where's the power coming from?"

Bella chuckled. "I told you I have my ways, no? This room is another, as you would say, pocket of reality, kind of like a nesting box, yes? Worlds within worlds. Unaffected by what transpired outside of it."

Something clicked for Jenny. "You're not really a follower of Milaar, are you?"

Bella laughed, a sound like chalk screeching on a board. "I was once an actress on the stage, a very long time ago, you know. And a very good one. Oh, yes, I have many talents, all of which are appreciated and rewarded by my master."

"Your master?"

"The Supreme First Lord of Aizenev. I am, how to say it, a clandestine agent. A spy for my Dark Lord."

"Damn you!" Jenny lunged for the woman, her hands going for the gun. The next thing she knew she lay on the floor on her back, looking up. Bella's hideous face floated above her.

The old woman smiled. She dropped her cane, her hunched frame straightening. Reaching up, she removed her eyepatch.

Jenny scooted back and rose to her feet. She held her ground at the frightening sight before her. Bella's bad "eye" appeared as a swimming oval of black. In its ebon depths, spiraling bands of red and white filament-like threads spun, dazzling, hypnotic. Despite her weakened powers, Bella exerted a powerful spell.

"I was to make sure the invoking of Orcus succeeded," Bella said. Jenny couldn't look away. The hideous eye kept her immobilized. She struggled to contact Kim with her mind but couldn't. Stupid! She'd waited too long. The power of that eye damped Jenny's resistance. Or maybe this bubble of reality blocked any such mental transmissions.

But she could still talk, barely. "Didn't work out for you like you thought, did it?" she whispered.

"Well, we underestimated you, did we not? You are more than you seem, Signora Sibulovich. From a frightened, cowering umana, you have transformed into someone to reckon with."

"I won't help you."

"We will see about that!" Bella's voice turned hard and cold. "You will pinpoint the next temporal displacement tremor. Another aftershock perhaps. I will take care of the rest. Do you understand?"

So, Jenny's hunch was right. But her frustration answered for her before she could contain herself. "No, I don't! If the Void is simply some kind of cosmic archive, how has it caused all this chaos?"

Bella paused, as if weighing her answer. "a'Kasha has become unstable," she said.

"a'Kasha? Is that the Void's name?"

"It is one of many. This thing you do will help to harness it and free our Lord Orcus and bring the First Lords of Aizenev back into power."

"Unstable." Jenny recalled Wayne's idea. "Or maybe a'Kasha has become rebellious instead."

"Be quiet!" Bella took a step closer, her eye burning into Jenny.

"All right. All right! You win. Let me examine the equipment."

Bella pulled the patch down over whatever her eye really was, mercifully covering it. The control over Jenny lessened, allowing her to turn to look at the computers. Slowly, she moved her hand into the pocket where Wayne had secreted some object. "You know, Wayne is the computer geek," she said, hoping to distract Bella. "He was a programmer for years. You should have brought him down here too."

"Indeed?" Bella glanced away as if considering that information. "Well that is interesting. Perhaps I was too hasty in sending him away."

A quick glance told Jenny the object she pulled from her pocket was a mini strobe/flashlight. She held it up and flicked on the strobe. With a cry, Bella threw her arms up and turned away from the brilliant flash.

At that moment a huge, black blur shot through the door and slammed into Bella, knocking her to the floor and causing her to drop her gun. Efficiently. Quickly. Hiroshi the Ōkami clamped his jaws onto Bella's shoulder and, with a flick of his great head, picked the woman up and flung her into the far wall. Bella crumpled to the floor and lay still.

Jenny jumped back as Hiroshi turned in her direction. "Uh," Jenny muttered, catching her breath, her stomach flip-flopping. "Th…thank you, Hiroshi." The beast was alone, no doubt Wayne having sent him back secretly to help her. But how had Hiroshi been able to get into this interdimensional area?

The Ōkami chuffed, impatiently Jenny thought, and trotted to a server rack. He looked back and gave Jenny a questioning look. Jenny forced down her nervousness at the wolf-creature's sudden appearance and joined him. She studied the servers mounted in their separate bays. Suspecting what the equipment might represent, Jenny looked down at the Ōkami, knelt and, fear replaced by excitement, grabbed Hiroshi's huge head with both hands.

"Yes," she said. "Thank you again, Hiroshi. This will do nicely, but I think we'll need your master's help."

CHAPTER 11

I will never stop, never slow down, until we have rid our world
of all these monsters. Human and otherwise.

Lenora Calabria

Zone of Concealment

If that freaking hag thinks I'm just going to abandon Jenny, she's even
more insane than she acts!

Wayne Brewster paused at the top of the stairs on the first floor. He
winced at the pain in his side where flying stone debris had struck him
in Dartham City. He didn't think anything was broken but, because he
had maybe bruised some ribs, some discomfort could be felt. Kneeling
in front of Hiroshi he placed a hand on each side of the Ōkami's head.

"Hiroshi, follow Jenny and the sorceress. Don't let Bella see you
but make sure Jenny remains unharmed and be careful. Do you understand?"

Hiroshi rumbled deep in his throat and wagged his tail. Although
Wayne had slipped a possible weapon into Jenny's pocket, Hiroshi would
provide more protection. Maybe even kill that evil witch!

No, no, he thought. Can't think like that. ArcNight certainly
wouldn't. ArcNight. Where was the masked hero? Wayne was certain
ArcNight had ended up in Venice, Wayne's Venice. But had he then
returned to Dartham City just as Wayne had returned here because
of the aftershock? Then again, strictly speaking, this wasn't Wayne's
Venice. The rules could be different. ArcNight could still be here.
Somewhere.

"Okay, boy. I'll be along shortly but I have to check on something
first. Go!"

Wayne watched the Ōkami lope back down the stairs, knowing the
wolf would protect Jenny. He marveled again how he and the mythical
animal had bonded. They had both been transported to ArcNight's
comic book city of Dartham, after the battle at Spirit Winds, Inc.
Deposited on a skyscraper's rain-swept rooftop, surrounded by huge
stone gargoyles, Wayne thought he'd have to face his dilemma alone.

But, putting aside their differences, he and the Ōkami became allies; an act Wayne knew helped keep him sane. Together, they fought desperately to save people from Orcus' rampage. Including an alternate Kim Yoshima.

Just like there's two of me, one in each universe, there's two of Kim, he thought. Hell, maybe more!

No time for that now. He needed to verify something. When he and Jenny watched the group of monsters gathering in the courtyard below, he thought he'd seen another denizen of ArcNight's reality. He looked out the window again. There! He was right. Among the milling creatures, one figure stood out, if only because Wayne recognized him. He'd met him before.

Wayne had no weapons. He'd have to improvise. At Spirit Winds, Inc., when he and Hiroshi had fought, he'd been weaponless. He figured he could handle this next fight, if it came to that. He'd done it when he first encountered this so-called super-villain in Dartham City. Whatever the case, he knew this would be a lot easier than facing Kim right now. He'd changed, become more certain of what he wanted, needed, to do. He hoped she'd understand.

That is, if any of them got out of this mess alive. He marveled how they'd managed to survive to this point. At what they'd gone through. No rest for the weary, he thought, and stepped up onto the window's thick stone sill.

Wayne dropped the short distance from the second-floor window to the ground, clenching his teeth at the ache in his side as he landed. Apparently, fixated on the sight of Orcus standing in front of them, the group of creatures didn't see or hear Wayne. Thankful for small favors, Wayne moved forward through the rubble and concealed himself behind a piece of a still-standing column. Orcus' head and shoulders were visible from his vantage point, above the heads and shoulders, such as they were, of the various creatures thronging the courtyard. All seemed oddly calm. Perhaps they smelled blood, eager to attack Orcus. The red aura of the demon flickered weakly, broadcasting his weakness.

Still, Orcus made the first move. With a loud sigh, the demon dropped to a knee, his head lolling to one side. As if by some unspoken command, a rippling of skin, scale, feather, and hide rushed forward. They swarmed over Orcus like a horde of army ants. If Orcus struggled or fought back, no sign was evident. No sound, no cry or shriek emitted from under the pile of flailing limbs, mandibles, tentacles, and tails. Silently, efficiently, the hideous mob went about their deadly work.

Brewster held his breath. Could it be that easy? Could Orcus be subdued that quickly, even while injured?

Apart from the teeming mass, that lone figure Wayne had recognized rose from where he crouched in hiding among the rubble. The Bespeller.

Show time, Wayne thought. He clenched his fists and stepped forward.

Rising up from where he crouched behind some rubble, the tall, face-painted, outlandishly dressed arch-villain of ArcNight's world turned to run. Wayne stepped out to intercept him. "Going somewhere, punk?"

"You again? Who the Hell are you?" The Bespeller threw Brewster the finger and sprinted in the direction of one of the canals, his top hat flying off his head. Brewster took off after him, ignoring the pain in his side. Rubble clogged parts of the canal. Wayne didn't think the Bespeller would swim but he could utilize the bridge of debris to get over to the other side. Wayne couldn't let the bastard escape. After what he'd seen him do in Dartham City, he couldn't!

The Bespeller reached the canal's edge and whirled. As Wayne got closer, he could see the panic in the villain's painted face. The approaching madness. "What is this? What's happening?" the Bespeller cried.

Then Wayne changed his mind, realizing ArcNight wouldn't seek such revenge. It was, after all, an unwritten code of super heroes, wasn't it? Maybe this creep could be of use. He stopped at the edge of the canal. "Listen to me," he said. "We can help each other. We..."

"Help? Help you?" The Bespeller brandished his knife, spit flying from his mouth. "I'll kill you! I'll rip your guts out!"

The water near the debris erupted. A huge gray-skinned humanoid broke the canal's surface and fell upon the Bespeller. Wayne watched in shock as the powerful creature grabbed the Bespeller and broke his neck, among other bones. He then lifted the dead villain over his head and flung him into the canal.

At least six feet in height with a muscular build, the thing sported a small ridge of cartilage from the top of its hairless head, down its back to the tip of its thick tail. Flashing wicked-looking talons from its webbed hands, the red-eyed being, gills quivering on its thick neck, swung its slavering attention to Brewster.

Quena, the man-shark, another of ArcNight's deadly foes. Evidently not a fan of the Bespeller either. "Youuuuu again!" Quena hissed.

Huh? Brewster thought. Me again? True, Brewster had encountered the Bespeller before, but not this monstrosity. Brewster backed up. He didn't think he could outrun the amphibious creature and certainly didn't want to fight him, especially with bruised ribs. He doubted Quena would listen to reason either.

A chorus of roars and screams behind him whirled Brewster around. With one eye on Quena, he saw the man-shark's attention had been diverted as well. The campo. The situation there had changed. Maybe that could help Brewster. Or maybe not.

Orcus hadn't been stopped. Covered in blood from multiple wounds, the demon had exerted a hidden reserve of strength and threw off some of the attacking monster horde. With his red aura pulsing brighter, Orcus stood, flailing his arms and sending bolts of some kind of energy at his adversaries from his hands. A few of the creatures hung on to the demon, continuing to fight back.

Okay, maybe reason might work. "There's your enemy, Quena!" Brewster shouted, pointing to the demon. In his research on ArcNight, Wayne now remembered, though all bad guys, Quena, the Bespeller, and Orcus had clashed as well, each one wanting to be the top dog of crime in Dartham City. Now that the man-shark had disposed of the Bespeller, Wayne hoped Quena's animosity toward the demon would be greater than going after him. "The others need help to subdue Orcus. Add your strength to theirs so we can all work together to get out of here!"

"Orrcusssss!" The man-shark seemed to consider Brewster's words. Then he ran toward the campo, his powerful legs skimming him over the rubble.

That was close, Brewster thought, hoping Quena's added strength would turn the tide against Orcus. Better get back.

Then paused to consider. Quena seemed to think he had met Brewster before. Instead, could it have been ArcNight, sans costume, in his own alter-ego of Wayne Brewster the man-shark had seen? That's probably it, Brewster thought. But where did that occur?

He turned and headed back toward the Maghi warren.

CHAPTER 12

Look for it, it cannot be seen.

Lao Tzu
Tao Te Ching

Venice, Italy

Cannaregio District

2011 C.E.

Lazo followed ArcNight's GPS signal on his phone, moving quickly through the narrow backstreets of the Cannaregio district where the Jewish Ghetto and Lenora's now-destroyed apartment were located. For a moment he wondered if Lenora and her son had safely reached their backup headquarters on the island of Lido. ArcNight had given Lenora a weapon he'd called an "aural disrupter." That calmed Lazo's concerns for the moment, but he'd need to call Lenora as soon as he could. She had, after all, volunteered to help him and Jenny at great risk to herself, without asking anything in return. When, not if, they got out of this mess, he needed to thank her.

ArcNight said something's finally gone our way, he thought. I hope the hell so!

The large sestieri or neighborhood ran parallel to the Grand Canal. At least that's what the description on his phone read but this section lay back from the water. Two and three-story structures, some painted in gaudy colors or emblazoned with crude murals, lined the streets. Lazo encountered very few people, only the occasional shopkeeper or passerby. He jogged over one of the many small, stone footbridges extending over narrow canals. He continued, then stopped.

It's saying I ran past it, he thought, studying his phone with a frown. He looked behind him. Nothing. No ArcNight. He walked back a few paces. Here, it should be right here. The entrance to an alley yawned before him. He took a step forward then backed off. No, no. I can't go in there. A sudden compulsion to turn away, to leave, washed over him.

"Sibulovich." ArcNight's voice sounded over Lazo's cell phone speaker. "Walk into the alley. I'm here and can see you. There's a kind of negation spell placed here to ward off snoopers. I felt it too. Just walk in, it's safe."

"Uh, okay." He did. Once he moved beyond the entrance, the alley no longer appeared empty. ArcNight stood a few yards away. But he wasn't alone.

"Damn!" Lazo pocketed his phone and rushed forward. He knelt beside an unconscious Daiyu, the woman covered in ArcNight's cape. Lazo had gone through some EMT training and had seen more than his share of injured and dying as a police officer, but Daiyu's condition baffled him. She seemed comatose but Lazo suspected her condition had to do with some magical aspect, just like the alley entrance. He turned to ArcNight.

"Do you know what happened to her?"

"Apparently she fought against one of the Maghi sorcerers, defeating him but was injured in the process."

"How badly…?"

"She should be okay," ArcNight said and told Lazo about the karura, the winged humanoid who had fought against Marceeka at the Grand Canal.

"Hawk Man's boss lady can help Daiyu?"

"Hopefully, yes. Providing he finds her." He then revealed who the young girl was.

Lazo stood, trying to grasp what ArcNight had just told him. "You're sayin' that girl over there," he said, pointing to Marceeka. "She's the bat-monster that attacked us at the canal?"

"Yes." ArcNight followed Lazo's gaze to where the young woman stood. Dressed in ArcNight's street clothes, head down, arms folded at her chest, she seemed lost in her own thoughts. "She's part of some curse or ritual where the monster side of her emerges at night."

"What happened?"

"I found her here in her human persona and helped calm her down. She's really afraid and confused. She, at least the part of her that's still human, doesn't want to be what she's been cursed to be."

"Okay, but what do we with her?"

"She's Marceeka, remember? I know, she doesn't look like much now, but she could be an asset." He indicated the space behind him. "I think she can help us get through that."

"Through what?" Lazo saw nothing but the alley extending into shadows.

"Ah, right. You can't see it. It's a barrier concealing an alternate realm or something, which I think can't be crossed unless you've got the key, so to speak. Among other things, your wife might be there."

"Oh, man…" Lazo's spirits soared at that remark, for the first time since Jenny had been abducted. They might finally be close to saving her! Still, his inherent concern and distrust drove his next words, "What's to keep Marceeka from turnin' back into that bat-thing and attackin' us?"

ArcNight shrugged, a gesture Lazo felt was at-odds with the man's powerful, decisive demeanor. For an absurd moment, Lazo wondered if the Wayne he knew could rock that super-hero suit like this Wayne did. "Don't know," ArcNight said. "But we have to use every advantage we have while we can."

"Does that include Hawk Man?" True, Lazo had seen what the karura could do but a healthy skepticism had served him well more than once. "Can we really trust him?"

"I think so. He could have handled me and Marceeka easily, but he didn't."

"I doubt it was for lack of tryin'."

ArcNight smiled. "True, but he's a helluva lot stronger and quicker than I am. In the end, he seemed reasonable and offered to help."

"Okay, okay." Lazo blew out a breath. "I guess we can wait a little longer."

Cannaregio District

Strada Nouva

I can't believe I'm taking the lead here.

David walked through the bustling Strada Nouva, his companions following. The shadow-thing had gone in this direction. Now and then David spotted it, elusive yet somehow only staying just out of reach. It darted like a gray ghost among oblivious visitors, residents, and tourists, pausing briefly to look back at its pursuers, then move on again.

What the hell is it doing? David stopped, an idea forming. Seiryuu, Jaraal, and Jonas gathered around him, once more an island of security and privacy created by Seiryuu surrounding them. "I've a hunch," he said. "Tell me what you think. I don't believe this thing, whatever it is, means us any harm."

"How so?" Jaraal asked.

"It does seem to be following us, but the way it's keeping its distance yet not wanting to completely get away from us reminds me of a cat who's cautious but curious. I think it noticed us when we first arrived."

"You," Seiryuu interjected. "It noticed you, David-san."

"Right. I don't why that is, but okay. It's been following us...me... since we got here. Its proximity to us is causing this interference with your karura, Seiryuu. It, evidently, has that effect. At least that's what I think."

"Sounds about right," Jonas said.

"Agreed," said Seiryuu.

"So how do we get away from it?" Jonas asked.

"Let me approach it alone," David said.

"That may not be wise, David-san," Jaraal said. The bakeneko appraised David with what David thought might be approval. "You have courage, but we do not know what this creature is capable of."

"Yes," David said. "You're right. But, I'm with a goddess, a yokai, and a were-shadow-tracker. If that isn't enough of the cavalry watching my back I don't what is! Let me try this."

"Very well," Seiryuu said. "We will stay back but keep you in sight."

David nodded and walked further down the street by himself. Above the heads of the crowd, he spotted the shadow-thing. It crouched on a second-story awning stretching over a trattoria's sidewalk seating. So it climbs, too, David thought. On a hunch, he walked toward the cafe. The thing's dark oval of a head followed David's every move. One outdoor table at the cafe was empty. Looking up at the creature, he walked to the table and sat down.

Ordering an espresso from the waiter, David waited.

In a moment, the shadow-thing appeared, slinking among the diners unnoticed. It stopped, waiting until after the waiter brought David's order, then moved closer. David remembered when he first met Zaronal, Jaraal, Seiryuu, and Thompkins. He should be getting used to these kinds of otherworldly encounters, but a momentary chill ran through him at the sight of the creature. It knelt across from David, its head peeking above the tabletop.

"Hey, buddy," David said softly.

The creature cocked its head at the sound of David's voice.

"How you doing?" David wasn't sure how to proceed. Making small talk with this thing didn't seem to be the most helpful. He'd once talked down an Iraqi villager who was about to kill himself because his home and family had been destroyed in a bombing run. That seemed simple now compared to this.

"Excuse?" A passing waiter stopped, thinking David was talking to him. David shook his head, pulled out and pointed to his cell phone. The man smiled, nodded and moved on to his next customer, completely unaware of the shadow-thing's presence. "Look," David said to the creature. "I don't know what your interest in me is, but you really need to go away. Understand?" David waved his hand. "Go away!"

Now he really did feel foolish, as some of the other diners to turn to glance his way. He smiled sheepishly, once more pretending to talk on his phone. The shadow-thing leaned forward. One of its strange, fingerless hands reached out and placed an object on the table in front of David.

Before David could react, a gust of wind blew through the sidewalk seating. A tingling warmth ran through David, causing him to gasp.

The shadow-thing's head jerked. It looked to the left and right, then to the left again. Once more David thought of the cat analogy, as if the being had noticed some bright, shiny plaything. It turned, rose to its feet, and zipped away.

"Was it something I said?" David joked quietly. He looked closely at the object the creature had left behind—a figure of a tiger. How the hell did that thing get this? he thought, shocked. He reached out and took hold of the small jade figurine, staring. His grandfather had some sculpted jade he'd collected over the years. This looked like part of that collection. My god. Was this why that shadow-thing was attracted to me? To give me this?

Seiryuu suddenly joined him, taking the seat on the other side of the table. "Is it gone?" she asked David, who quickly pocketed the figurine "I cast a wide swath of distractive energy to hopefully get its attention. I saw you talking, as if to yourself, so I knew you had succeeded in drawing it to you. While it was thus occupied, I cast the energy."

"Yes," David said, relaxing. "It's gone. Like I said before, it was like a shadow in human shape."

"There are a number of spectral beings which assume that aspect."

"Well, anyway, thanks."

"You are the one to be thanked." Seiryuu bowed her head.

David felt a little embarrassed by the goddess' attention, and by not telling her about the "gift" the creature had left behind. He had to think about that first. "Are you, uh, able to sense your karura now?"

The goddess' eyes suddenly closed as if she heard something far away. "Yes." She opened them and smiled. "Renta'Mur, I have found him. We now have contact."

It turned out they didn't have to wait that long.

Lazo looked up. The karura warrior gently dropped from above between the two buildings abutting the alley. He stood a few feet away, his wings furling behind his armored body. He pointed a taloned hand at Lazo. "You are an ally of Kim Yoshima."

"Uh, yeah." Lazo sized up the winged being. "Lazo Sibulovich, at your service. What about you?"

"I am called Renta'Mur and I, too, am an ally."

Good thing for us. "Thanks for your help and welcome to the club."

"Did you find your mistress?" ArcNight said to Renta'Mur. "The Azure Seiryuu?"

"Seiryuu?" ArcNight hadn't mentioned that small item. Lazo said, "You talkin' about the Guardian Spirit Dragon of the East goddess? That's his mistress?" Man, Kim had told Lazo there'd been some heavy shit going down back home but what exactly had he missed?

In answer, four figures appeared at the alley entrance. Unlike Lazo who had walked right by the alley entrance, these four entered without question. As they approached, Lazo recognized David Amamoto, even though the security chief of Spirit Winds, Inc. wore casual clothes rather than his usual uniform. Another of the men was a young African-American who carried a small backpack. The third man, dressed in jeans and wearing a hoodie and sunglasses, looked to be something else entirely. Tall and graceful, he removed his sunglasses. His eyes momentarily became visible beneath the shade of the hood. Cat eyes.

And the woman wearing the long skirt, blouse, denim jacket and a wide-brimmed sun hat had to be Azure Seiryuu. ArcNight had mentioned something might be going their way. Seiryuu had to be it.

Lazo stepped forward but Renta'Mur blocked his bulky body with his own. "Look," Lazo said, his anger rising. "Seiryuu's got to help Daiyu so they both can help us find my wife. Do you understand, Hawk Man?"

ArcNight placed a hand on Lazo's shoulder. "She will, Sibulovich. Let's give her some space."

Renta'Mur moved aside. Seiryuu stood before Lazo and ArcNight. Lazo thought she was probably the most beautiful woman he'd ever seen. More than that, in spite of her simple clothing, a palpable energy emanated from her. One both calming and immensely powerful. "Peace," she said. "These servants with me are here to help. I will see to the one called Daiyu, Lazo Sibulovich. Please stay here for the moment."

Lazo just stared. She knew his name. "Thank…thank you," he finally murmured.

"You, masked defender," Seiryuu said to ArcNight. "Please accompany me."

ArcNight seemed to be as much in awe of Seiryuu as Lazo was. "As you wish," the hero said softly as he walked with her toward Daiyu.

"Mr. Sibulovich, glad to see you're okay."

Lazo jumped. "Sorry," David Amamoto said. "It took me a while to get used to Seiryuu, too."

Lazo shook Amamoto's hand. "Yeah, she' somethin' all right. Thanks for comin', Amamoto. I won't ask how you got here."

Amamoto snorted. "I'm not sure I can answer that myself. Who's the costumed dude? He looks familiar."

"ArcNight."

"Never heard of him. He reminds me of Mr. Brewster."

"Yep." Lazo chuckled. "That he does. Long story."

"Like to hear it." Amamoto jerked a thumb toward the young African-American. "This is Jonas Thompkins. He's a long story too."

Lazo shook the man's hand, but a sudden uneasiness came over him. "You're one of them, aren't you?" he said, releasing his grip and taking a step back. "A shadow-tracker."

Thompkins raised his eyebrows. "How'd you know that?"

"Let's just say I've had some experience in that area." Lazo studied the man. "But you're different. You're human and yet you're not."

"I'm on your side, man," Thompkins said. "I follow Seiryuu now. I did some fucked-up things, I admit, and I'm not proud of that, but those days are over. Seiryuu saved my ass and I bet she's doing that with your two girls over there right now."

"It's true," Amamoto said. "I had my doubts too, but I can vouch for him. What he did as a shadow-tracker wasn't really his fault, kind of like Marceeka, I would say." He turned toward the bakeneko. "And this is Jaraal, a yokai."

Lazo looked at a being part man, part cat. Powerful and intimidating. "You sensed Jonas' true nature," Jaraal said softly. "Interesting."

Wow. "Yeah, well, uh, with all this magic runnin' around, some of it was bound to rub off." Like Lazo's connection with Jenny, their "personal force," his perception had become more acute. Like now. "You're Hideo, aren't you? Kim's cat."

The bakeneko smiled and nodded, as if approving of Lazo's statement. "Indeed."

Lazo laughed. "Shit. I've held you in my lap!"

"So you have. And fed me pizza."

"Uh, yeah, well, sorry about that. I know Kim didn't want you eating that kind of stuff."

"Not at all. The pepperoni was quite good."

"Check it out," Thompkins said.

Marceeka had come out of her funk upon seeing Seiryuu. She fell to her knees, sobbing. "Splendid One," the girl said, her voice breaking. "Please forgive me. I didn't want to serve the Maghi in this way, to kill, to cause harm. I had no choice!"

"I know, child," Seiryuu said. "All is forgiven."

Sudden tears ran down Marceeka' face. "I am a monster! I have killed. How can such crimes be forgiven?"

Seiryuu placed a hand on the girl's cheek. "You are not to blame. Do not despair. There is someone here who shares your pain. Perhaps you can both help each other to atone for your perceived sins." She turned toward Thompkins. "Jonas," she said.

Thompkins tilted his head. He touched a finger to his chest. "Me? How can I help her?"

"You are both alike in many ways. Trapped in a violent duality not of your choosing. Come, speak with her."

As if in a trance, Thompkins moved forward. ArcNight stepped aside, allowing Thompkins to face Marceeka. After a moment, Thompkins and the girl began to talk, a murmuring of voices from two people in pain. Lazo watched as Marceeka sighed and slumped forward. Thompkins took hold of the girl and gently held her. Marceeka's manner calmed, her features relaxing, her eyes clearing.

Lazo turned as Seiryuu knelt beside Daiyu. The goddess placed both hands on the side of the sorceress' face. Lazo discerned a faint shimmering in the air around both women. Daiyu gasped, her body arching upward. ArcNight went to her side. After a moment, he and Seiryuu helped a now conscious Daiyu to her feet.

Yes! Lazo thought, about to say something to Daiyu. But he held himself back as Daiyu bowed to the goddess, briefly speaking to her while ArcNight stepped away. At a gesture from Seiryuu, Renta'Mur joined the two women, acknowledging Daiyu with a short bow. Again, a short discussion ensued. Then Daiyu turned and directed her appreciative gaze to the group gathered in front of her. Her eyes lingered on Marceeka, Thompkins, and ArcNight. Both the young girl and Thompkins seemed awestruck while ArcNight nodded, his manner respectful.

"My friends," Daiyu said. "Thank you for your help. It's good to be back."

CHAPTER 13

"Interdimensional Leakage" is a more common
phenomenon than previously thought.
How else can you explain the alternate realities of
certain political figures and news outlets?

T'sai the Huntress

Zone of Concealment

Maghi Warren

2011 C.E.

Brewster reentered the Maghi warren, his eyes and ears alert for any noise or movement. Outside, the sounds of the battling monstros had ceased, becoming a murmurous undertone of hisses, spits, and growls. He paused to look back out onto the courtyard through the broken window. Once more a standoff seemed to be in progress. Orcus stood quietly, bloody wounds oozing, his great chest heaving. The bodies of several creatures lay broken and burned around him. Brewster spotted Quena among the throng, the creature's headlong charge halted. He stood apart of the others, facing Orcus directly. Evidently some kind of agreement had been reached or silent command or point-of-honor obeyed. Brewster wondered if Quena desired to fight Orcus by himself and had been granted that request.

Somehow, that seemed like the comic-book thing to do.

Then, as if a switch had been flipped, Orcus whirled and ran, stumbling back the way he'd come. The chimeric-mob stood watching and, then, quietly, slowly, began to follow him. The reptilian/feline being motioned to Quena, who joined her and the komainu at the front of the mob.

Brewster turned away and carefully descended the steps Jenny and Bella had taken to the so-called laboratory on the floor below. A scuffling sound reached his ears ahead of him. A large, shadowy, bestial shape appeared at the bottom of the stairs. Its tail wagged.

"Hiroshi," Brewster said, reaching the Ōkami and rubbing his head. "Everything okay? Where's Jenny? Is she all right?"

In response, the Ōkami turned and darted down the dimly-lit hallway. He waited for Brewster at an archway at the end of the dank, rubble-strewn corridor. Wayne couldn't see anything beyond the opening, only a deep darkness, like a black hole. As if impatient, Hiroshi trotted back to Brewster and gently took his hand in his great mouth. Tugging Brewster along, Hiroshi pulled him into the archway and the darkness.

A feeling like pushing through jello surrounded Brewster, as if he penetrated a gelatinous membrane. Then he was through and blinked in the brightly lit, modern, hi-tech room he found himself in. Jenny Sibulovich stood a few feet away in front of a server rack. She turned as Hiroshi came to her side. "Wayne," she said smiling. "Glad you could make it."

"Jenny, are you all right?"

"Yes." She indicated the computers and equipment. "Pretty amazing, huh? Bella described this as another pocket of reality within this Venice simulacrum."

"Speaking of Bella." Brewster pointed to an unconscious Bella lying on the floor.

Jenny chuckled. "Thanks for the strobe light. It came in handy. Hiroshi helped too."

Brewster smiled. It appeared Jenny and Hiroshi had neatly gotten out of what might have been a very bad situation very quickly. "The laboratory, I presume?" he asked.

"Yes, I'm going to need your computer skills here."

Brewster walked to Jenny's side, studying the servers. "This? For what?"

Jenny closed her eyes, folding her hands at her chest. Brewster marveled at the change in his friend, the courage and strength she'd found to fight against this unnatural, deadly threat. Not many people he knew could do that. Lazo was indeed a lucky man. She opened her eyes and met Brewster's gaze, her expression grim. "We're going to contact the Void. We're going to convince it to get its cosmic shit back together!"

———————————

Jenny figured it would take a lot to surprise Wayne Brewster, especially after all that had happened recently. From the expression on his face, her statement had done it.

"Contact the Void?" He eyed Jenny curiously. "And how do you propose we do that? I mean I like the idea, of course, but I doubt my long-unused IT knowledge would be of much help here."

"Maybe not. Yeah, we may be out of our league, but I have an idea." Jenny looked at the still-unconscious Bella. "And it involves our friend over there." She reached down to rub the Ōkami's head. "And Hiroshi too."

The wolf chuffed at Jenny's touch then swiveled his attention to Brewster and back to Jenny again.

Brewster crossed his arms at his chest and gave Jenny a tentative look. "Something tells me this isn't going to specifically be a scientific operation, is it? More info from the Akashic Records?"

Jenny shrugged. "Not sure but we've got a sorceress and a mythological wolf with us. There's got to be some energy there we can use."

"Again, how?"

Jenny knew her idea would sound pretty fantastic and not based on anything logical but something, something, told her this might work. She placed her fingertips to her temples and closed her eyes.

The Akashic Records

Well, hell, why not?

Bella groaned.

"We've got to keep her senseless," Jenny said as she, Brewster, and Hiroshi walked to where the sorceress lay. Bella looked to be regaining consciousness. Hiroshi growled, placed his head inches from Bella's and licked her face. The Ōkami's saliva sparkled for a moment on the woman's cheek then evaporated.

Bella sighed and slipped back into unconsciousness.

"Well," Jenny said. "That was convenient."

"You know, Hiroshi, that's the second hidden talent you've demonstrated since we hooked up." Brewster rubbed the big Ōkami's head. "What else do you have up those furry sleeves of yours?"

Hiroshi made a noise Jenny guessed was the Ōkami's version of laughter.

"We need to act quickly now, Wayne. I'm going to remove her eyepatch where an unusual and powerful aspect of her magic is concealed. Even though Bella's out, don't look directly at her face. It might still exert some negative power. Besides, it's pretty damn ugly." Jenny took hold of Bella's eyepatch and carefully lifted it.

"Man!" Brewster explained. "It looks like a mini-black hole."

"She mesmerized me with it before Hiroshi came to the rescue." She knew what she'd say next would be even more startling. "Wayne, can you find the server or domain controller here? We'll need some kind of a power cable or USB hookup to connect the controller to Bella's eye to bypass the network."

If Brewster was startled, he gave no sign of it except for a shadow of a smile. "Uh huh. Using Bella as a power source. Gross, but interesting." He stood and walked into the server racks.

"All right, Bella," Jenny whispered. "Let's see if you can do some good here for once in your vile life."

A few minutes later, Brewster helped Jenny place a server cable's IEC connector into Bella's eye, or the shimmering cavity that passed for an eye. "I don't know whether to laugh or throw up," Brewster said. He had to admit he felt a little unsettled at this bizarre idea, but Jenny was no one to argue with, especially now when she might be getting help from the ether somewhere.

After all, he and Hiroshi had just gotten back from a trip to a comic book universe so why would this be any more fantastic? Still...

"If this works," he said. "Then it'll mean Milaar had the means to possibly transport Orcus to our world right under her nose."

But Jenny wasn't paying attention. Kneeling beside Bella, she placed one hand on the sorceress' chest and the other on Hiroshi's back as the wolf sat beside her. It looked like she used the Ōkami and the Maghi as terminals or conductors for whatever type of energy might be called up.

Sure enough, the space around the threesome shimmered. Jenny, Bella, and Hiroshi became surrounded by a glow of faint, flickering iridescence Jenny and Hiroshi didn't move. No pyrotechnics, no conflagrations or explosions happened. Just the light and silence.

Brewster moved closer to Jenny. If anything went wrong, he would yank her and Hiroshi out of here. For a heartbeat, a memory flashed through his mind. Similarly, he had watched over Kim and Shioko in the Old Books and Research Haven. Kim had psychically entered Shioko's mind to bring the little girl out of her fear-driven trance after the shadow-tracker attack.

In this case, he didn't have to wait nearly as long as he had during that incident. With a moan, Jenny slumped sideways to the floor. The "connection" apparently broken, the light dissipated. Brewster picked Jenny up and carried her to the small couch in a corner of the lab. He turned to see Hiroshi taking hold of the cable with his teeth and pulling it away from Bella.

I've got to read up on Ōkami, he thought. This guy is full of surprises.

He lay Jenny down on the couch. "Jenny," he said. "Can you hear me? Are you okay?"

No response. Jenny looked to be breathing regularly but the movement beneath her closed eyelids reminded Wayne of REM sleep. He ventured a guess as Hiroshi joined them. "Hiroshi, can you do a wakeup lick as well as a knockout one?"

Hiroshi growled softly, positioned his head over Jenny's, and, true to his understanding Brewster Lassie-style, licked her cheek. Like before his saliva glittered for a second.

"Oh!" Jenny sat up, eyes wide.

"It's okay, Jenny," Brewster said, gently taking hold of her shoulders. "Are you all right? Did you contact the Void?"

Jenny looked like she'd stuck her finger into an electrical socket. "I...yes. Yes! But it was nothing like I could ever imagine."

No doubt. "And?"

"It, she, communicated with me but I can't explain how. I didn't really see her..."

"Her?"

"Yes, the Void is a female entity but definitely not human. But she's not gone rogue, Wayne. As you suspected, a'Kasha, that's the Void's name, is acting on her own volition. She's out to try and fix what she considers the problems with the cosmos, to change the way the universes are run." She shook her head. "Wow. And...and..."

"Yes?"

Jenny looked at Brewster. "It's like I thought. a'Kasha has been feeding Kim and me information almost from the beginning, without our knowing it. Ever since Kim first discovered her psi powers."

"The repository part of the Void. The Akashic Records."

"Yes!"

At that moment, Hiroshi whirled toward the lab entrance. Brewster turned as the wolf bared his fangs, hackles raised, and growled.

CHAPTER 14

There are no illusions in magic. Only illusions in perception.

Akihiko Sato, Court Magician of the Jade Court, The Veiled Years

Venice, Italy

Cannaregio District

2011 C.E.

"**D**aiyu!" Lazo finally cried, exhaling a relieved breath. "Are you okay?"

"I am now," the sorceress said. Black jeans and a long-sleeved, blue linen shirt, both ripped and dirty, clung to Daiyu's slim frame. Her straight dark hair hung disheveled around her shoulders. Despite her seeming disarray, her copper-colored skin, green eyes, and Asian features were striking, her manner confident. A slow smile spread over her face as she pressed her palms against her chest. She glanced at Seiryuu and the karura. "Thanks to the Guardian Spirit Dragon and her servant, Renta'Mur. And to all of you for staying by my side."

She looked again at Marceeka, who stared fearfully at Daiyu. "Have no fear, Marceeka. I know what you are but will not harm you."

"You are Maghi." Marceeka said softly.

"She's on our side, kid," Lazo said, instantly wondering what side Marceeka was really on. Despite Seiryuu's calming influence, Lazo sensed the girl needed even more than a goddess' help.

"He's right," ArcNight said, coming to the girl's side. "You're among friends."

The girl cast a softened look at the caped hero. She's seems to trust him, Lazo thought. That's one good thing.

Daiyu ran her hands through her hair. "I have no quarrel with you," she said to Marceeka. "Let us work together."

At that moment a soft humming sounded from the alley entrance. Lazo turned. The air, the space, above the alley floor shifted, becoming angles of fractal movement. A man stood in that spot, which had been empty moments before. Unblinking white eyes looked out of a sharp-featured face, neither young nor old. Braided white hair hung past his shoulder. His tall, black-robed body stood completely still. Lazo tensed at the sight of the strange-looking figure. He's outnumbered, he thought, aware of the sudden tension emanating from his comrades. But since he's here alone, he must be pretty powerful. Or pretty stupid.

Renta'Mur's wings furled. He raised his taloned hands and stepped forward.

"Hold!" Seiryuu ordered, her voice suddenly sharp and commanding. She walked toward the figure. "Agura the Hunter," she said. "What brings you here?"

Lazo gaped in surprise as the man, instead of attacking like Lazo thought he would, bowed to Seiryuu. "Splendid One," he said in a silky, soft voice. "I have been tasked to find you and your karura comrade. I am gratified you are both safe."

Seiryuu turned to Lazo and the others. "I and Renta'Mur must converse with Agura. Please remain here." She and the karura walked to speak to the imposing Hunter.

More delay! Lazo thought, slapping his hand against his thigh. What's going on now?

"Who's that guy?" Amamoto asked before Lazo could. "Agura the Hunter? What the hell does he hunt??"

"He is a servant of the Sanctuary Elders," Jaraal answered.

"Ah, that explains it," Amamoto cracked. "Sorry I asked."

Jaraal smiled, revealing sharp fangs. For a moment, Lazo thought of the Cheshire Cat. But one with a definite razor edge. "Someday, David-san, you and I will have a long conversation."

"Fine. As long as beer is involved. I need a few drinks after this."

"Enough of the freakin' banter!" Lazo said, throwing his hands up. "We've got to get inside that place and find Jenny!" He turned to ArcNight. "You and me, hero. You said Marceeka had the key to gettin' in there. Let's go!"

"Not like this, Sibulovich," ArcNight said. "I understand your frustration, but you need to calm down. We've got to have some kind of plan."

For one moment, Lazo wanted to shout, "I'm a cop, damn it!" but, upon realizing the hilarity of that comment, threw his hands up and shook his head.

"Chill, brother," Jonas Thompkins said. "The costumed dude's right."

Lazo whirled on Thompkins. "Don't brother me! I can't stand this anymore. My wife's been taken from me. Don't you understand that?"

"Lazo," Daiyu said, taking hold of his arm. "Please. We do understand, but you…"

"You're a damn magician! Can't you just do something with your magic, for God's sake?"

"Yes," Daiyu replied softly. "I can." She touched the side of Lazo's head. Her fingertips felt warm against his temple.

Lazo's eyes squeezed shut. His breathing slowed, his anger receded. "I... I'm sorry," he said, opening his eyes. "I didn't mean to lose it like that. I know I'm not the only one with problems here. Thanks, Daiyu."

Daiyu smiled. "Seiryuu comes." She frowned. "And I suspect not with good news."

"We cannot come with you."

David looked sharply at Seiryuu, as surprised at the goddess' comment as the rest of his comrades. "Why, Seiryuu?" he asked.

"Indeed, Splendid One," Jaraal added. "Why can you not?"

Seiryuu stood with Renta'Mur and the strange man, Agura the Hunter, a regretful expression on her face. "Renta'Mur and my parts in this are done," she said. "Urgent matters are afoot in the ambient-milieu I must attend to. Agura informs us certain events have transpired during my absence that are of great concern. My Guardian Spirit Convocation requires my presence. I have done all I can for you."

"Now wait a minute..." Sibulovich's temper once again ignited, his fists clenching.

This time David tried to reassure him. He knew the big man had been a cop and David, himself, was ex-military. Neither experience could prepare anyone for the kind of situation they found themselves in, despite their training and first-hand knowledge. Still, they had to keep their wits about them. That kind of discipline got David through Iraq and the battle at Spirit Winds, Inc. and he knew Sibulovich also possessed the same quality. "We've got Daiyu now, Mr. Sibulovich. Plus Jaraal and Thompkins. Trust me, they're more than capable. Not to mention your buddy ArcNight over there."

"Okay, okay." Sibulovich backed off, holding his hands up. "You're right. You're right."

"Mistress Seiryuu." Jonas Thompkins looked stricken. "I've just found you and now you're leavin'?"

The Guardian Dragon placed her hands on each side of Thompkins' head. "Be at peace, Jonas-san," she said softly. "I will never leave you and you have not only found me but these friends around you as well. Plus, you now have a purpose. One not defined by evil."

A moment passed, David thinking a type of silent communication

133

between the two ensued. Thompkins chest rose and fell, his eyes closed and opened. His face seemed to light up from within. "That's…that's what you want me to do?" Thompkins asked as Seiryuu stepped back, lowering her hands.

"It is your decision," the goddess answered. "It may seem to be a small matter, but its outcome has great significance. So, I put it to you first. It is dangerous and does entail a great sacrifice on your part so, please, do not agree in order to simply please me. You must do this for yourself, for the right reasons."

David glanced questioningly at Sibulovich, who simply shrugged.

"Jonas-san may not be accompanying us any further," Jaraal said. "I think the Splendid One is offering him another role to play."

"I'll do it," Thompkins said. "I got a lot of bad shit to make up for and, really, it ain't that much of a sacrifice. I want…need to do this, to have a life of my own, if I survive. Or a death of my own choosing."

Seiryuu smiled, dazzling and beautiful. She reached out her hands again. "Then go, Jonas Thompkins and live in glory."

"Thank you," Thompkins said. "Thank you. I'll… I'll never forget you."

And, just like that, Thompkins no longer stood there. He'd simply vanished.

"Seiryuu, what…? David began. But a gentle squeeze of his arm by Jaraal quieted him.

Seiryuu turned back to the group. "Do not grieve or fear for Jonas-san. Rest assured his part in this journey was written long ago. His willingness to fulfill it allows us to continue our fight."

Before Jaraal could stop him again, David asked, "Where did you send him, Seiryuu? And for what?"

"All is well, David-san," Seiryuu said. "I know you did not compl- etely trust Jonas Thompkins, but he is the only one who could accomplish the task I have given him. The only one who will accomplish it."

David nodded, not pressing the matter. He'd learned pretty quickly most questions he asked of these magical beings would rarely be answered. "I… I'm glad for Jonas, then, Seiryuu. I…know what it's like to go through life with regrets, with wanting to make amends. It can eat you up inside. I saw it in the service, when I served in Iraq, growing up with my family."

He turned toward ArcNight. "I said something to Mr. Brewster once, not you, but the other one. I fight against all injustice. The Totou, the Taliban, Al-Qaida, racists, neo-Nazis, or any other megalomaniacal group or individual won't succeed on my watch. And that goes for these freaking Maghi too!"

"Good to know, Mr. Amamoto," ArcNight said. "But I already pegged you as one of the good guys."

Again, Jaraal squeezed David's shoulder but this time the bakeneko gave David a look, despite his inhuman features, which registered respect. Sibulovich held out his big hand. "Glad to have you on our side, David," he said.

For a moment David's eyes stung. He blinked and said, "Okay. What now?"

Seiryuu continued, cast an approving look at David and the rest. "As some of you have heard me say, my powers are very different than what exists in this realm and might function erratically within the Zone of Concealment. But, yes, David-san is correct. You are a mighty force. Plus, Daiyu has a connection to the magic that has created the zone and will not be obstructed by the barrier."

Seiryuu's eyes focused on Marceeka. "Lucia Digregorio."

Her human name, David thought. And she's another one who acts like she needs to atone for something.

"I fear you can go no further either, child," Seiryuu continued. "Your part in this is also done. Your destiny lies on another path." Again, a silent exchange occurred between the two women, David was certain. Marceeka nodded. "I understand, Splendid One." Casting a quick glance at ArcNight, Marceeka calmly walked away and exited the alley.

We're being whittled away one by one, David thought.

"Seiryuu," ArcNight said. "What's going to happen to her?"

"I only know her ending, as with Jonas Thompkins, is not here with us. She too has another role to play."*

David thought ArcNight might protest but the man remained silent. David spoke, "Seiryuu, you haven't mentioned your friend Agura. Will he be joining us?"

"Ah..." Seiryuu turned toward the Hunter.

Agura spoke, his white eyes and stony features unreadable. But David discerned sincerity, perhaps even regret, in the Hunter's words. "I would be honored to help you find your comrades, but I cannot. I too must depart."

Seiryuu steepled her hands in front of her. "Good hunting and good luck to you all. It has been a privilege to be aligned with such courageous and righteous beings."

David's spirits rose, again in awe of Seiryuu and her words. But he

---

* As depicted in "The Raptor and the Lion" by Larry Ivkovich in Star Quake I Anthology, 2009.

knew not to get too confident. He thought of his wife, which made him smile. And more determined to see this through, if not for his sake, but for hers.

I'll get back to you, Lu, he thought, absently fingering the jade carving in his pocket. I promise. He blinked at the empty spot in front of him. Seiryuu and Renta'Mur had vanished. Agura stood, his arms folded at his chest, his hands hidden with the sleeves of his robe. Then he too was gone.

Daiyu stepped forward and held her arms out at her sides. "Now, everyone," she said, a glimmer of a smile on her lips. "Let us find Lazo's wife and end this!"

David pumped a fist. "Now we're talking!"

David winced. He brought his hand out of his pants pocket, holding and looking at the jade tiger. The figurine had become warm, almost hot to the touch. It glowed with a soft green light.

Wrapping it in his fist, he held it down at his side. In that moment, David knew what the figurine was.

CHAPTER 15

"The zeta-beam of the Adam Strange comic books
has to be a version of the Spirit Winds."

Wayne Brewster

"Star Trek's transporter ain't got nothin' on
temporal displacement tremors."

Lazo Sibulovich

Zone of Concealment

Maghi Warren

C. E. May 2, 2011

Brewster stood at Hiroshi's warning, his own defensive mode activating.

"Wayne," Jenny breathed. "Who is that?"

A tall black man dressed in a blue business suit, white shirt and black tie and shoes stood in the laboratory doorway. He regarded Brewster quizzically, seemingly as surprised to see Brewster and Jenny as they were to see him. Wisps of blue smoke curled upward from the floor around the man's feet, a faint odor of burning wood drifted on the air.

Brewster put a hand on Hiroshi's back, feeling the wolf tremble, his sidekick barely holding back his primal urge to attack. "Who are you?" he demanded of the stranger, a chill running through him. "How did you get here?"

"Hmmm," the stranger said. "This is interesting."

"What?"

The man held a hand up, palm outward, and Brewster immediately shut up. A fuzzy warmth traveled the length of his body. For a moment, he felt as if he could lie down and just go to sleep. But then, just as suddenly, he snapped to his senses and became alert again.

Hiroshi abruptly quieted and sat down at his side. Brewster glanced at Jenny who had placed one hand against her chest, the beginnings of a smile beginning to form on her freckled face.

The developing tension and sense of danger had gone. Brewster stared intently at the man. He did something to us, Brewster thought.

To take away the surprise, to defuse the situation.

The man entered the lab, an unreadable expression on his face. He spoke in a soft voice, a slight unrecognizable accent evident in his English. "I've administered a neural massage to calm you and your friends here," he said, confirming Brewster's guess. The stranger shot a quick glance at Bella. "Except for that bitch. She appears to be calm enough."

Jenny abruptly laughed, her eyes wide. "She is that," she said.

"This…adventure gets more and more interesting," the stranger continued. "If someone would have told me so much of an unexpected nature would happen after I got promoted to a Sanctuary Elder, I would have laughed."

A what? Brewster shot a confused glance at Jenny who just raised her eyebrows.

For a moment, the man's features changed, shifting and blurring, revealing another countenance, if it could be called that. Brewster started. A face? He wasn't sure exactly what he saw in that moment, but that second visage seemed more nebulous, not human at all.

"Wayne," Jenny said, reaching out to take Brewster's hand. "I… I think he may be okay."

"It's true," the man said. "I am…okay although I didn't expect to pop up here. I don't usually get surprised very often. And I'm not really a 'he,' per se, but I do possess the powers of a metamorph and can shift my shape when needed." He looked at Jenny. "Dr. Sibulovich, right?" he addressed her.

"How do you know me?"

"Before I manifested to this level, I picked up on your conversation with that Maghi sorceress, Bella. I regret at that moment I wasn't able to help you. My apologies."

"That's…that's quite all right," Jenny said.

"Bella told you this place was a pocket of reality, right? One she created herself?"

"Yes. She did say that."

The man shook his head. "Not entirely true. In fact, it's bullshit. This laboratory and the outside environs resembling Venezia are, in truth, part of the Mystic Realm, annexed by the Maghi for their own purposes centuries ago."

"The Mystic Realm?" Brewster said.

"Yes, an offshoot of what we call the ambient-milieu. The beasties of the Italian mythos who inhabit the Mystic Realm have been diminished, exiled, cut off from the other realms of the multiverse by the First Bastards, I mean Lords, of the Maghi. Only when the present cataclysm weakened the Veils Between Worlds, did they find the strength and resolve to attempt to finally fight back."

"And you're one of those Mystic Realm beasties? Wearing a business suit?"

"No, I'm not." The man smiled. "I took on a form you'd be familiar with. As for the Mysties, as I call them, I'm basically just working for them. The organization I belong to received a kind of distress call from an outcast Mysty, a papstesel, a patchwork being, as it were, a chimera made up of several different aspects."

An image formed in Brewster's mind. A being with the head of a donkey, a snake for a tail, flesh and scales covering a mostly female body with one foot clawed, the other a hoof. The head of an old man peeked out from between its shoulder blades.

Patchwork? Brewster shuddered. He'd never heard of the papstesel but felt that brief look was more than enough.

"This papstesel, who insists on remaining nameless, rebelled against his own kind centuries ago to help a mortal being, a renegade sorceress named Daiyu. Do you know of her?"

"No," Jenny said.

"Me neither," Brewster added.

"Trust me, you will." He held up a hand. "Uh uh, don't ask. I can't reveal any spoilers, you know."

"Can you help us?" Jenny asked. She rose from the couch and stood next to Brewster.

"Yes! Why not? I've broken just about every rule of metaspace administration since I got elevated to this position as an Elder. One more cosmic indiscretion surely wouldn't hurt." He looked away and smiled. Then, almost to himself, "Besides, I guess I'm feeling frisky today."

He sighed. "I can tell you this—from within the Mystic Realm, the Mysties are hard at work to release this so-called pocket of reality from its interdimensional construction and return it to its rightful place within their own spectral landscape. The current rupture of the Veils Between Worlds has given them back the ability to repair it, albeit slowly." He held up a finger. "Ah, excuse me. I have to take this."

The Elder paused, closing his eyes as if listening. "I don't have much time," he continued after a few moments. "Whatever magical detour brought me here is about to release me. So, I can only warn you. The Mysties, with my help, may succeed at any time to regain control of their domain. You must leave here as soon as possible. Return to your own reality before this 'pocket' collapses."

"We have friends in trouble here," Brewster said. "We won't leave without them. Isn't there anything you can do?"

"You are a loyal, strong, and courageous man, Wayne Brewster. Good looking, too."

"You know me? How?"

"Neural signature. It's like a mental fingerprint within the ambient milieu that is a slipstream or network, if you will, of mental wavelengths accessible by all creatures providing they know how to access their personal entry point. Every sentient being possesses a signature uniquely their own."

"Yes, yes!" Brewster's patience had worn thin enough without all this talk! Brewster felt exhausted by the man's long-winded explanations. "We know what a neural signature is!"

"Oh, right. Kim would have explained that all to you."

"For God's sake, are you going to help us or...?" Brewster jerked. "Kim? You know Kim?"

"Again, no spoilers. You'll find out soon enough. In the meantime, I'll try to convince the Mysties of your urgency, and to hold off a little longer in order for you to get to your friends and beat feet. I'm sorry, but that's all I can do at the moment. As a Sanctuary Elder, I normally have more leeway in executing these types of, uh, magically cosmic tricks, but I'm on a deadline here and, quite frankly, acting independently, which is a big cosmic no-no."

Jenny took a step forward. "Sanctuary Elder," she whispered. "I... I think I've heard of that."

"Hmmm," the man looked thoughtfully at Jenny, cupping his chin in a hand. "You've contacted the Void, haven't you?"

"You know that, too, it seems. Yes, I have."

"You have a certain, shall we say, aura about you. Huh. Curiouser and curiouser. Something tells me, Dr. Sibulovich, you and I will meet again. Good luck."

"Wait a minute!" Brewster cried. Hiroshi ran toward the stranger.

The man flickered as smoke arose around him, encircling him in a cloud of blue mist. In a moment, he had simply disappeared.

Brewster gritted his teeth. "How's that for gratitude?" he snapped. "That cataclysm and rupturing he talked about was basically your doing, Jenny. He could have at least thanked you!"

"She, Wayne. I think he was a she." Jenny lay a hand on his arm. "At least she warned us. It looks like we're here on borrowed time."

"As if we didn't need any more pressure, but you're right. But how does he or she know Kim? And what did she mean saying those things about you? That you'd meet again?" Now it was Brewster's turn to study Jenny. "You know what these Sanctuary Elders are?"

"It's just a feeling. I don't completely understand it yet. Remember what I said about getting information from a'Kasha? It's like that, sudden knowledge filling my mind like air filling a balloon. At the same time, it makes me calmer, more relaxed and accepting of that knowledge."

"Instant explanation and reassurance," Brewster said. "Just add thought. Okay, let's get the hell out of here and find Kim!"

"I'll try to contact Kim mentally again, but I can't go with you."

"What do you mean?"

"I need to stay here for a little while."

"Why? Jenny, what's up?" The Void, Brewster thought. This has something to do with her contacting the Void.

"I can't explain it now. Just, please, do as I ask. I'll be along later." She looked toward Bella. "And, if you will, take that out of here."

CHAPTER 16

Metamorphosis, transmutation, holometabolism, whatever term is used, can never truly describe and explain the process of complete and utter biological and alchemical change.

An element of the numinous must also be present.
Alberta Portero
The Mystic Realm: My Ancestor's Spectral Voyage

The Month of Marzo

Time of Constant Battle

2007 C.E.

Venice, Italy

They'd fled, having been defeated. Humiliated.

The Totou, his cowardly masters, had used him, creating his hybrid nature in order to further their own goals. And then, after their abject failure, they'd planned on terminating him, deeming him too dangerous and expensive an experiment to continue.

Jonas Thompkins raged silently as he remembered that time. The time before he escaped the Totou during their retreat and so-called "relocation." When the Cabal withdrew to lick its wounds after succumbing to the Shuugouteki's power. The time when his Mistress' Maghi agents had found him and had taken him from the streets after his escape—homeless, drug-riddled—to keep his morphing at bay. The time before he'd been molded, fashioned, and trained in the ways of the Maghi in their Venetian warren.

Now he faced his first test as part of his Mistress' inner circle.

In his shadow-tracker persona, he crouched on the roof of a house overlooking a small, neighborhood canal. His muscles tensed beneath the layer of black fur covering his humanoid body. His pointed ears pricked forward. His yellow eyes pierced the semi-darkness, only lit from a single standing streetlight.

The sidewalk edging the canal lay empty of life; no one walked its tiled length. The houses bordering each side of the narrow waterway sat darkened, quiet. And no wonder. This place was a crossroads of time and space, one designated Between.

A battleground for the Hunt. A killing floor.

The chiming of church bells, which always rolled through the winding maze of narrow, crisscrossing streets and canals comprising the city, suddenly stopped. As if heralding the approach of another and the impending battle.

Jonas sniffed the night air. Ah, yes, there. Someone did come. Not just a human, or umana, as the Maghi called them in Italian. But a special being, powerful, full of magic.

The human vessel of a Lion of the Venedetto. One of the two warring factions of the Maghi. Jonas remembered his Mistress' teachings.

The leaders of those ancient tribes known only as the Shadow Clans had cursed the Lions' and the Raptors' human families long ago for opposing the Clans' corrupt dictates. A Blood Pact had been written, passing down its precepts through countless generations of unsuspecting umana.

One month every generation, the Time of Constant Battle would allow the Raptors and the Lions to take form. Once, every twenty years, after being suppressed by an umana psyche as the Curse dictated, the two factions' animal natures would emerge to hunt and fight again.

The city had been a collection of fishermen's stilt-huts in those times, dotted throughout the islands of the lagoon and ruled loosely by the Shadow Clans and their supporters, who would eventually become the Maghi. The Shadow Clans clandestinely orchestrated the ascension of the first ruling Doge and propelled Venice to power as the longest running Republic in the history of the world.

The Pact had been written to assure the Hunt would never interfere with the growth of the city. That it would, in fact, contribute to its growth. That the energy expended in battle, and the blood sacrifices taken by the Raptors and the Lions would give the city its strength and dominance. Almost as if Venice were a living thing, feeding on its own people.

So much had Jonas learned! How proud he felt to be chosen for this powerful ritual!

His hackles tingled. He licked his fangs in anticipation. Normally one of Solomon's Raptors would face off against a Lion, competing for the blood of the city.

But, tonight, his Mistress had appointed him as a combatant. As the Lion changed below him, bursting out of his human clothes into its leonine form, Jonas jumped from the roof to the killing floor.

Ōiso, Japan

Jade Court Era, The Veiled Years

C.E. 1543

Thompkins took a deep breath. Alive. He was alive! And the air he breathed…so clear, so pure. Except for the smoke. From his hidden vantage point behind a pile of charred, fallen timbers at the end of a narrow dirt road, he saw fires raging in the distance. Destruction lay all around him. A great battle had been fought here in this town of…Ōiso.

I'm here, he thought. I'm in the freaking past. In…in freaking Japan. Seiryuu did it!

His body thudded with the hammering of his heart. No turning back now. Seiryuu had told him what he had to try and do. Whether or not he succeeded or even survived was up to him.

I can do this. I can do this. I got to!

Just as Seiryuu had described without speaking, the thoughts and words forming from her mind to his, two buildings stood across the street from one another. One was a religious shrine to the town's protective kami, damaged but still mostly intact from whoever had attacked this town. Sounds of a struggle came from within. Shouts, curses.

The wind shifted. The hairs on Thompkins neck and arms prickled. A gamy odor drifted on the breeze from the other building, a barrel-maker's shop. He watched, fascinated, as two figures emerged from the building.

Shadow-trackers.

Thompkins gritted his teeth, his fingers digging into the dirt. He'd never encountered another shadow-tracker before. These were the original models, not like him. They were shorter and less stocky than he but that didn't mean they'd be easy to take down.

The two beasts paced before the shrine, snapping their jaws impatiently. The doors to the shrine burst open. Three hooded soldiers, samurai, exited. Two of them dragged a fourth man, a robed priest.

They threw the priest in the dirt at the shadow-trackers' feet. The priest rose to his knees, defiant, his expression hard and unrelenting. The shadow-trackers lifted him to his feet and pulled him into the barrel-maker's shop.

Thompkins removed his backpack where he'd packed extra clothes in case he had to morph quickly. His shadow-tracker persona stood over seven feet tall. If he had clothes on when he changed, they'd be shredded.

For one absurd moment, he thought of The Incredible Hulk television show where David Banner always seemed to have an inexhaustible supply of shirts, shoes, and pants after hulking out and ripping up the ones he wore.

This ain't TV, Jonas thought. Closing his eyes, he morphed, allowing the beast within to emerge.

Leaping out from hiding, he rushed toward the three samurai. The soldiers' complete surprise helped lead to their undoing. Thompkins took them down easily, his claws ripping through their puny armor and skin like paper.

Whirling toward the barrel-maker's shop, Thompkins spied one the shadow-trackers watching in surprise from the doorway. He'd gotten their attention. Silently he charged, slamming into the other beast. They fell back onto the floor, knocking over a lantern and two barrels. Pinning the shadow-tracker, Thompkins grabbed the beast's throat with his claws and ripped it completely out.

Just like he'd done with his hated partner, Andera Martouse, in another time and place.

Thompkins regained his feet as the second shadow-tracker howled. It launched itself from the back of the shop where it had dragged the priest. It slashed at Thompkins, raking its claws over his chest. With a howl of his own, Thompkins grabbed his attacker's head and twisted.

Its neck snapped, the shadow-tracker dropped dead to the floor. Thompkins raged triumphantly over his victory, his animal nature asserting itself. He yelped at the smell of smoke, realizing the interior of the shop had caught fire, probably from the fallen lantern.

Regaining control, he rushed toward the priest. The man was unconscious with some cuts and bruises. The shadow-trackers hadn't had time to wreak their bloody toll upon him. Thompkins picked him up and, leaping over and through the flames, ran out of the shop.

He turned for a moment to witness the shop become engulfed in fire. Too late, he heard the strum of an arrow being released. The feathered projectile arrow found his neck, piercing his thick hide. One of the samurai he'd attacked. Somehow the soldier still lived, getting to his knees, nocking his bow and shooting him.

Another arrow. This time directed at the samurai. It imbedded itself in the man's already slashed chest, felling him completely.

Thompkins turned toward the shrine, blood forming in his mouth, his breath ragged. The arrow had to have struck a vital artery. Even

146

for one as strong as he, he knew he'd bleed out soon. A young woman stood at the shrine's doorway, a bow in her hands. She stared in wonder at Thompkins, then beckoned him to enter the shrine.

Staggering, his vision blurring, Jonas Thompkins carried the priest into the shrine.

INTO THE AKASHIC

The realm of the Myriad Things is only a thought away.
But it must be the *correct* thought.

Samuel Kim

THIRD INTERVAL

Venice, Italy

1457 C.E.

Daiyu moved quickly through the narrow, darkened street, her breath catching in her throat. Pulling her cloak tightly about her slender body, she forced herself to run faster. Only moonglow and the occasional torch inset in the stone wall sconces illuminated her way with dancing, checkered light.

Any late-night, wandering umana would only notice a passing rush of air, a faint odor of jasmine, perhaps a movement from the corner of their human eyes. The air was cold this autumnal eve, and even through the warm cloak Daiyu wore, she shivered from something other than the season.

The Maghi and their creatures pursued her. If caught, they would show her no mercy. She had defied and betrayed them and been found out. Despite the magical abilities she herself possessed, she would be helpless before their combined might.

Her only hope waited for her at the lagoon's hidden quay—her lover and fellow Maghi Marcello. Their small boat was ready; together they would escape the fate awaiting them both. Together they would warn those outside Venezia of the threat the Maghi posed and the great evil they presided over.

"Daiyu!" A shadowy figure appeared in front of her, blocking her path.

Daiyu raised her hands, ready to strike. Then she recognized the voice. "Amedio?" she said.

"Yes." Maghi sorcerer Amedio Zaronelli stepped into a circle of wan light.

Daiyu bristled. "So you've come for me too?"

"No, Daiyu. I'm here to warn you." Amedio's dark features were set like a mask, emotionless, hard, but his eyes revealed a great fear within their depths.

"Warn me?" Daiyu lowered her hands, surprised by the sorcerer's sudden appearance. Amedio had always been supportive of her, had taken her side in one or two disputes with the other Maghi. He had never acted like the other sorcerers with their deadly, power-hungry aspirations and their distaste for the "outsider" in their midst. At least he had always seemed so. At times even more so than Marcello who was always more cautious.

But why was Amedio really here? She knew many of the Maghi had their own self-serving plans, subservient to a degree to the First Lords but always scheming on their own behalves. Always. In the end, why would Amedio be any different?

"Yes." Amedio looked stricken. "Marcello has betrayed you. He has no intention of helping you to escape let alone accompany you."

"What?" Daiyu rose up. "I don't believe it! How would you know this?"

"It's true. He desires power, nothing more. He uses you to gain it. Go no further. Turn back."

"You lie!" Daiyu always suspected Amedio favored her more than just as a comrade. Could he be lying about Marcello in order to gain her favor for his own ends? How could she herself not know if Marcello possessed such duplicitous aims? Was Amedio implying she herself had been somehow secretly bespelled? "I thought you were different but you're just as conniving as the rest of the Maghi."

"Please believe me, Daiyu, you're running into a trap. Come with me, I beg you."

"Get out of my way!" Daiyu shoved forward, an unfamiliar anger burning within her. Amedio turned away as if struck, allowing Daiyu to rush past him. She fumed. Marcello loved her! He would never do such a thing as Amedio accused him of!

But as she stepped from the street into a small campo, the tiled courtyard shimmering softly in the light of the moon, she realized her mistake. The air suddenly felt lighter. Her skin tingled, the hair on the back of her neck rose. Outside the boundaries of the campo, the fishermen's huts, the clouds scudding across the night sky, the flicker of torches, took on a blurred, unearthly aspect, as if time itself had slowed.

Strade Trasversali. Crossroads, a place Between, one of Power and invisible to the umana whenever the Maghi so wished it. Daiyu had indeed walked into a trap. She who had been the betrayer had now herself been betrayed. And stupid and naive. She had let her guard down for someone she thought she loved, for a passion she'd never known before.

Marcello. What have you done? How could I believe your lies?

As if in answer to her unspoken questions, the shadows took shape, moving, coalescing. Cloaked and masked figures stepped into the campo like hooded spirits. They formed a circle of black to surround Daiyu, the power radiating from them almost as tangible as a physical blow. Like grotesque Carnivale revelers, the dark forms stood statue-like, the eyes behind the masks they wore blazing with an angry light.

Two such eyes she recognized. Marcello.

Too late Daiyu realized why Marcello had urged her to come this way, through the Jewish Ghetto. From sunset to dawn, those living here were forbidden by law to be outside their homes. There would be no one to help her or, at least, witness her fate. Some umana possessed the ability to see into the Between realm. Not so here. She would die alone and unnoticed.

Then again, perhaps not. Amedio Zaronelli, familiar to her even behind his own mask, joined the circle. Amedio, why didn't I listen to you? Would he help her now? Or would he play the part of the powerful and judgmental Maghi, his powers directed against her in order to save himself?

One of the masked figures spoke, "Daiyu," the male voice intoned, low and menacing. "Sister of the East. Our castaway from La Cina. Why have you rejected our teachings?" Daiyu felt a buzzing in her head; a strange sensation coursed through her body. "You are unique, different," the voice continued. "We have always suspected that. Your eastern blood infuses you with a mysterious inner strength. We thought we could tame and harness that strength. But no. You, who have showed so much promise, have disappointed us greatly. You have become the outsider, the alien, among us in more than just your race."

Daiyu tamped down her fear and fought against the encroaching unreality, using mental techniques taught to her by the Maghi when she had been an obedient and blind disciple. Ah, but it was more than that, she realized. The forces of the Cinese mo fa which had lain dormant within her for so long, those magical workings of her eastern heritage, began to stir. "I follow my heart," she answered, her own voice calm and steady. "My eyes have been opened. It is the Maghi who have disappointed. Mad with the lust for power, corrupt, eager to control and destroy all who oppose them."

An angry hiss sounded around her, a chorus of hatred that made her heart jump.

"Kill her."

"Burn her."

"Destroy her."

The speaker broke the circle and approached Daiyu. A chill ran through her. She thought she knew now who this was, who they all were. Tall, feral-seeming, exuding raw power, their bejeweled, beaked plague masks repugnant. Though she had never been privileged enough to meet the Primi Signori, the First Lords, those who had formed the Maghi so long ago, she knew she faced them now.

Including Marcello and Amedio.

But was it the magic and its blood payment that controlled and manipulated Venezia and its umana denizens for centuries, which was now directed at Daiyu?

No. Instead, the First Lord struck Daiyu with the back of his long-nailed hand, viciously, brutally, like some umana thug. With a surprised cry, Daiyu's head snapped back and she dropped to the pavement. With a gasp, she looked up to see Amedio rush forward. He stood between her and the First Lord.

"Listen to me, my Lords," Amedio said. "Daiyu can still be of use to us. Do not harm her."

The First Lord pointed to Amedio. "We can tolerate a transgression or two among our kind," he said. "But to love this alien traitor? That, also, will not go unpunished. We banish you, Amedio Zaronelli. You are no longer Maghi."

"Then banish us together!"

"No! She will die and you will suffer the memory of it. That is our judgment."

"Your judgement?" Amedio said, pointing to one of the robed figures. "Or is it hers?"

Daiyu watched, puzzled, as one of the robed figures broke the circle, walking toward Amedio. A woman. No! More than a woman.

The woman raised her hands and removed her mask. Daiyu rose to her feet. This was no Maghi! The woman facing Amedio was of the Dark Demesne!

"Estansa Milaar," Amedio spat. "So you and your filthy kind add your powers to the Maghi." He turned away from the lamia. "My Lords, how can you allow this? Nothing good can come from such an unnatural union!"

In reply, each First Lord pointed a long finger at Amedio. Amedio jerked as the combined power of the sorcerers struck him. He bent over, falling to his knees.

"Stop! Amedio, protect yourself!" Daiyu tried to rush to Amedio's aid but the power of the First Lords overwhelmed her. An unseen binding encircled her mind and body. She plummeted into an endless abyss.[*]

* As depicted in "The Turin Effect" by Larry Ivkovich in Penumbra Online Magazine, 2011.

CHAPTER 17

They say, "Everyone makes their own Hell."
The same can be said of the Dark Demesne.

Kim Yoshima

The Dark Demesne

"It is getting more difficult to bring you here."

The Dark Demesne. And Omori again. "You did a pretty good job just now. I tried to fight you off, but it didn't work."

"And that has fatigued me."

Kim placed her hands on her hips and allowed herself a satisfied smirk. "What a shame. Maybe you should start working out."

Omori glared at her, giving new meaning to the phrase "If looks could kill."

This time around the stark landscape of the Demesne exhibited a little more color and substance. Some bluish thatch-like ground cover stretched away from Omori's dais. A few scraggly, leafless trees dotted the harsh ground in the distance. The sky had turned a light green with two small moons hanging over the horizon.

Were those changes a good thing? The warlord said he was having a more difficult time. The landscape had changed to reflect that. Maybe.

Kim tapped her lip with a gloved finger. She narrowed her eyes at the warlord. "I think I know who's competing with you for my attention. Remember that spider-demon I mentioned. A jorōgumo. Goes by the name of Damara."

Omori's face lit up with interest. "Ah, so. And?"

"Something latched onto her spirit-avatar from what she referred to as an imprisoning nether-realm and freed her. At least I think so. She mentioned someone helping her and I suspect that someone came to collect payback for their help."

"So, there is this spider-demon, myself, and a'Kasha all vying for the vaunted Yomitsu's attention. You are indeed in great demand."

"Tell me about a'Kasha."

"A great celestial power. We know It as the Void."

"The Void? It has a name? So it's...it's sentient?"

Kim looked away, somehow not completely surprised, though why it had centered its attention on her was still a mystery. She looked back at Omori. "Does this a'Kasha know you've intercepted me? Will it interfere with what you want to do?"

"If we do not act quickly, yes. I have been fortunate in concealing my presence from it but feel I cannot keep that up for much longer."

"You still haven't convinced me of anything."

Omori hissed between clenched teeth. Kim sensed some kind of internal struggle going on behind that scarred exterior. The sky abruptly roiled in whirlpools of red and gray. "Though it galls me to ask this," he finally said. "You must help me."

"What?" This was unexpected. And ludicrous. "You can't be serious."

"I am nothing but. Through my talent at deception, I was able to contact and convince a certain servant of Orcus to believe I was indeed her demon master. A faithful, if incompetent servant who bungled an attempt to free me and bring me back into corporeal existence. You must aid this servant to complete that task. That is why you are here."

"Uh huh. You fooled someone into thinking you were the devil? That wouldn't be hard to do."

"You make light of this?"

"That's like the cat asking the squirrel to let him into her nest. Why would I help to free you?"

Omori bared his teeth. "To get me out of your head. Is that not reason enough?"

He had her there. "So then, what? You can unleash your evil on the world again? I'm willing to sacrifice my sanity to prevent that." Kim surprised herself by meaning just that.

"How noble you are! And how foolish."

"Fuc…"

"Listen to me, my Great Enemy. I am the key to restoring the Balance."

Kim snorted. "Oh, please, that expression is so damn clichéd. You can do better than that."

"Why do you think my Parker-incarnation was able to splinter my spectral essence before he died, to cast each separate shard into another neural realm? Into Shioko and the ambient-milieu itself. To resurrect himself afterwards? How a shard of my spirit-avatar almost took control of the milieu, yes? I had studied and exploited the weaknesses of that realm which allowed me to attack it. I was able to absorb the powerful energies abiding there and use those against it."

Kim bared her own teeth. "But you failed. Mitsu stopped you. Let me remind you again—she lopped your ugly head right off."

Omori craned his neck toward her. His twisted features flickered as if trying to hold back a smoldering rage. "Yes, she did, did she not?"

And he's still pissed about it. Good!

"Do you think all that was coincidence?" Omori spat. "I, in some form, was meant to survive through the ages, to this moment, to take my rightful place in the multiverse."

"What B Sci-Fi movie did you escape from? That's super-villain-talk 101. You're insane! I'll kill myself first before I allow you to go free. In any form."

"Not even to help your nephew?"

Bobby. Kim felt like she'd been hit over the head. "What are you talking about?"

Omori smiled. "Did you not realize what I'd just said?"

Kim blinked. The words had just washed over her. "You...you said Parker resurrected himself."

"Indeed, and he has taken your nephew."

"Liar!" Kim snarled, her body shaking. "I killed that maniac! I killed him twice!"

"And yet he lives. I do not lie in this matter."

"Damn you." As if she didn't have enough to worry about. Now this. She couldn't ignore this. Omori might be lying to get her to help him but, then again, he might not. Bobby's life could be in danger.

"Listen to me, Kim Yoshima. I can help your nephew if you help me. The servant of Orcus I mentioned has vanished from my awareness. As I weaken, I can no longer exert my will as strongly as I could."

Okay, okay. Kim took a deep breath. "Because, as you say, a'Kasha has changed. What's the Void have to do with this?"

"I am unsure of that. I only know a great upheaval has occurred in the multiverse, partly as a result of a'Kasha's instability. That instability once helped me to expand my power and now depletes it."

Kim tried to process this new information. She said carefully, "All right. You're able to detect my presence within the displacement tremors and reroute me here through my lizard brain or whatever the hell it is. Except you can't hold me for long, can you?"

"Just so. But I can keep you here long enough to explain how you can help to release me."

"All right. I'm listening."

"I mentioned a servant of Orcus I had misled. Yes? Estansa Milaar, Grand Mistress of the Maghi. Do you know of her?"

159

"The Maghi, yes. Milaar, no. Should I?"

"She controls the Maghi in the mortal realm of Venice. As a lamia and one of Orcus' servants, she possesses great powers."

A lamia. In Venice. Did she have something to do with Jenny's disappearance? "So, Milaar's a vampire and she's missing, is that it? What of it?"

"The Maghi attempted to control your scientist friend..."

Another punch to the emotional gut. The Maghi did take Jenny!

"Ah, I see you know her."

"Yes, I know her!" Kim glanced away, trying to maintain a neutral expression. First Bobby and now Jenny. Turning back to Omori, she said as calmly as she could, "Go on."

"Milaar attempted to establish your scientist as a Nexus Point. She wanted to manipulate those forces known as the Spirit Winds in an effort to bring Orcus into our world, not knowing my true identity, but failed."

"Is my friend all right?"

"So far, I believe she is."

Kim held back the revulsion forming in the back of her mind. "What is it you want me to do?"

"Locate Estansa Milaar and take her back to the Maghi Summoning Chamber in their Zone of Concealment. She must recommence the ritual to free me, this time with you as the Nexus Point. Despite her failure, Milaar holds the key to my freedom. You must locate her."

Goddess, help me! "How? I don't even know where to begin to look for this person."

"You must..."

"You must, you must, you must. Damn you!" Kim spat. "I'm not going to help you find this damn vampire, until my nephew and Jenny are safe!"

Fists clenched at her sides, Kim let her anger overcome her fatigue and disgust, releasing it in a psychic beam straight at Omori. It widened, bathing the warlord in a wave of dark emotion. Omori flinched as Kim's rage struck him. His body shivered, his hands shook. A great sigh, like a hot gust of wind, escaped his mouth. He moved, bringing his arms up, bending his knees, slowly, as if he felt great pain.

Kim suddenly felt better, her healing telekinetics aside. Her fatigue and nausea had completely abated. It seemed a little brute force against this old enemy had done wonders for her.

"You do have great power." Omori dropped to his knees on the dais, his head down. The chains loosened around him as their tautness relaxed. "Look what you have done," he said, shooting a reptile gaze at Kim. "Though still bound, I am free to move again. After all this time. You are more powerful than you know."

Kim shuddered at the sight. "That's not what I intended! You did that to yourself. I refuse..."

"If you do not find Estansa Milaar in order to free me, your nephew and your friend will die. That much I do know. Everything will change."

"Because of you? You think you're that important?"

"It is much more complicated than that. I am one of many. As you are. As there are countless Balances existing in countless worlds. We both have a role in maintaining the equilibrium of the multiverse. If... our universe is unduly affected, so will the others be. Our goals are the same."

"Never." Kim turned away, pressing her clasped hands to her chin. "Wait a minute. Back when I first entered Parker's mind, someone else was there. I saw a person, a man, at least a silhouette. Who was that?"

Omori stared. "You saw nothing."

He's lying. "You know I did. Who or what else was in Parker's mind?"

Omori suddenly reared up, his mouth opened wide as if in shock. The warlord shook his head, eyes blinking rapidly. Kim started as Omori groaned, his head lolling onto his chest, his body slumping forward.

He's unconscious, Kim thought. For a moment, her head swam. She placed her fingers to her temples, taking a deep breath to dispel the dizziness.

She looked up...

The sounds of bells drifted over the plain. A sweet smell of incense enveloped her. In the distance, wavering shapes appeared, enormous, alien.

Like before, the landscape shifted.

CHAPTER 18

The inner self holds the true power;
the outer exists only as a vessel.

Samuel Kim

The Teachings of Yira - The Five Precepts to Enlightenment

The Void

Guess Omori and I didn't act quickly enough.

Kim stood in a sunlit garden, one of indescribable beauty. Scarlet-leafed maples, flowering yews, orchids and other lush vegetation encircled her. Finely-cut grass lay beneath her booted feet. Another dais made of intricately-carved and bejeweled stone rose waist-high and twice as wide in the middle of a circular glade.

The space above the dais glimmered, as if from a fallen star. Unfurling in shadowy tendrils, a smoky essence drifted in waves to the ground, roiling and unfolding. It coalesced in streamers of luminous color, forming substance, becoming a woman.

But not just any woman. Of inestimable beauty, she stood shining in a long, white robe, an aura of spectral brilliance surrounding her. Her silver hair fell shimmering to her ankles. Her eyes gleamed bright blue, golden motes floating within each orb.

"Kim Yoshima," the woman said in a smoky, deep voice. She moved closer, floating rather than walking. Like something out of a vision, her form shimmered with a soft glow. She bowed her head. "An honor to meet you again. Fabulous outfit. Onna-bugeisha, right?"

Kim gawked, astonished, unable to speak. Then it hit her. Surely, this was Amaterasu! Well, an Amaterasu who talked very un-goddess-like. But who else could it be? Kim blurted out, "Please, great sun goddess, my friends and my nephew are in trouble. You have to help them!"

"I'm not Amaterasu," the woman said, "Though I appreciate the comparison. I borrowed this appearance from one of the sun goddess' gorgeous servants. Sometimes I miss my old human persona. Plus, I like to make an entrance. I think this's a good look for me, don't you?"

Kim's spirits fell. To have met the sun goddess! What an experience that would be. Then again, after all that had happened, Kim would probably rip Amaterasu a new one!

"I…yeah, you look, uh, marvelous," she replied to the woman's bizarre question. "But, my concern still stands. My friends. My nephew Bobby…"

The woman waved a dismissive hand. "Your friends and your nephew are safe for now. Trust me."

"Trust you? Who are you?"

"A friend also. Someone who's been, shall we say, following your career. I felt it time to intervene in this hot cosmic mess. I'm here to help."

"A friend, huh?" Kim said. "You know, I feel like I'm going through this revolving door of magical beings popping up and telling me absolutely nothing! Directing my every move. I need to be free, to make my own decisions, to act, not react. Can you give me some concrete answers for a change?"

Amazingly, the woman laughed. "Most mortals would stand in awe of my presence but you're not most mortals, are you?"

"Let's just say you're not my first mythological deity rodeo. I've become pretty jaded when it comes to this kind of thing."

"I'll bet," the woman said. "Unfortunately, there are some things you have to find out for yourself. Take it from me. I've been there. That's just the way things work."

Kim threw her hands up. "I knew it! Another dead end."

"Now hang on." The woman floated closer. "I'm a member of the Sanctuary Conclave, an Elder, though I don't feel so old. Then again, it's not the years but the mileage, isn't that what they say?"

"Just tell me what you are, what the Sanctuary Elders are."

"That's going to have to wait, I'm afraid. You've got some pressing matters to attend to. I've intercepted you from a'Kasha's phase-shifting stream…"

"Whoa, hold it! You've got that kind of power? This is a'Kasha we're talking about, right?"

The Elder spread her arms. "Yet, here you are. a'Kasha's stretched pretty thin right now. Even as powerful a force as the Void can take on too many problems, exert too much energy. That overload has given me a chance to sense you in the phase-shifting stream and contact you."

Like Damara and Omori did, Kim thought.

The Elder's features hardened. "Kim, your nephew Bobby is safe at the moment, but he's in danger. However, you have to wrap up your current mission before getting back to Pittsburgh."

"And how am I supposed to do that? I'm not exactly in control here.

What's happened to Bobby? Can't you intervene?"

"You are in control, Kim. Think about it. That's why I brought you here, to assure you of that. You know, a cosmic pep talk."

"Hold on," Kim said, remembering something. "You said earlier it was an honor to meet me again? We've never met before."

"Ah, but we will. Things flow in a non-linear way around here, sometimes. We'll meet again, or I should say, we'll meet for the first time. But, trust me, I won't look like this."

"How will I know you?"

"Let's just say I bear a resemblance to someone very familiar to you." The Elder closed her eyes. "Oops, sorry, a'Kasha's re-exerting control. Gotta go. Good luck."

Before Kim could scream in complete frustration, the phase-shifting stream took hold of her.

CHAPTER 19

The Ancients have long told of realms different from our own; realms
existing just over our shoulders, from out of the corners of our eyes,
in the darkest depths of shadows.
The Veils Between Worlds wall off and protect each
place from the other.
Some of these realms are unnatural, peopled by creatures neither
human nor spectral; creatures which have no earthly ties but,
instead, are bound to the powers of
distant stars. If the Veils are weakened, broken, or collapsed,
what unnamed horrors would be unleashed?

The Chronicles of the Dragon's Conclave

Carnegie Museum of Natural History

Pittsburgh, Pennsylvania

C.C. May 1, 2011

The heater grate opening behind the bookshelf looked way too small for Joe Martin's tall frame and broad shoulders. In fact, the janitor's closet he stood in was cramping him. "I doubt I can squeeze through there," he said to his diminutive companion.

"We will assist," Talera said, no longer hiding invisibly at Joe's side to avoid attention. The opening widened, like magic. Of course, since Talera was a jinni, it was magic. But her child-like face, wrapped in a headscarf, took on a pained expression. She staggered.

Joe knelt and took hold of her shoulders, steadying the djinn. Through the robe-like abaya Talera wore, her trembling was evident. "Are you all right?" he asked.

"I…" Talera seemed weakened, dizzy. She'd just referred to herself in the singular. That can't be good, Joe thought. As one half of a "dual entity" Talera needed to find and rejoin with her escaped other half, her "sister," before they both became dangerously unstable. Brought into Joe's world from their own by the errant Spirit Winds, Talera had been drawn to Joe by his proximity to Kim Yoshima, the Yomitsu. "The…the separation from our sister is sapping our strength. We must to get to them quickly."

"Can you at least sense Bobby from here?"

"Yes. The boy is near."

Good. After Joe had been approached by this strange magical being (in the shape of a hideous bat-like creature), after he'd realized he wasn't dreaming or hallucinating, he and Talera had followed Talera's sister to the Carnegie Library in Oakland, the university district of Pittsburgh.

Once inside, the spectral trail led from the library to the natural history museum, of which the library was part of and connected to. Then, the trail wound to a basement section of the museum, where the few staff working were completely unaware of Joe and Talera's presence, thanks to the Jinni's magic. Bobby's mother Marjorie, Kim's sister-in-law, waited anxiously above in the main part of the museum. It was she who had called Joe, initially wanting Kim, to tell him of Bobby's dissappearance. Joe had urged her to contact the police, but Marjorie had been reluctant, hoping to keep this disappearance under the radar.

"Is Bobby unharmed?" Joe asked Talera.

"Yes." Talera seemed to regain her former strength. "But he is not out of danger."

"Okay, after you."

Talera slipped through the grate and Joe followed, his tall, muscular body easily fitting through the enlarged opening. They came out into the dusty, cobwebbed hallway of an apparently abandoned and walled-up area of the museum. Yet, a couple of still-powered, flickering overheads shed a muted light.

Enough light for Joe to see the two figures at the end of the hallway. Who the hell is this? Not Bobby or Talera's other half. He and Talera walked toward them, Joe unholstering his Beretta 9mm from under his leather jacket.

A man and a woman turned at Joe and the djinn's approach. The man, of Asian descent, dressed in casual slacks and shirt was Ken Yoshima, Kim's brother. The woman…

"Damn," Joe Martin said, pointing his revolver at the woman. "You sure look like Kim Yoshima, but I bet you're not her at all. Care to enlighten me?"

"I'd enlighten you anytime, handsome," the woman purred in Kim's voice, winking. She wore a blue, skin-tight cat-suit, and held a crossbow-pistol in one gloved hand, pointed right back at Joe. Her dark eyes, staring out of Kim's face, however, focused intently on Talera. "More to the point, who are you?"

K en Yoshima recognized Joe Martin immediately. He'd met Lazo Sibulovich's security man the one time Ken had visited the Old Books and Research Haven to pick Bobby up from a visit there. But what was Martin doing here? And who was the little middle-eastern girl with him? T'sai seemed to take a sudden interest in her.

"Joe... Mr. Martin," Ken said. "You won't need that gun with T'sai."

"Mr. Yoshima," Joe said. "Maybe you can tell me what's going on."

"Please, Joe, T'sai, lower your weapons," Ken said. "Bobby's missing. T'sai's helping me to look for him."

"Huh." Joe lowered his gun. "That's why Talera and I are here too."

"Excellent!" the Kim-twin T'sai exclaimed. "We can join forces. Now, who's your little friend here? Talera, is it?"

"You are of a spectral nature," the little girl said. "But not of the djinn."

"Djinn? You're a jinni? I thought you guys were all giant, green, and bald."

The girl smiled, her expression very adult and very menacing. "We could crush you like an egg."

"Hmmm. I'd like to see you try, genie-girl."

"T'sai," Ken said. "Let's not get distracted. We're here to find Bobby." That's all they'd need for these two to get into it. Ken had seen and experienced enough in the last two weeks to recognize another non-human when he saw it. The little girl said she was a djinn and he believed her.

He'd come this far to find his son and didn't want anything to keep that from happening!

Joe Martin leaned down to say something to Talera, obviously on the same page as Ken. Good! The girl backed up a step. "Talera's pretty sure her, uh, sister is the one who's taken Bobby," Martin added quickly.

"Why?" Ken asked, looking at Talera. "Why did she take Bobby?"

"That's a long story, Mr. Yoshima," Martin said with a sigh. "I suggest we find your boy first before we get into any long-winded explanations, even though I'd love to know why your friend T'sai here looks exactly like Kim."

"Well," Ken said. "That's another long-winded explanation."

"You know, boys," T'sai said. "I'm standing right here."

"Mr. Yoshima, your wife is upstairs. She's the one who contacted me about Bobby being missing. She's pretty worried, so, as you suggested, T'sai, let's work together to find Bobby."

"Excellent idea...Joe," T'sai said. "I can call you Joe, can't I?"

Marjorie, Ken thought. Bobby. Kim. Damn it! I won't disappoint any of you again.

Just then, Talera glanced to her right. She said, so softly Ken almost couldn't hear, "There is someone else here."

When Ken looked to T'sai for confirmation, T'sai was gone.

Venice

Zone of Concealment

Maghi Warren

2011 C.E.

Creatures the like Amanozako had never seen before stared at her through the bars. Each imprisoning cell held at least one monstrous being. Some hissed, reaching a clawed hand or a barbed tentacle through the bars. Others growled or chittered. Wolfine, insectoid, reptilian, staring at her with an intensity that burned like fire.

"Brothers and sisters," she said, slowly, carefully, hoping they could understand her. "Attend me. I sense you have been misused and lied to by your loathsome mistress, the lamia Milaar. Is this true? Do you comprehend my words?"

A chorus of hisses, chuffings, and grunts echoed throughout the chamber. All the beasts pressed against the bars of their cells, some shaking uncontrollably, some beating their heads against the cell walls. Whether they understood her words or not, her intentions had broken through to them.

"I can free you. Yes, it is true. Will you join me to bring down your cruel and unjust mistress?"

A cacophony of wailing, screaming, and roaring answered her. The creatures rattled their bars, shrieking their agreement. Whatever control held these beasts in captivity had been shaken apart.

Amanozako felt a rush of power and pride. The wing stumps on her back fluttered in anticipation. I am a leader again, she thought. And this time I, we, will not fail.

Amanozako, the metengu and demon-goddess, looked with satisfaction at her monstros "army." For too long Amanozako had borne the stigmas of being the only female tengu, and of her violent, disgusting birth from the vomit of the storm god Susanoo. Now, she had a chance to redeem herself from the humiliating defeat of the yokai in the mortal realm.

But not in the way she would have done before. Now, she would do some good. Now she would strike back at the power threatening to overturn her realm and that of the humans. It would start here with the lion-dog komainu's help.

Once released from their holding cells, the myriad creatures imprisoned by Estansa Milaar, eager for revenge, joined her and the komainu enthusiastically. They showed her a large door at the rear of the prison chamber, which would allow them all to exit more quickly and efficiently than by using the much smaller elevator. Through the door, a torch-lit ramp led to the upper levels of the Maghi structure.

"So, dog," Amanozako said to the komainu, once an enemy, now a comrade. "Shall we proceed?"

The komainu growled, also eager, she knew, to escape this foul prison and cause some damage.

As they ascended the ramp, Amanozako and the komainu in the lead, voices sounded ahead of them. Two human figures stood at the top of the ramp in front of a large set of wooden double-doors. Maghi. Though not hooded and cloaked like the other sorcerers Amanozako had encountered, a certain power radiated from them. These two wore mortal clothes, their tattooed faces unhooded. Supernumeraries. Perhaps they considered themselves great sorcerers but, to Amanozako, they were nothing more than thugs. They would be no problem.

Before the surprised sorcerers could act, Amanozako grunted to the eldritch creature on her left. The huge beast, possessing multiple eyes and shifting tentacles hanging from its jaws, rushed forward on two powerful legs. It reached out its ropey arms and grasped the Maghi by their throats in its clawed hands and crushed them.

What power and speed the beast possesses! Amanozako thought, impressed. Yet the lamia was still able to entrap it like the others. Like she and her servants caught me and the komainu. But now, she was certain, the lamia's power wouldn't be able to stop her and the monstros collectively. They were united...free! She had thought the Guardian Spirit Dragon Seiryuu had forsaken her, had abandoned Amanozako here in this gods-forsaken place to die instead of returning her to her own realm. Now she knew the goddess of the East had worked to send

171

her here to regain her honor and purpose.

And faith. Amanozako had been ripped from her world like so much offal. In the end, the Spirit Winds had not discriminated between those who dwelt on the mortal planes and those who ruled above them. She had thought then there was no difference between the two in the eyes of those who governed the Great Ending of all things. She feared her knowledge and experience of the worlds was false and twisted.

Well, as she realized now, perhaps not false but certainly a little twisted. She would enjoy this while she could.

She smiled in approval as, tossing the broken corpses aside, the eldritch creature kicked the doors open. The monstros streamed into a long corridor, a wave of unleashed strength and anger, not to be denied. Adding her voice to the chorus of roars and bellows, Amanozako led her followers forward.

The element of surprise and the anger pent up for their long imprisonments infused the monstros. The Maghi sorcerers, male and female and their mortal servants, attempted to stop the wave of relentless savagery aligned against them.

But, unable to group together quickly as an effective fighting force, the Maghi were cut down in twos and threes on the floors and in the many rooms of the warren. Their own powerful magic was ineffective against the complete and utter rage of the monstros to enact their revenge, to allow their long-subsumed power to be released.

Amanozako ripped and tore, giving her own primal energies full rein. She and her army rampaged, gloriously, joyously, and with great satisfaction.

When it was done, when the Maghi had been slaughtered or had fled, much of their warren wrecked, Amanozako and her army stood in the ground-level floor of the warren, triumphant, exultant. The creatures howled and shrieked their pleasure, stomping their feet, raising their talons.

The komainu growled softly and faced Amanozako. The lion-dog had wreaked much havoc himself. Amanozako was proud to have him by her side. A communication passed from the lion-dog to the goddess. "Indeed," Amanozako said. "Our victory is not complete. The Maghi mistress, the lamia, is not here. Neither are the ones who took you and me from the place of worship. The Maghi Roberto and the beast Marceeka. Had they left before we escaped? Perhaps they are in another lower level of the structure. We know there are many such floors and passages within it."

The komainu stilled, raising its head, its nostrils flaring. The other monstros became quiet, their attention riveted. Amanozako felt it also, a tremor, not unlike the force which had brought her and the lion-dog to this place. But different. More subtle. More dangerous. "A threat approaches," she said. "Quickly, brothers and sisters, we must get outside."

As they exited onto a wide courtyard, the entire city trembled as if struck by a shaking of the earth. Buildings swayed, the pavement heaved. In the distance, the air wavered and bent like a heat mirage. It rippled toward them in a great pressure wave, distorting and shifting.

"An incitement of ancient power!" Amanozako shouted, bracing herself. "Stand against it, brothers and sisters!"

***

Some time had passed. She and her followers survived the mysterious cataclysm that had destroyed the city. Now, they looked to her for answers. Even the komainu chuffed questioningly. A presence had manifested before them, a tall, monstrous figure lumbering out of the smoke and debris.

A demon. One who had no right to be here.

"So," Amanozako said, the komainu growling at her side. She flexed her claws. "It appears we have company."

CHAPTER 20

The Self cannot truly exist on its own. There must be Others.

Samuel Kim

The Teachings of Yira - The Five Precepts to Enlightenment

The Void

(**A**n odor of incense, sweet, pervasive)
Some force overpowered Omori. Something created in my own mind?

(Drum beats and a soft tintinnabulation)
No. I felt dizzy as if some outside force affected us somehow. Something other than the phase-shifting stream.

So much had just happened, so much had been revealed to Kim, so much allowed for her to see and feel. It was so hard to process, to understand.

An outside force.

(Whispered chanting and the nickering of horses)
Her thoughts whirled. Bobby and Jenny were in trouble.

Bobby! Jenny!

(A swishing of metal against metal)
She rubbed her face and calmed herself, looking to her right. Omori was gone. His dais was nowhere to be seen. Could this still be the Dark Demesne of the exiled ones? No, no, another place. Somewhere outside…of everything.

Warm sunlight embraced her in a pleasant haze. She stood on a vast desert. Black volcanic sand stretched behind her to the horizon, interrupted by tall, rippling dunes. Once more the sounds of bells drifted through the dry air. The smell of incense struck her as her mind cleared. She turned around.

A tall obelisk fronted the entrance ramp of an enormous structure. A ziggurat of massive proportions, it put the estimated size of Iraq's Great Ziggurat of Ur to shame. The step pyramid's multiple receding terraces vaulted upward into the sky as far as Kim could see. A statue stood at the top of the obelisk, flashes of gold sparkling off its smooth surface.

A larger-than-life muscular figure dressed in a knee-length kilt.

Dazzling gemstones lined his garment. A man with a blank, featureless face. He held a golden sphere aloft in one hand.

The first one, Kim thought, knowing who the statue represented. The first Void.

Kim blinked and, appearing out of a shimmering haze, a group of people approached from the front of the obelisk. Kim didn't have to form her esper-sight to see who or what this group was, as its members got much, much closer in a matter of heartbeats. Made up of several individuals, two sat astride armored sleek, horse-like animals. The riders wore a kind of stylized samurai armor, the helms completely covering their heads and masking their faces. They appeared to be guards or escorts. Four loin-cloth garbed, muscular bearers carried a large, elaborately decorated palanquin, its passenger's form vague and shifting as if seen from behind misty glass. A trio of brightly outfitted musicians marched in front of the group, the source of the drums and bells. All were led by a robed woman swinging an incense censor and chanting in a language Kim didn't recognize.

Kim watched fascinated, her anxiety and concern momentarily abated. The entire party halted. The musicians ceased their playing and, with the robed woman, moved to one side. The bearers lowered the palanquin to the sand. One of the samurai guards rode closer, pulling his strange mount up a few feet in front of Kim. She noticed the muscular equine left no hoofprints in the sand. The guard's armor shone as if polished and untouched by battle. Faint colors snaked over its surface like that of a rainbow. The samurai spoke, his male voice low and steady. "You are the Yomitsu."

"Yes," Kim answered. "That's what I'm called. And you?"

"We are servants of a'Kasha the Archive. You know her as the Void. She wishes to speak with you."

Kim was long past being surprised at almost anything anymore. Anger and frustration took over and she almost laughed out loud. "So the Void's finally going to show its face? Good, because I have some questions for it. For example, has it simply gone batshit crazy? Is there any real purpose to anything that's been happening? My nephew's in danger!"

The eye-slits in the samurai's helm glowed. "You will show all due respect in a'Kasha's presence and refrain from insults."

Kim shot her arms out in front of her, readying a psi-stun. "Or you'll do what, samurai-boy? Slap my wrist? You know who you're talking to? I'm the freaking Yomitsu! The Luminous One! A goddess-damned Warrior of the Light! And I'm sick to death of this whole lunatic nightmare!"

The samurai urged his mount forward, his metal-gloved hand grasping the pommel of his sword.

<<Peace.>>

That single word, uttered in a soft, calm, almost hypnotic voice, caused several things to happen. The tension between Kim and the guard vanished. The samurai stopped, backed his mount up, and joined his fellow guard standing to one side of the palanquin. Kim lowered her arms, the anger gone. 'Do you know who you're talking to?' Did I really say that? Kim reproached herself as a sudden shame came over her. What was I thinking? I'm better than that. I'm so worried about Bobby.

The samurai and musicians bowed their heads as the figure in the palanquin rose up. The palanquin's beefy carriers knelt on the ground, also showing obeisance. The figure stepped out of the palanquin and walked toward Kim.

No, not walked. Floated.

The figure stopped a few feet from Kim, hovering. Its form flickered, shifting, its features cloudy, continuously moving as if blown by the wind. Nebulous, seeming to break apart and reform instantaneously. The voice intoned again. <<This entity is designated as a'Kasha, the Archive. And so we meet, indigene of Earth.>>

Kim closed her eyes and opened them. The type of communication a'Kasha employed was unlike anything Kim had experienced, either spoken or thought-sent. The words just happened, sounding all around her, through her. Her breath quickened, her heart thumped.

"You...you're the Void." Kim tried to control the emotions stirring inside her. Some anger returned, yes, along with resentment, disbelief, astonishment. "You're the cause of all this...this chaos! The controller of the temporal displacement tremors, the Spirit Winds. And what do you mean, and so we meet?"

a'Kasha drifted closer and became whole. Or, at least, she projected an image Kim could understand. Sort of. An emerald-green robe, lined with ruby-red highlights, draped a'Kasha's tall, slender frame. Four arms hung at her sides. Her black hair framed a long, blue-skinned face with vaguely Asian features, a wide mouth, aquiline nose, high forehead. Large, red eyes flashed, devouring Kim.

Another emotion clutched at Kim. Fear. She began to tremble in front of this terrible being, the one who'd started all the temporal displacement tremors, a being Kim realized she feared more than any other she'd faced, including Omori and Orcus.

<<This entity will not harm the indigene.>> a'Kasha touched the

tips of one long-fingered hand to Kim's forehead. <<The indigene and this entity must converse.>>

Kim closed her eyes and relaxed at a'Kasha's warm touch, her mind clearing. She took a deep breath. We must converse? That's got to be the ultimate understatement! She opened her eyes…

A cavernous chamber surrounded her. Kim gawked, dumbstruck. A vast domed ceiling loomed above her, supported by enormous columns of ruby-red stone veined with golden threads. The inside surface of the dome churned with colors, ever-shifting, coiling and expanding, shrinking and blooming.

Large orbs of soft light floated throughout, illuminating the chamber's wonders. Enormous bookstacks, some constructed of wood, others of stone, still others of metal and glass, spread out in front of her on the marble floor. Lined up across the vast width of the chamber, the stacks stood dozens of feet tall.

As if pulled by strings, Kim walked to the stacks' entrances, peeking her head in to look at their contents. Cuneiform stone tablets, glyphs, scrolls, parchments, codex, books, every type of medium Kim could imagine were stored there.

Behind her, a long corridor stretched into infinity, intermittent arches spanning above its length like the giant ribs of a leviathan.

"Wow," was all Kim could say. "This…this is wonderful."

<<A simple construct for you to identify with.>> a'Kasha said. Her uppermost set of arms rose, the hands clasped.

"Simple?"

<<Indeed. The Archive's true aspect would only confuse and perhaps frighten you. The knowledge stored here is mutable, constantly changing and evolving. Its form is that of thought, stardust, matter, and energy>>

Kim looked above and around her. She remembered the World War I song, "How You Gonna Keep 'em Down on the Farm After They've Seen Paree?" That's how she felt.

But she needed answers.

a'Kasha smiled as if detecting Kim's thoughts, which she probably had. <<The indigene has questions.>>

"I…" Kim had to tear her eyes away from the incredible sight around her. "Yes, as I hinted to your samurai, about a billion." Where to start? "Are you a god? Goddess? Demon?"

<<Others have deemed this entity all of those appellations.>>

Kim remembered many Hindu gods and goddesses being depicted with blue skin and multiple arms. Ancient astronaut theorists posited those descriptions as proof of alien visitations to Earth in the far distant past. "An extraterrestrial?"

<<Yes, though not in the sense the indigene is familiar with.>>

Okaaay. "My friends, Jenny, Wayne, Daiyu, Lazo. Are they safe?"

<<For now.>>

"My nephew Bobby?"

<<Yes. Do not fear for your nephew. All will unfold to ensure his safety. This entity assures the indigene.>>

"Thank…thank you." At least that's a relief, if I can believe her. I have to. "So what's going on? Forgive me for being so blunt but have you lost control of…of whatever you do? This archive?"

<<In part. Yes>>

Kim blinked. She hadn't expected an equally-as-blunt answer. Or the statement that followed it.

<<But this entity has chosen to relinquish that portion of control.>>

"Why?"

<<Things are amiss within the multiverse and have been so even before this entity sensed the indigene's presence. Certain safeguards must be recreated despite what the Sanctuary Elders think. To do so means long-standing protocols must be abandoned and new ones instituted.>>

"This isn't the first time I've heard of the Sanctuary Elders. Who or what are they?"

<<Guardians and administrators of the ambient-milieu. Ancient entities.>>

Kim stood silent, waiting.

<<This entity requires the indigene's assistance as a Warrior of the Light in instituting those safeguards.>>

Kim blinked. "You want me to help you?"

<<Just so. Realize the indigene has already begun that assistance.>>

"Yeah, without my knowledge or consent."

<<A necessary action. The indigene is part of the reason this entity relinquished control though the indigene has never been aware of that and is not to blame. The forces of the Dark, using the warlord as a vessel, exerted their power. As such…WE must work together to correct the Balances. But on this entity's terms.>>

"Balances as in plural. More than one?"

<<Like individuals and universes, there are innumerable Balances. The indigene must help to maintain a particular Balance, yes.>>

That's what Omori indicated. Kim folded her arms and eyed a'Kasha curiously as the Void continued.

<<The entire multiverse has been affected by this recent imbalance. There are others like the indigene, Luminous Ones of other cultures, other worlds, other universes, who attempt the same actions as the indigene. Essentially, the indigene is part of a cosmic congregate with each member affected by their own history and myths and culture.>>

Bobby popped into Kim's mind again, something he'd said about a comic book team of galactic law enforcers—the Guardians of the Universe and their Green Lantern Corps. "That's good to hear. I've been thinking this is way too much responsibility for just one person. But why can't you fix this? And, if there's a team of Luminous Ones out there, why are we just running around on our own? There's no 'I' in Team, you know."

<<The indigene is not alone. Those entities known to you as Daiyu, Amedio Zaronelli, Wayne Brewster, ArcNight, Jenny Sibulovich. Jackson Yamaguchi. Your grandmother. Your forerunner. And others unseen and unknown throughout the ages. All have been involved.>>

Obaachan. "Thank the goddess. I guess I never thought of that. I'm not so damned important after all."

<<This entity did not say that.>>

Kim remembered something the Sanctuary Elder she'd met had said to her. "You're the one who's been taking me through time and space by the Phase-shifting stream."

<<Yes, though certain other entities seem to have interfered without this entity's knowledge until now. That will not happen again.>>

"But why are you doing this to me?"

<<In order for events to proceed to the correct balance point, the indigene had to assist in past manifestations.>>

"In other words, I had to help myself, my past-selves."

<<Correct. This must be done to ensure the stability of the timelines, among other concerns.>>

"I still don't completely understand."

<<This entity exists as and within what the indigene's kind term the Void. But this entity's existence is more than a Void. This entity possesses the knowledge and history of the Myriad Things. Everything. Everyone. Everywhere. Every time. This entity was initially brought into existence after the Great Beginning to be a record keeper. An archive. To take the place of the first one.>>

The Myriad Things. A concept of Taoism. A memory sparked in the back of Kim's mind at the mention of a record keeper. The sound of a'Kasha's name reminded Kim of something she and Jenny had talked about once or twice, that Kim had read about a long time ago. A cosmic repository.

"The Akashic Records."

<<That is one such designation of this entity's purpose.>>

"But you've evolved into something more, is that it?"

<<This entity possesses a protean nature. Yes. The evolution the indigene speaks of began when this entity sensed the presence of the indigene's forerunner.>>

"Yoshima Mitsu."

<<Indeed. Never had so primitive a being been able to attract this entity in so powerful a fashion. Others have done so over the millennia but not in such a personal, emotional, selfless manner.>>

"Mitsu wanted to save her little sister, Shioko. To transport her away from danger."

<<But, even then the balance had shifted. Somehow manipulated in favor of the Left Hand Path due to its warlord servant.>>

"Omori Kadanamora."

<<This entity had become restless. Bored. Upon reaching beyond this entity's existence, the forerunner and the warlord were detected.>>

Bored and restless, Kim thought. Like me. Feeling directionless was one of the things that started me on this crazy journey.

<<This entity became curious about the indigene's forerunner and allowed her venture to go forward.>>

Like praying to a deity and having the prayer answered. Kim hazarded a guess. "That's when things went wrong. More so when I became involved along with my forerunner, Mitsu."

<<Yes.>>

"I and Mitsu are that important? That powerful?"

<<The indigene, you, know it is so. The indigene is a harbinger of a new age.>>

"No! I reject that. Why me?"

Incredibly, a'Kasha shrugged. <<I have foreseen it. Realize it is so. One such harbinger comes into being every millennium. You are she.>>

"What do you expect me to do? Despite what you say, I'm only one person."

a'Kasha once more placed her fingertips against Kim's forehead. Again Kim calmed. <<This entity regrets what has transpired but cannot right the Balance by Itself. This entity must assist in correcting the Balance of the Myriad Things before the Sanctuary Elders find this entity and the indigene and stop…US. Will the indigene allow this entity to transmit additional understanding to the indigene?>>

"Yes. Please! But..." Kim paused. "But why do these Sanctuary Elders want to stop you?"

<<A reason as old as time. Long-held power corrupts and is difficult to surrender. Often the reasons for initially gaining that power are forgotten or perverted.>>

"a'Kasha, I..."

<<The indigene wishes to assist its comrades.>>

"Look, I know you can manipulate time and space, whether you're supposed to do that or not. You've been bouncing me around my own past the last however long it's been. Right? But, please, I've got to go back and help my friends. My nephew."

<<Indeed. And the indigene must also comply with the warlord's request to locate this so-called Mistress of the Maghi.>>

"You would allow that?"

<<Yes, but not for the reasons the warlord has told the indigene. The warlord lies to only free himself and once more wreak havoc and chaos.>>

"I knew it! But then why find this Milaar?"

<<Despite what the Sanctuary Elders think, this entity must proceed with these plans which include the warlord and the lamia. They are, as you say, wrenches in the works. The warlord must be united with the Mistress of the Maghi but on this entity's terms so both the warlord's and the mistress' existences may be controlled.>>

"Must get tiresome trying to keep up with all of this."

<<That is why this entity also searches for the one who will come after this entity.>>

"You're looking for, what, a replacement?"

<<Yes. A temporary one. One outside the politics and strictures of the Sanctuary Elders. One selfless enough to give everything up, to sacrifice all for the common good for but a short time only. Yes, this entity has become, as the indigene says, unstable, but not in the true sense of that word, and not enough as yet to ignore this final responsibility. A new Archive must be appointed so this entity can, as you would also say, take a break.>>

Kim didn't, couldn't say anything. Then, "Do you have anyone in mind?"

<<Perhaps. It is still too early to tell.>>

"Well, what is it you want me to do?" Kim asked, knowing full well she wouldn't get an answer. But, again, a'Kasha surprised her.

<<This entity will transport the indigene to where the Grand Mistress of the Maghi has been taken. But first the indigene must assist in a

number of final past manifestations.>>

"Past manifestations? No! Please, let me get down to business. No more distractions!"

<<These are not distractions. The indigene will appreciate and understand why this entity empowers these next events. Do not struggle or protest. Go and be enlightened.>>

"STOP! Please." Kim trembled. Fear, anger, impatience, all combined to break out of a'Kasha's calming influence.

Incredibly, a'Kasha paused, watching Kim curiously.

"a'Kasha, I can't wait anymore. Can you speed my traveling up?"

<<The indigene already travels at the speed of thought.>>

"What I mean is, can you make me appear in more than one place and time at the same moment? You know, what's it called? Bilocation or superposition." Jenny had described those concepts to her, superposition being an idea of quantum mechanics.

<<Such a spatial and temporal adjustment will take its toll on the indigene. Physically. Mentally. Emotionally.>>

"So, it is possible?" Jenny had told Kim superposition wasn't supposed to work with macroscopic bodies like humans.

<<It is possible but at a price.>>

"Please, a'Kasha. I'm already at the edge. I need to do this."

<<Very well, but this entity will give the indigene a weapon to assist in those endeavors.>>

A flash of light and Kim held a small object in her hand. A green paper unicorn, constructed much like the origami creation of Jackson's.

"This is a weapon?"

<<Just so. The indigene will know how to employ it when the time comes.>>

This time, as Kim got swept up in the slipstream, she felt herself pulled in opposite directions.

Literally.

PART 2

Karma

All Things Have a Beginning…

Lao Tzu

DREAMSCAPE

In rare cases, the individuals involved will experience, not so much a true dream state, but more an alternate reality, one in which the "dreamer" inhabits the guise of another, ostensibly real person. This person will engage in his or her day-to-day activities in this reality with the dreamer simply tagging along for the ride, observing through that person's eyes. This type of lucidity can be disorienting and frightening. The origin of this state is, as yet, unknown, but it has been posited that perhaps, in unique individuals or those who have been exposed to some traumatic mental stimuli, there exists a connection or thread to, in fact, another point in the mental universe, one in which the dreamer is actually connected to another, separate entity's mind by way of some telepathic interdimensionality. This has lately been credited as explanations for flashes of déjà vu or sensing fleeting glimpses of a parallel world.

Dr. Lilith Cardazio
Dreams and the Unmapped Territories of the Mental Universe

FOURTH INTERVAL

Totou Safe House

Somewhere in the Laurel Highlands of Pennsylvania

C.E. April 30, 2011

11:37 PM

The six members of the DragonEye Hunter-Squad moved swiftly through the dark, forested landscape. Wearing camouflaging crypsis skinsuits and flexible body armor, they blended into the shadows as silently as ghosts. With no moon visible, the Dark Sky above the Laurel Highlands displayed a breathtaking panorama of stars. The filmy haze of the Milky Way stretched across the horizon, an errant brushstroke of gauzy white. Had the Shuugouteki hunter-squad's mission not been so critical, team leader Peter Gurkovsky would have found the glittering firmament beautiful, would have stopped to admire the dazzling heavenly vista. It was a sight he never tired of.

But he had no time for stargazing tonight. Armed with M16 assault rifles, Glock pistols, and stun grenades, Gurkovsky's team exited the woods to face their target. On his order, the squad split up, with second-in-command, Steven Kikuchi, taking two DragonEyes around to a point behind the target. Gurkovsky and the other two squad members took up positions in front of the Totou safe house. That's how their intel had described the multi-story Tudor mansion before them. At least what was left of it.

Fire still smoldered in parts of the blackened ruins, sparking and flashing in the darkness. The charred timbers and stone columns of the structure and its surrounding scorched acreage appeared gutted and abandoned. The tall brick wall encircling the mansion had been breached in several places as if rammed and knocked down. The bars of its metal gate stood crumpled and open. It looked as if the safe house's occupants had fled with no intention of returning. If any had survived at all.

What had happened here? Gurkovsky's intel had provided the location of the safe house based on satellite images of the fire, cross-referenced with cell phone transmissions from the same area. Magnified shots picked up an image of the Totou ouroboros sigil within the conflagration. A recon drone flown in from the squad's deployment site a half-mile away confirmed this was, in all likelihood, a Totou hideout. No signs of life had been detected.

Gurkovsky hoped this wasn't another dead-end. The Hunter-Squads had experienced too many disappointments of late, too many false leads. Though the Totou had been defeated, its members had proven very adept at concealment. While the Cabal licked its wounds, its members had to be rounded up before they regrouped and re-consolidated their power. That order had come straight from Director Cheng, the head of the Shuugouteki Pittsburgh, PA region, and this year's acting Shuhan (leader/CEO), himself.

"Kikuchi," Gurkovsky spoke sub-vocally into his shoulder comm. Ludicrously, he always felt like a ventriloquist when initiating that select mode of speech. "Picking up anything at the rear of the house?"

Kikuchi's voice broke over Gurkovsky's comm. "There's a stable and some outbuildings back here, Team Leader, pretty intact and untouched by the fire. Damn." A pause. "Got some bodies here, too. One of them looks like Xavier La Tan."

La Tan, the so-called "Illustrious Master of the Totou," exiled, fallen from the Cabal's grace. "Damn is right," Gurkovsky muttered. La Tan had been the brains behind the Totou's activities for the last thirty years. Who had caused all this destruction and brought the man down?

"Sir?" Kikuchi continued. "The rear of the house is as much a mess as the front but there's a below-ground entrance to what looks like an old bomb shelter or bunker. Permission to investigate."

"Granted and watch your backs. We're going in for a closer look on the first floor. Frankovitch, O'Dell, with me." Gurkovsky and his two DragonEyes crept through the front gate and slunk closer to the ruined structure. They clung to the shadows, their infrared goggles allowing them to pick their way carefully. Gurkovsky hand-motioned Nick Frankovitch and Maureen O'Dell to split up to his left and right.

"Team Leader," O'Dell motioned to Gurkovsky. Like all the squad members, O'Dell's face was covered in camo webbing. Before her lay a body. Twisted, Broken. Not human.

"What the hell?" Gurkovsky knelt over the corpse. Humanoid and simian-like in appearance, tall and powerful-looking, the creature, nevertheless, had been felled by some unknown force. "It looks like freaking Bigfoot!"

His comm sparked to life again. "Got some bodies in the bunker, Team Leader. And they're not human."

"We've got one of those here as well. Explain."

"The bunker's made up of several rooms. One looks like a lab of some sort. Another is a refrigeration unit containing several dead shadow-trackers zipped up in body bags."

"Shadow-trackers?"

"Whoa! Peter!" Kikuchi cried suddenly over Gurkovsky's comm. Kikuchi never called Gurkovsky by his name when out in the field. Unless something was very wrong. "Something shot out of the bunker. It must have been hiding somehow and, just, uh, popped up. Hard to track on the imager. The thermals keep flickering in and out, but it looks like it's…there's three of them. Tall, really tall. They're moving towards the front of the house on the ground floor."

For a moment, Gurkovsky paused, a rough chill running up his back. They had all heard the rumors about the exiled Totou searching for and, in some cases, supposedly finding what they called the "Displaced." Fabled creatures from alternate realities that hadn't returned to their own worlds by the temporal displacement tremors, too far away from a Spirit Wind event or its aftershocks to be sent back.

Gurkovsky had never witnessed such creatures or experienced a displacement tremor. He'd never met Kim Yoshima or Wayne Brewster; only saw them from a distance a couple of times. He thought the incredible tales and the stories of the Yomitsu had been inflated, blown up out of proportion in order to further the Totou's agenda of ridding the world of the Shuugouteki.

Which was fine with him. Agents of the Shuugouteki had killed his parents and sister. He would do anything or follow anyone to bring such murderous scum to ground. "Roger that," Gurkovsky said. "Sweep the rest of the bunker and follow all protocol. We're on it up here." The space between Gurkovsky's shoulder blades tingled. His own wrist-thermal imager began to beep. Wavering blobs of heat signature appeared on the small screen.

"Headlamps on," he ordered, activating his operator cap light and turning his goggles off. "Everyone move up." Powerful beams from the small lights illuminated the front of the shattered safe house.

Three large, bestial shapes erupted from the smoking interior of the safe house. The head lamps revealed tall, shaggy, man-like creatures with jagged horns sprouting from their heads. No, not horns—antlers. Making no sound, the creatures split up, rushing toward the DragonEyes.

One of the creatures charged straight at Gurkovsky. Christ, it was a monster! Gurkovsky stood six feet tall but this creature towered easily several inches above him. It looked like a combination of bear, ape and deer. Gurkovsky recovered enough from his shock and prepared to fire. But the creatures stopped their swift approach. The one standing before Gurkovsky appraised him with glowing amber eyes.

"We never desired this," the monster crooned in a voice low and rumbling. Startlingly, the words were spoken in...Russian! Gurkovsky understood the monster, having grown up speaking both English and his parent's native tongue. "We never desired to be here in this foul, alien land."

Gurkovsky responded in kind, forming the words in Russian carefully, slowly. He felt as if he were dreaming. "Who...what are you?" he asked, suddenly wanting to know the answer to that simple question more than anything. "Where did you come from?"

The beast moved closer, the face beneath the tall, pointed antlers fully revealed in Gurkovsky's cap light. It looked as surprised as Gurkovsky must have, as if thinking this human wouldn't be able to understand it. The team leader gaped in recognition. Monstrous as it was, it was a face he knew, one he'd read about as a child.

Leshii. Mythological Russian forest guardians.

A sudden blue light bathed the front lawn. Even the leshii turned at its brilliance. Another creature appeared from a side of the ruins, the light emanating from it like a newborn star. It shook its long-maned, single-horned head and stamped a hooved foot.

The three leshii fell to their knees and bowed their heads as if paying obeisance to this magnificent horse-like beast.

"A unicorn," Gurkovsky muttered.

"No, not a unicorn." Steven Kikuchi walked out of the front of the smoldering rubble, his two squad members behind him. "A kirin."

Yes, now Gurkovsky could see the differences between the two mythological animals. The kirin was a chimera, a hybrid of horse, deer, and ox. Its multi-colored mane flowed like water. Knowing the kirin could call down lightning as a weapon, Gurkovsky had a feeling he looked at the cause of the safe house's destruction.

Which meant, he hoped, the kirin was on their side.

The beautiful, graceful animal moved closer, a naked human figure slumped over its back and neck. The kirin nickered and turned its head sideways as if indicating its passenger, as if giving permission to... help. Both Gurkovsky and Kikuchi ran to the kirin and gently lowered an unconscious woman to the ground. Blood smeared her pallid face and shoulders, one arm appeared to be broken. "O'Dell," Gurkovsky said. "Get our chopper here now. She needs medical attention."

"Yes, team leader."

But before O'Dell could radio their pilot awaiting them at the deployment site, the kirin bowed its head and touched the woman with the tip of its horn. The woman moaned, the blood she had shed simply vanishing. Her breathing strengthened, her arm straightened, her color improved.

Gurkovsky gaped, flabbergasted. Then he recognized the woman.

"Christ," he muttered. "It's Rebecca Parantala."

"The Totou Inquisitor?" Kikuchi asked. "The one with the eidetic-type memory?"

"Yep." He looked at the kirin. "I sure wish you could talk, my magical friend." Gurkovsky had a thought. He turned back to the leshii he had spoken with. "What is your name, Old One?" he asked in Russian.

"I am called Loam."

"Can you speak with the kirin, Loam?"

"I can," he said. "I can convey the Radiant One's thoughts to you in speech."

Gurkovsky smiled and shook his head. You couldn't make this stuff up. How incredibly wrong he'd been to doubt! "Please," he said to the leshii. "Ask the…Radiant One who he is."

"What did it say?" Kikuchi asked as Loam walked to face the kirin.

"Hold on a minute," he said to his Second. Loam bowed and addressed the horned beast. The leshii backed up, turning to Gurkovsky. "The Radiant One must depart."

The kirin reared up on its hind legs. A pinpoint of light flashed at the tip of its horn, expanding to a whirling sphere of fire. The kirin vanished.

"Wow," Kikuchi whispered.

"Loam, what did the Radiant One tell you?"

"The Radiant One was called away by another great power. The Radiant One is needed elsewhere. And…"

"Yes?"

"He told me his name," Loam said. "The Radiant One's name is Trell."

CHAPTER 21

We will never succumb, never submit, never surrender.
To either the enemies within or without.

Takeo, Sohei Warrior Monk

Outside Osaka, Japan

March 1985

Kim

First Iteration

<<**B**ut first the indigene must assist in a number of final past manifestations>>

―――――――――――

"**W**e will not see each other again, Kimmy-san."

Looking up at her Grandmother Mitsu's remark, Kim Yoshima smiled. "Don't be silly, Obaachan. Of course we will. I'm planning to be back next spring-break for another visit and you better be here!"

Kim and Mitsu sat in the tea room of her grandmother's small house near Osaka as they had done so many times before over the years. Mitsu's home was a simple dwelling but scrupulously clean and meticulously arranged. And, oh, so comfortable! Mitsu had lived here ever since marrying Kohoshi Jirou, a kind and gentle man who had died many years earlier.

Interestingly, unlike many women of her culture and generation, Grandmother Mitsu had reverted to her own surname after Jirou had died, with his blessing. That had to be pretty revolutionary, Kim reasoned. It spoke to Mitsu's strength and Jirou's open-mindedness, two amazing people definitely ahead of their time. Mitsu had explained she felt it necessary to use her name again as a form of empowerment for her children. Jirou had died suddenly while Mitsu had been pregnant with their son, Kim's father. Once Kim's father had been born, Mitsu gave him her surname, to be passed on to his own children.

Mitsu never remarried. Kim had always felt very lucky to be part of her life, though she wished she'd known Jirou.

As Kim had expected, Mitsu wore a brightly-colored kimono and had performed the traditional tea ceremony for herself and her granddaughter. As part of their tradition, Kim also had donned a kimono, one Mitsu kept just for her granddaughter. Both women now knelt on tatami mats, sipping their rock tea on opposite sides of a low kotatsu table. The tea, also as expected, was delicious.

Mitsu was ninety-four years old, yet looked and seemed much younger. She was still beautiful, the wrinkles on her face and hands finely drawn and barely noticeable. Her white hair was fashioned in its usual topknot, the slim body within the obi-belted kimono still strong, her brown eyes shining. "Ah, I will have crossed over to the Plain of Heaven before you return, Little One."

"Ha! You're going to live forever," Kim laughed, trying to ignore a sudden uneasiness. "Look at you! I only hope I'm half as healthy and young-looking as you when I'm your age. If I even make it to your age!"

Mitsu smiled, a hint of sadness revealed in her upturned lips. "And you will, Kimmy-san. You will. A little kami told me."

Kim sat silently for a moment, realizing there'd come a time when her beloved grandmother, her obaachan, wouldn't be there for her anymore. But not now, not yet. Kim was only twenty. She wanted, needed, to spend a lot more years with Mitsu. Her parents and brother were distant, their interests and concerns very different from hers. Mitsu was Kim's only family member who truly seemed interested in what Kim did with her life, had always been so.

Especially now. Kim had earned her associate degree in law enforcement and planned on taking criminal justice classes in preparation for applying to the police academy. To become a police officer was a career choice she'd thought about since she'd been a child but one her parents were never happy about.

Grandmother Mitsu, on the other hand, seemed particularly pleased about Kim's decision. "Hai," she had remarked. "You will do well in such a profession. As I have told you before, Kimmy-san, you have the courage of a dragon and the heart of a warrior. It is your destiny to fight for balance, for karma, in our troubled world, like a true samurai."

Kim had laughed, not seeing herself in those ways at all, just wanting to help people and make a difference. Sometimes, Grandmother could be overly lavish in her praise. If only the two women lived closer to each other, if only Kim could visit Mitsu more often.

Kim had managed to save enough money for the trip to Japan by working after school in a local dojo, teaching self-defense and martial arts (and winning some prize money from a couple of competitions). She had earned a black belt in aikido when she turned eighteen and was certain her skills would help her when…

Kim suddenly gasped, placing her fingertips to her temples. "Oh. Oh my." She bowed her suddenly spinning head, breathing hard. "Well," she muttered between breaths. "I'll be damned." She chuckled at her words. Better not say that in front of Orcus!

"Kimmy-san?" Grandmother Mitsu reached out and touched Kim's arm. "Are you unwell?"

No, just the opposite, Kim thought in wonder. But her friends were in danger.

Yes, she knew, but calmed even more, realizing because she traveled through time, she could still help Amedio and Jenny before anything happened to them. At least she hoped so. But now, right now, Kim allowed her spirit to soar. Grandmother Mitsu had been dead many years. To see her, to interact with her, once more, was a gift beyond measure.

And Mitsu could see her so that must mean Kim had been taken out of the phase-shifting stream. a'Kasha had allowed her to bilocate.

Kim enfolded Mitsu in a tight embrace, tears welling in her eyes. This vastly different time-travel event allowed her to inhabit her much younger self, living the experience instead of just observing. Once before, while dreaming, Kim had inhabited her six-year old self, also visiting her grandmother. Sitting here now, though dreamlike, wasn't a dream. Once again, this stop on her astral voyage had deviated greatly from what she knew, being more encompassing. When Kim looked up, she took another deep breath and smiled. "Obaachan," she said softly. "Grandmother. It's so good to see you again."

Her grandmother pulled gently away, staring. The puzzled expression on the old woman's face gave way to a look of wonder. She lightly touched Kim's hair. "Little One," she said softly. "It is you, is it not? Not of the now but of what is to come. The future, yes? I can sense it, see it in your older, much wiser, yet pain-filled, eyes."

Kim nodded, feeling the rapt expression on her own face. She hadn't remembered this so her younger self's persona must be gently subdued and would not recall what had happened. She took hold of her Grandmother's hand. "Obaachan," she said excitedly. "There's so much I want to talk to you about, but I don't know how much time I have here."

Yoshima Ayako Mitsu smiled, acting as if this was just another everyday occurrence. "I understand, Kimmy-san, my granddaughter of power. It is enough you are here at all."

Why exactly am I here? Kim thought for the millionth time. That question had become a mantra for her. She took another deep breath, centering herself. She met her grandmother's suddenly intense gaze, that same gaze that had mesmerized her as a child. The strength reflected in obaachan's youthful eyes stunned her, even after all these years.

There was something. Jackson Yamaguchi and her grandmother. Why suddenly did Kim feel a connection between the two existed. a'Kasha told Kim she would be "enlightened."

That's why Kim was here.

"I must gain entry to your mind, Grandmother," Kim said, reining in her excitement." I need you to show me through your mind's eye what Pascal Lunguku, the Exalted Sir, looked like."

A bust of the legendary Shuugouteki operative stood on display in the Spirit Winds, Inc. Lobby, but it had been somewhat stylized. No accurate description of the man had ever been found. But Kim had an idea, one fueled by her memories and of Jackson disappearing after the battle at Spirit Winds, Inc.

"Is that possible?" Mitsu cocked her head, pursing her lips. "Surely you already use much of your power to inhabit your younger self at this moment. Hai?"

"I...I'm being helped in this, Obaachan. Another force guides me on this mental journey of mine."

"Another force. Ah, so." Mitsu nodded and smiled. "I wish you could tell me all that has befallen you, Kimmy-san, but I know that is impossible. I too, have kept things from you, but it was necessary. It was all part of a promise I made long ago to the Exalted Sir."

"It's a story I do need to share with you, obaachan, and to hear yours as well. But time is of the essence. I'm sorry."

"Then do what you must. My mind is open."

"Grandmother Mitsu," Kim said with a smile. "You rock."

She entered Mitsu's mental landscape.

Ambient-Milieu

Kim remembered her entry into Shioko's neural realm at the Book Haven. Shioko's terror of Omori Kadanamora's shadow-trackers had driven the young girl into a fear-driven emotional withdrawal. The mental scenario Kim encountered had been a mix of virtual seascapes, underwater caverns, and a myriad ocean dwellers. All of which had been created by Shioko's imagination in the ambient-milieu to keep her subconscious hidden and safe.

Grandmother Mitsu's neural realm was completely different.

Kim stood across a large pond fronting a familiar Japanese structure or, at least, the psychic-virtual image of it. The Zen temple Kinkaku-ji, the Golden Pavilion. Three stories tall with each floor surrounded by an outside balcony, much of its wooden construction covered in gold leaf. A stylized bronze Phoenix sculpture adorned the rooftop. Kim took a deep breath. She had visited the real Kinkaku-ji once with her obaachan.

As if guided by an outside force, Kim took a step forward directly onto the pond's glimmering surface. And was immediately transported.

Kim found herself inside the Golden Pavilion but, as so often happens in dreams and visions, the temple interior looked vastly different from what Kim remembered.

A long hallway stretched before her, alight from an unseen source. Paper shoji screens lined both sides, concealing numerous rooms. Yet Kim continued walking, once again gently guided by that mysterious force. Even as some of the screens slid back to reveal the rooms within, Kim didn't stop. Though she did glance into the interiors as she passed.

Grandmother Mitsu! Kim thought in wonder. Yoshima Ayaka Mitsu as a young girl, playing with her friends in the poor neighborhood in Osaka where she grew up.

Another room. Mitsu working to help support the family.

And more. Grandmother's memories, Kim thought, awestruck. Has to be. But I'm not seeing them through her eyes but, rather, as an outsider, a witness. And this one. What's through here?

Mitsu at the Ise Jingu.

Kim stopped. Ise Jingu, the Grand Shrine in the city of Ise, dedicated to the sun goddess Amaterasu. She turned and stood at the open shoji entrance to the room, staring open-mouthed. Like viewing an old, hand-colored kinescope recording, she watched a young girl wearing a kimono and clogs, her hair done up in an older, more mature style, exit the shrine. She crossed the Uji Bridge straddling the Isuzu-gawa river, which flowed through the shrine's peaceful parklands. The sky shone a brilliant blue, scudding clouds mere wisps of feathery whiteness. Twittering birds and the sound of running water shed a soothing comfort throughout.

There she is, Kim thought, her heartbeat racing. It's her as a sixteen-year old, paying her respects to Amaterasu as her mother had done. This would have been around the nineteen-twenties

At the end of the bridge, Mitsu stopped as an old black gentleman dressed in a suit, tie, and hat appeared. He leaned forward on a cane, which appeared to be damaged. His clothes were dusty as if he had fallen, perhaps in the street.

Pascal Lukungu, Kim thought. It's him. She stepped into the room's landscape, feeling a rush of warmth flow over her body as she became immersed in the memory. She walked closer.

"Hello, little sister," Lukungu said to Mitsu kindly.

This is where he gave her the book, Kim thought. But, his voice. I know that voice. She wanted to see more but then the gentle guiding force took hold of her again. She turned and reluctantly exited the room. The shoji screen closed behind her.

And another opened.

CHAPTER 22

How Can You Be in Two Places at Once
When You're Not Anywhere at All?

Fireside Theatre

Venice

Zone of Concealment

Maghi Warren

2011 C.E.

Kim

Second Iteration

<<**B**ut first the indigene must assist in a number of final past manifestations>>

Somewhere else in space and time, Kim sped instantaneously to another destination. True to her word, a'Kasha had allowed Kim to exist in multiple locations at the same time.

Superpositioned. Bilocated.

Kim was cognizant of everything happening with her grandmother, up to the point of her entering obaachan's mind and witnessing her as a young girl.

Now Kim's awareness, this second iteration of herself focused here…

A vortex, a maelstrom, the Void churns with unlimited power, its spectral surf crashing onto galactic shores. Intertwined throughout space and time, It thrashes and shudders in a clash of opposing primal forces. Ancient, unknowable, It strives to unleash itself throughout the ages and branches of the multiverse, to keep Itself in check within the nexus of existence in order for the Balance to be maintained. Its powerful duality, formed during the Great Beginning, wars constantly. To contain Itself and the annals of knowledge It stores of all times and places. To unleash Itself to share that knowledge, to advise, to cajole. To contain Itself. To unleash itself. Over and over infinitely.

Arcs of blue lightning, temporal energy surges, convulse like enormous, flailing tentacles. Streamers of coronal flares explode, erupt, cascading outward. Across the multitudes of stars, galaxies, nebulae, dimensional and temporal rifts, the Void spreads Its churning winds of cosmic energy, only to be reined back into Its numinous, whirling heart…

———————

Kim put her hands to her chest where the beating of her heart shook her whole body. Grandmother Mitsu, she thought, taking a deep breath. I was, I am with her. She recognized me as my older self.

Then Kim realized she possessed no hands, no chest. No heart. Her vision, her essence, expanded. Kim watched, floating, non-corporeal, invisible. She felt as if she used her esper-sight, her body located somewhere else, much like when she witnessed Wayne in Dartham City. Only her awareness existed here, a frightening tableau unfolding before it. One part of her mind visualized a'Kasha in its true nebulous form.

The other part of her mind showed Jenny Sibulovich lying on a stone platform within a large, columned chamber. The bright light and heat from a glowing portal bathed her in waves of flickering crimson. Four Maghi supernumeraries surrounded her, animal masks covering their faces.

A woman entered the chamber, her body moving effortlessly, a long tail curling behind her. She wore her own mask, a starkly simplistic, white, human face. Kim knew this was Estansa Milaar as a rush of knowledge revealed itself to her.

From the Void. The Archive. The realm of the Myriad Things. It had been a'Kasha, keeper of the Akashic Records itself, who had been feeding Kim information all along. Knowledge. Since the beginning. How to employ and control her esper powers, how to predict and call forth the temporal displacement tremors, how to survive within the phase-shifting stream. How to figure out what the Totou planned. Everything. All in an effort to right this so-called cosmic imbalance.

As if her mind couldn't be boggled any further.

The lamia Milaar chanted, a litany of spells to summon her demon master into the world.

Orcus.

Kim moved her attention closer to her friend. Twin bite marks puckered Jenny's neck. The vampire's work! Jenny no longer had any real control over her actions. She would become Milaar's Nexus Point, a compass indicating the location of the temporal displacement tremors.

And Kim must help her. She must help Jenny bring the alternate Orcus of ArcNight's world into her world instead of the real devil. The right sequence of events had to play out, no matter how painful that was.

No! Kim protested as cruel irony overwhelmed her. If I do so, I'll help injure Amedio and destroy Edmondo. I wanted to save them. Please…

But she knew she must. Incongruously, tragically, in order to thwart Milaar's plans, she had no choice.

A large crystal orb hung suspended in the chamber. It, too, radiated a rhythm like a beating heart. Jenny, Kim thought-sent. It's Kim. Kim felt a rush of heat shoot through Jenny's body. Spiderwebs of sparkling radiance danced over her supine form. Jenny struggled, trying to break free of the invisible force constraining her.

Kim reached out and touched Jenny's mind, allowing the image of the Void to appear in her friend's mind. Kim suspected Jenny only sensed Kim's presence peripherally, like a hunch or idea. The displacement tremors, Jenny. Jenny immediately became rapt and composed at the sight of the Void. The same image metamorphosed within the crystal orb like a recording plucked from inside her. Estansa's voice rose triumphantly, an excitement, an anticipation of victory sounding. Bravely, Jenny strained against her invisible bonds. Pain gripped her.

Kim formed a spark of hope, sending it flickering into her friend's mind. We can do this, Jenny. We…

Kim's astral-self recoiled. No! Not we but Jenny. Jenny herself! There, revealed in Jenny's mind lay a long-dormant, what? How could Kim describe it? A kind of genetic marker? Identifying or pointing to a sub-conscious and inert ability, like a power switch turned off. Now visible to Kim, it explained Jenny's passion for physics and cosmology, her desire to understand the workings behind the multiverse. For her willingness to put herself in this dangerous situation.

To touch the Void.

I can't help her, Kim thought. I'm not supposed to. Only, what? Simply watch? Nudge her in the right direction?

Kim sensed Jenny's thoughts—My…my conversations with Kim about the displacement tremors, the aftershocks, my own research and writings. There's got to be something in all of that I can use to stop this.

That's it! Kim sensed a mounting expectancy within Jenny's mind.

She has to be on the right track.

Jenny's thought continued, a burning fire within the neural realm. Af…aftershocks occur from inside a ruptured area of the Void, a rift, caused by the tremors.

Kim concentrated. There, Jenny, look there.

That cut, that dark spot I see. Could…could that be one of those ruptured areas within the Void? If I disrupt it further, direct it against the Summoning Portal's energy, could I set off a premature aftershock? Stop Milaar's plans? I have to try.

It's a'Kasha, Kim thought. It's activating that marker, turning the switch on, giving Jenny the knowledge and power.

The lesser Maghi added their voices to Estansa's. Their dark energy rose, magnified by the forces of the gateway portal. Kim felt the opposing power as the Maghi's attention focused on the Void. For a moment, Jenny faltered.

Kim! she screamed in her mind, trying to keep anchored onto the aftershock rift. Kim, can you hear me? Kim! Lazo!

It's Kim! I'm here! But she knew Jenny couldn't hear her. But to sense her, yes! Kim knew Jenny might and that could be enough. It might…

The world exploded.

Ambient-Milieu

"Jenny! Jenny!" My friend, what's happened to you? "Oh!" Kim cried out, tumbling through a whirling, serpentine vortex. The concussive event in the Summoning Chamber had thrown her second iteration out of the phase-shifting stream. She could feel the difference! See it in the flashing, gleaming arcs of iridescence spiraling around her.

She twisted and turned, as if caught in a vast wind tunnel. Lightning-like bolts flashed; fiery tracers cascaded. She'd rarely felt in control during her temporal journeys, either in the displacement tremors or the phase-shifting stream. But this felt completely random and unstoppable. And fatally out-of-control.

Her stomach roiled, her head spun. She barely managed to jerk her body away from one of the tracers as it shot past her. "No!" She tried to bring her esper powers to bear but they didn't respond. Damn it! Not now!

Wa…wait! Kim grasped at the straw forming in her mind. The unicorn. Kim grabbed her belt-pouch and managed to get a hand inside it. The spectral wind whirled her around as she fought the darkness threatening to overcome her. She'd placed the origami figure given to her by the Sanctuary Elder in her pouch. The Elder said the unicorn construction was a weapon. But surely Kim could use it for another purpose. Wouldn't fighting back against this maelstrom need a weapon?

She held onto the paper figure tightly with both hands, afraid it would be torn away by the vortex's brutal buffeting. The Elder said Kim would know how to use it when the time came. That time was now! She placed the paper unicorn against her chest, willing it to do something. Anything.

"Ahhhhhhhh!" Kim's arms and legs splayed as something bumped up below and against her. Frantically, she took hold of a…horse's mane? Powerful muscles beneath her coiled and stretched like pistons, supporting her prone body.

A horse, a unicorn… No! A kirin elongated beneath her. A kirin! A hide of many colors covered its muscular equine body. A single-horned head rose upward on a thick-maned neck. The kirin turned to look back at Kim, its beautiful eyes shining.

Yomitsu, the thoughts reached Kim's mind from the animal. It is gratifying to see you again.

"Trell" Kim shouted over the surrounding tumult. Kim didn't know whether to laugh or cry out in astonishment. Trell was the origami weapon? How did that happen?

Please, Yomitsu, hold on tightly. Kim didn't need to be told twice as she wrapped her hands around Trell's neck, pressing her knees against the beast's great flanks.

The kirin righted Kim's fall, corrected her course, and, though wingless, flew and veered away from and out of the vortex. Using his horn and front hooves, Trell broke through the imprisoning walls of the vortex, and glided into a calmer space, one devoid of color or shape.

Except for the glowing blue sphere blazing ahead of them (Or was it behind? Above?) Kim cried out as Trell flew into the sphere.

The kirin descended through a thick cloud cover. The wind rushed through Kim's hair as she and Trell broke through, wisps of cloudstuff clinging to their bodies. Kim stared in wonder at a jeweled city, glittering below like a billion earth-bound suns.

Rising from an island floating on a crystal blue sea, the city looked like it had been born straight out of a Thousand and One Arabian Nights tale. Towering minarets, domed mosques, tiled streets, all surrounded by four high, circular stone walls. Between each set of walls, gardens bloomed, shining pools glistened in the sun.

In the middle of the island, on a hill overlooking the city, stood a huge palace. Constructed of stone, marble, and gold, the palace vaulted into the sky as if it might take off like a rocket.

Where is this place? Kim wondered. Why am I here?

You will see, Trell thought-sent.

The kirin dropped lower, heading for the uppermost ramparts of the palace. Trell settled lightly on a tiled outdoor terrace. Near one corner, a tall date palm tree grew right up through the tile, its branches overhanging two people. One, a young boy…

It's Bobby!

A woman stood with Kim's nephew. Green skin, ruby-red eyes, dressed in a long, diaphanous robe. Dark hair whirled as if wind-blown about her frightening face. She gazed at Bobby as if controlling him.

Trell bent his front legs, lowering himself to allow Kim to dismount. Bobby didn't react, as if not seeing Kim or her extraordinary steed. The woman, however, turned a surprised glance in their direction. The woman walked toward them as Kim strode quickly to meet her.

"What have you done with my nephew?" Kim demanded, facing the fearsome-looking woman. It was all she could do not to strangle the green-skinned witch!

The woman scowled. "Who are you? How have you gained entry to this level?"

"Let Bobby go!" Kim cried. "Bobby! Can you hear me?"

The woman tossed her head, a haughtiness in her demeanor. She held up a ringed finger. "He cannot. I protect him here, keep him safe. You and your creature will leave immediately."

"Like hell we will."

She pointed that red-nailed finger at Kim. "I am Nolu of the Djinn. You have no power here."

A jinni! "You think so?" Kim barely controlled her anger. Who did this Nolu think she was? "We'll see about that."

Trell suddenly trotted between Kim and the djinn, his imposing body keeping them apart. The kirin speared Kim with an intense look. Not yet, he thought-sent to Kim's mind. Safe for now. Come.

Reluctantly, fighting back tears of rage, Kim climbed back on the kirin. Evidently, she'd been brought here to see that what a'Kasha had told her about Bobby was true. Trell lifted skyward while the djinn Nolu simply watched.

"I'll be back, Bobby!" Kim cried. "I promise!"

Not this iteration, Trell thought-sent. But another.

How many of me will there be? Why…?"

CHAPTER 23

Do not be afraid to open one door; be wary of the many.

Samuel Kim
The Teachings of Yira ~ The Five Precepts to Enlightenment

Ambient-Milieu

Kim

First Iteration

A different room. A different memory. This one more detailed, more revelatory.

And even more immersive. Grandmother as a young woman again but this time I feel her emotions and thoughts, see and remember what she does.

Kim, this Kim, let herself be swept up in Mitsu's life.

Outside of Nara, Japan

C.E. 1912

Kohoshi Ayako Mitsu walked slowly through the central corridor of the long, one-story building. She looked around in wonder at the western-style interior, so different from the outside. The exterior façade of the structure had been designed in an architectural style much like the Ninomaru palace of Nijō Castle which Mitsu had seen in photographs. The tiled roofs, pointed gables, and intricate wood carvings made her heart flutter.

She followed a few steps behind the western-dressed man who had driven her and her husband Jirou to the outskirts of Nara from Osaka by motorized omnibus. The nurse who had been their companion on the trip stayed close by her side, her arm linked with Mitsu's.

Mitus's mind whirled with the events of the last few days. An omnibus! Truly a marvelous creation. Jirou had transported the two of them from their small, humble home by ox cart to the countryside west of Osaka. There the both of them waited. When Mitsu's husband saw the large mechanical vehicle pull up in front of them under its own power, his surprise and awe had been hard to conceal.

The nurse who had traveled with them on the two-day journey had looked after the pregnant Mitsu as if the young woman had been her own daughter. She made sure Mitsu had everything she needed and slept in the room next to her and Jirou's room at the teahouse inn the night before.

Mitsu had been a little embarrassed by the attention. The nurse's presence had eased her husband's concern and softened his stance on allowing her to go in the first place. She was, after all, seven months pregnant and the trip in the omnibus would undoubtedly be uncomfortable. Plus, these people were unknown to them. Could Mitsu's welfare be entrusted to strangers?

Surprisingly, the old African gentleman, whose real name Mitsu had never known, had requested her presence. And hers alone. The gentleman escorting her and the nurse had asked Jirou to stay in the clinic's reception chamber to wait for her, which Jirou begrudgingly agreed to. The old gentleman's personal messenger had visited Mitsu's home a week earlier to extend the invitation to the clinic, identifying the gentleman to Mitsu by using the honorific Mitsu had called him. 'The Exalted Sir'. That was when they had met at the Grand Shrine of the sun goddess Amaterasu at Ise Jingu. She couldn't refuse his summons, though her husband had objected. It had been two years since their first meeting at the sacred shrine and Mitsu thought she would never see the Exalted Sir again. How grand to get his invitation! She had to go!

In the end, it wasn't hard to allay Jirou's fears and convince him they should go.

Mitsu had dressed in a floor-length, loosely sashed white robe and sandals, had arranged her hair in a traditional nihongami style, her long dark locks pulled up toward the top of her head, rounded and fitted with combs and small ornaments.

She had applied only a small amount of makeup to her face. Mitsu did not want to appear as a geisha or shirabyoshi.

Now a respectable married woman eighteen years of age, she was literally full of life, just as the Exalted Sir had predicted. She placed one hand on her extended belly, feeling the movement within. A son, she thought with a smile. He told me I would have children and grandchildren and I just know this first one will be a boy.

The clinic was located in a rural area outside of Osaka, its grounds dotted with gardens and cobblestone walkways. A wide driveway led to the front where Mitsu and Jirou had disembarked from the omnibus.

The clinic interior was quite organized and professional, well-lit, and very clean. Mitsu marveled at the doctors and nurses attending to the patients. Everything and everyone seemed very efficient, from the greeter at the reception chamber to the staff members who mopped sections of the wooden floor. She had been told this was a private clinic, meaning (according to her husband) that some individual or group owned, operated and maintained it. How fortunate for the Exalted Sir to be able to afford such personal care.

She noticed, though, some of the workers at the clinic stopped what they were doing to stare at her as she passed. Some whispered among themselves. Mitsu thought she heard one of them say, "She-Who-Comes-Before."

Finally, the omnibus driver stopped in front of a patient room, bowed and motioned for Mitsu to enter. The nurse smiled at her and nodded. Mitsu bowed, thanked both of them, and walked into the room. The door closed quietly behind her and, to Mitsu's surprise, she found herself in a large and pleasant space, more so than she had expected.

The patient rooms in the small hospital in Osaka could barely fit three people in them. This room was wide and spacious. A single window, with the curtains pulled back, allowed sunlight to brighten the interior. A ceiling fan slowly turned above the wooden floor. Mokuhanga block prints hung from the walls. A faint smell of incense wafted through the air and small ikebana flower arrangements were situated throughout

The Exalted Sir lay in a bed near the window. Though it was a lovely spring day, a blanket covered his thin frame. His once gray-haired pate was now bald, his features gaunt and sunken. The silver-tipped cane Mitsu remembered him using (or one very much like it) leaned against a bedside table. But his tired eyes brightened when he saw Mitsu. "Ah, little sister!" he exclaimed hoarsely in perfect Japanese, his dark, weathered face breaking out into a smile. "How wonderful. Did you have a good journey here?"

Mitsu caught her breath, returned his smile, and bowed. "Oh yes, Exalted Sir. My husband and I were escorted here by a very respectful gentleman and a caring nurse."

"Good. Good. It's lovely to see you again. Your beauty and maturity have flowered with your pregnancy. Come closer."

Mitsu felt herself blushing as she approached the bed. "You honor me. I am glad to see you although I am saddened at your state. The only other time I met with you, you were injured. And now, you are ill?"

The old man coughed. "Unfortunate, yes, yes. You've never seen me in my best condition. But for men of my age and profession, these types of injuries and illnesses are a common occurrence. In the parlance of the world I once belonged to, it comes with the territory."

His profession, Mitsu thought. What could that be? And what is this world he speaks of? "I have thought of you often, Exalted Sir, and hoped to see you again. There is so much I still do not understand, so many questions I want to ask."

"I know, child. I wish I could explain everything to you, but there's a great deal even I don't know. For instance, though the secret texts of the times-to-come described one of my order finding you, I didn't know I would be the one so privileged, or that it would be at Amaterasu's holy shrine. Alas, my time is short now. I'm dying, you see."

Mitsu felt a great sorrow come over her. Though she barely knew the old gentleman, he had affected her life greatly. "I am grieved to hear such news."

The old man shrugged. "Such a fate comes to us all, does it not? I've been both blessed and cursed to have lived so long and to have experienced so much. Yet, even after all these years, all these adventures I've participated in, these lives, all that I've won and lost, not all is clear." He coughed again, this time producing a deep, rattling sound. Mitsu poured some water from a pitcher resting on the bedside table and gave the glass to the old man.

He drank deeply and sighed. "Thank you, child." He looked at her then, his gaze intense. "Though we've only met these two times, I know all about you, the person you are now and the person you will be. As I told you that day at the holy shrine, you are She-Who-Comes-Before, the forerunner of the Yomitsu. You will teach your granddaughter the old ways, relate to her the ancient tales and myths and educate her from the book I gave you, The Teachings of Yira--The Five Precepts to Enlightenment. This you must do for history and legend to come together. Your granddaughter will be the focus of this in order to stop the chaos that will otherwise ensue."

Such strange words! "The Yomitsu, Exalted Sir?"

"Your granddaughter. It's one of the names she will be known by when she's grown into an adult. But you mustn't tell her this. Do you understand?"

Mitsu frowned. "I think so. Yes." Though she really didn't. She felt so small, insignificant and confused. How was it this strange man felt she was so important? And what did he mean by "the secret texts of the times-to-come?" So much mystery!

"May I ask what my granddaughter, the...Yomitsu, will do and why she will be so important?" She had put the same question to him that day two years ago but had not received an answer. She had been satisfied with that. Now, she wanted to know.

"I'm sorry, child, but I still can't tell you." The old man looked at her, his face overwritten with guilt. "Even though you're crucial to your granddaughter's development, the less you know the better. Some knowledge can't be yours to possess in order for your family to remain safe. That's all I can say. Unfortunately, we all have our secrets to keep."

Mitsu pursed her lips, disappointed but knowing she must obey. "I... I have read and reread the book you gave me on that day, Exalted Sir," she said. "I know Yira's precepts by heart and have tried to live my own life by them."

"Good, good. You're a wise and brave child. But there's something I am permitted to tell you, that I must tell you. It's why I sent for you. Please, come closer, sit."

Mitsu sat on a chair by the bed. This close, she could smell the old gentleman. An odor of great age, of sickness and, Mitsu reasoned, of the modern medicines used to treat him emanated from his person. Had the traditional acupuncture and herbal treatments not worked? The Exalted Sir must be ill indeed to have come here to receive such current remedies. Yet his eyes were now alight with an inner strength.

She took the empty glass from him as he spoke. "How much and to whom have you spoken of me?" he asked.

Mitsu sat with her hands folded on her expanded belly. Through the open window, she could hear birds and the conversation of other visitors walking in the gardens. The slow whirring of the fan above. "Only to my husband," she answered truthfully. "I never wanted to let people think I was unseemly by accepting gifts from, forgive me, strange men. But I could not keep such a thing from Jirou. Besides, it was an innocent passing. You just gave me a book, and he understands."

"Not just any book," the old man corrected her. "It's a copy of our Sacred Artifact. You must remember that."

"Of course," Mitsu agreed, wondering he meant by our Sacred Artifact.

"You were wise to not tell too much, and I apologize for asking your husband to not accompany you to my bedside. It's easier for me to speak to you alone. I beg you to continue your silence. It will be difficult, but no one must know the particulars of your visit here today. Except for Jirou. Of course, you must tell him."

A relief swelled with Mitsu. She rejoiced she wouldn't have to face whatever this was alone. "Thank you. I... I told my neighbors and friends I was visiting an uncle." She looked down, ashamed of telling a lie.

The old man's face broke out into a smile again. "That's accurate enough. Very good and don't feel bad about that. Sometimes an untruth is necessary. And I must say your husband sounds like a good man."

Mitsu blushed again. "Oh, he is. Jirou is very kind and he treats me like a princess."

"As you should be treated. Now, my dear, there is something else I must give you, something as equally important as the Five Precepts."

"Oh?" Mitsu replied without thinking. Why would the old gentleman need to give her another gift?

"It's there, child," he said, pointing a gnarled finger to his bedside table.

Mitsu looked and, to her surprise, saw a small green figure sitting by the water pitcher where she was certain none had been before. She looked questioningly at the old gentleman who nodded.

Gently, she picked up the figure. It was an origami-constructed dragon, created entirely from green-colored paper. She smiled at the intricacy of its making. Its body curved as it appeared to be walking forward. Its fierce-looking head, positioned atop a long neck, held an angled face possessing two blue eyes. Its whiskered jaws opened, studded with paper fangs. The dragon was truly beautiful. So intricately folded, so carefully designed. "Wonderful," Mitsu breathed. "Exalted Sir, did you make this noble piece of art yourself?"

"Indeed, child, and you must keep it. When you return to your home, unfold it and read the instructions within. It affects both you and Jirou."

"Exalted Sir, I do not understand."

The old man sighed. "I know, I know, all this is so vague and confusing, isn't it? I wish it could be otherwise but, I assure you, what you read will be direct and you must follow the instructions to the letter. Believe me, it will be a great help to you, your husband, and your future granddaughter. Now, if you don't mind, child, I grow weary. I must rest. Return to Osaka safely and live your life well."

More mysteries! What did all this mean? Mitsu bowed her head. "Yes, yes, Exalted Sir. I understand. Thank you." Mitsu stood but continued looking, transfixed, at the dragon. She knew it was simply made from paper but somehow it seemed so much more. What hidden message did it contain? She held it in both her hands and pressed it to her breast.

Oh, there was one more important question she wanted to ask. "Exalted Sir, forgive my forwardness and if it please you, what is your name?"

The man smiled, his eyelids fluttering with apparent fatigue. "I have had many names," he said mysteriously. "Most recently, however, I have been known as Pascal. Pascal Lukungu." Then the old man abruptly fell asleep, his breathing deep, his chest rising and falling with each breath.

But what is your real name? Mitsu wondered in resignation, sudden tears blurring her eyes. One more thing I may never know. She did know for certain, however, that this would be the last time she would ever see the old gentleman. But I have a purpose now, more than just being an ordinary wife of a laborer. I pray I can live up to his expectations and faith in me.

Kohoshi Ayako Mitsu stood, bowed to the sleeping African for the last time, turned and walked to the door.

Kim found herself back in the hallway of the Golden Pavilion, a shoji screen closing before her. She didn't remember exiting the room but the memory of what lay behind the screen burned in her mind. Grandmother Mitsu had met with Lukungu a second time. Why had the old man really desired that meeting? What did the paper dragon contain that was so important?

That was Pascal Lukungu! But, goddess, he reminds me of someone.

Kim remembered Jackson once saying Lukungu was his great-grandfather. But he also said he was a direct descendant of two of the Jade Court—Princess Midori and Chancellor Hiroshi. How could that be? Regardless of the seeming discrepancy, maybe that's why Kim thought Lukungu familiar. A family resemblance of some sort.

Two rooms down on the left, another screen slid aside, beckoning. Kim approached it and walked through the entrance. A young Japanese woman and man knelt on the floor at a hadoken box table. Their peasant-style clothing hinted this was once again a time period further in the past, though after the previous scenario. The woman held a green origami dragon, staring at it silently. Candles cast flickering light over the table while a faint odor of cooked fish, garlic, and ginger still lingered. Outside, a lone catbird trilled in the night.

Grandmother again, Kim thought, standing in a corner of the room. And grandfather Jirou. Kim had never known Jirou, who died before Kim's father had been born.

She watched in wonder as Mitsu held up the paper dragon given to her by Lukungu.

"Aieee, Jirou-chan, this…this is such a wonder," Mitsu said.

"Is it truly from him?" Jirou asked. "The man you met at the Ise Jingu two years ago? You were so silent on the omnibus trip back here."

"Because of the nurse and the driver. I was told not to reveal any of this except to you. At the clinic the Exalted Sir told me I am to unfold the dragon and read the instructions written within."

"Instructions? Ah. Then, please, do so."

Mitsu shook her head. "But, husband, how can I undo this origami marvel? It is a work of art. Such a wonder should be forever shared and treasured."

"But the old gentleman wishes you to." Jirou smiled at his wife. "I suspect you are afraid, hai?"

"But what are these instructions I must follow? Yes, I am afraid, Jirou-chan. What if this changes our lives?"

"They have already been changed, Mitsu-chan, by your meeting with the Exalted Sir at all. In his giving you the book, The Five Precepts to Enlightenment."

"The book I am to give to our future granddaughter of power." Mitsu sighed. "It is all so mysterious! Very well, I will unfold the dragon."

"So many strange things you have told me." Jirou touched Mitsu's arm. "But know this. Whatever resides within the dragon, we shall face it together."

"Oh, Jirou-chan."

Open it, grandmother, Kim thought. Just for a second, Mitsu turned in Kim's direction, her brow creased. Then, with trembling hands, Mitsu gently, and with great care, peeled apart the dragon's wings and tail, its body and head. She flattened the paper out on the table, peering intently at the writing upon its surface. A chop mark adorned the upper left side with elegant and flowing script running the length of the page. Kim held her breath as Mitsu began to read. And, then, when finished, started crying.

"Mitsu-chan!" Jirou cried. "What is wrong?"

With a tear-stained face, Mitsu smiled. "Oh, husband! A fortune. Jirou-chan, the Exalted Sir has left us a fortune!"

So that's how obaachan got all that money, Kim thought with a smile. Good old Pascal. It also explained the source of the inheritance

216

Kim had received from her grandmother. Kohoshi Ayako Mitsu had been bequeathed a large sum of money and, possibly, investments, from the man Jackson believed had been his great-grandfather.

She never told me or Ken, Kim marveled. Did our parents know? How difficult it must have been to have kept such a secret. Yes, she left me the book, but I never really suspected this part of the story.

When it had been determined Kim's grandmother had been "She-Who-Comes-Before," the Yomitsu's precursor out of Shuugouteki legend, it had taken Kim some time to accept it. It was too much of a coincidence, she thought. But, of course, it wasn't. Grandmother Mitsu had been given the book by Pascal Lukungu. The Five Precepts to Enlightenment had been written by a man named Samuel Kim, describing the work of an ancient philosopher named Yira. Then Mitsu secretly passed the book down to Kim. But was there more to that story? Who the hell were Samuel Kim and Yira? How did those two mystery men fit into this?

Kim turned and exited the room.

CHAPTER 24

A rotting of the soul, the inner self, displays without, revealed to all.

Samuel Kim
The Teachings of Yira ~ The Five Precepts to Enlightenment

Aizenev, Lost City of the Maghi

Somewhere Other in Time and Space

Kim

Second Iteration

The lamia, Estansa Milaar, stumbled along the Royal Canal of the desolate city of Aizenev. Two robed and cowled Maghi guards accompanied her, each holding a staff of power. She was, in effect, being escorted, not as the visiting Grand Mistress, but as a prisoner, a fallen Maghi.

She had been saved by these very two guards from the conflagration within the Void in her Zone of Concealment warren. If saved was the correct term. She had no doubt she had been brought here to be judged. To then be punished, a fate worse than anything she could imagine.

A purple and gold serpent-head mask concealed the upper half of her face, her white hair streaming out from under and behind it. Beneath the floor-length feather cloak wrapped about herself, her body ached, sore and bruised from the explosion, or whatever had befallen her and her followers. Trailing behind her, her tail dragged flaccidly on the tiled sidewalk.

As always, the sky over Aizenev loomed gray and depressing. As such, no bright sunlight in this realm could harm her, could destroy her vampire aspect. Small comfort as she anticipated the confrontation with the First Lords of this realm.

The water of the city's myriad canals rippled murky and grease-spotted, sending forth a dead, fishy smell. A smoky pall hung over the empty buildings, strada, and campos with an overriding odor of decay and great age. Trees and plants stood bare of leaves, stark and brittle in the wan light. No birds flew in the sky, no insects flitted. It was neither cold nor hot, but a constant neutral dullness.

By Orcus, how she hated this place! The other Maghi who had fled to the earthly Venice had thought the mortal world they had re-discovered would be their salvation. Once they had wiped out the inhabitants living here in Aizenev, and turned it into a dead world, a desire to take back their old "feeding ground," the earthly Venice some had fled so long ago, had grown.

It hadn't been as easy as they thought. Through the centuries, two Maghi factions had formed in the earthly Venice, those that had remained behind—Solomon's Raptors and the Lions of the Venedetto. Their struggle for power had weakened both sides with much loss of life. And to what end? The Maghi had undermined itself to the extent that both sides' power dissipated in time. They had thought to regain that power with Estansa's summoning of Orcus.

The few Maghi inhabitants, hidden in their own beast masks, who walked the otherwise deserted city, stopped and bowed to her, offering their respect to the Grand Mistress of their order. Despite her obvious prisoner status.

She had been brought here by Aizenev's own Primi Signori. They had summoned her here for the first time in decades. Not for any honor, she was certain. Her great plan had failed.

As she attempted to bring Orcus from the under-realm, there had been a rupture in the Void, a collision of opposing forces. The scientist! The mortal Estansa had abducted whose knowledge had been crucial to the task of delivering Orcus. "Dr. Jenny Sibulovich," Estansa murmured, spitting out the cursed name. Sibulovich had done something at the end of the ritual, interfered somehow. A mere mortal! How could that have happened?

She hoped she lay dead in pools of her own blood and filth.

After some few moments (for time knew no measure on this different plain) she and her guards stepped onto the cracked, faded tiles of the Plaza of Saint Koronan. Nothing had changed since last she beheld the vast public square. The top third of Michaela's Obelisk lay broken on its side, torn from the rest of the pillar's body. The Duka's Keep and the Great Library's burned-out hulks lay silhouetted against the gray sky at the edge of the lagoon like the skeletons of beached leviathans.

But where were the Primi Signoris of this alternate plane, including their Supreme First Lord? Would they not allow her to defend herself? Would they not take the pleasure of seeing her grovel? For the first time in a very long time, Estansa felt powerless and afraid. Had she been too full of herself, too sure of her own control? She had let matters slip and become unprotected. Worst of all, she had underestimated the humans.

"Help me," she whispered to no great power in particular, the words like salt in her mouth. A hissing sound, accompanied by a musty odor of age and rot, swept over her. Gasping for breath, she looked to the center of the plaza.

As if in answer to her silent question, one of the First Lords of this alternate plane had appeared. Ah, this wasn't just any First Lord, Estansa realized. A hunched-over specter of a figure, the Supreme First Lord was the oldest of the Maghi in either realm. Thin, bony hands sprouting bird-like claws pressed together as if in prayer. His glowing red eyes were the only feature visible within his dark robe's cowl.

The Supreme First Lord and his most loyal followers had stayed behind in Aizenev for reasons unclear and murky. Yet, they allowed those who had left to do as they would. They still retained some power and influence. And, from time to time, they exerted both on each world.

The guards walked Estansa to within a few feet of the sorcerer. One of them reached over to Milaar and removed her mask. The guards bowed repeatedly and backed away. "My Lord," Milaar said, swallowing her fear, attempting to still the fluttering of her heart. "How may I serve you?"

"Estansa Milaar, Grand Mistress of the Maghi," the Supreme First Lord said, his voice like crackling, dried leaves. "In order to understand our summoning of you, you must observe what is transpiring in your warren at this very moment."

With that, the First Lord gestured, and a glowing crystalline globe materialized. This world's Orb of Orcus, it floated in the space between the First Lord and Estansa. The view within its crystalline depths grew in size, shocking Estansa at what it revealed.

Orcus had been freed! The Maghi's master stood grand and beautiful, his golden hair and porcelain skin shining. Her plan had worked! But...but...

The Venice of her creation in the interdimensional Zone of Conceal-ment lay in ruins, shambles. Buildings had been toppled, sidewalks split, windows smashed, fires burned. The great rupture within the Void had practically destroyed that realm. Yet, the barrier between her warren and the earthly Venice still held. In the midst of that ruination, Orcus raged, rampaging through the ruins.

"You have caused great destruction to be wrought," The Supreme First Lord said.

"But Orcus has been brought forth!" she protested, a semblance of courage rising.

"Has he? Look again."

Orcus raised a hand, now clawed and dark. He changed, becoming monstrous, alien. He raised his bestial head to the dark sky and howled.

"He...he has been corrupted!" Estansa felt herself deflate, her legs weak. Then, the full truth hit her. "He...he is not Orcus."

"He is not our Orcus." The Supreme Lord passed his taloned hand over the Orb. "There is more."

More images appeared. A horde of monstros ran rampant through her secret warren. She choked back an angry cry. Her collection of pets, her menagerie, had escaped! Before her eyes, the veilant, the carnesca, the eldritch spawn, and the other myriad creatures she had captured and ensorcelled, broke through the debris of collapsed walls and ceilings, overpowering what remained of Estansa's Maghi despite the sorcerers' powers. They stampeded through the stairwells and hallways of the buildings, bellowing, shrieking, striking down her servants and guards. How can this be? She had placed the creatures under her control and had kept them in captivity for so long.

Their apparent leader spurred them onward as they wreaked destruction and death. The strange beast found in the church by her slave Edmondo and her Second, the First Lord Roberto! The tall, feline-reptile hybrid strode through the secret chambers, a giant lion-dog at her side. The statue it had been found with? Like one of the Lions of the Venedetto, the statue had transformed into a living thing.

How had she not foreseen this?

Somehow the combined might of the beasts overwhelmed her own followers. Such power they must possess! "My Lord," she said, her thoughts awhirl. "I do not... I..."

"We will not risk our own safety for your mistakes," came the cold, emotionless reply.

"Cowards!" Estansa spat, sudden anger and resentment rising. She bared her fangs, hissing. "You hide here in this rotting city like mice!"

The Supreme First Lord made a slicing motion with his hand. Estansa sucked in her breath, her words silenced. "Control must be exerted, the Balance maintained in our favor," the Supreme First Lord rasped. "You have failed in this."

"I have been a faithful servant!" Fear surged through Estansa. She knew what would come next.

"You have become too arrogant and disobedient. So, we have found another."

222

"Someone to take my place?" Estansa quivered, becoming more afraid.

The Supreme First Lord placed his clawed hands together in front of him, his red eyes burning. "She...it...is of a different race and mythology of the Left Hand Path, as you are, but she originates from an Eastern milieu, not the Dark Demesne. We discovered her essence banished and floating in a nether-world between worlds, not fully dead or alive, and rescued it. We reconstituted her body and mind. She is known as a yokai, from the Eastern realm of Nippon. She has power and is eager to use it."

The Supreme First Lord directed Estansa's gaze to an abandoned coffee shop situated among the storefronts which once thrived along the edges of the Plaza of Saint Koronan. What looked to be a human, an umana, female emerged from the open door, accompanied by two First Lords. She walked barefoot and wore tunic and trousers. Her long hair tumbled behind her as she approached Estansa.

Estansa laughed, despite herself. "This is she who will succeed me? A mere umana cow?"

At those words, the female raised her head, her Asian eyes defiant, piercing Estansa with a bold look. Behind those dark orbs, a flashing of power and strength no umana could possibly possess, simmered.

"Well, what is it you are called then?" she demanded of the female, refusing to submit. "What is your name?"

The woman scowled, a slight twitching below one eye. "I am Damara, the jorōgumo," she said softly with a short bow. "The Spider Demon. I have a score to settle with both the umana and the yokai. The Supreme First Lord has resurrected me, and I will now do his bidding, which will allow my own vengeance to be taken."

Damara looked to the Supreme First Lord who nodded. The Spider Demon then changed. Sharp, erect hairs sprouted over her exposed flesh, her hands, feet, and face. Multiple eyes shifted and floated in in a twisted, hideous face. Her fingers elongated, forming long pointed claws at their tips.

She viciously lashed out at Estansa with one of those deadly hands, slicing through the lamia's shoulder. Estansa gasped more in surprise than pain, blood and steaming life-force erupting from the wound. So, the Supreme First Lord had given the jorōgumo additional power, as he had once given it to Estansa, when she had been his favorite. The First Lord had found a new pet and had empowered her to destroy the old one.

Estansa tried to laugh, as the jorōgumo readied for another strike.

A burst of blue light blinded her. The pavement rumbled beneath her. Cries of confusion whirled around Estansa. Explosions reverberated throughout the plaza, smoke, flame, dazzling tracers of radiant fire. The jorōgumo shrieked and raised her arms above her head.

A woman winked into existence as if from the air itself. Dressed in warrior garb, she stepped in front of the jorōgumo and opened her gloved hands. A flash erupted from her palms.

A horse, rainbow-hued, a long horn projecting from its forehead, stood on the plaza. No, not a horse...

As if from some unseen command given by the woman, the equine beast reared up on its hind legs. The tip of its horn gleamed, a beam of light shot upward from the horn into the sky. The beast came down, a front hoof striking the jorōgumo in the chest.

The spider-demon flew backward, tumbling and skidding over the plaza tiles. Blazing arcs of lightning rained down upon the plaza, exploding among the surprised Maghi. The sorcerers cried out in confusion and terror.

The warrior, a Japanese woman, gestured to the equine and turned to Estansa. "So you're the Grand Mistress," the woman said in Italian. "Something tells me you've seen better days. You better be worth it."

Estansa hissed, more in amusement than anger. Though she had never met this woman, she knew instantly who she was.

The Yomitsu, she thought. It's the cursed Yomitsu.

CHAPTER 25

When everything is said and done, we're all just
products of another's imagination.

Dr. Lilith Cardazio
Dreams and the Unmapped Territories of the Mental Universe

Ambient-Milieu

Kim

First Iteration

few more steps brought Kim to a different type of door. But instead of facing another paper shoji screen, she stood before a plain wooden one. With a soft click, it opened inward revealing a room Kim had seen before, the patient room in the Osaka clinic. Pascal Lukungu, dressed in a suit, slumped asleep in the chair by his bed. A suitcase and his cane lay by his feet.

Kim approached him, gently nudged forward by her unseen guide, and once more experienced the warmth of memory immersion. Once again, something about Lukungu's face struck her. Something recognizable, like his voice.

But where was her Grandmother? Why the wooden door instead of a shoji screen? This memory and scene played out vastly different than the others.

A shimmering of the air behind the old man formed into a human shape. A man. But very unusual in his appearance and manner. Tall and thin, yet resonating great power. He wore a floor-length black robe. Long, braided white hair hung down past his shoulders. His angular face, neither young nor old, held two pure white eyes, perpetually staring. He smiled, revealing pink teeth.

"Yomitsu," he said softly, a sibilant undertone to his voice. "And so we meet. Interesting I would find you here."

Startled, Kim stepped back. "You...you see me?"

"Indeed. I have that ability." He regarded Kim, coolly appraising her. "You are well known within the ambient-milieu. I am honored. I wonder though how it is you inhabit the phase-shifting stream."

Honored. I wish they'd stop saying that! "Phase-shifting stream? So that's what I've been experiencing rather than the usual temporal displacement tremors?"

"Of a sort. Phase-shifting is an offshoot of the tremors but is able to be controlled by those who are shifting." Agura smiled. "Except in certain situations."

"Like what I'm going through now. Sending me off on these trips into the past? The Dark Demesne?"

Agura looked thoughtful. "The Dark Demesne. Yes, you mentioned that the first time."

"Who are you and why are you here?" She peered closer. "Have we met before?"

The man smiled, revealing pink teeth. "In a way, we have."

"More secrets!" Kim shook her head. No time for exasperation now. Goddess knew she'd experienced enough of it! "Why did you say it was interesting you found me here? Who are you and what are you doing here?"

"I am Agura the Hunter," he said. "I am on a multiple-entity hunt. You and the old gentleman are two of those entities."

"So you've found us. Now what?"

"Before, I had little time to converse with you. You see, I am, as you would say, replaying this encounter. In essence, we've lived through this particular experience before but, initially, I was unaware of the interest in you and was not yet contracted to find you."

"You manipulated time to meet me again?"

"In a way. Of more concern at the moment is the journey the old gentleman must make, with me escorting him to his destination. Still, you and I have a little time to talk. One of those who procured my services is known to you. Yoshima Mitsu, the Luminous One."

"Mitsu! Why did she...procure your services?"

"She can no longer sense your presence in the milieu, realizing you didn't end up where she thought she'd sent you. Your inhabiting the phase-shifting stream is, no doubt, the reason for that."

"Are you going to get me out of this and take me to Mitsu?"

"I'm not sure I can. If what I believe is correct, I won't be allowed to interfere any further."

What a surprise. Kim focused her attention on the old man. "This is Pascal Lukungu but...not really. Is he?"

"Yes and no. He was once known to you as a much younger man, by another name in a future age."

226

"But this isn't my grandmother's memory. Why am I here?"

"Your grandmother? Unknown. This scenario may have been granted to perhaps edify you. a'Kasha the Archive will sometimes allow deserving souls certain insights." He smiled again. "I suspect a'Kasha has deemed you one of those worthy souls. It is she who may be, as you say, pulling the strings."

That's for sure. She looked down at Lukungu. Here, this close, he seemed more than simply Jackson's ancestor. Even beneath the ravages of age and illness, the resemblance was uncanny. Too much so. Especially the eyes.

They possessed epicanthic folds. Asian eyes.

A chill ran through her but not one of dread. She looked questioningly at the strange creature Agura. "Jackson?" she whispered. "Pascal Lukungu was, is, Jackson Yamaguchi?" The import of that realization slammed into Kim. If that was true, then Jackson must have been sent back to when? The late 1800s, after the battle with the yokai at Spirit Winds, Inc. He lived and grew old, joining the Shuugouteki, and taking on the persona of Lukungu. In essence, living a second life.

Agura nodded. "I see you understand."

Kim waved an impatient hand. "Not really. How can Jackson be his own great-grandfather?"

Agura smiled. "Because he is not. Many, there is an expression, red herrings have been created to confuse and hide certain parts of history, which was necessary for the timelines to run correctly. But know this and be comforted. I will take Jackson Yamaguchi back to a time long ago, to be young and well again, and to live a fulfilling life with those he loves, including the Glorious Ko."

"Shioko?" Kim didn't dare to believe. "Really? You can do that?"

"In this case, I can. I have certain powers permitted by the Sanctuary Elders I can bring to bear when deemed necessary. Plus, I am here as part of an agreement I've consented to."

"What kind of agreement? And how do I know you're telling the truth?"

"I am here for the old gentleman at the behest of one who serves the Glorious Ko."

"One who serves Shioko?" Kim placed her hands to her chest and shook her head. "This person then is the other one who secured your services along with Mitsu?

"No, that is one of the karura who looks for her missing comrade. This is a different agreement."

"Karura. I've met one of those." Now she had Agura's attention.

Interesting. "That important to you?"

"Perhaps. Was the karura named Renta'Mur?"

"Yes. He was in Venice, Italy in the present, looking for his mistress."

"Seiryuu. I wondered if Seiryuu and Renta'Mur might be connected to you. Thank you, Yomitsu, you have made my hunt much easier as I thought you might. I am indebted."

Everything's connected. "Can you pay that debt back now? Can you allow me to talk to Jackson before you go? Is it possible for him to see and hear me?"

Agura paused, nodded, and stepped back.

Kim knelt at Jackson's side. She placed her palms on Jackson's chest. The old man didn't stir, his eyes still closed. He's so old, she thought. I can't even imagine what he's gone through. How he's survived.

She concentrated, sending her thoughts to Jackson's mind. A tiny tendril of thought answered. A sense of surprise and then recognition blossomed there. Jackson opened his eyes. "Ms. Yoshima? Kim!"

Kim smiled as she took Jackson's gnarled hands. "Hello, my brave friend. I'm so glad to see you again."

Jackson's face lit up. "And I you. But how are you here?"

"It's a long story, Jackson, and I can't remain much longer. But, there's someone with us who'll be taking you back to be with Aimi and Rinji again. To be young again."

Jackson shook his head. "Ah, I must be dreaming."

"No, incredible as it sounds, it's true. I promise. Go and be happy, you deserve it. And, please, if you remember, give Shioko my love."

"I... I will."

Kim stood, backed away, and looked to Agura. "Thank you, Agura," she said. With that, the Hunter placed his hand on the old man's shoulder, leaned down, and whispered in Jackson's ear.

As if on cue, Kim once stood more in the hallway outside her grandmother's memory rooms. She wrapped her arms around herself, trying to keep from laughing out loud. How wonderful! Finally, something good had happened. She had found Jackson and knew what would happen to him.

Thank you, Amaterasu. The name of the sun-goddess just popped into her mind as it done many times during this journey. Was she the deity Kim must follow now? One from her own heritage and not of the Christian pantheon?

So be it. Kim felt oddly comforted at that thought. By that decision.

She wondered for a moment why Amaterasu herself hadn't made an appearance yet. Ah, well, mysterious ways, etc., etc.

A schussing sound indicated another wooden door opening, the entrance to a second memory of somebody not her grandmother. Kim entered.

Once before, while dreaming, Kim had dreamed and inhabited the mind of Aimi, Jackson's wife from feudal Odawara. Kim had seen, heard, and felt from Aimi's perspective, as if she were Aimi. Kim had never understood why and how that could have happened, though because of that encounter, she had learned of Jackson's plans to return to the past by the displacement tremors. The same immersive experienced had just happened with her grandmother at the Osaka clinic.

Now, Kim stood in a corner of the beautiful indoor meditation room in Odawara Castle called the Moon Shadow Garden Chamber, where her previous encounter with Aimi and Jackson had occurred. This time, Kim viewed apart, watching. She wondered briefly what controlled her being corporeal and not.

It depended on if and how she was to interact in whatever place and time she resolved, of course. In this case, she was just an observer.

Aimi, with her and Jackson's young son, Rinji, sat quietly in a wall niche, heads bowed in front of a small shrine. Aimi's hands lay folded in her lap. The black kimono she wore indicated she'd felt Jackson would never return. Rinji looked very serious, very intent. His dark-skinned brow furrowed, no doubt trying hard to communicate with the kami to bring his father back.

The sound of footsteps caused Aimi and Rinji to raise their heads and glance to their right. Kim did likewise to see a young Jackson Yamaguchi appear from around a tall, planted copse of decorative grasses, still dressed in that old, wrinkled suit.

Young!

Aimi rose. "Honorable Husband?" she whispered. "Jackson-chan. Is it you?"

"Father!" Rinji's eyes widened, his mouth open in a surprised O.

"Yes, Aimi-chan, my love," Jackson said in the Japanese he knew so well, his voice hoarse and trembling, his eyes shining wetly. "Rinji, my fine young warrior. It's me." He reached into one of his jacket pockets and pulled out a beautiful ring. Aimi cried out at the ring's silver, red-eyed dragon inset, so intricate and lovely and, Kim guessed, something very personal and meaningful to her and Jackson.

Rinji was the first to move. He ran crying into his father's arms.

Aimi followed, wrapping her arms around Jackson's neck. Behind them, Shioko and another woman appeared, both beautiful in white kimonos. Shioko's hair fell loosely about her neck and shoulders; the other woman's much shorter hair had been intertwined with a small lotus blossom. They held hands and, they too, looked happy together.

Yes! Kim thought, her heart soaring. Shioko once told Kim she had loved someone in Odawara during her time there but didn't reveal who that was. Now she knew. Another moment to cherish among all the terrible ones.

At that moment, the other woman left Shioko's side and walked toward Kim. She paused at a flower arrangement as if appreciating its beauty, but her dark eyes slid up to focus on Kim. Happening again, the figures of Shioko, Jackson, Aimi, and Rinji became immobile as if a cosmic Pause Button had been pushed.

"Honorable Kim Yoshima," the woman said. "Yomitsu. It is a wonder to meet you. Shioko has spoken of you often."

"Oh, tha…thank you," Kim replied. She and Shioko had reconciled just before the moment the displacement tremors had arrived at Spirit Winds, Inc. She was so glad Shioko hadn't forgotten her! "You can see me. I guess I'm not surprised yet it appears you know me, but I don't know you."

"I am Izanami of the Jade Court and I promise you needn't worry about Shioko and Jackson and the others any more. They are safe and well and have much more to do during the Veiled Years."

"I'm glad. More than you can know." For a moment Kim didn't know what else to say. Izanami's presence was more than reassuring. It was magical. "You're Izanami-no-Mikoto, the goddess of creation and death, aren't you?"

"Once upon a time, yes. Back from my own death, you might say. I now reside here as attendant to the Glorious Ko and interim Regent of the Jade Court."

And more, I suspect, Kim thought with a smile. "You mentioned the Veiled Years. Is that the part of Odawaran history that's been hidden, unrecorded?" Kim remembered she and Lazo talking about that omission in the texts they'd researched.

Izanami nodded. "The Spell of Unknowing will keep these next several years shrouded until their remembrance is needed."

"Spell of Unknowing. Your doing, no doubt."

Izanami bowed her head. "Indeed, but it was Shioko's idea."

Kim smiled. "Somehow I'm not surprised. And you're the one who made the deal with Agura to bring Jackson back, yes?"

Izanami's smiled. "Yes."

"Thank you." Kim took a deep breath. "Can you help me further, Izanami? Is there anything more you can tell me?"

"There is no time to speak further. You have more important work to attend to. Be assured all is well."

Izanami was right. Kim had found what she needed to know. I wish I could stay here longer, she thought wistfully. No rest for the weary. "Thank you, Izanami."

Izanami's face spread into a smile. "The multiverse works in mysterious ways, yes? Go with grace, Kim Yoshima."

The mental tether once more took hold. Just as Kim began to evanesce, normal time resumed. She heard Jackson say something odd. Something about writing a letter to himself and sailing to Africa to deliver it.

Kim

First Iteration

Kim gasped, finding herself back with her grandmother in Osaka. She leaned forward in the chair, once more exulting in what she'd seen and heard. Jackson and Shioko! They had survived. Both her friends had once more ended up in feudal Odawara. No wonder Kim couldn't contact them on their cell phones!

And Izanami. Now that was a story Kim wanted to hear. She began to giggle, her eyes misting.

"Kimmy-san?" Her grandmother leaned forward, concern written on her beautiful face.

Kim smiled, tears of joy and relief running down her cheeks. "I did it, obaachan. With your help, I did it and found out more than I needed. Or, really, all that I needed. It's wonderful!"

Mitsu nodded. "As I knew you would. Good. Very good."

"My friends Jackson and Shioko have been missing. I feared the worst but, instead, both lived and were safe, and it was Jackson Yamaguchi who became the Exalted Sir and met with you that day at Ise."

"So that is his name!" Mitsu's face lit up, yet those wise eyes of hers reflected no real surprise. That's when Kim knew that gentle force directing her in Mitsu's mind had been some aspect of Mitsu herself.

"How wonderful, but sad for him, hai? To be taken from all he knew and loved?"

Kim nodded. She could relate. "No, it couldn't have been easy." She thought of Izanami again. "But a little kami of my own says he lived a fulfilling life and it sure looked to me like he would." She stood and embraced her grandmother. "Thank you, obaachan, thank you. I'm so glad I was able to be with you again."

"No, little one, it is I who must thank you. I am so proud of you. Now I know the acts of the past, however strange and mysterious, have indeed fulfilled the promises of the future. Your harmony and karma empower you and all those in your circle. You are indeed my granddaughter of power, a warrior."

"Oh, obaachan, I'm going to have to go. I feel..."

"Sleepy, yes?" Mitsu smiled. "Remember you fell asleep and, upon waking, did not recall what you've just done as your future self."

"Ha! You're right. And you kept it a secret. Just like the real reason you took back your birth surname."

"Yes, you couldn't very well be the Yomitsu with the name Kohoshi. Jirou himself suggested, insisted upon, it."

"I wish I'd known him." Kim smiled. "It couldn't have been easy to keep such secrets."

Mitsu touched Kim's cheek. "It isn't something I relish but only because it's necessary. Or was necessary because I know I've passed on and am no longer in your life. Go now, little one. You have much work still to do."

Kim hugged her grandmother, both women clinging to each other. "Mitsu, you'll always be in my life. I love you."

"And I love you."

Kim pulled back to look one last time at her Grandmother...

CHAPTER 26

Take the initiative before your opponent takes your spirit.

Takeo, Sohei Warrior Monk

The Dark Demesne

Kim

Second Iteration

Kim and Estansa Milaar flashed into existence on the barren plain of the Dark Demesne. Trell once more reverted to origami form, lying at Kim's feet. "Thanks, my friend," Kim murmured. She quickly picked Trell up and tucked him in her pouch.

A faint thought entered her mind, a warning from Trell. Be on guard.

Sure enough, a confused-looking Estansa Milaar stood defiantly, hissing and baring her fangs at Kim. Her tail snaked behind her from beneath the feather cloak she wore. "Yomitsu!" she snarled. "At las..."

"At last we meet," Kim finished, unsheathing her dagger. "Yeah, I get that a lot. So you're the one who took my friend, Jenny. If it was up to me, I'd send you packing straight to Hell instead of bringing you here, although this would be my second choice."

The lamia cocked her head. "And where exactly is here? I suppose I should thank you for saving me."

"Ask him." Kim gestured toward Omori. "That's your Orcus, not the real one, but a trickster, a liar. He used you to set himself free but, instead, brought a false demon into the world. And now he wants you."

Milaar glared at Omori. "So it was you! The Supreme First Lord told me of this. How could I be fooled by one such as you?"

"It was not I who brought the false Orcus through!" Omori protested, tugging at his chains. "That was never my plan."

"But your subterfuge and interference didn't help any either," Kim said. "Now Milaar's here. What are you going to do with her?"

"You were not to bring her here but take her back to the Summoning Chamber!" Omori roared at Kim. "I warned you..."

"You will do nothing to me!" Milaar shrieked, throwing off her cloak. "I will kill both of you."

Kim crouched, her kaiken blade held in front of her. A sudden intake of breath from Omori turned both her and Milaar's attention back to him. Omori, stared straight ahead, mouth hanging open. "What is that?" he said, his voice catching. "What is that?"

Kim turned. A strange, hideous figure approached, running swiftly on multiple legs, getting larger by the second.

A giant spider.

"Damara!" Kim cried. "How…?"

"You fool, Yomitsu!" Omori shouted, tugging at his chains. "You allowed it to follow you here in your esper wake."

"What?"

The spider-demon launched itself at Milaar. The lamia held her hands up, as if to cast a spell at the oncoming creature. With no effect. At the last moment, Milaar spun away from the creature but one of the spider's legs struck her in the back. Milaar fell to the ground, the spider's huge mandibles snapping after her. Kim stretched out her arms, tried to call up a psi-stun or bubble. Nothing happened. Those abilities of hers wouldn't work here, just like before.

As, evidently, Milaar's powers were likewise affected.

"Save her, Yomitsu!" Omori shouted. "I need her!"

The spider-demon whirled toward Omori. It cocked its head. Several arachnid eyes considered the captive warlord.

"You save her!" Kim retorted. "I'm tapped out."

Omori squirmed. "I cannot! I no longer possess my strength. This realm has been disrupted. Help me!" Omori showed true fear, the same as when he'd encountered Shioko at the Pavilion of Black Dragons.

How can I help him? Kim thought. Should I help him? I won't stand a chance against Damara without my powers. There's no point even trying to run away. She concentrated on Trell. The kirin, too, seemed spent, having accomplished his task.

This is what a'Kasha meant. When she said she'd allow Kim to bring Milaar here. Not to help Omori but to be controlled. On a'Kasha's terms.

But she didn't foresee this new "wrench in the works." She didn't foresee Damara!

Damara leaped at Omori. Mounting the dais, the spider-demon tore open Omori's throat and chest. She ripped a gurgling Omori from his chains, threw him to the ground, and shredded him to pieces. Ravenously, she devoured the remains of the hapless warlord.

Damara stood in front of the dais, blood covering her mandibles and head. She shuddered and began to change. The huge arachnid, the same as Kim had seen at Spirit Winds, Inc., shook, splitting apart. In a matter of moments, Damara stood as a monstrous hybrid of human and spider, just like Wayne had described to Kim after Damara had attacked him.

A brutish, hulking creature faced Kim. It stood nearly seven feet tall on two multiple-jointed legs, its powerfully muscled body covered alternately with spiky fur and hard, chitinous scales. A set of four arms flailed the air, each ending in a wickedly taloned hand. Two other limbs hung at its sides as if useless. From a spider-like head, those same compound glowing yellow eyes stared above a gaping mouth full of razor-sharp teeth. The creature spoke, not in its own voice, but with that of Omori Kadanamora.

My goddess, Kim thought, repulsed at the sight of what Damara and Omori had become. a'Kasha didn't get this one right at all.

"Ah, I see it now," the spider-warlord-chimera said in a hoarse, grating tone, the fear the warlord had felt replaced by surprise and... satisfaction. "This is the way it must be. No matter. As long as I kill you, Yomitsu."

Milaar screamed, having regained her feet. Kim had almost forgotten about her. "It has consumed his essence," the lamia cried. "The spider now possesses his anima!"

The creature rushed forward, four arms outstretched.

Time slowed as Kim remembered, a sudden insight blossoming. But this knowledge wasn't from the Void. This was her, Kim Yoshima, figuring it out as she always did as a detective. Her deductive mode went into overdrive.

The Dark Demesne was like Damara's nether-realm, a type of limbo, where exiles like Omori were sent or fell into of their own accord. Omori had said he'd brought Kim here, redirected her from the phase-shifting stream. But had he really? Had he really done that or had Kim herself, subconsciously following the trail Omori had left in her mind, knowing on some level a remnant of the warlord was still out there. Somewhere.

The same with Damara. Had some connection been made to the spider-demon through Kim's proximity to Wayne, or at Spirit Winds, Inc.?

But Kim knew one thing for certain. She'd rescued Milaar and returned here rather than the Summoning Chamber by her own will, not by the kirin's power. Not by Omori's. Not by a'Kasha's.

On her own.

She was tired of being yanked around by forces out of her control. She would control this, damn it! She pulled the paper figure from her pouch. She'd call the shots!

As time sped up and the spider-warlord-chimera hung in the air inches from her, Kim held up the paper kirin. A weapon, she thought, feeling the origami figure grow warm in her fingers. Come on, Trell, fire one last shot!

Just then, Kim caught a glimpse of Milaar leaping toward her.

The kirin fired.

CHAPTER 27

Do not believe in miracles. Perform them.

Samuel Kim
The Teachings of Yira - The Five Precepts to Enlightenment

Carnegie Museum of Natural History

Pittsburgh, PA

C.E. 2011

Kim

Third Iteration

Superpositioned. Bilocated. No. Tri-located.

Now Kim's awareness, a third iteration of herself focused here...

Bobby's here, she thought. a'Kasha kept her word.

A dimly lit hallway lay before Kim. A dull, dusty suit of armor stood against the stained, wooden wall. A dust-covered model of a Pterosaur hung from the high ceiling, its wings spread, its needle-toothed mouth agape. A grimy glass display case below it contained samples of sea stars and mounted, stuffed fish. A moldy smell, a stale odor of disuse and abandonment, hung in the air.

Four people stood in the midst of this neglected arcana, none of them a Past-Kim. Kim had thought a link between her past and her present selves, or with one or both of the Mitsus pulled her, initially connected her to each of the events she'd been involved in. But here, like at Odawara Castle, nothing. What had drawn her here?

She looked more closely, recognizing the tall, strongly built African-American man holding a gun in one hand. Her friend, Joe Martin. Beside him stood a little girl dressed in some type of middle-eastern clothing. A purple, robe-like abaya draped the child's body. A matching headscarf covered the top, back, and sides of her head and neck. Yes! Kim thought. I'm no longer in the past. This is happening now. But what has Joe gotten into?

She looked to the Japanese man facing them.

Ken! Kim couldn't believe her eyes. Her brother. Could this get any stranger? But who is the girl and this other one? The woman standing next to Ken Yoshima turned around, fixing a piercing gaze in Kim's direction.

Though the woman's hair was much longer and clothing very different, it was as if Kim looked in a mirror. She stared at herself, or, a doppelganger of herself. And the doppelganger stared back.

Not the Kim she'd seen in Dartham. A third one.

The hairs on the back of Kim's neck tingled. She sees me. Just like Agura and Izanami. The woman moved, her body shifting, and she strode toward her. Garbed in a blue, form-fitting, one-piece catsuit, her body pixelated as if moving through a damaged video. Behind her, Ken, Joe, and the girl looked frozen, unmoving.

"Kim Yoshima," the woman said. She held a crossbow pistol pointing downward. "The famous Yomitsu?" She tilted her head and pursed her lips as if studying Kim. "A pleasure to meet you."

"And you are?" Kim ventured.

"T'sai, although I'm sure you can guess we're basically two-of-a-kind." She paused, tapping her lips with a gloved finger. "Or, more like three-of-a-kind, I think. You're spreading yourself pretty thin, girl, with the multiple iterations."

She's how I ended up here, Kim reasoned, her esper-sense flaring. Besides Bobby, she's the link. Has to be. "Just telling me your name doesn't tell me anything."

"I've been looking for you, my quantum clone sister," T'sai said. "Considerate of you to drop by and make my life easier. We need to talk."

Kim smiled. "No shit," she said. "What are you doing with my brother?"

T'sai chuckled. "Don't worry. Nothing untoward, I assure you. That would be rather too familial, wouldn't it? I'm helping Ken to rescue his son."

"So Bobby is here! Is he all right?"

"Well, that's the question, isn't it?" She turned to glance back over her shoulder. "That hot, sexy black man apparently knows you. The little girl, who is just now realizing I've phase-shifted between temporal nodal points, is more than that. Notice she's turned her head just a little in our direction? I suspect she's got some powerful juju at her command."

"Damn it, what about Bobby? And how did Ken and Joe hook up with you?"

"I'm a hunter," T'sai said. "There have been many of us through the millennia. You may have heard of some us. Kilah, Orion, Agura."

"Agura? I've met him."

"Ah, so you know of my counterpart in this sector of the multiverse. We've served many masters on many worlds, like the Sanctuary Elders, though these days, I mostly work freelance. Can't speak for Agura."

"The Sanctuary Elders again!"

"So you've heard of them?"

"More or less."

"They're the head honchos of the ambient-milieu. Evolved energy beings, you know, like in cheesy science fiction stories. Anyway, my present ability is phase-shifting to, through, and between dimensions and timelines. That's how I can see you since you're essentially doing the same thing, although I suspect you've been separated into a number of iterations, yes? And none of you are in full in control."

"You know I'm, uh, tri-locating?"

"Tri-locating. That's cute. I do, and I can tell you if you proceed any longer, you may hurt yourself."

"That's what I've been told. Let me worry about me. Why are you here?"

"As I mentioned, I'm on a hunt right now for your nephew Bobby who appears to have been whisked off by some powerful, supernatural entity. I was able to track them here with Ken in tow when, Joe, is it, And the girl showed up. It's the girl who I'm worried about."

Kim looked at the girl who had indeed turned her head even more in their direction. "If you have to deal with her, I can find Bobby," Kim said, deciding quickly. "But what's your real motive?"

T'sai grinned. For one absurd moment, Kim wondered if she looked that devilish. "Well, I hate to break the news to you, but there's a matter of an old friend of yours, one Parker, just Parker, who's still alive and still causing trouble."

"So it is true!" As Omori said. Kim had killed Parker the first time when he and Martin Sakai had invaded her apartment by taking Joe Martin hostage. Then, the second time, in a hidden recess within Shioko's mind where a small part of Parker's essence had found refuge.

Hearing Parker's name reminded her again of the figure she'd seen in Parker's mind when Omori, in the Dark Demesne, had allowed her to remember their first encounter. The figure she had never recalled seeing there before.

Somehow, that fact was important.

"True story," T'sai said, studying and probably misunderstanding Kim's reaction. "Somehow Parker reabsorbed that little bit of his essence you thought you'd destroyed in Shioko's mind though he's now a mess physically. He was pronounced dead."

"He was dead. I killed him with a naginata."

T'sai shrugged. "Hey, you should know by now the multiverse works in mysterious ways."

"That's one way to describe it."

"Anyway, Parker got spirited away from the morgue by a big hunk of burning muscle named Mr. Tammelou. Parker threatened Ken's family to try to get to you and when that failed, went after Bobby, certain you'd ride to the rescue. I, in turn, had found Parker during my travels and thought he might be useful in helping me round up some stray beasties who had become separated from their dimensional herds, so to speak. But I decided to help Ken, literally out of the goodness of my heart."

"I don't buy it."

T'sai's mouth formed a circle of mock surprise. "Suspicious? Of moi? I'm shocked."

"Do not mess with my nephew and my friends!" Kim glared at T'sai, the strangeness of seeming to talk to herself replaced by fresh anger. "I've been pinballed around the ambient-milieu, phase-shifting stream, superpositioned, and whatever other interdimensional, alternate reality level mode of travel for it seems like forever and I'm in no mood for joking around."

"Understood. Sorry about that." T'sai glanced to her right. "Seriously, though, I need to see to this little girl with your friend Joe. Will you, at least, trust me enough to do that?"

Kim looked also. The girl had turned her head completely toward her and T'sai and had taken a single step toward them. "Don't you hurt Bobby, Joe, and Ken, do you hear me?"

T'sai's expression softened. "I promise you I won't harm them. I can't say the same about the girl and whatever's taken your nephew."

"A djinn named Nolu."

"Ah, good to know."

"I'm surprised that surprises you." She narrowed her eyes. "You know, you remind me of someone." Or something.

"Look in the mirror."

Kim sighed. "Okay, I'll defer to you. I have no control on how long I stay in these iterations and with this phase-shifting whatever. So, since

Ken's trusting you, despite our past differences, I will too."

T'sai nodded. "Can you contact me psychically when you find Bobby? I'm guessing our neural signatures are the same or pretty close. I don't think Bobby's far, but I bet you can find him faster than I."

Kim nodded.

T'sai turned and walked away, her body once again shifting like pixel blocks. Kim closed her eyes and sent out a psychic search net, looking for Bobby's neural signature. It only took a moment to locate. There it was, so familiar to her, so dear. It led away down the opposite end of the corridor.

He'd better be safe!

Kim released her esper-sight. She could see and feel the surfaces and empty places within what now revealed itself to her mind's eye as a remote, mostly unused part of the Carnegie Museum in Oakland. Her mental vision winged its way down the musty corridor to its end where a wooden door faced her.

Bobby was behind that door.

Kim retracted her esper-sight and ran down the corridor. Almost immediately an unseen barrier stopped her at the door. Some invisible force blocked her. Kim pushed harder and broke through a protective field of some kind, reminiscent of the one at the box factory where she fought the spider-demon. She wondered at the ease of penetrating this particular barrier. Damara had wanted Kim to enter her "realm" within the box factory and so allowed her through her barrier. Possibly whoever erected this one didn't foresee someone in phase-shifting mode being able to breach it. She moved through the door to enter the room behind it.

A room, small, but brilliantly decorated and furnished. The ceiling hid above a tent-like canopy. A red carpet covered the floor with billowing curtains, and plush floor pillows. Candles and incense burned on a round, wooden table. Arabesque patterns adorned the walls.

Bobby lay on a pile of large, thick cushions against the far wall, his eyes closed. A movement to the right pivoted Kim's attention. A tall, shifting column of white smoke had appeared in the middle of the room. It coiled and wavered, forming a vague human outline. It drifted to where Bobby lay, its amorphous blob-of-a-head looking down on him.

Kim could see Bobby's chest rising and falling. She gently nudged his slumbering mind with a mental probe. She found he wasn't really asleep, but not unconscious either. He was alive but in some kind of trance or fugue state, existing in that neural fantasy "level" with the djinn Nolu. She feared trying to wake him in case it might harm him.

T'sai! Kim thought-sent, sending her mental voice unerringly to the hunter. This way!

The smoke-being shifted its position, turning toward Kim but not in slow motion as had happened with the girl. Like T'sai, its form flickered and morphed. "Get away from him!" Kim cried, realizing this creature, like T'sai and the strange little girl, could detect her, could move within the phase-shifting stream. "Bobby! Wake up!"

Bobby stirred but didn't waken. The smoke-being reached a misty tendril out toward Kim.

The door splintered open and slammed against the inside wall. The young girl dressed in the abaya and headscarf stepped into the room. "Sister!" she cried to the smoke-being, her eyes flashing. "We have been searching for you." T'sai, Ken, and Joe followed.

"Bobby!" Ken cried. He moved toward where Bobby lay but Joe held him back.

"Mr. Yoshima," Joe said. "Not yet, please."

Reluctantly, Ken nodded, his chest heaving. Kim risked a peek inside Ken's mind. Anger, remorse, guilt. He needed to save Bobby. But not for appearance's sake. For love of his son.

The smoke-being fluctuated again, turning an angry red. It reformed, shrinking and becoming…

Shioko. Shioko as a little girl dressed in modern clothes.

"Why will you not leave us alone, Talera?" the Shioko-thing said plaintively. "We want to be free!"

"We cannot allow you to take advantage of these mortals, Nolu," the girl said.

So she's Nolu. The one at the golden palace, Kim thought.

"You know this. You must rebind with us. We must be together again as a complete entity. Talera and Nolu, a djinn made whole."

More castaways from the Spirit Winds.

The djinn Talera continued. "Apart, we will begin to deteriorate, to waste away, to lash out destructively. Already we have both begun this devolution. We have terrorized, lied, threatened, and grown weak and dangerously inward."

"Got that right," Joe muttered. Kim wondered what the jinni had done to him. She picked up an image of a skeletal, winged, bat-like creature flashing through his mind.

"We saved this boy!" Nolu cried. "He was about to be taken by force. We foresaw the abduction and intervened."

"Saved, yes, but then you saw a reason to keep him with you, to use him for your own selfish purposes. Even now he slumbers in a state not truly sleep and dreams in a realm which is not truly of the living. Is that not so?"

"He is happy! He is loved!" Nolu shot a defiant gaze at Ken. "You! His father. You do not care about him. You never have!"

"That's not true!" Ken retorted. "He's my son and you have no right to do this!"

"He must be released!" Talera continued. "You cannot hold the boy by such unfair means. Release him so he can be with his parents and we can be whole again. The final stage of our separation will weaken us beyond saving, as it has already begun. Please, sister! Take our hand before it is too late."

"Unfair? Then who is the one hidden there?" Nolu pointed in Kim's direction. "An unseen force waiting to strike us down?"

T'sai spoke for the first time. "As I've explained to Talera, the 'one hidden' only wants to get the boy back like we all do. She helped me to find you and means you no harm. As long as you don't act against us."

Frowning in tandem puzzlement, Joe and Ken stared at the indicated spot where Kim stood, invisible to them. Evidently, T'sai's explanation of her had only been for Talera's and Nolu's ears.

At that moment, as Nolu became distracted by T'sai, Talera rushed forward and embraced her sister, twin, half, duality, whatever she was. A sound like a thunderclap erupted. A blinding implosion of light shot out and sucked back into a red pinpoint.

"No, no!" Kim cried as she rushed forward. "Bobby!"

The djinn had vanished, leaving only a few wisps of smoke and an acrid odor behind. T'sai abruptly appeared beside Kim, phase-shifting. She put her arm around Kim' shoulder and whispered something unintelligible in her ear. Kim gasped. Her body jerked as if shocked.

And then nothing.

Or something.

"I've taken you out of the phase-shifting stream, girlfriend, this iteration of you, that is," T'sai said. "You're welcome."

"Kim!" Ken and Joe cried together, astonishment written on their faces.

But Kim's attention focused entirely on Bobby. He lay as he had before, seemingly unresponsive.

She leaned over her nephew. His breath had become shallow, his color paler, his eyes had opened but had turned milky white.

"What is it?" Ken asked, joining her.

"Something's wrong."

T'sai placed a hand on Bobby's chest. "His mind is still trapped in whatever this realm Talera mentioned Nolu put him in. The djinn are gone but Nolu's control over Bobby's still strong."

"How is that possible?" Kim said. "Can you free him?"

T'sai shook her head. "I'm not sure."

"Damn it! Then I've got to try."

"What are you going to do?"

Kim had performed a mental probing once before when Shioko had initiated her fear-driven fugue state. Could she do the same thing here with Bobby?

"I'm going to enter Bobby's mind, his…his neural landscape, you know like a Vulcan Mind Meld thing. I was already taken there briefly but wasn't able to do anything. I need you and Ken and Joe to babysit the both of us while I give it another shot."

"You could be putting Bobby in more danger."

"Then what do you suggest?"

"Do it, Kim," Ken said. "If anyone can help Bobby, it's you."

Kim regarded her brother, almost like a different person than the one she'd known all her life. T'sai, a grim set to her lips, nodded. "Thanks, Ken, T'sai. If you see anything odd happening to either of us, well, just slap the shit out of me. Okay?"

T'sai grinned. "That might be fun."

"Kim," Joe said, gently gripping her shoulder. "Be careful."

Kim smiled and, without thinking, placed her hand over Joe's. She knelt at Bobby's side and locked eyes with her nephew. Before, with Shioko, Kim' ancestor Yoshima Mitsu had advised her, guided her. Plus, she and Shioko, like Shioko and Mitsu, were connected, as teacher and student, like siblings, like mother and daughter.

But she and Bobby had a connection too, possibly stronger. They were blood family and Kim counted on that to make this succeed. It had to!

She closed her eyes and sent a thin beam of her esper-sight into Bobby's mind…

PART 3
KEEPER OF THE ARCHIVE

A life fully lived can't really be done in one lifetime. Or two.

Jackson Yamaguchi

THE WARRIOR AND THE WARLORD

You can go home again. It just might not be one you recognize.

Dr. Lilith Cardazio

Dreams and the Unmapped Territories of the Mental Universe

FIFTH INTERVAL

Closure and Justice are vital. But nothing is as satisfying as revenge.

Takeo, Sohei Warrior Monk

Eastern Shore of the Lido

Venice, Italy

The Villa Francesca

1991 C.E.

"**B**runo, listen to yourself. Do you hear what you're saying?"
Lenora Calabria stared at her husband, incredulous at the unbelievable tale he'd just told her. Pacing back and forth in the living room of the small villa Lenora inherited from her father, Bruno sounded like a madman. His handsome features were grimly set, outwardly giving nothing away. Yet other emotions Lenora had never sensed in him before enveloped him. Determination, complete and absolute, mixed with a touch of fear.

"You've got to believe me, Lenora," Bruno said, pausing and facing her. He looked a mess. His polo shirt was drenched in sweat, his white slacks rumpled and stained with dirt. He ran a hand over his thinning, brown hair. "I saw them. Monsters. I tell you they are real. This isn't a relapse of my disorder, I can assure you."

Lenora stood up from the couch. Through the open window, the sound of waves breaking upon the Adriatic shore added a surreal soundtrack to Bruno's story. Her husband had become abruptly fixated the last two weeks, staying out late multiple nights, glued to his laptop as he obsessively researched…something.

Lenora had begged, demanded, threatened him to tell her what troubled him so. Bruno took medication for an anxiety disorder, but that condition had been under control for years. Now this sudden bizarre turnabout shocked and frightened her.

It was late, after midnight. Lenora had donned her robe after being roughly awakened by her husband. He had been reading in his study when she'd gone to bed. She hadn't realized he'd once more left to go

249

out. "Tesoro," she said. "Darling. You…"

"I can show you!" Bruno took hold of Lenora by her shoulders. His brown eyes flicked back and forth. "Come with me. I couldn't tell or show you this until I was certain."

"Come with you? Now?"

"Yes. To the Alberoni Dunes. That's where I've been. There's a portal, a gateway there that connects this world to the world of the monstros, allowing access to and from both. I've seen it."

Lenora backed away and threw up her hands. "Bruno, this sounds like a fiction. Some tale of fantasy."

"Please, my love. Let me prove it to you. I'm not crazy! I've met someone who'll help to convince you."

"Who is this person?"

"A woman who's lived in the monstros world but now rejects them and those who control them."

"I…"

"We must hurry! Please, Lenora."

"All right, all right." Lenora quickly dressed in sweat pants, sneakers, pulling a sweater over her tousled brown hair. She, at least, had to mollify Bruno until she could reason with him. Something had upset him, that was certain, but these monsters, this gateway? And who was this woman he mentioned? She followed Bruno out of the villa. As she locked the door behind them, Lenora noticed Bruno had taken his camera with him.

After a several minute walk in the cool night air, with Bruno practically dragging Lenora after him, they arrived at the famous dunes of the island/sandbar that was the Lido. Deserted at this time of night, the Alberoni beach shimmered under the light of a half-moon. Bruno pulled Lenora down behind a dune. "There!" he hissed, pointing. "We arrived just in time."

Lenora squinted. A blinking point of pink light hovered over the shoreline. It expanded, pulsing with a flickering energy, like a star fallen to earth. A whirlpool of red, blazing energy, it resolved into a large, glowing sphere.

A figure walked out of that sphere. Shadowy and indistinct, the figure stood on the beach, its form backlit by the light, translucent and ghost-like. It turned toward where Lenora and Bruno crouched. "Signore Calabria?" a soft voice said. The figure approached, revealing itself to be a thin woman, possibly in her fifties, with gray-streaked short dark hair. She wore a long cloak, its hood thrown back.

"Here," Bruno said and stood, urging Lenora up with him.

"My god, Bruno, who is this?"

"Lydia," Bruno said. "This is my wife, Lenora. Lenora, this is Lydia Carpenscu, the woman I told you about."

"Signora," Carpenscu said with a slight bow of her head.

"Who are you? What's going on? Bruno!" Lenora held onto Bruno's arm, trembling, dizzy, absolute astonishment overwhelming her.

"The monsters I told you about, Lenora, exist in a realm, another Venice, reached by that portal. Lydia has asked for my help. I'm going to take pictures, to prove the threat to our own world."

"It's true, Signora Calabria," Carpenscu said. The woman's gentle but powerful gaze took hold of Lenora's own frightened one. Lenora calmed, her breathing slowed. Carpenscu continued, "I can't explain much now but I promise I and your husband will tell you everything once we return. But this world is in danger, I assure you.

"There is a faction of malevolent sorcerers reconstituting its forces in Venice, planning on regaining power first there by blood sacrifice. A war between the Lions of the Venedetto and Solomon's Raptors has been waged for centuries to feed the city's power, the lifeforce that might allow Venice to once more become a world power.* But these sorcerers need help from the Supreme First Lord in Aizenev to accomplish that heinous task. I have hope now we can stop that. Signore Calabria has agreed to help me." She reached to her neck and pulled forth a small, silver amulet in the shape of a twisted horn. "He was able to procure this for me, a cornicello gemstone, protection from the Evil Eye. But it can be much more powerful than that. It will help me break the bonds of captivity that have held me prisoner."

Bruno took up the tale. "Two weeks ago, I found Lydia here on the beach, wandering, weak. She'd found a hidden branch of the gateway leading to the Lido and used it to escape from Aizenev. But only temporarily. The hold on her was too great. She had to return but not before she asked me to find a cornicello for her."

"Why do you have to do this, Bruno? Why can't..." She turned to Carpenscu. "Why can't you with your magical protection? Why involve my husband?"

"I am leaving Aizenev, the alternate Venice. I've been essentially a prisoner there for years, enslaved by the Maghi and their Supreme First Lord. Now, with your husband's help and courage, I can finally

* As depicted in "The Raptor and the Lion" by Larry Ivkovich in Star Quake I Anthology, 2009.

break my ties with them. In turn, I'll help provide him with proof of what lies beyond that portal."

"I want to do this, Lenora. Lydia needs help. She didn't force me into this. I've already been through the portal once with her and returned. What I saw there about drove me crazy. But a real danger to our world exists."

"Then I'm coming with you."

Carpenscu frowned. "Signora Calabria, that may not be a good idea."

Bruno shook his head. "She's right, Lenora. I can't let you do that."

"I'm coming with you!"

***

They had done it!

Lenora, with Bruno and Carpenscu, fled back through the portal from the alternate Venice to the Lido. On the other side, Bruno had captured images too bizarre and unbelievable for words to describe. Another City of Masks, decaying, crumbling under great age and rot, ruled by decadent sorcerers, who hid there amidst dying dreams and forgotten magical glory. Aizenev.

Bruno had taken pictures of masked revelers, the inhuman residents of Aizenev, and their monstrous servants.

Somehow, through it all, Lenora had kept her sanity, her focus. The portal flared behind them as they ran onto the beach. "Bruno," she said, embracing her husband. "Forgive me for doubting you. This... this is incredible!"

"Nothing to forgive, my love," Bruno said, kissing her.

"What now?" Lenora asked, looking at Lydia Carpenscu. "Should we contact the police? If the sorcerers plan on helping this faction in the real Venice you spoke of, surely we'll need help."

"Well, what have we here?" a sibilant male voice interrupted.

Lenora and her husband jumped at that sound. She placed a hand over her mouth to stifle a scream.

A group of darkened figures congregated near the surf. Scaled, furred, feathered, some possessing multiple limbs, others nothing but mouths and teeth. Monstros.

Three of those approached. Two looked human, cloaked like Lydia. How had they arrived here so silently? "Ah," Lydia said softly. "We have been discovered."

The face of the man who had spoken was hooded, like something out of a stereotyped black mass. Within the hood, two eyes glowed bright red. Beside him stood a nightmarish creature. Easily seven feet tall, it revealed itself in the moon's light as a bat-like humanoid, winged, taloned, horrific.

"Marceeka," Lydia said. "I am so sorry Signore and Signora."

"My god," Lenora whispered, knowing these were members of the faction Lydia had mentioned. "My god."

"Lydia," Bruno said, shoving his camera into the woman's hands. "Protect Lenora. Run!"

Lenora cried out. What was Bruno doing? "No, no, Bruno…"

Bruno shoved Lenora away from him and ran in the opposite direction. Lydia grabbed Lenora by the arm, holding the cornicello amulet out in front of her. As Lydia pulled her away, Lenora watched in horror as the bat creature caught up with her husband and fell upon him, ripping and tearing. Lenora tried to scream, to call out his name, to deny what she witnessed, but her body and mind refused to obey her.

The third figure, a woman, appeared, seeming to float over the sand. A tail trailed behind her. White hair snaked around her bare head, neck and shoulders. She studied the retreating Lenora and Lydia with dead eyes.

"Mistress Estansa," the man said. "Shall I have Marceeka dispatch them as well?"

The woman waited a heartbeat before answering. "No, Roberto. No one will believe the umana female and her mind won't be able to survive what she's seen here tonight for very long." She waved a long-nailed hand. "Despite Lydia's traitorous help. Let them go. There's nothing they can do against us now."

Lenora let Lydia take over. They turned and ran.

Lenora had gone a little crazy after that. Her mind almost didn't survive. But shortly thereafter Lydia brought Daiyu into her life. Both women rescued Lenora from the brink. After that, Lenora found her resolve and began her mission. She wouldn't stop until the Maghi, their Grand Mistress Estansa Milaar, and her monstrous servants Roberto and Marceeka were crushed.

She vowed Bruno's death would not be in vain.

Eastern Shore of the Lido

Venice, Italy

The Villa Francesca

Monstros Hunters Backup Headquarters

2011 C.E.

Lenora clutched the small, rectangular weapon ArcNight had given her, the aural disruptor, in one hand. She had arrived too late. The Villa Francesca had been breached.

"Gino," Lenora spoke into her cell phone. "Are you and Luca there?"

No response. Her bodyguards were supposed to have arrived at their alternate residence on the Lido before them, to open up the villa and begin preparations for their defense against the Maghi. Lenora's Venice apartment and primary headquarters had been destroyed, blown up by Lydia in a final effort to stop the Maghi assault team in the Jewish Ghetto.

The foul sorcerer Roberto had led that attack. Somehow Lenora knew he'd escaped the explosion and arrived here before them. Her cell phone vibrated.

Lenora answered. "Antonio," she said to her son. "What is it?"

"Mama," Antonio replied. "I'm on my way to the villa now. I can't let you do this alone."

"No, please, Antonio. We talked about this. Stay with the boat."

"Mama…"

"I have the gun and the disruptor. I'll call you back shortly."

Lenora stood in the front doorway. The hallway leading to the living room looked scorched, as if by fire. She walked slowly, tightening her hold on the aural disruptor. ArcNight had explained the weapon would skew any creature's hearing, confusing and disorienting only those it was directed against. She glared in anger at the condition of the house. The living room was in shambles, the furniture overturned, broken.

Two bodies lay on the floor. Lenora gasped and looked away. Gino and Luca, torn, broken, bloody, and beyond help.

A noise behind her…

Lenora turned. A desiccated figure stood in the hallway. Roberto. The Maghi First Lord, servant of Estansa Milaar, had been ravaged.

His face burned and scarred, one red eye gouged from his face, his body bent, one arm hanging limp. Only a magical assault could have caused that much damage.

Lenora smirked. "Daiyu," she said. She felt no fear of Roberto anymore. Only revulsion.

Roberto wheezed out an angry reply. "Yes, that bitch! But I hurt her as well before escaping."

"Hurt," Lenora said with a sneer. "Not kill."

"Do not look so smug, Monstros Hunter. The traitor Lydia was not so lucky."

"I know. But Lydia had more courage than any ten of your kind."

"Yet I still live."

"If you call that life!" Rage burned within Lenora. "You helped to kill my husband."

"And?" Roberto stumbled toward her a step. "What are you going to do about it? You see what I did to your so-called bodyguards, even as weakened as I am. Do you think you can do any better than they?" With a wave of his skeletal hand, the aural disruptor became scalding hot. Lenora cried out and dropped it, her hand throbbing with burning pain.

"Now what will you do, Lenora Calabria? Most of your vaunted group is gone, its members dead or dying. Daiyu, Edmondo, Lydia. Gino. Luca. There's nothing and no one here for you anymore. Once I kill you, then I'll go after your beloved son. He's almost here. He's near, coming to his mama's rescue."

"You bastard!"

Roberto clapped his hands, releasing a bolt of energy straight at Lenora. She cried out as a grip of iron smashed against her, knocking her back against the wall. Groaning at the pain inflicted on her, she managed to keep her feet. Feeling her life slip away from a lethal blow, she pushed herself away from the wall.

Lenora knew the only way Roberto had killed Gino and Luca had been by surprise, considering the First Lord's condition. And he had done the same to her. But she still survived and, in Roberto's current state, he could be stopped in a non-magical way. She reached into the back pocket of her slacks, pulled out the gun, and fired, once, twice, three times. The bullets struck Roberto in the head, blowing out the back of his skull. He toppled to the floor.

Lenora stood over him, her legs trembling, her vision blurring. "For Bruno and the others," she whispered and shot him one last time, right through his black heart.

She dropped to the floor just as Antonio burst into the house.

CHAPTER 28

Daiyu and Roberto had become as still as statues. Both magic-wielders stared at each other, unmoving, unblinking, fighting their battle on another plane of existence...

Venice, Italy

Cannaregio District

C.E. May 2, 2011

A surge of real hope coursed through Lazo. With Daiyu back in action, they had a good chance of rescuing Jenny! It felt like forever since he'd seen his wife, talked to her, held her in his arms. They'd been a team for twenty-five years, supporting each other, loving each other. They'd decided long ago they didn't want to have children, preferring to be a couple, to do all they things they really wanted to do.

He'd become a police officer, she a scientist then a writer. They'd been all over the world, formed real, long-lasting friendships, helped many people along the way, created the Book Haven together. He couldn't let this damn abduction be the end of their life together. He had to find her! He would find her!

And Kim too. He knew his friend was behind that invisible barrier as well. He wouldn't abandon her either!

He looked toward ArcNight as the hero's cell phone buzzed. ArcNight took the phone from its belt clip and glanced at the screen. "It's Antonio Calabria," he said. Lazo, Kim, Lenora, Antonio, and ArcNight had exchanged cell numbers.

For a second, Lazo wondered why Lenora was calling ArcNight, then shook off the feeling, trying to ignore his momentary unease.

ArcNight answered. After a moment, he spoke, "Damn, I'm sorry Antonio. You don't have to stay there..." Another pause, longer this time. "All right, I understand. We'll be in touch. Be careful."

Lazo watched ArcNight closely. Something was wrong.

"I...have bad news," the hero said, his face visible beneath the cowl hardening. "I'm afraid Lenora's dead. Gino and Luca too. Killed by the Maghi Roberto."

"What!" Lazo cried. He hung his head, the hope he's just felt turning to ashes. Lenora had been a powerful ally. She, Gino, and Luca had found Lazo in his wandering, helpless state at the bridge in Venice. There, he'd confronted the one-eyed woman who'd taken Jenny, who just vanished before his eyes. Lenora had taken him in and given him hope. She knew she'd been targeted by the Maghi but that hadn't stopped her in her crusade against them.

He'd liked her, respected her. And yes, been attracted to her. He couldn't deny that although his love for Jenny outweighed everything else. Still, this was crushing news. "How? What happened?"

"**W**hat have I done?"

Daiyu cried out, startling everyone. She bent forward, falling in upon herself. "No, no!" She staggered as if struck. She'd failed. Failed! Strong but gentle hands took hold of her. The masked warrior called ArcNight stood at her side. "Are you all right?" he asked.

"Daiyu, what's wrong?" Lazo Sibulovich asked.

Daiyu closed her eyes, wondering why and how it had all gone this badly. "It's my fault," she said, tears welling. "Lenora and the others are dead because of me."

"What do you mean?" ArcNight asked.

Daiyu sighed, wiping her eyes with her fingers. "I fought against the First Lord Roberto on the ambient-milieu's Plain of Becoming. Though defeating him, I see now I didn't destroy him completely as I'd thought. That defeat has cost the lives of ones dear to me. First Lydia and now Lenora, Gino, and Luca!"

"That's not your fault," ArcNight said. "You almost died fighting Roberto."

Daiyu shook her head. It didn't matter. She'd failed. "What...what did Antonio tell you?"

"He heard several gunshots and, upon entering the secondary Lido headquarters, found Lenora had killed Roberto before collapsing herself from injuries inflicted by him."

"Damn that Maghi scum!" Lazo exclaimed.

"Lenora succeeded where I failed," Daiyu said.

"At least that's some consolation," David Amamoto added. Something in Amamoto's voice got Daiyu's attention. The man looked pensive, holding a clenched fist at his side.

"I grieve for you, honorable Daiyu of the East," Jaraal said, also coming to Daiyu's side. "But you did not fail. You, without a doubt, sorely injured the sorcerer Roberto in your fight against him. Lenora may never have been able to defeat him otherwise."

"He's right," ArcNight said. "Antonio said Roberto looked like hell, torn up, emaciated. Lenora and Gino and Luca are avenged."

"No, it's not on you," Lazo said. Daiyu gasped as the big man enfolded her in his arms. She felt engulfed in comfort by his powerful presence. She also felt his sadness. "Don't beat yourself up about it," he continued. "We need you now at your best and, let's face it, Lenora wouldn't want you to feel this way. We've got to carry on with her vision, her strength."

Lazo released her from his gentle bear hug. Daiyu looked at each one of her companions. "You are right," she said. "Thank you. Let us finish what we've started."

"There's something else you should know," Jaraal spoke again. "An ally hides on the other side of the barrier who can help us. The Demon Queller, known to us as Zaronal the Sleeper."

"Zaronal?" Daiyu asked, starting at the sound of the name.

"Yes. Once the Maghi Zaronelli."

"Amedio..." Daiyu breathed.

"You know him?" asked ArcNight.

Daiyu smiled. "Yes. I do." Amidst the tragedy, some wonderful news! "Come." She turned and approached the barrier, easily visible to her magicked sight. And halted.

She stared at the barrier, placing a palm against it. Warm and tingling to the touch, it would normally have yielded to Daiyu's presence, allowing her entry. Now, though she discerned the barrier with her senses, she couldn't traverse through it.

At all.

Daiyu could only assume she had been gone too long, her aspect changed from her absence. The girl, Lucia, would have had no difficulty getting past the barrier, being marked by the power of the Dark Demesne. But Lucia, Marceeka, was gone. How had Amedio accomplished it? Surely his existence here and now boded a similar problem for him as it did Daiyu.

She turned back to her companions. "We have a problem," she said and explained the situation. Again, she focused on David Amamoto. He had been very quiet. Now he raised his fist and opened it. He looked at Daiyu and held out his hand. A glowing jade tiger figurine rested in his palm. "Will this help?" he asked.

"**W**here did you get that?" Daiyu demanded. It was obvious to David the sorceress' anger and self-reproach vanished at the sight of the tiger. Did she know what it was?

"The shadow-being," Jaraal said. "Yes, David-san?"

David nodded and explained to Daiyu what had occurred at the sidewalk café in the Strada Nouva. "It gave me the jade carving."

"Why didn't you tell us about this sooner?" ArcNight asked.

David had wondered about that himself. "I'm not sure," he confessed. "It was as if I had to find out what it was myself before I revealed it. You know, what passed between the shadow-thing and me, it seemed somehow personal. I know that sounds crazy but, well, that's how I felt. My grandfather collected jade carvings and this one could have come right out of his collection. I was strongly reminded of him when I held this."

"Do you remember what I told you, David-san?" Jaraal said. "That the shadow-creature was drawn to you because of your unique makeup and family history? Because of your grand-sire?"

"Yeah but what was the damn shadow-thing anyway and how did come by this carving?"

"Questions we must ponder another time," Daiyu said. "You said you needed time to discover the figurine's purpose. Have you?"

"I think so." The glowing around the carving shimmered brighter. David felt it tugging at him, pulling him toward the interdimensional barrier. "I think it's a key."

"Yes," Daiyu said. "I think so too. One of a magical kind. In answer to your question, I believe it can help us gain entry to the Zone of Concealment."

"Only one way to find out," Lazo said.

David took a deep breath and, turning toward where ArcNight had indicated the barrier stood, held out his hand.

CHAPTER 29

A tiger in the hand is worth two in the bush.

David Amamoto

Venice, Italy

Lazo sucked in his breath at the sight of the space, the air itself, in front of him moving, separating, churning apart. A swirling tunnel, for lack of a better description, opened in the invisible barrier surrounding the Zone of Concealment.

Created by the jade tiger David Amamoto held.

Beyond the tunnel, a scene of devastation lay. Still somewhat indistinct because of the tunnel's rolling, liquid-like state, the site appeared to be a courtyard where no courtyard should be. But broken and damaged as if by some natural disaster.

Natural? Lazo doubted that.

"Come," Daiyu said again, taking hold of David's hand. "Link together."

Lazo took Daiyu's and ArcNight's hands with Jaraal bringing up the rear of their living chain.

As they entered the tunnel, Lazo lowered his head, his eyes closing. He'd recognized Jaraal as Hideo, Kim and Shioko's cat. He'd sensed Jonas Thompkins was a shadow-tracker. He'd told Jaraal his perception had become more acute, like the intimate connection he had with Jenny he called their "personal force."

He'd sensed Jenny's danger more than once.

Now, he sensed her again. Closer.

Jenny, he thought, feeling an unseen grip take hold of him, strong and purposeful. I'm coming.

The pressure around him, the sense of place, shifted.

He opened his eyes.

Zone of Concealment

The destruction David faced looked like the proverbial bomb had gone off. "What could have caused this?" he asked, his voice raspy in the thick, dusty air. With David leading the way, the jade tiger had opened a path into and through the barrier, allowing David and his unusual team entry into the hidden campo.

At least what was left of it.

"We are here," Daiyu said. "We are in the Maghi's interdimensional realm." She looked around. "Despite the destruction, there is still strong magic present, but it has been disrupted, replaced by a far darker force. The Maghi have always been able to straddle worlds, dimensions, other plains of existence, but this is something different, much like the alternate Venice, called Aizenev, where they sometimes retreat."

"How many of these Venices are there?" David asked.

Daiyu smiled. Indulgently, David thought. "More than you can imagine."

"Those pictures in Lenora's apartment," ArcNight said. "They were of that other Venice."

"Yes," Daiyu said. "Taken by Bruno, Lenora's husband, when they infiltrated Aizenev with Lydia's help. But this place straddles Aizenev and Venice, a hidey-hole, if you will for the Maghi warren. I've been here before, long ago. Estansa and her kind are creatures of the Dark Demesne, an offshoot of the Left Hand Path with its own levels like that of the ambient-milieu."

"Say," ArcNight said, looking behind them. "Where's Sibulovich?"

David and his companions turned. Lazo was gone. "Wait a minute," David said. "Daiyu had hold of his one hand."

ArcNight nodded. "And I had the other."

"I sensed, felt nothing untoward," Daiyu said.

"Me neither," ArcNight added.

"Jaraal?"

Jaraal growled softly. "I am not sure. I sensed no danger, but Lazo-san has simply vanished."

"It's okay," David said. The jade tiger flashed in his hand. "Mr. Sibulovich is okay."

"How do you know?" ArcNight asked.

David smiled and held up the figurine. "A little tiger told me. Seriously, it's like it doesn't actually talk to me, just implants, I don't know, feelings, hunches, ideas in my mid. It just didn't pinpoint where Lazo's gone but it's really nothing to worry about."

"The figurine is from the Void," Daiyu said. "A talisman to provide assistance. I am sure of it."

"Which means the shadow-thing was also from the Void," David said.

"Perhaps."

"All right," ArcNight rubbed his gloved hands together. "Let's get back to business."

"Agreed," David turned to the bakeneko. "Jaraal, can you sense Thompkins' mistress now?"

"No," Jaraal replied. "But that does not mean she has been destroyed."

"She may have fled to Aizenev," Daiyu added. "If, in fact, she escaped this destruction. Can you sense Amedio Zaronelli, Jaraal?"

"Unclear," Jaraal said.

"Hold on," David said. "The tiger's directing me again." He's like a freaking living GPS!

"Over here." ArcNight had walked away from the group, scanning the area. It looked like he beat David's jade figurine to the punch. He stood over a pile of rubble, this one looking to have been arranged to cover something.

Or someone.

Daiyu knelt at the pile, staring intently at the mound. She hung her head. "It is Edmondo Vincherra," she said softly. "He too is gone."

"Someone basically buried him," ArcNight said. "Kim, I bet."

"Yes," Daiyu said, standing. "I think so too. David?"

David felt like a puppet, being pulled by his strings as the jade tiger once more urged him in another direction. "There's something else over here," he said, walking away from the others. He stopped, seeing nothing out of the ordinary except broken mortar, glass, and assorted debris. "I don't see anything but..."

Again, Daiyu concentrated her attention of the spot David indicated. "A concealment veil," she said. "Someone or something is hidden here."

David turned around. The tiger once again guided him. David squinted at the smoky horizon. "Everyone," he said. "I think we have company."

A grotesque figure lumbered out of the misty shadows. Though tall, it walked slightly hunched, as if in pain. A weak red glow surrounded the creature. Blood stained the creature's chest and torn kilt. What looked like multiple claw and bite marks scored his torso. Scorch marks covered his legs.

"Holy crap," David whispered.

"It's Orcus!" ArcNight exclaimed. "I've fought him before in my own world. What's he doing here?"

Amamoto's arm jerked toward Orcus. "The tiger's pointing in the direction beyond that monster!"

"Go!" ArcNight ordered. "I'll keep Orcus occupied and distract him away from you. You search for the others."

Daiyu took hold of ArcNight's arm. "I will help…"

"No, Daiyu. You've got to go with them, to use your magic to help find Kim and Lazo's wife. Don't waste your power here, especially after you've just recovered from your injuries, I don't care how magical the cure was. You're needed more with them. I can take care of myself."

A glimmer of smile touched Daiyu's face. "Of that I have no doubt."

"Then take the tiger with you," Amamoto said, holding out the figurine.

"No, for the same reasons. You'll need it more than I. But thank you both."

"Then I will join you," Jaraal said. He pulled off his hoodie, the fur covering his torso rising as if by static, claws unsheathing from his fingertips, his mouth spreading in a wide, toothy grin. "I am in the mood for a good fight." ArcNight looked at Jaraal closely for the first time. It was obvious he wasn't human, yet a shade of the human clung to him. More importantly, a feeling of power emanated from him as he seemed to gather that power to him.

The power of magic. And of the beast.

"I will not be dissuaded," Jaraal said.

"Can't argue with you on that," ArcNight said, glad Jaraal was with him. "But the rest of you, go!"

"Very well," Daiyu said. "Be safe."

ArcNight ran toward the demon, Jaraal loping at his side. ArcNight had been hunting Orcus in Dartham City at the exact moment he'd been snatched up and transported away from his own reality. Evidently, so had Orcus at some point, which was a relief. At least the demon wasn't able to cause any more damage to Dartham. But Orcus looked like he'd already been in a fight. And been beaten up pretty badly.

"ArcNight!" Orcus bellowed. "How…is it you are here?"

ArcNight and Jaraal stopped, appraising their demonic adversary. "Just lucky, I guess," ArcNight cracked. "Looks like someone messed you up, Orcus. Maybe you should lie down and take a nap." ArcNight saw Daiyu and Amamoto head around Orcus, using what structures remained standing for cover.

"I will attack," Jaraal said. "Draw its attention further."

"Orcus can shoot deadly energy from his hands," ArcNight said. "It might injure even someone like you."

"Noted." Jaraal growled but before he could act, Orcus held up his hands.

"Help me," the demon said, surprising the hell out of ArcNight.

"Jaraal, wait," ArcNight said to the bakeneko. Then to Orcus, "Help you?"

"I am pursued."

"You're also insane if you think I'll help you." ArcNight took a four-bladed throwing star from his service belt.

"He is afraid," Jaraal said, his nostrils flaring. "I smell his fear."

"And weakened. That red aura of his is always brighter than it is now."

"Ah," Jaraal pointed behind Orcus. "There are his pursuers."

A group, a mass of frightening-looking individuals approached. "Monstros," ArcNight muttered. "The ones Lenora described hunting."

Yes, judging by their appearances, that assessment made sense. But ArcNight intuited no danger from the oncoming creatures. At least to him and Jaraal. As they got closer, moving slowly, their attention focused solely on Orcus.

Fear glittered in Orcus' bestial eyes; spittle flew from his open, fanged mouth. He reached out a taloned hand toward the oncoming throng. ArcNight spun his throwing-star toward the demon. The sharp-edged blades struck Orcus' wrist and threw the demon's aim off.

The fiery tracers spitting from his clawed fingers went wild. The army of creatures attacked, moving swiftly and with purpose. They overwhelmed Orcus, burying him beneath scores of snapping jaws, ripping talons, sharp proboscises, crushing tentacles.

"Looks like you'll have to fight another day, Jaraal," ArcNight said.

"Hmph. Indeed."

Three of the monstros stood apart from the grisly work. "Quena," ArcNight whispered, recognizing another of his enemies.

The man-shark glared back at ArcNight. "Hooow," he growled. "Did yooouu get here soooo soooon?" Quena turned and sprinted away, his powerful legs speeding him to the remains of a still-existing canal. ArcNight watched Quena dive into the canal, wondering what the man-shark meant.

The other two monstros walked toward ArcNight and Jaraal. One looked like a hybrid of cat and reptile, tall and imposing. The other seemed familiar to ArcNight but only as a symbol, a piece of sculpture, a komainu lion-dog, the Japanese version of the Chinese Foo Dog. ArcNight stood his ground, ready for anything.

But he was still surprised when Jaraal said, "Hold," and strode forward to meet the fearsome-looking twosome.

"**A**h, Komainu," Jaraal said, grasping the huge head of the lion-dog. "It is good you are safe." The komainu extended a wide tongue and licked Jaraal's face. Grinning toothily, Jaraal pressed his forehead against the lion-dog's.

He, Komainu, Trell, and Zaronal had worked together to watch over Kim Yoshima, Wayne Brewster, Shioko Yoshima, and Jackson Yamaguchi. Jaraal in the cat-guise of Hideo, pet to Kim and Shioko Yoshima. Zaronal in his ability to transport himself over vast distances, essentially rendering himself invisible, in order to protect Brewster, and Komainu in his statue configuration to guard Jackson. And Trell, the kirin, to use his mystical powers to protect all of them, all without the notice of those they guarded.

They had formed this clandestine team to keep four of the Warriors of the Light crucial to the safeguarding of history out of danger. As Jaraal had said once to Zaronal the Sleeper, "The kami work in strange ways. We are here by the celestial design of others. At least that is what I think." No orders had been given, no instructions. They just knew what they had to do.

If only their comrade Trell, the kirin, were here too.

Jaraal turned toward the goddess, acknowledging her with a short bow. Once an enemy, she appeared to be continuing her allegiance to Seiryuu and the Yomitsu formed at the battle of Spirit Winds, Inc. "Amanozako," Jaraal said in Japanese. "It is an honor to have you with us."

Amanozako's eyes flashed, her scaled and furred face breaking into a smile. Of sorts. "The honor is mine," she responded in kind.

"Jaraal." ArcNight appeared at the bakeneko's side. Both Amanozako and Komainu turned their awesome gazes to appraise the costumed newcomer. Jaraal made the necessary introductions then asked Amanozako. "Honored One, these creatures who follow you. How...?"

The komainu suddenly darted forward, running past Jaraal and the others to the spot Daiyu had described as being hidden by a concealment veil. The komainu raised a huge paw and held it above the spot. No, Jaraal realized. The paw actually rested on some solid surface, invisible to all but the lion-dog.

The air rippled and flashed, dissolving to reveal a man lying among the stones. One Jaraal knew.

"Zaronal!" he cried, rushing to the sorcerer's side. Fully revealed unhelmed, wearing trousers, short tunic and slippers, the sorcerer, nevertheless, exuded a familiar aura.

"No more, my friend," the unarmored samurai said, grasping Jaraal's huge hand. "I am Amedio Zaronelli from this moment on."

A thrill of relief and gladness swept through Jaraal. His comrade had returned! "Indeed you are. It is gratifying to see you again. Although, now that I think about it, I have never really seen you. Until now."

"Yet you have always known."

"As I told you once before." Jaraal's nostrils flared. "Your spoor. You have a certain air about you."

Jaraal helped a chuckling Zaronelli to his feet. The sorcerer thumped Komainu affectionately on the lion-dog's side. In turn, Komainu gave a gentle bump to Zaronelli with his great head.

"You have suffered a grievous wound," Jaraal said.

Zaronelli placed a hand against his blood-stained side. "I have recovered," he said, though Jaraal wondered if that was entirely true. "And now we have work to do."

Jaraal whirled toward where the monstros had worked their savagery upon Orcus. All the creatures stood, ignoring the bloody corpse, staring to their right. An event approached. "Zaronelli-san, ArcNight!" Jaraal cried. "Get back!"

A great light surged upward over an area near the monstros feeding ground. It blossomed wide and high into an oval of blue radiance. Jaraal watched in wonder as it drew in upon itself, imploding, dissipated into streamers of coiling mist.

Another of the implosions reared up a distance away among the ruins. Then a third, farther still from the second.

Jaraal's meta-vision zoomed in on the first and closest. A wide oval of a mirror-like surface had been pressed onto the ground, as if the implosion had turned the rocky surface into glass. A woman lay upon it. Despite the different garb she wore, Jaraal knew her.

"Quickly," Jaraal said, racing toward the site of the implosion. "It is the Yomitsu!"

CHAPTER 30

The Mystic Realm has remained hidden and
inaccessible for millennia.
Now, it seems, we must...go public.

Papstesel

Zone of Concealment

Maghi Warren

"Thank you, Wayne," Jenny said as Brewster carried Bella's limp form toward the black lab/dimensional entryway. Brewster stopped, turned and faced Jenny. Hiroshi stood at the doorway.

"Be careful, Jenny," he said. "I know you don't want to tell me what's going on but, please, be safe."

"I will. You too."

"I'll be back."

No, Jenny thought. You may not. She watched Wayne, Bella, and Hiroshi vanish into the doorway back to the Venice simulacrum. Neither of us may.

She clasped her hands together to stop them from trembling. She had a lot to think about and she wanted to do it alone. A decision had to be made. A big one.

The Void

What seemed like minutes to Wayne had been much longer to her. A giant library spread out before, around, and above her. Jenny stared, the vastness and beauty of the enormous domed chamber overwhelming. Breathtaking. All those books and scrolls! "Wonderful," she breathed.

She stood in a side alcove, hidden in the shadows of a row of book-stacks. In the middle of the marble-floored chamber, two women faced each other, conversing.

It's Kim! Jenny thought. And...a'Kasha. The Void. The Akashic Records. And who knew what else? Her first thought was to run out and greet her friend, to ask her about Lazo. But she didn't. That's not why she was here. She hadn't contacted the Void through Bella and Hiroshi.

The Void had contacted her.

Jenny blinked and Kim no longer stood there, vanished. Jenny took a deep breath and stepped out of the alcove. a'Kasha turned toward her.

<<Welcome, indigene of Earth.>>

Jenny moved forward as if sleepwalking. Spellbound, she felt the knowledge contained in this chamber, this place. Science, culture, art, history, of all things. The Myriad Things. Its combined energy so profound it filled the air itself with sparkling motes of thoughts and ideas.

Jenny could see them, feel the power of the information they contained.

a'Kasha reached out and touched Jenny's forehead with her warm, gentle finger. Jenny relaxed, watching, wondering, filled with a great anticipation.

But of what?

<<This entity would like the indigene to consider an offer.>>

"An...an offer?"

a'Kasha nodded and smiled.

Afterwards, as Jenny dematerialized, she caught a glimpse of another person stepping out of the same alcove she'd been in.

A man. A big man. With a beard.

To leave everything and everyone I know. To abandon Lazo. How can I do that? I can't! I can't!

The Void needed a temporary replacement, an entity who could be the record keeper until a'Kasha returned from her sabbatical, wherever that would be and whatever that would entail.

The Void had asked her to be that entity! To be the keeper of the Akashic Records.

Even if Jenny wanted to, the responsibility, the enormous obligation, the sacrifice. It was too big, too crazy! Too fantastical.

And yet...

The wonders she'd see and experience. The mysteries she could solve. The good she might be able to do.

My god, what should I decide?

"Take the job, Jenny. You'd be perfect at it. And you wouldn't have to do it alone."

Jenny cried out. Lazo stood in the middle of the laboratory. Wearing a torn, dirty, T-shirt and rumpled trousers, his hair mussed, he beamed at Jenny with that infectious smile she'd always loved.

"Lazo!" Jenny ran and threw herself into his arms. Lazo enfolded her and kissed Jenny again and again. Both shed tears of joy.

"Is it really you?" she cried.

"In flesh. God, girl, I thought I'd lost you."

"And I knew you'd never give up looking for me." She pulled back from his embrace.

"Wait a minute. You are Lazo right, my Lazo? Not some shapeshifter from god-knows-where."

"Did you get a whiff of me? I haven't showered in a while."

"You're right!" Jenny laughed and once more embraced him. "Nothing could imitate that smell!"

"Are you okay?"

"Yes. You? And how'd you get here? What did you mean I wouldn't have to do it alone? Do what alone?"

"Don't play dumb. You know. The job I mentioned. a'Kasha interviewed me too."

"That was you I saw!"

"Yep. As the new keeper of the Akashic Records you'll have an assistant. Yours truly. My previous experience with the Book Haven made me a shoo-in for the position."

The reality of the situation slammed into her. Jenny walked away, throwing her hands up. This was crazy! "We can't just decide like that! We need time..."

"That's just it, babe. There is no time."

"I know. Damn it, I know."

"And it won't be forever. Just until a'Kasha gets her cosmic shit together."

"And how long will that be?" Jenny snorted. "Listen to us! It's like we're discussing a lateral promotion at some Fortune 500 company, for God's sake!"

"Lateral? I don't think so. And I don't think God has anything to do with this."

"How will our absences be explained? What about our jobs? Our friends and families?"

Lazo shrugged. He was taking this a lot better than she was. "You'll be the Void. You can make anything happen."

"Yeah, but do I have that right? Look what happened to a'Kasha!"

"You're not a'Kasha. She picked you for a reason."

Jenny touched the fingers of one hand to the side of her head. "a'Kasha said it was in my DNA. Some kind of genetic marker."

"Right. In other words, you were born for this job!"

Jenny's mind was afire with objections, excuses, and…possibilities. "But, for all intents and purposes, we won't be completely human any more. a'Kasha explained we'd have to become part of the energies that power the Void."

"But we'd be able to change back whenever we want to. Just like a'Kasha does."

"Why are you so calm and accepting about this?" Jenny shot Lazo what he'd dubbed the "hairy eyeball."

Lazo's expression hardened, all traces of his good humor gone. "I've been through Hell tryin' to find you and I know you've been through the same. We've seen what the dark side of this world and other worlds are like. We might be able to help make things better. Even just a little. This is a chance to do that on a ginormous scale! Don't you think?"

"Yes, yes. I've thought of all that too." She closed her eyes at a sudden idea.

"I see those gears workin' in your head," Lazo said with a smile.

"Just a thought." She cupped her chin in her hand. "We may also be able to manipulate time to make our stay seem, perhaps not short, but shorter. Perhaps a matter of a few months. It would be longer for us but a lot less time would pass in our world."

"Relatively speakin', that's what I got out of what a'Kasha told me. And, personally, I want to find out for sure who Jack the Ripper really was among other things."

"Ah, that might be considered an abuse of power, my love."

Lazo chuckled. "Speakin' of time…"

"We have a little yet."

"A little."

"Then let's go to our friends. I need to see them. Talk to them."

Lazo gestured toward the portal. "After you."

"No," Jenny said, taking Lazo's hand. "Together."

As they entered the outside hallway, what sounded like thunder rumbled in the distance. "Sounds like a bomb or two went off."

"I don't think so," Jenny said. "Not quite."

They hurried to the steps and ascended to the first level. Wayne, Hiroshi, and Bella were nowhere to be seen. But looking out the same window Jenny and Wayne had gazed from, she and Lazo saw three blue spheres vaulting into the sky. Then folding back in upon themselves.

"They're like implosions," Lazo said. He looked at Jenny. "Now what the hell's goin' on?"

"Hmmm," Jenny said. "I think this may be a good thing. At least part of it."

"Let's go..."

"No, wait, Lazo." Jenny paused a moment, her mind once again expanding, reaching out and being answered in turn.

"Damn girl, you're glowin'."

"We're staying here." She nodded. "We're where we need to be. Everyone and everything will come to us."

CHAPTER 31

Left to its own devices, the multiverse runs pretty smoothly.
Simply put, don't fuck with it.

Shioko Yoshima, the Glorious Ko

Dreamspace

Kim

Third Iteration

Kim felt a tightening rush, as if drawn inexorably forward toward some actual physical destination. A flash of white light encompassed her.

She stepped into that light, recognizing this neural doorway, an entrance to Bobby's mind, much like she'd experienced with Shioko. And like that time, a soft, lambent cocoon surrounded her with no beginning and no end, no horizon, no up or down. She stood? Floated? On, over, within, a flickering, misty landscape, shimmering like the soft-edged remnants of cloudstuff.

And then everything changed.

Ambient-Milieu

Once more Kim stood on the upper terrace of the golden palace. But, this time, only Bobby's astral-persona remained. Nolu's spirit-avatar was nowhere to be seen. But something was wrong. The once-clear sky had darkened to an angry red. Part of the brick-and-marble construction of the palace had tarnished, becoming soot-dark and cracked.

The terrace tiles heaved upward. A hot wind blew. The date palm uprooted and fell over. Bobby still stood in the same spot, smiling vacantly, oblivious to his surroundings. Without Nolu's control, Kim thought. This ambient level is falling apart.

Kim rushed toward Bobby, dodging a section of the spire that had been knocked off its base. She jumped over an opening fissure and exploding tiles, darted through a cloud of dust, and grabbed Bobby by his arms.

"Bobby!" Kim said. "Bobby, kiddo, it's me, Aunt Kim."

Bobby smiled dreamily, his eyes blank and staring. Kim sent her thoughts to Bobby, mentally probing. "Okay. Everything's all right." She felt her psychic energy flowing into Bobby, like it had when she'd rescued Shioko.

But nothing happened. Bobby's expression didn't change. So, as the palace began to completely disintegrate under their feet, Kim tried a very non-esper action. She slapped her nephew across his face.

<hr />

Carnegie Library of Oakland

Pittsburgh, PA

C.E. 2011

"**A**unt Kim?" Bobby awakened and stared at Kim with sleepy eyes. He put his hand to his cheek where Kim had mentally slapped him. "Ow."

"Bobby? You can see me?" Kim let out a breath, realizing she and Bobby were back in the museum.

Her breath. Her breathing came shallowly. Tired. She was so tired.

"Duh. Yeah, I can see you! Cool uniform."

Kim smiled. "Hey, kiddo," she said, running a hand down the side of Bobby's face. "You okay?"

Her hand shook.

"Yeah, I guess." Bobby sat up, rubbing his eyes, then focused an accusatory stare Kim. "Hey, Aunt Kim. How come you didn't come to my soccer match?"

Kim laughed, one filled with great relief and released tension. But the sound came out hoarsely, wavering. She pulled Bobby to her and hugged him hard. "I'm sorry, baby, I'm sorry. It's a long story. I'll tell you all about it someday."

Bobby's voice tickled her ear. "It's okay."

Kim pulled back, woozy. "No, it's not. You've been through those broken promises too many times. Never again, at least not from me. Not..."

She released Bobby, putting a hand to her head.

"Aunt Kim, are you okay?"

"Kim?" T'sai put her arm around Kim's shoulders. "What's wrong?"

"I... I feel so strange."

"It's the bilocation. It's breaking up in your physical state. I've got to get you back into the phase-shifting stream…"

Ambient-Milieu

Gone again.

Ripped from another place, another time.

At least Bobby was safe.

And…and… Grandmother Mitsu. What a joy to see her again!

The Damara/Omori/creature. Had it been destroyed? She doubted it.

All happening at once.

a'Kasha and T'sai were right.

Too much. Too much.

I can't stop now, she thought. It's not over yet. Not over… Not… NO!

She screamed into the ether, praying she could contact her super-positioned selves, struggled to pull them together. There, one iteration leaving Grandmother Mitsu for the last time, the other with Trell and Estansa Milaar. And this one, the third and final one.

Not final, she thought. The…one…in…control.

She came to a decision. She had to believe Bobby was truly safe. The huntress T'sai would help in that regard. Since they were "quantum sisters" Kim was certain the woman wouldn't let any harm come to Bobby. And Ken and Joe were there.

But Jenny and Kim's friends, the chimera created by Damara. a'Kasha. Those issues were still unresolved.

She cried out again, her spirit-avatar reaching out.

And got an answer.

BLOOD SACRIFICE

The Most Serene Republic of Venice—*Serenìsima Repùblica Vèneta*—is a living organism, a creature of thought and appetite created and maintained by the dark magic of the First Lords. Birthed by an ancient war and a final damning curse,

Solomon's Raptors and the Lions of the Venedetto take form one month every generation.

Living as *umana* by day, they turn at sunset to hunt and kill in their bestial forms.

Appeased by the Hunt, the city retained its power and world influence, with the *Maghi* as its grateful stewards.

But that power has faded in recent centuries, rendering the *Maghi* weaker and Venice merely slumbering.

That will soon change.

Estansa Milaar, Grand Mistress of the Maghi

SIXTH INTERVAL

Ōiso, Japan

Jade Court Era, The Veiled Years

C.E. 1543

Hiroshi Yoshida, Chancellor of Princess Midori's Jade Court, sat astride his war-mount, Kanaga, in the main street of Ōiso. He narrowed his eyes through his horned kabuto helm and appraised his surroundings—the smoldering ruins of what used to be the coastal city's mercantile district.

The burning skeletons of shops, vendor stalls, and teahouses stood starkly against a smoke-filled sky. The samurai warriors of the Jade Court, including the princess' Jade Guard, had fought a great battle here against a mysterious contingent of masked and hooded samurai. With no sigil or markings of any kind on their armor, they had swarmed into Ōiso to take control in a surprise attack. A carrier fowl released by one of the townsfolk had reached Odawara to report the assault. By that time, even though her goddess powers had been vastly reduced after casting the powerful Spell of Unknowing, Izanami had sensed the attack and warned the court. Hiroshi and his warriors had arrived and engaged the enemy. They emerged victorious but with a great loss of life and destruction.

After the fall of the Eminent Lord, the maniacal warlord's forces had scattered. Some had gone into hiding in the wilderness of the outlying Kanto Plain. Others committed ritual suicide. The treaty negotiated by the Jade Court and the various warring daimyo factions still held and had kept the peace within the environs of the Jade Court.

But Hiroshi long suspected some of Omori's surviving and rabid old guard, their loyalties still gripped by their master's madness, might someday reform and retaliate, refuse to relinquish their power, to admit defeat. Was this attack on Ōiso a first strike? If so, they had to be rooted out. All supporters of Omori had to be put down so the terror of the Eminent Lord could be forgotten.

Hiroshi steeled himself. The post-battle duties were when the true consequences of war became horrifically vivid. The death, destruction, the maimed and uprooted. Such actions against the helpless and unprotected were abhorrent to him.

Sobs and scrabbling sounds alerted him to displaced townsfolk emerging from where they'd tried to hide from their brutal attackers. Some wretched survivors crawled from beneath charred timbers and fallen masonry. They bowed before Hiroshi in the dirt, thanking him and his samurai for defeating their oppressors.

"No, gentle people," Hiroshi said, addressing the growing crowd. "Please, citizens of Ōiso, heap no praises upon us. The threat has been stopped but much rebuilding needs to be done. In order to defeat the forces of the Left-Hand Path, we too inflicted much damage. For that we beg your forgiveness. The enemy was strong, and it was necessary to strike at them in a like manner. Princess Midori and the Glorious Ko have promised aid. We will help you all we can."

The crowd cried out gratefully. Except for one.

"Curse you, Chancellor of Lies!" an old woman shouted. "May you rot in yomi forever!" Stepping forth boldly from the crowd, the crone leaned on a wooden staff, shaking a gnarled fist in the air. The people stepped away from her, as if she held some power.

Though Hiroshi's leather and metal armor was bloodied, scratched and dented, he, nevertheless, sat tall and imposing in his saddle. Kanaga himself was a strong, noble beast, able to instill fear in those he opposed in battle. Yet, wearing only a torn, gray robe over her skeletal figure with white stringy hair framing her lined, weathered face, the old woman seemed completely unimpressed in the chancellor's presence. Courage? Stupidity? Madness? Hiroshi had to give her credit, no matter the reason for her daring.

"You are no better than the so-called Eminent Lord. Like him, you have no honor!" She spat on the ground. "You ask for our forgiveness but how will that bring back those we have lost?"

The rest of the crowd seemed to recover their courage as they angrily shouted at the woman. Some reached out for her.

"No," Hiroshi said, holding up his hand. "Let her go."

"Pah!" the crone cried. Shooting Hiroshi a final, fierce gaze, she turned and hobbled away.

One of the Jade Guard hailed Hiroshi. "Lord Chancellor!" Masaaki, his second-in-command, approached on foot, his mustached and bearded lips turned downward in a rare frown beneath his winged helm. He stood apart, not coming any closer. In each gloved hand, the samurai held two bloody hemp sacks. Hiroshi started at the sight.

Kanaga snorted, tossing his head and backing up a step. The warlord Omori had required his samurai to bring him the heads of certain enemy combatants, those officers, commanders, and daimyo who had opposed him the most vehemently. Was Masaaki imitating this revolting practice? Hiroshi had given no such orders!

"What is the meaning of this, Masaaki-san?" Hiroshi demanded, pointing at the sacks as he joined his second.

"I beg your forgiveness, Lord, but you must see this. I... I did not want the citizens of Ōiso to witness such a horror." With those ominous words, Masaaki placed the sacks on the street. Carefully, as if they might burn him, he upended them.

Two grisly, bloody heads rolled out of each sack.

"Huh!" Hiroshi dismounted and knelt to study the heads. Blackened and scorched by fire, they, nevertheless, were recognizable. Not human, they resembled both man and dog.

Shadow-trackers. Hiroshi sucked in his breath and shot a glance at Masaaki. "Your suspicions appear to be correct, Lord," Masaaki said, a tinge of fear underlying his words.

"So it would seem." Hiroshi stood and folded his arms across his breastplate. His mind whirled furiously. After Midori had been rescued from the now-dead majo, Eela, she had described an assistant of the witch. A man named Takeshi. Hiroshi frowned. Even now, months after Eela had died by Midori's hands, Midori lay bedridden in Odawara, still possessed by memories of her forced transformation by Eela into a shadow-tracker, the one known as the Source-of-all-Things. Takeshi had been allowed to escape with some of the hybrid beasts in order to continue Eela's breeding program.

A decision which enraged Hiroshi, but the Glorious Ko had convinced him it was necessary so future history would play out as it should.

Hiroshi wondered if Takeshi had organized this mysterious faction of samurai. It must be so. Who else could control the shadow-trackers? "Where?" he asked, pointing to the heads.

"We found their remains across the street from a nearby shrine in a burned-out barrel-maker's shop. A trail of blood led from the inside of that shop, so we followed the trail back. We think the beasts and their killer fought within."

Who could have killed them? Hiroshi wondered at yet another mystery. "A brave and strong warrior indeed to face shadow-trackers, let alone kill them. Perhaps then, in the heat of battle, a fire had been ignited."

"Yes, Lord. We thought so too. Though already dead, we removed the beasts' heads so, if such horrors have a place in the Plain of Heaven, they now cannot attain it."

"Mmm. You did well."

"Plus, Lord, at the side of the building lay three of the enemy samurai, dead, their armor and bodies torn open, as if by the shadow-trackers."

Hiroshi frowned. "Odd. It would seem the enemy and the shadow-trackers would work together, not oppose each other."

"Indeed, Lord."

"Show me where the shrine and this other structure are and then burn these abominations further until only ash remains."

———————

Hiroshi stood in front of the shrine, most of which still survived despite the damage it had sustained. Its gabled roof had collapsed. Its torii gate lay overturned. Sections of the high wooden fence surrounding the shrine had been broken. The burned structure opposite the shrine was a skeleton of charred timbers, making its former barrel-making purpose unrecognizable. Masaaki and three more of the Jade Guard placed the shadow-trackers' heads back inside where they'd found them and started their remains ablaze a second time.

After dismounting and tethering Kanaga to the fence, Hiroshi had examined the three samurai corpses Masaaki had described. They indeed looked to have been ravaged by beasts. Again, Hiroshi wondered. Why would the shadow-trackers turn on their allies? If, in fact, that is what happened.

The trail of blood led to the steps of the shrine's shattered wooden entrance door. Hiroshi climbed the stairs. The blank stone eyes of two guardian komainu statues on each side of the door seemed to stare right through him, making him strangely uneasy. He stopped, looking down.

A faint bloody footprint lay at the threshold. Hiroshi recognized it. One of the shadow-trackers? But, judging by the size of the footprint, larger than any Hiroshi had ever seen. A possible third one? He withdrew his wooden fighting staff from its shoulder sheath and cautiously entered the shrine.

Inside, the smell of incense overwhelmed his senses despite the reek of death and destruction without. Stone lanterns had been pulled down throughout the Hall of Worship, curtains and decorative roping ripped from their moorings. Sukaki, ceremonial tree branches, lay scattered. The local kami enshrined here had been defeated easily.

The blood trail led through fallen roof debris to the front of the main altar of the Hall of Worship. There, a naked black-skinned man lay on his stomach, an arrow protruding from the side of his neck.

Hiroshi knelt down at the man's side. Dead, he thought, checking the man's breath, seeing the man's lifeless, staring eyes. But who is this? He is not Japanese. Hiroshi stared down at the corpse, more bewildered than repulsed at the sight of the dead man. Did this strange-looking person encounter the shadow-trackers, escaping only after being mortally wounded?

Hiroshi stood, a startling thought manifesting. Could this man be the killer of the shadow-trackers and the samurai? Remembering the bloody footprint, he took stock of his surroundings more carefully. Backtracking he studied the floor. There and there! Other faint outlines of a shadow-tracker's foot but then...

A fourth footprint, closer to the dead man looked more human. Hiroshi examined the corpse again. The man's left foot was partially covered in blood. As were his hands.

What could this mean?

An intake of another's breath alerted him. Bringing his staff up, he darted behind the altar where he found an older man garbed in a long black robe and a young girl. The girl was a miko, a Shrine Maiden, dressed in red trousers and white kimono jacket, her hair tied back in a single braid. She knelt, holding a bow, its arrow nocked and pointed at Hiroshi. The man lay on the floor with his head resting on a pillow. Eyes closed, neck and shoulder covered in blood, his chest rose and fell faintly. The kannushi, the Chief Priest or God Master. He still lived.

"Honored Miko, what has happened here?" Hiroshi asked.

The girl didn't lower her weapon, challenging Hiroshi with a defiant expression. "Have you come to send us to yomi, the World of Darkness, oh brave and noble samurai?" the girl spat, her voice full of hatred and disdain. "Will you keep us from attaining the Plain of Heaven as you have so many others here? Are you so brave now to remove the mask your kind so cravenly hid behind?"

Hiroshi's features twisted in pain. Here was a second courageous yet bitter woman to face him this day. Unlike the crone, however, the miko was young, her life still before her. All too soon, she had been cruelly violated by the devastation visited upon her city, her shrine, her priest, and herself.

"I am Chancellor Hiroshi of the Jade Court," Hiroshi said. "I am not your enemy."

The girl's expression fell. She lowered the bow. "Oh, Lord Chancellor, forgive me. I thought…"

"It is all right. Can you tell me what happened?"

"Three masked warriors. They inflicted the damage you see here. Our God Master made me hide from them while he attempted to stop the destruction. The cowards took him outside where…where their shadow-trackers awaited like trained beasts."

"Shadow-trackers. Two of them?"

"Yes."

"Tell me, these warriors. Do you know who they were?"

The Shrine Maiden's face hardened, anger flashing in her eyes. "I saw it from where I hid," she said softly. "A tattoo on the wrist of one of them."

"Yes?"

"A dragon devouring its tail."

Hiroshi clenched his teeth. "The sigil of the daimyo Omori Kadanamora." Just like they had discovered on the corpses of other fallen attackers. "The dark-skinned one, who was he?"

The miko's eyes widened. "A shadow-tracker! It's true. But he saved our God Master. I came out of hiding to try and help the priest. I was so afraid but could not abandon him. At the door I saw it all happen. The shadow-trackers dragged our God Master into the barrel-maker's shop across the street, the warriors remaining outside. Suddenly another shadow-tracker, bigger and stronger and so fierce, attacked the warriors, killing them and then ran inside the shop. I heard the sounds of great combat, brutal, vicious. Then…"

"This shadow-tracker saved your priest and brought him back here." After killing the enemy shadow-trackers.

"Yes, though terribly wounded himself. One of the samurai still lived and shot him. I… I, in turn, managed to kill the samurai." The miko hung her head. "I have never killed before."

"You are very brave."

"I sensed the shadow-tracker wouldn't harm us. He carried our God Master here and then he turned into a man as he died. I swear it is true!" The miko's eyes glimmered with tears. "What magic is this, Lord Chancellor?"

The same as what happened to Midori? No, this is different. Izanami may know the how of it. "A magic of a strange and different kind," Hiroshi said quietly. "One for good, I think. You are safe now and we will help your people. I promise you that."

Masaaki entered the shrine. Hiroshi gently pressed the miko's shoulder, stood, and turned to his second-in-command. "I must leave for Odawara, Masaaki-san. Take charge here and render as much aid as possible until I return. See to this young girl and her priest. And give the dead man at the altar a full honorable burial."

"Hai, Lord Chancellor!"

Turning his back on Masaaki, the miko and the kannushi, and the dead man, Hiroshi exited the shrine. The rising smoke and flame across the street spiraled into the air. Mounting Kanaga, he didn't have to urge his mount out of Ōiso in a gallop, Kanaga eager, as always, to run. The great steed could cover the distance to Odawara in a very short time.

The wind whipped behind in Kanaga's speeding wake. Unfamiliar tears of rage and sadness blinded Hiroshi. I must report to Izanami and the Glorious, Ko, he thought. They must know of this.

Dreamspace

She stood at the edge of a great forest. Trees with vast, gnarled trunks and grasping limbs reached to the sky. An undergrowth of thick, bushy greenery, saplings, and tall, wide-stemmed flowers spread below the mighty canopy. A warm breeze blew at her back. Shafts of orange sunlight lanced through a scudding cover of clouds.

She blinked, confused, wondering where she was. Short-cropped grass tickled her bare feet. She looked at her clothes in surprise. She wore a laborer's pants and shirt. A short sword sashed at her waist, rested against her thigh. She held a fighting staff in one hand. A pang of memory swept through her. This is what she wore at the battle of Odawara-Jo when she led the Sleepers against the forces of Omori, the Eminent Lord.

Before she became the Princess of the Jade Court. When life was simpler as the proprietress of a teahouse. Before she became jaded and angry. And envious of the Glorious Ko and the Principal Advisor. Before she began to shut Hiroshi out of her life.

A shadow detached itself from the treeline. She gasped as a figure emerged from the forest, moving sinuously, expertly, like an animal. Midori instinctively assumed a defensive stance, holding her staff out in front of her. The figure walked into the sunlight, revealing itself fully. Midori gasped. She knew this creature. She had been a part of Midori and Midori had been a part of her. She had given Midori purpose and hope. Midori had felt her die.

"By the kami!" Midori cried, lowering the staff. "It is you. The Source-of-All-Things."

The shadow-tracker cocked her bestial head, her sleek, fur-covered body supported on two powerful legs, her yellow dog eyes flashing in the sunlight. She spoke. "Midori Nakamura. It's good to be with you again."

Midori backed up, her mind awash with foreboding. "Where is this place? Why are the both of us here? Have I died then too?"

"No." The shadow-tracker spread her arms out at her sides. "This is a place of dreams, your dreams. And I've been allowed to be a part of them."

"For what purpose?"

"I'm here to urge you to let go of your demons. Don't let Eela win."

Midori frowned. "What…what do you mean? Eela's dead! You helped me to kill him, Great Mother. How can he win?"

"Look at yourself. You still cower at the slightest noise. You awake screaming at imaginary dangers. You continue to stare in the mirror as if you expect to see…"

"You! I expect to see you! Please forgive me. I know you're not a monster but…but I'm so afraid."

"You have no need to fear me or Eela. Or anyone or anything anymore. Release that fear. Allow it to fade away. Reject it. You have a life to live as Princess of the Jade Court. Your people, your Chancellor, need you in these veiled times. Your time is not yet over. In many ways, it's just begun."

"Hiroshi. Ko. I'm so ashamed of what happened, of my weakness. I fear facing them."

"You showed no weakness and your friends risked their lives to rescue you. They need you, Midori, just as you need them. Realize that Eela empowered you, though that was the last thing he intended. Because of what he did, he allowed me to exact my revenge through you and to help free you. Remember that. Eela's gone forever but dangers still abound. Rise up! Be the leader you were meant to be. I know you can. I felt your strength, your courage and determination when we were linked. Don't let my death be in vain, I beg you."

Midori felt a surge of power blossom within her, one of determination and atonement. Her chest swelled with a fervor she'd long missed. She raised her eyes to the fierce gaze of the shadow-tracker.

"Yes, yes! Oh, Great Mother, I will, I will. Thank you. Thank you!"

Odawara Castle

Jade Court Era, The Veiled Years

C.E. 1543

"**O**h!" Midori jerked, sitting up from her bed, her hands flailing, her legs kicking the blankets covering her. "The Great Mother. The Source-of-All-Things!"

"Midori!" A woman's voice reached her through a veil of mist and shadows, softly, yet filled with calming strength. Gentle hands took hold of her and pressed her back onto the bed. Midori lay, gasping, her chest heaving.

"She's returned to us," the same voice said. "It's different this time. It's good."

"Shioko-san?" Midori said, struggling to see through her cloudy vision. "Glorious One?"

"Yes, it's me, Midori. Welcome back." The Glorious Ko beamed at Midori, her beautiful face alight with relief and, yes, love. Midori felt that love a sister feels for another, for one who had been lost and now had been found.

"Oh, Ko, I… I… But who is this?"

"Hello Midori-san." A man, a non-houjin, stood beside Shioko, a smile lighting up his dark-skinned face. Long…dreadlocked hair fell about his shoulders. He wore a blue kimono and trousers. "I'm back too."

Midori cried out. "Jackson-san! By the kami, is it really you?"

"In the flesh."

"Oh, how wonderful. Praise Amaterasu." Tears sprang to her eyes at the sight of the Principal Advisor. He leaned in and took Midori's hands in his.

Then she remembered. Midori tried to speak around the emotions swelling in her throat. "Zaronal. He is gone, yes?"

"Yes," Shioko said, a tinge of sadness creeping into her voice. "He saved us all."

"Ah, Zaronal. My brave and selfless demon-queller. How I will miss you." Fighting back the trembling in her voice, she asked, "Where is Hiroshi? And Izanami?"

"They're outside in the hall, conferring. Hiroshi has some news," Shioko's face darkened. "I'm afraid it's not good."

As if on cue, the bedroom door opened, and the Chancellor and the Goddess entered.

"Midori!" With a cry, Hiroshi ran and knelt at Midori's bedside, enfolding her in his arms. "You're back! You're back."

Midori returned Hiroshi's embrace, tears flooding her eyes. "Oh, Hiroshi-chan, I'm so sorry. So very sorry."

"No, no, my love," Hiroshi said, his voice breaking. "It was not your fault. I am equally to blame."

In the distance, as Midori buried her face in Hiroshi's shoulder, Izanami's voice sounded. "I must go to Ōiso at once. The reign of the Jade Court faces its first crisis."

"In that case," Shioko said. "I'm coming with you."

CHAPTER 32

The power of the mind and spirit is sometimes
too terrible to put aside.

Yoshima Mitsu, the Luminous One

Zone of Concealment

Kim

Second Iteration

The kirin fired.

Kim struggled, pushing upward toward a light glimmering over-head as if swimming up from the bottom of the ocean. A binding, an unseen constriction, gripped her body. Her mind tried to break through the murkiness clouding it.

She gasped, crying out as she rose up from some hard, smooth surface. She lay back down, breathing hard, her stomach queasy. Dust whirled around her, causing her to cough. She rubbed her eyes, glancing to each side of her. She lay on what looked like a giant mirror inset into the ground. Remnants of blue mist spiraled upward. A burnt smell drifted in the air. Beyond her, a stark version of Venice lay in ruins.

Still clutching the paper kirin, she placed it against her chest. The Zone of Concealment. Kim knew without a doubt. And…and I'm…

She closed her eyes. Not whole again. Not completely. Just two of me.

Her attempts to reunite her iterations had only partially worked, her first iteration, the one who'd interacted with her grandmother, had rejoined with her, its manifestation complete. Now she'd only have to be in two places at once! Still, Kim felt better as a result, stronger. Now she just felt like hell instead of death-warmed-over. Muscles sore, head pounding, vision cloudy. Goddess, she needed a vacation! Maybe in some nice, quiet war zone.

Damara/Omori-chimera!

What had happened to it? She and the spider-warlord hybrid had been blasted from the Dark Demesne by her and Trell's combined power. But she saw no sign of that hideous hybrid. Or the lamia Milaar.

Kim got to her feet and stifled a cry. A group of…monsters stood, crouched, and slithered several yards away, returning her look with curious ones of their own. At least, Kim hoped it was curiosity, it being difficult to gauge the expression of some of the monstrosities. A large carcass lay behind them. At least what was left of it.

She formed her esper sight, still a little shaky from her "reforming." Orcus, she marveled, recognizing the kilt, the skull-head. He's been torn to bits.

"Yomitsu!"

Kim turned at the sound of that oddly familiar voice. Two figures rushed toward her. She held out the paper kirin, hoping it had more juice, but the origami figure crumbled to dust. "Trell!" Surely this wasn't the end of the kirin!

Needed elsewhere, a fading thought echoed in Kim's mind. Travel in light, Yomitsu.

And you! Taking hold of her dagger, Kim readied for an attack.

An attack that never came.

"Jaraal!" she cried. Her headache abruptly gone, she threw herself into the powerful arms of the bakeneko, embracing him hard. To think she once feared this pussycat!

"Please, Yomitsu," he purred. "The kaiken blade."

"Oh, yes, yes! Sorry." She sheathed the knife and laughed out loud as ArcNight joined them. She looked at ArcNight and nodded. The costumed avenger held out his hand. Kim took it, glad he wore his cowl. It was enough right now to have Wayne's eyes appraising her from the face of a virtual stranger. She didn't need to be reminded of her Wayne's loss any further.

And not just his physical loss.

"I like the new look," ArcNight said, a ghost of a smile appearing.

"Indeed," Jaraal added. "What has happened?"

Quickly Kim described the metamorphosis of the spider-demon, the psychic remnant of Omori, and her encounter with the lamia Milaar, the reappearance of Trell, which elated Jaraal. She left out a lot of her story. There just wasn't time. "I don't know what became of them."

"There were two more of the same implosive events like yours," ArcNight said. "Could be them."

"It appears the devil Omori just will not die, will he?" Jaraal said.

"That seems to be contagious, like Damara too," Kim said.

"Another symptom of the weakening multiverse," the bakeneko offered.

"If, in fact, that's what the other two implosions imply," ArcNight added.

"I don't doubt it. Did Lazo and Lenora and Antonio make it to the Lido hideout?"

Jaraal and ArcNight exchanged a look. "What's happened?" Kim demanded.

ArcNight paused, a shadow passing over his face. "I'm sorry, Kim, but Lenora's dead also," he said. "Her men Gino and Luca too. They were attacked by a Maghi sorcerer who Lenora finally killed before she died."

Kim closed her eyes. Damn it! She hadn't known the woman very well at all, but she'd shown great courage and determination. "Edmondo is too," she said sadly. "Lenora's son?"

"He's safe on the Lido. Sibulovich is gone but we've been assured he's safe," ArcNight said.

"Gone?"

"Truly, Yomitsu-san. Daiyu feels he is in no danger."

Kim gasped. "Daiyu's alive?"

"Indeed."

"She and David Amamoto split off while we tried to distract Orcus."

"Thank the goddess." Kim shook her head. "Well, you can tell me later how all of you got here. I can't wait to hear that, but is there any news on Jenny?"

"She's here, we think," ArcNight said.

Kim focused, seeking out Jenny's neural signature. Nothing. No trace of it but that didn't necessarily mean she was gone. Some force could be blocking her.

Just then Kim saw a huge animal approaching. A man walked by the beast's side.

"Is that Jackson's komainu?" Kim asked. "And is that...? Goddess!"

Before Jaraal or ArcNight could react, Kim sprinted to meet the oncoming duo. "Amedio!"

Zaronelli slid down the komainu's flank, allowing Kim to embrace him. He tightened beneath her arms. Kim pulled back, concerned. "You're not completely healed," she said.

Zaronelli quickly erased the pained expression on his face. "I am healed enough. Our numbers are increased now. We will prevail no matter my condition." Zaronelli smiled. "Besides, I would not miss this for anything."

"Okay." Kim squeezed the sorcerer's hand. "Okay. And you," she said to the lion-dog. "You're Jackson's statue, aren't you? You and

Zaronal, Trell the kirin, and Jaraal the bakeneko worked together to watch over Jackson, Shioko, Wayne, and me." A low rumble emanated from the komainu's throat. The huge creature stepped up to Kim, its nose just inches from hers.

A chill ran through Kim, not of fear, but of wonder. She slowly raised her hands and placed them on each side of the komainu's face. It was warm and furry, not like a piece of stone at all. It smelled very alive. "Jackson's safe," she said, praying it would understand. "He's with those he loves again." The beast blinked and, amazingly, purred.

Kim realized another had joined her, Zaronelli, and the komainu.

"Yomitsu," the creature said in Japanese, its voice like grating sandpaper. The komainu barked softly, as if to say, "She's okay."

"You know this creature?" Zaronelli asked.

Kim nodded. "Although we've never been properly introduced. You led the attack against Spirit Winds Inc." Kim faced the battered yet still formidable-looking creature who had addressed her, having to look up because of the thing's eight-foot height. Kim spoke in Japanese also, not sure if the creature could understand any other language.

"Hai," the thing replied. Its face was a combination of reptile and feline, almost beautiful in its hybrid construction. "I know now it was a mistake which I regret and must atone for. Yet here we are, part of a larger plan of the kami. I am Amanozako, once a goddess, now a warrior for a just cause." She pointed to the group of monsters who had killed Orcus. The motley, monstrous crew had gotten closer, creeping, crawling, walking to gather near.

Kim looked at the frightening group Amanozako led. One, in particular, a tall humanoid with multiple eyes and facial tentacles. It was as if it had stepped out of an H.P. Lovecraft story. "These are your cause?" she asked.

"To free them, yes." Amanozako's arm flung out to her side, the gesture encompassing the fantastic entities. She seemed proud and determined. "We have escaped our prison and caused much damage in the process. But the leader of those we attacked was not present."

"You've seen this leader?" Kim asked.

"Yes. She is a female of a vampiric nature."

"Estansa Milaar," Zaronelli said. "The Grand Mistress of the Maghi."

"Unfortunately, we've met."

ArcNight and Jaraal joined them. Kim smiled at the incredible group.

This was a summit meeting of the ages!

"Amanozako," Kim said. "Did you see any others there? Humans? There is one like us who was being held captive, a female with red hair."

"Yes," the creature answered, blinking her eyes slowly. "The structure where we were imprisoned is large and labyrinthine. I do not know where the lamia held your friend."

"Can you take us there? Would you be willing to go back to help us free our friend?"

The komainu chuffed, the lion-dog turning its maned head toward Amanozako. Some understanding seemed to pass between them. Amanozako nodded and then said to Kim, "Would you be able to exert your powers to send us back to our own worlds as you did many of us before?"

Only fair, she thought. If I can do it again. "I will try. Yes."

A chorus of howls, hoots, whistles and grunts echoed throughout the destroyed campo. The army of creatures waved their appendages in the air; some stomped their feet or slapped their tails against the tiles; still others ran in circles.

"Real party animals, aren't they?" ArcNight cracked.

"Then," the former goddess said, "we will help you."

"Thank you. Let's..."

"Can you truly trust these creatures, Kim?" ArcNight interrupted, turning serious.

"Yes," Zaronelli interjected. "I believe they can be trusted. And, I doubt, in any case, these monstros had served Estansa willingly. They serve no one now but themselves. That is the intent I see, that I feel."

"As do I," Jaraal said.

"Okay," ArcNight said. "I'm in."

"Oh!" Kim jerked in surprise, putting both hands to her head. Her scalp tingled, a jolting thought searing her mind.

Kim! Can you hear me, sense me?

Jenny! she thought-sent in reply. Are you all right? Where are you?

Yes. Lazo and I are in the former Maghi warren. Can you follow my neural signature?

Lazo's with you? On my way! Keep sending your thoughts to me!

"Kim," ArcNight said. "What's wrong?"

"Nothing," Kim replied, her heart soaring. "Finally, something's going right!"

Just then, Zaronelli climbed back up on the komainu. With a

rumbling growl, the lion-dog ran off. "Follow!" Zaronelli cried over his shoulder.

"They're heading toward the site of one of the other implosions," ArcNight said.

"Well, that's on our way," Kim said. "Let's follow."

CHAPTER 33

The metamorph's true identity lies in its surrogate forms.

Jaraal, the *bakeneko*

Zone of Concealment

"**T**o me!" Daiyu shouted, spreading her arms above her head.

David didn't need to be told twice as he hunkered next to the sorceress. A billowing cloud of blue light erupted right in front of them. Shooting into the sky and then falling back to earth, its reverse energies sucked at him and Daiyu like David imagined a black hole would. Daiyu created a barrier against it, forming a magical "force field" very much like David had seen Kim Yoshima do with her esper-bubbles.

In a moment the event was over. A large oval of what looked like mirrored glass spread out on the ground where the blue implosion had occurred. A woman knelt on the glass surface, her head down, tendrils of blue mist twining around her.

She stood—pale-skinned with shocking, long white hair and eyes the color of blood. Dressed in a sleeveless, thin, black robe, she looked like a witch or some pagan priestess. Except for the tentacle that trailed behind her like a tail. The air crackled above and around her.

"Estansa Milaar," Daiyu hissed.

"Daiyu of the East! You are alive?" Milaar showed true surprise. It was evident the two women knew each other. Snarling like an animal, the lamia shook, her head thrown back. Her body rippled, bulged. She transformed, turning into a huge glistening serpent the size of a school bus. Spreading its jaws wide, the serpent lashed out at Daiyu's barrier.

Its mouth struck the unseen field, sparks glinting off very long, sharp fangs. In a heartbeat, it coiled its thick body around Daiyu's barrier. "I cannot hold this for long!" Daiyu cried. Sweat popped out on her forehead.

"Not on my watch!" David shouted. Again, he knew what to do. No time for fear or disbelief now. The jade figurine, given to him by the shadow-thing, possibly a servant of this Void he kept hearing about, warmed in his hand. "Daiyu, lower your shield." He held up the figurine.

Daiyu paused only a second and complied. Holding back his fear, David thrust the tiger at the serpent. "Take this, bitch!" he cried.

The serpent screamed in a woman's voice, uncoiled and jerked its head back. David stepped closer to the shuddering reptile. The tiger flashed in bright green light. The serpent whirled and slithered swiftly away.

"Damn," David muttered. His legs and hands trembled. He stared at the jade tiger. *Just what the hell is this thing?*

"Well done, David," Daiyu said, placing a hand on his shoulder.

"You know that snake monster?"

"Once. Long ago." She turned back the way they'd come. "Others approach."

Oh no… David looked back, readying for another assault. Then smiled.

Kim

Second Iteration

Kim, Jaraal, and ArcNight reached the second implosion site just as Zaronelli slid off the lion-dog. Kim looked in surprise at Zaronelli, whose own face registered shock. "Daiyu!" he said upon seeing the sorceress.

Daiyu, too, looked like she'd just found out she'd won the lottery. "Amedio. That was you in the concealment veil." Her eyes found Kim. "And Kim!"

"The gang's all here," Kim said with a smile. She and Daiyu embraced. "I wasn't sure I'd see you again after you faced off with Roberto," Kim said.

"Or I you,"

"I'm sorry about Lenora."

"Yes, as am I." Daiyu said, although her eyes strayed to Zaronelli as she spoke.

Kim sighed. "Unfortunately, we really can't spend any more time catching up." *Time again.* Though most of what they'd gone through had to do with some aspect of time, there never seemed to be enough of it.

"Ag…agreed," Daiyu said, albeit, Kim saw, reluctantly.

"Indeed," Zaronelli spoke, his own gaze locked onto Daiyu.

"Kim," David said. "The lamia was here."

"I detect her spectral spoor," Jaraal said. "It is as I found in Jonas Thompkin's blood and leads in that direction."

"Daiyu and I both have a history with Milaar," Zaronelli said. "Though it has been a long time, we know what she is capable of and should be able to confront her."

"She turned into a giant snake and attacked us," Amamoto said.

"Hmm," Kim said. "Wonder why she didn't do that before."

"It takes a great deal of power for her to transform," Daiyu explained. "In that serpent form, she cannot utilize her other abilities. She became weakened enough that David's jade tiger drove her off."

"Well done, Amamoto," ArcNight said.

"You were right, ArcNight," Kim said. "No doubt, the Damara/Omori hybrid came through at the third implosion site." She took a heartbeat to make up her mind. "I'll go after it."

"By yourself?" Amamoto asked.

"I have an advantage with my psychic abilities, my esper powers," Kim said. "Besides, part of that creature is Omori and I need to finish him once and for all." She paused. "Jenny psychically contacted me. Lazo's with her in what she described as the Maghi warren. It looks like they're both safe. They're in the building the lamia used as her base here."

"Yes!" Amamoto pumped a fist into the air.

"But they are not the same, I wager," Daiyu said. "Lazo vanished from our presence and Jenny has been a captive for a long time. He and Jenny were chosen, I think. For something of the Light."

"Chosen for what?" Amamoto asked.

"We'll have to talk of that later," Kim said. "Although I agree with you, Daiyu, I get the sense it's a choice they were given, that it isn't a bad one." It's her, Kim thought. a'Kasha wants Jenny to replace her and maybe Lazo will be with her. "I was going to follow Jenny's neural signature to where she and Lazo are but Amanozako here has volunteered to lead you there. Follow her and her friends and get to Jenny and Lazo. Not to mention Milaar while I go after Omori and Damara. Be careful of that one."

"There are plenty of us to spare," Amamoto said, indicating the monstros. "You don't have to do that alone."

"I'll go with you."

Kim looked at ArcNight, impressive in his uniform. She too wore a uniform of sorts, she thought. Smiling, she allowed a small laugh to escape.

"Something funny?" ArcNight asked, folding his muscular arms across his chest.

"Well, since we're both dressed for it, I guess I'm your sidekick, huh?"

ArcNight pursed his lips. "I think it's the other way around."

"Okay. I'll be glad for the company. Thanks."

"I'll meet you there." ArcNight ran off, his costumed, muscled body a blur of dark motion.

The komainu stepped up, rumbling in its throat. "Ah, yes," Kim said approvingly. "You beat Damara before. Your presence will be a good psychological factor for us."

The komainu knelt down on all fours, inviting Kim to climb up on his back. Kim did so and looked at the eclectic members of this fighting force, this otherworldly army, which had come together in this strange part of the multiverse. David Amamoto and Jaraal stood side-by-side, a determined set to their vastly different features.

Daiyu and Zaronal looked everywhere but at each other. Yet, Kim felt some type of communication passed between them. They had known each other once. Yet another story Kim wanted to know. She hoped she lived to hear it.

Amanozako and the monstros. Well, who could tell what such creatures thought or how they really felt? But a burning anticipation emanated from them. Kim sensed a desire for a final vengeance, a yearning to be free.

"Good luck!" Kim said. "I... I love you all."

The komainu bounded away.

CHAPTER 34

The further you go, the less you know.

Lao Tzu
Tao Te Ching

Zone of Concealment

No need for subtlety anymore. No need to hide in the shadows. An invasion of brute force was the order of the day, it seemed.

Daiyu walked in the middle of the column of monstros, whose members employed various types of mobility to move away from the implosion site. She felt as if she participated in some surreal parade of grotesque and bizarre creatures out of someone's imagination.

Lorenzo Portero's imagination perhaps, inherited from his grandfather. For the first time in a long while, Daiyu thought of her friend. She recalled him regaling her with so many stories of his travels, his family. It had been Lorenzo's grandfather who had come up with the idea of holding vinegar in small compartments within plague masks to help deter the spreading of the horrible disease among the Venetian physicians.

Once dying, Lorenzo had been healed. Once a man of vision and ingenuity, he had been chosen to participate in an endeavor to save history.

She remembered being with him when the Sanctuary Elder transported him to the realm where he would begin his work. She and Lorenzo sat in her underground refuge, waiting. Lorenzo had not been afraid; in fact, he'd been jubilant, anxious to be on his way.

He'd embraced her, tears in his eyes, and was gone. As a result, he'd helped to set certain cosmic events in motion.

I wish I could speak with him again, she thought.

"What are you thinking?"

She turned to Amedio Zaronelli, who walked beside her. Back, essentially like her, from the dead. How strange and wondrous! "I am thinking how I misjudged you, wronged you. You tried to warn me, to help me. I never thought to see you again."

"Nor I you. It seems we've both cheated our deaths."

"And we both have a second chance." Without thinking, Daiyu took hold of Amedio's hand. She leaned into him and kissed him. "A second chance at everything," she breathed.

"I look forward to it," Zaronelli whispered and returned her kiss.

Clasping hands, they continued, with Amanozako and the monstros leading the way. Daiyu and her companions followed closely behind the giant former goddess and the living statue. She wondered how Edmondo would have reacted to this scenario. Some of these things had killed his sister, after all, and had taken him to the lamia who placed him under her insidious control.

But not entirely. Despite Edmondo's small size and unassuming aspect, he had been no thrall to Milaar, instead exhibiting great courage and resolve. And Lenora and Lydia. Daiyu cleared her mind of those dark thoughts. Time to grieve later.

The street and what remained of the ruined city's buildings flanking them were deserted, the only sounds the marching and dragging of dozens of feet and the occasional hissing or grunting of the monstros.

"How much farther?" she asked Amanozako.

"We are almost there," the once-goddess replied. From this angle, Daiyu could see the burnt and torn wing stubs on Amanozako's back. She wondered how that had happened.

Up ahead, a great jagged hole in the bottom story of an unusually tall tower-like building loomed like an open mouth. Bricks and masonry were scattered about the courtyard facing the structure.

As well as blood and several bodies. Monstros. Dead, no doubt by Orcus' hand.

The air around and in front of the broken wall shimmered a ghostly light. Daiyu got the impression of a body trying to heal itself, throwing up a protective membrane in front of a serious wound. Milaar, she thought. She is here and trying to rejuvenate her power.

"David, can the talisman gain us entry?"

Amamoto looked at the jade tiger he'd been holding onto. "I don't think so, Daiyu. It's not emitting any warmth." He looked at her, disappointment lining his Japanese features. "I think it might be used up."

Before Daiyu could comment, the huge, tentacled monstros charged through the opening.

A flash, like that from a camera only bigger and brighter, winked in and out of existence at the creature's magical penetration. Amanozako and the rest of the monstros rushed forward, pulling Daiyu and Zaronelli along with them in their frantic wakes.

Inside a shattered chamber, crumbling doorways with cracked hallways and stairways greeted them. From the shadows of the damaged corridors and adjacent rooms, four shadowy robed figures emerged, facing them, their faces hidden by their cowls except for their red, glowing eyes.

A loud whooshing sounded behind Daiyu and the others. The hole in the broken wall had sealed, a blank black field of spectral matter shutting them in.

The monstros became agitated, shuffling about and skittering.

"A trap! Come close, all of you," Daiyu said. "We need to combine our powers to protect ourselves."

"Amedio Zaronelli," a sibilant voice hissed. "You too have returned from the grave."

From a far hallway, a woman emerged. Still wearing the same clothes as she had at the implosion site, the lamia looked stronger as if, in just that short time, she had completely rejuvenated herself. The air seemed to shimmer around her like a heat mirage.

"Estansa Milaar," Zaronal hissed.

"And some of her surviving Maghi," Daiyu added. "Not all were destroyed."

Amanozako roared, her claws extending at the sight of the lamia. Milaar pointed to the goddess/warrior. "I should never have allowed Roberto to bring you here, monster. You and that wretched statue."

"Speaking of Roberto," Amamoto said, holding up the tiger and impressing Daiyu once more with his courage. "He's dead. Lenora killed him."

Estansa turned her baleful gaze to the security guard. Daiyu saw him shudder at the dark depths of those reptilian eyes fixed upon him but he didn't turn away. Milaar hissed. "And you, talisman wielder, you will make a good addition to my new menagerie."

"Not in this life," David said. "In case you can't count, you're outnumbered."

"There will be no more menagerie, Estansa," Daiyu said. "No more blood sacrifice. Your and the Maghi's time is finished, your reign over."

Milaar raised her hands, screaming a command, a bespelling. "She calls on her hidden power!" Daiyu shouted, raising her own hands. "Her desperation, her madness! Beware!"

Behind them, a second black barrier rose, walling off the monstros. "Now we are evenly matched!" Milaar screamed. "Attack!"

The four Maghi sorcerers rushed forward.

CHAPTER 35

There's a certain school of philosophical thought that states there is no time. The world doesn't change, it just is, and the past, present and future are merely conveniently invented labels. Which would imply our actions have no consequences. And so-called 'objective reality' is really based on the perception of the moment by any number of perceivers.

In other words, no *karma*. But I don't believe that.

Everyone has a destiny to fulfill.

Kim Yoshima

Carnegie Library of Oakland

Pittsburgh, PA

C.E. 2011

Kim

Third Iteration

"**G**lad you made it back, girl" T'sai the Huntress said. "Let's try this again, shall we? Your physical form outside of the phase-shifting stream should be more stable now that you reintegrated two of your three iterations"

"How do you know that?" she asked T'sai.

"Ssshhh. Just go with it. Look."

Just like what Agura the Hunter had described to Kim about "replaying" a moment in time, Kim knelt over Bobby again.

"Aunt Kim?" Bobby awakened and stared at Kim with sleepy eyes. He put his hand to his check where Kim had mentally slapped him. "Ow."

"Bobby? You can see me?" Kim let out a breath, realizing fully she had a second shot at this moment.

"Duh. Yeah, I can see you! Cool uniform."

Kim laughed. "Hey, kiddo," she said, running a hand down the side of Bobby's face. "You okay?"

"Yeah, I guess." Bobby sat up, rubbing his eyes, then focused an accusatory stare Kim. "Hey, Aunt Kim. How come you didn't come to my soccer match?"

Kim laughed, one filled with great relief and released tension. She pulled Bobby to her and hugged him hard. "I'm sorry, baby, I'm sorry. It's a long story. I'll tell you all about it someday."

Bobby's voice tickled her ear. "It's okay."

Kim pulled back. "No, it's not. You've been through those broken promises too many times. Never again, at least not from me."

Bobby looked behind Kim. "Dad?"

Kim turned around. Ken stood there, watching them, his expression full of heartbreak and regret. Ken had never been much of a father to Bobby. Now, Kim had a feeling that was going to change. She hoped it wasn't too late.

She stepped back and allowed father and son to embrace, at first tentatively, then tightly and strong. "Bobby," Ken said. "We've been worried about you."

"How come? Hey, where are we? Is Shioko here?"

<hr />

"He doesn't remember anything after arriving at the library with Marjorie," Ken said, watching Bobby talking with Joe. Joe had volunteered to keep Bobby occupied while everyone else conferred.

"That's probably a good thing," Kim said. "But you're saying Parker forced you to lure Bobby to his hired thug?"

"Tammelou. God help me, yes. But Parker said he'd harm Marjorie and Bobby if I didn't comply. I didn't know what else to do."

Kim nodded. "It's okay, Ken. I know how persuasive Parker can be. I would've done the same."

"Look, Kim..." Ken sighed and glanced down at the floor, as if trying to organize his thoughts. "I don't pretend to know much about what's been going on the last year or so, but I'm sorry for the way I've doubted and treated you. Bobby's safe now, and Marjorie and I need to understand what's this has all been about, if you can even explain it. I've seen and experienced things that are just unbelievable. When you're done with whatever you're doing, please, please call me."

"I will, Ken. I will. And, I'm sorry, too. Thank you for being there for Bobby."

Ken nodded and looked away, suddenly awkward. Kim knew she should take the next step and embrace him, but it was too soon. There'd been too many angry, regrettable moments between them over the years. A real reconciliation wasn't going to happen overnight. Maybe, hopefully, later.

If there was a later.

"But, let me tell you, Kim, he fought back," T'sai said, shooting a quick glance toward Ken. "He grew a pair and did what he had to, namely letting me help."

"More like you forcing me to let you help," Ken said. "But, thank you, T'sai. I mean it. Except for one thing."

T'sai smiled knowingly. "The dwayyo, right?"

"What's that?" Kim asked.

"Appalachian mythology beasties," T'sai replied.

"One is held captive by Parker," Ken said. "It, she, told me T'sai wasn't to be trusted and that she wanted the dwayyos for some purpose of her own."

"No. That's what they think, I'm sure, because of how Parker and his goons have treated them, and I had to keep up that same nasty appearance," T'sai said. "The dwayyo probably figured if she turned you against me, that would be enough of a distraction to help her escape. I just want to help them, believe it not, on my own."

"You have a funny way of going about it. You allowed one of the dwayyos to be killed then imprisoned and threatened another!"

"You think I wanted that?" T'sai's expression turned dark. "I found myself in a particularly strange situation when I arrived at Castle DeGroot, searching for the dwayyo pack. There was some strange shit going on there with Parker and his crew, complex, bizarre energy. Then you came along, Ken, complicating things further. Despite the powers I possess, I felt I needed to take everything slow and not give myself away or make matters worse. I needed to see what was up.

"There's a certain order and balance to the multiverse that has to be maintained. You know, entropy? Parker, and others like him, had been either killing or collecting creatures like the dwayyo, helping to upset that balance. Those beasties have to be returned to where they belong."

"But the balance was upset before with the displacement tremors sort of running amok, for lack of a better term," Kim said.

"Yes, starting with your ancestor, Yoshima Mitsu, directing the Spirit Winds to scoop up the little girl, Shioko, and the warlord Omori making a pact with the Left Hand Path. Before that, the temporal displacement tremors were relatively inactive and benign...and few and far between."

Kim nodded. "Right. Once Mitsu detected the Spirit Winds, she subconsciously sent her thoughts through what she called the Dreamspace, or ambient-milieu, into the Void and got a'Kasha the Archive's attention."

"You know of a'Kasha?"

"Yes, we've met."

"Really? Well, you really are special."

"Through Mitsu, a'Kasha directed the tremors to save Shioko. Mitsu was more powerful than she thought, she just didn't know how to focus and control her powers well enough. The Archive was already becoming restless, but when it sensed Earth and Yoshima Mitsu and Omori, that's when a'Kasha began to act independently and this mess started."

"Who's a'Kasha?" Ken asked. "And, Kim, how do you know all this?"

"Long, long, long, long story, Ken. Like you said, I promise to tell you everything. But right now, how do you know all this, T'sai?"

T'sai laughed. "Really, Kim? After all you've experienced, you ask me that? I'm one of the good guys, believe it or not, a Warrior of the Light and follower of the Radiant Way." She shrugged. "When the mood suits me, I admit, and using my own methods. Plus, I've been an agent of the Sanctuary Elders. I've picked up a few pieces of information along the way during my very long and varied life."

"Then why subject me to talking with the imprisoned dwayyo?" Ken said. "What was that all about?"

A shrug. "Just covering all the bases. The dwayyo was interested in you because it sensed your connection with Kim. I needed to see how that would play out, if it could help me to find Kim. That's the information I hoped to get from the dwayyo."

"Finally." Kim asked. "Why do want to talk to me?"

For the first time, T'sai looked uncertain. She licked her lips. "Because you know something about me I don't, some future event. I sensed a huge change in my own timeline, something I wasn't able to access. But you, Kim. I did sense you there. You were there when this change happened."

Ah, that's why she reminds me of someone. Kim smiled. "Yeah, you're the one. You're going to get a promotion."

"A promotion? From who?"

"The Sanctuary Elders, T'sai. They have a job opening they think you'd be a good fit for."

"What?"

"They want you to be a member of their council. An Elder yourself.

Probably so they can keep a closer eye on you, but trust me, that won't stop you."

Before Kim could say anything else, T'sai threw her head back and laughed. She turned to Ken. "Don't worry, Ken. The dwayyo will be all right. Now, go to your son." Stepping forward, she whispered again in Kim's ear.

CHAPTER 36

Harmony, karma, concepts I've always respected, tried to follow and invoke in everything I do. It's not always easy, sometimes near impossible. But, they're necessary in all aspects of life. Without them, chaos gets its foot in the door.

Kim Yoshima

Zone of Concealment

Kim

Second Iteration

Kim and ArcNight crouched within two still-standing walls of what used to be a structure of some kind. The komainu lay on the ground, stock-still, blending in with the fallen stone and assorted rubble as if it had turned back into its statue persona.

Dust had settled here though Kim wrinkled her nose at a smell of fire-scorched wood. From her much closer vantage point, she could clearly see the surrounding remains of the devastated city beyond, illuminated in whatever passed for sunlight in this pocket of reality. The ruins appeared as if out of an end-of-the-world scenario, silhouetted eerie and stark against a purple horizon. For a moment, Kim thought of the Fukushima Daiichi Reactor again. Of Susanoo, the god of sea and storms, who had caused the power station disaster but yet agreed to help Kim.

Susanoo, are you still out there? she thought, suspecting the punk-looking god was done with her, now that he'd kept his promise to help her. Which brought to mind the karura, Renta'Mur, who'd come to her aid at Susanoo's urging. Where were they now?

Directly in front of Kim and her companions lay the third implosion site. The mirrored surface glittered darkly in the wan light. Kim knew better than to get angry, but a certain frustration bubbled to the surface. How had a'Kasha allowed this to happen? She wondered again how the Void's supposed plans had been foiled.

"It's the Omori/Damara chimera, all right," she said, shoving her annoyance aside. The komainu chuffed, rising and veering toward a

311

jumble of wrecked structures.

"He or she went that-away, I presume," ArcNight said.

"Looks like it. Let's…oh." A tingling in her mind.

"Kim?"

"One second."

Wayne?

Kim? Wayne Brewster's thoughts, faint, fading in and out. Where…?

Wayne! Is it really you?

As far as I know. Kim sensed the smile in those thoughts. It was her Wayne. No, she realized. He'd never really been hers. And shouldn't be. He belonged to a wider experience, something bigger than just the two of them. That realization made her both sad and somehow…free.

I thought I'd lost you, she thought-sent.

Me too. I'm glad you're okay.

Is Jenny all right?

The last I saw of her, yes. At her insistence, I left her to throw out some garbage, so to speak.

"A Maghi?"

"You got it. The garbage in question isn't dead but should be inactive for a while.

Why did Jenny insist you leave her?

Not sure but, are you ready for this? She contacted the Void.

Ah.

You don't sound surprised.

I've spoken to a'Kasha too.

A sense of laughter in the ether. I should have known.

A pause. Kim got the impression of Wayne taking a deep breath. Listen, Kim, I need us to join forces. I was on my way to rejoin Jenny but saw a creature like that spider-demon I told you about heading for what used to be the Maghi warren. That's where Jenny is. I doubt I can confront that damned creature alone.

We're looking for the spider-demon too. It is the same one you fought.

Damn! But you said 'we'?

Yes. Follow these mental bread crumbs I'll send you and I'll explain when you get here. Can you sense them?

Yes.

We'll wait.

On my way.

"Well," Kim said to ArcNight. "Your twin will be here shortly."

ArcNight's cowl covered the upper half of his face but Kim was certain he cocked an inquisitive eyebrow.

It only took a couple of minutes for Wayne to show up, slipping among the ruins toward Kim. Kim's breath caught at the sight of him. It had been so long. She hadn't known if he was still alive or dead.

Brewster paused at the sight of the komainu, then reached out a hand to touch the lion-dog's nose. The komainu shook its great head and looked curiously as a wolf trotted up to Brewster's side.

No, Kim realized. Not a wolf, an Ōkami.

As the Ōkami and the komainu appraised one another, Kim and Brewster drew close. They both looked at each other and then, silently embraced. Kim fought back tears, not just at seeing Wayne safe again after all this time but at a feeling, a sense, something had changed forever between them. It was there, in his touch, his...his aura or energy. Kim didn't scan him with her powers, but she could feel the difference. "I'm glad you're safe," she said as they parted.

"Same here."

"Who's your Ōkami friend there?"

"That's Hiroshi."

"Hiroshi? As in Yoshida?"

"Sort of." Wayne smiled, an expression that used to thrill Kim. Now, she felt somehow resigned. And a little sad. "The Ōkami I fought at Spirit Winds, Inc. The displacement tremor took both of us to ArcNight's world in Dartham City. We wound up working together."

A momentary cloud passed over his features, then was gone. "I've got a lot to tell you, Kim"

As do I, she thought. But not now. She turned and gestured. "Wayne, meet ArcNight."

"Oh my god," Brewster said. "It really is you."

"Hello." ArcNight held out a gloved hand.

"Uh," Wayne stammered. "We won't blow up or anything, will we?"

"Not in this world." The two men shook hands, Kim marveling at the sight.

"You should know," Brewster said. "Orcus caused a lot of damage to Dartham, but he got sucked up here too."

"I know. Orcus is dead."

Brewster nodded. "Good. So is the Bespeller. But Quena's here."

"Hmmm. I ran into Quena in the real Venice and wondered what happened to him afterwards."

"He thought I was you."

"Aren't you lucky?"

"Also…" Brewster paused, glancing at Kim. "There's another Kim Yoshima in your world, ArcNight. And she's okay, at least the last I saw of her. She seemed concerned about you."

"Yes, I know of her." ArcNight also flicked his eyes toward Kim.

Well, this is strangely awkward although I'm not sure why. "Okay, guys," Kim said. "I know this isn't your normal meet-and-greet but enough chit-chat. Let's go find Omori/Damara."

Kim's esper-sense burned. The air in front of her a few feet away flickered. The rubble strewn around them quivered, the ground vibrated.

The komainu roared. The Ōkami snarled. Brewster whirled toward Kim. "Kim…?"

"Look out!" Kim screamed.

The ground erupted in a geyser of fire and debris. Shrapnel in the form of stone, brick, wood, and metal spewed up and outward.

Something hard hit Kim in the shoulder, piercing through the leather armor and into her skin. As she fell, ArcNight caught her and covered her with his body. A mass of rubble and flaming detritus crashed down upon them.

"**K**im!" Brewster shouted.

He and Hiroshi dove for cover from the flying debris caused by the explosion. But he'd seen Kim and ArcNight go under a flaming mass of scree.

The komainu shrugged off the fire raining down and faced in the direction of the explosion. The spider-demon/warlord chimera emerged from the smoke. Hulking, hideous, its many eyes flashed, its four working arms outstretched at its sides.

"Komainu!" it shrieked, pointing a clawed finger at the lion-dog. Its voice grated, alternating between male and female. Omori and Damara. "And Wayne Brewster! How gratifying to be able to kill the both of you at once."

"Like hell you will!" Brewster got to his feet, rage coursing through him. Before he could act, the komainu charged the chimera.

Another explosion ripped through the ground directly in front of the lion-dog. With a combination whine and roar, the komainu pitched over on its side and lay still.

"No!" Brewster ran toward the fallen komainu. Hiroshi loped at his side, barking at the chimera.

"I have been given superlative powers by the Maghi," the chimera hissed. "And in my semblance of both Damara and Omori, I can do anything!"

"Damn you!" Anger overcame Brewster's common sense as he knelt at the komainu's side. Beneath his fingers, the wounded yokai shuddered, growing smaller, until its statue form lay in its place.

Hiroshi yelped. Brewster looked up to see the Ōkami enshrouded in some kind of webbing. The wolf rolled on the ground, trying bite and claw his way out of the thick cocooning substance.

The chimera turned toward Brewster, strands of the web hanging from its hideous mouth. It lunged toward him.

Kim

Second Iteration

Kim's shoulder burned as if on fire. She writhed in pain, her vision cloudy. Blurred shapes twisted and ran before her tearing eyes like dripping paint.

"Aunt Kim. Aunt Kim!"

A young man's blond-headed, bearded face resolved, hovering over her. Long hair hung down past his shoulders. He had her nephew's eyes. "Bo...Bobby?"

"Yeah, it's me!"

"Bobby? How...?"

Bobby's T-shirt and shorts-clad body came into focus. Bobby? Bobby!

"Yes! My girlfriend, Marlene, and I are here. You've traveled forward in time to our future."

A young woman's face floated beside Bobby's, her own sweater and jeans startling to Kim in their simplicity. Behind them, walls, a ceiling, chairs and a desk became clear. Posters. A laptop computer. A dormitory room?

"You've been injected with spider venom," Bobby said. "We've got the anti-venom shot ready for you just like you told me. Marlene's a biology student and was able to get some. She'll give you the shot."

"What? What?"

"Aunt Kim! Please listen. You've got to remember so you can explain it all to me, as crazy as it sounds. You're here after being caught in an explosion caused by Damara, the spider-demon hybrid. She's infected you with her venom. Somehow, the explosion and maybe another force caused you to travel here, seven years into the future."

The future.

Kim felt a needle prick her arm. "I'm sorry, Ms. Yoshima," the woman, Marlene, said. Kim took notice of how pretty she was. "I hope we meet again under better circumstances."

"Kim," she said absurdly. "Please, call me Kim."

"You'll be yanked back to your own time in a minute," Bobby said. "It's because you've traveled forward in time, something about gravity and time dilation in reverse."

"Okay." Kim felt herself becoming unstuck, losing her connection to this time and place.

"You rock that outfit, Aunt Kim," Bobby said.

"Ha." Kim found herself smiling. Her shaky hands grasped both Bobby's and Marlene's. "Thank you. Thank you. I...won't forget, I promise. I...

Zone of Concealment

Kim pushed her psi-bubble upward, enlarging it enough to break through the imprisoning rock and stone covering her and ArcNight.

"Glad you got that shield up in time," ArcNight said as he stood and helped Kim to her feet.

"I couldn't have if you hadn't covered me," Kim said, breathing hard. "Thanks." She touched her shoulder. It was a little sore but not from the spider venom.

"Any time. You okay?"

Bobby and his girlfriend. In the freaking future. "Yes, it was just a glancing blow, luckily." I traveled to the future.

"Look!" ArcNight said. He and Kim ran over to a struggling Ōkami, completely wrapped in a web-like material.

"It's like spider's silk," ArcNight said.

I hope it's not venomous like what hit me. Kim carefully used her telekinetics like scissors to split the webbing. Hiroshi leaped to his feet, shaking off some of the leftover substance, sneezing and growling. He looked okay. "Where's Wayne and the komainu?" Kim asked the wolf, not knowing if she'd get an answer of not.

But Hiroshi trotted over to a statue lying on the ground.

"The komainu," Kim said, touching the warm stone. "In its alternate configuration."

"Perhaps it was injured," ArcNight ventured.

"Or maybe just knocked out."

ArcNight picked up the statue. "Whatever, he's coming with us."

Kim turned toward Hiroshi. "Wayne?"

Hiroshi barked and began sniffing the ground. Kim opened her mind, trying to find Wayne's neural signature.

"Anything?" ArcNight asked.

"No. He's being blocked somehow." She looked at ArcNight. "I wonder if your presence here cancels out his neural realm and vice versa."

"Go ahead. Take a look."

Kim attempted to peer inside ArcNight's mind. "No," she said. "Nothing there either. No offense."

ArcNight smiled. "None taken. I know what you meant."

Just as she sensed an approaching presence herself, ArcNight said, "Kim, something's coming." She and ArcNight ducked behind a fallen pile of rubble as Hiroshi crouched low.

A strange-looking quadruped came into view, moving swiftly but silently through the wreckage to her right. About the size of a horse, the tawny animal's head, affixed to a long, spotted neck, looked more like a bird. Behind it, two more beasts appeared--one an alligator-like creature with green feathers covering its long, tailed body, and a type of hominid, part ape, part human. It turned its brutish face toward Kim and ArcNight, then away, and continued on its lumbering way.

To Kim's left, a number of other odd beasties came into view, all moving in the same direction Omori had gone. But Kim detected no danger to herself from this motley group, but a purpose, yes, indistinct, but driving them all.

"Something's drawing them," Kim said.

"In the same general direction Hiroshi sniffed toward."

A familiar sense shot through Kim's mind. More than a tingle, a fiery mental alert. One she hadn't experienced since the battle at Spirit Winds, Inc.

I can feel it.

"Kim, what is it?"

"A temporal displacement tremor. The Spirit Winds. One's coming here. A big one with an accompanying aftershock."

"Maybe eight-point-zero on the Yoshima scale?"

"My nephew said you make a lot of wisecracks in your comic book. But this tremor'll be here soon and that's no laughing matter. That's why those stray creatures are moving this way. They sense it too and want to return to their true worlds."

317

"Sorry. My wisecracks are a defense mechanism. Even we super-heroes get nervous once in a while."

"I really wouldn't know about that."

"Oh, I'd say you fit very well into the super-hero category."

An impatient bark from Hiroshi kept Kim from responding. The Ōkami turned and loped off.

Kim rose and followed with ArcNight, the komainu clutched under one muscular arm, right behind her.

CHAPTER 37

Embrace the darkness; our birthing springs from the abyss.

Samuel Kim
The Teachings of Yira - The Five Precepts to Enlightenment

Castle DeGroot

Center Point, West Virginia

Kim

Third Iteration

The sub-basement beneath Castle DeGroot. She walks a long hallway lit by ambient ceiling lights. Passing closed doors interspersed at intervals, she finally stops in front of one particular door. An entry sensor and its control panel are inset in the wall alongside it.

She passes her hand over the sensor. The door opens.

A figure rises at the opposite end of a padded room. A dwayyo, recovered from the tranquilizer given it.

"You're free," she says.

The dwayyo lunges toward her.

"Ugh!"

Kim fell back against a hard surface, her back and head bouncing up against a wall. A small rug she must have slipped on lay bunched up at her feet. She lay there for a moment, her head throbbing, before realizing she wasn't alone. She looked up.

Joe Martin knelt at her side. "Kim, you okay?"

"Joe! What in heaven?" She looked past Joe who, she noticed, wore a shoulder holster strapped on beneath his T-shirt with its accompanying firearm.

T'sai stood behind him, one hand on her hip, the other holding her crossbow pistol. The three of them were in a large bedroom. "Not as smooth a trip this time, huh?" she said. "Sorry about that. Your friend

Joe insisted he come with us, and who am I to refuse such a gorgeous hunk?"

"I wasn't about to let you out of my sight again," he said. Then with a wry grin, "Besides, with Kim 2.0 here, how lucky can a fella get with two Kim Yoshimas?"

Kim smiled. "Smart ass. But thanks."

"You bet."

Joe helped Kim to her feet. She winced at a shot of pain in her elbow. "What have you done?" she demanded of T'sai, rubbing her arm. Then, to her friend, "Joe, how the hell did you get hooked up with that…that…djinn, for heaven's sake!"

"I'll tell you all about it later. It's pretty involved."

"Yeah, relax, girlfriend, chill," T'sai said. "It's okay. Bobby's back home with a newly enlightened father."

"Joe?"

"It's true, Kim."

Wow. Kim felt a surge of relief well up within her. "Are they safe?" she asked both Joe and T'sai.

"Talera and Nolu have been reunited and are back where they belong. They won't be bothering anyone in this reality anymore."

"Where are we?"

"Where and when. We're several hours ahead of the previous temporal nodal point at the library. You know, just a little further ahead in the timeline to give your other iteration some time to do her thing. While you traveled here, I was able to delay my and Joe's arrival to sync up with yours until we got Ken and Bobby settled. Welcome to Castle De Groot. I believe you have some unfinished business to settle with its owner."

"Both of us do," Joe added grimly.

"Don't tell me," Kim said, searching Joe's face. "Parker."

"Oh, yeah," T'sai said.

Kim flinched, as much as from the irony of the situation as the danger of it. "Okay, as eager as I am to stop Parker once and for all, I…we, need to wrap this up asap, so I can get back to the Zone of Concealment."

Joe frowned. "The what?"

Kim threw her hands up. "This is so damn frustrating. I…" Kim paused, reining in her annoyance. "Okay, okay, sorry, Joe. I'll explain later. What do we do now?"

Joe held up a fist. "I don't know about you but I'm going to kick Parker's ass."

Kim found herself grinning despite herself. "Get in line, Mr. Martin."

"That might not be so satisfying," T'sai said. "As I mentioned earlier, Parker's in pretty bad shape. His 'resurrection' has taken its toll on him. Kim's nephew Bobby could probably take him. However, I could see Joe and Parker's man Tammelou engaging in a pretty mean cage match."

"Bring him on," Joe said.

"All right, let's figure this out first," Kim cut in. "Make a plan. How many security or followers does Parker have here?"

"Around twelve total since the dwayyo killed four. Though six of those twelve remaining were injured in the dwayyo attack, three who didn't sustain serious wounds were immediately back on the job. So, along with Tammelou, that makes ten. Of course, I'm not a part of that force any longer."

"So you say."

"You still don't trust me? I'm shocked, sister. You should know me, or you, better than that."

"Please, Kim," Joe said. "I know you've been through a lot, but we need you to calm down and focus. You've got to be at your best here. Believe it or not, I trust Kim 2.0. She helped us out with Bobby."

"What if this is a ruse just to get me here for Parker?"

T'sai snorted. "It's always all about you, isn't it? The vaunted Yomitsu. The center of the universe."

"Well, all these spectral beings I've been encountering tell me what an honor it is to meet me. I think you better treat me with a little respect. Sister."

"Yo, ladies." Joe held up his hands. "Peace, okay? Kim, I reckon if T'sai wanted to deliver us to Parker, she wouldn't have brought us to this room. Just saying."

"Thanks, handsome," T'sai smirked. "Well, Kim?"

Kim sighed. "All right. So, you know this place, T'sai. Where do we go from here?"

"Hey, check this out." Joe motioned to Kim and T'sai to join him at one of the windows.

"Huh," T'sai muttered. "I wonder how that happened."

Kim stared down at the grounds outside the castle. A wide, finely manicured lawn had become a killing ground. Seven men and women lay scattered, parts of their clothes bloody.

She remembered.

"Damn," Joe muttered. "That's some nasty work."

"No, they're not dead," Kim said. "Just unconscious though beaten up."

"How do you know that?" T'sai asked.

"An hour ago, relatively speaking, I exited the slipstream and made sure the captured dwayyo could get loose and the rest of her tribe join her before we arrived. I hoped they might wreak some havoc, which it looks like they've done."

"Well," T'sai snorted. "You're just full of surprises, aren't you? Just how did you know where to go?"

"From Ken's mind. His memories were pretty solid. Plus, with some information from a'Kasha, I was able to split off and get to the sub-basement."

"Why haven't you done that before?"

"I think I may have." Kim smiled. "You said it, T'sai. The multiverse works in mysterious ways."

"And why didn't those creatures kill anyone?" Joe asked.

"That's not what they do," T'sai said. "They're not killers."

"I sensed that," Kim said. "Else I wouldn't have released their leader."

A thrupping sound broke in on the conversation. Kim looked up. Two military-style helicopters dropped from above, a familiar logo emblazoned on their sides. "Spirit Winds, Inc.," she said. "The Shuugouteki are here. That is, one of their Hunter-Squads."

Below, the dwayyo came into view, waving their arms, snarling and shrieking at the choppers. The helicopters set down on the huge lawn, their doors opening. Sure enough, men and women wearing the uniforms of a Collective Hunter-Squad exited, leveling their weapons at the dwayyo.

Then…

"Huh!" T'sai said. "What are those?"

"I think I know," Joe said. "I've read about them. Leshii, Appalachian folk monsters."

Four of the leshii stepped down from the second chopper, holding out their long, rangy arms in front of them. The foremost leshii cried out in an unknown language, directing its words at the dwayyo.

"That your work too, Kim?" Joe asked.

"No, but I think it's a good thing."

"We need to get down there," T'sai said. "I need to herd those beasties and you two have to find out where Parker and Tammelou are."

"If they're still alive," Joe said.

"I'm pretty sure they are." With that, T'sai exited the room. Kim and Joe followed. They ran down a long, carpeted staircase to what appeared to be a sitting room or some kind of parlor.

One that, Kim thought, had seen better days.

Chairs, tables, and lamps had been overturned and broken. The stained glass of a huge bay window had been shattered, brocade curtains slashed. A chandelier had been ripped from the ceiling, pieces littering the wooden floor. Books were upended from floor-to-ceiling shelves and scattered.

Two bodies were sprawled, mangled, broken, covered in blood. There was a smell...

"Parker's men," T'sai said. "That's nine out of ten dead. This way."

The huntress ran through what remained of splintered wooden doors onto a large outdoor patio. Kim looked at Joe who returned her concerned gaze. They ran after T'sai.

The chopper blades had slowed but the wind caused by their rotating still whipped across the lawn. Kim held back the hair from her eyes as T'sai went straight to the group of leshii and dwayyo. The creatures stood facing each other, some type of communication taking place.

"This is weird," Joe said. "Then again, most things that have happened since you came along, Kim, have been weird. But..." He took her hand. "I wouldn't change a thing."

Kim smiled. "But we're not done yet."

"Parker and his thug."

"Right."

Two of the hunter-squad approached. One was tall and Caucasian, the other of medium height and Asian. Both wore crypsis camouflage skinsuits, impact helmets, and flexible body armor. Behind them, other members of the squad began tending to the fallen Totou.

"Kim Yoshima?" the tall one asked. "The Yomitsu?"

"Yes. And please don't say it's an honor to meet me."

The man grinned. "Yes, ma'am. I guess you get that a lot, huh? I'm DragonEye Hunter Squad leader Peter Gurkovsky, and this is my second-in-command Steven Kikuchi."

"Konichiwa, Yomitsu-san," Kikuchi said with a bow.

"Pleasure, both of you. This is Joe Martin. You don't seem surprised to see us."

"Our sensors picked up your heat signatures. Yours is rather unique and matched what we have on file, so we suspected you might be here."

Ah, technology. Kim looked behind the two men. A tall, dark-haired woman had just gotten out of one of the helicopters. She wore prison fatigues, a blinking shock-anklet encircling one calf. "Who's that woman?"

Gurkovsky said, "Rebecca Parantala, the Totou inquisitor."

"I've heard of her. She's got the special memory, right? More than eidetic. Has she turned?"

"In a sense. She really didn't have a choice. Her detailed recollection of Parker's connection with Martin Sakai led us here. Sakai's family used to own this place."

Parantala turned to look at Kim. Something sparked in the beautiful Totou agent's eyes, something that sent a chill through Kim. This woman, despite her capture and cooperation, was still dangerous. Perhaps deadly.

"Keep her under wraps," Kim said.

"Yes, ma'am, we intend to. She's got a head full of information that may prove valuable."

"What about the leshii?"

"The leshii were able to pick up on the dwayyos presence here. Some kind of cryptid ESP thing, I guess. They insisted they could help so we brought them along. We recovered them from a Totou safe house in West Virginia where the late Xavier La Tan had taken up residence. That's where we found Parantala. Lying unconscious on the back of a kirin, of all things."

"A kirin? Named Trell?"

"That's the one. You know him?"

"Yes. He's one of the good guys. Team Leader, have you picked up any other heat signatures besides the ones here?"

"No, ma'am." Gurkovsky tilted his head, possibly listening to what Kim assumed was his shoulder-comm. "Excuse us. We've got to finish securing this area."

"You think Parker and his goon got away?" Joe asked as Gurkovsky and Kikuchi walked back toward the choppers.

"We need to look but let's check with T'sai first." Kim paused. "You were right about trusting her, Joe. Thanks."

"Hey, I think I'm a pretty good judge of character." He frowned. "Except for my ex-wife."

Kim snorted. "I can relate. My ex-husband wasn't who I thought he was. Too bad my esper powers weren't active during my marriage."

"I hear that."

When they joined T'sai, the leshii, and the dwayyo, one of the leshii was speaking to T'sai in English, angrily it seemed to Kim.

"We were afraid you would keep us away from our home," the leshii said.

"I wanted to return you to your home," T'sai retorted.

"This world is our home." The leshii bristled. "The land the humans call Russia. Here, in this world."

"As our home is in this world also, the realm of Appalachia," the dwayyo added. "Not in some other distant time and place."

Kim and T'sai looked at each other. "So they're real," Kim said. "Real in our world, not just legends at all."

T'sai smiled. "I'll be damned."

The dwayyo noticed Kim. "You are the Yomitsu. You set me free."

"Yes. My brother Ken wished for me to help you."

"I remember your brother. You and he have our thanks."

A familiar sense shot through Kim's mind. More than a tingle, a fiery mental alert. One she hadn't experienced since the battle at Spirit Winds, Inc.

I can feel it.

"Kim, what is it?"

"A temporal displacement tremor. The Spirit Winds. One's coming here. A big one with an accompanying aftershock. T'sai, you need to take the leshii and the dwayyo to the site of the impending tremor so they can return to their homes in Russia and Appalachia. It's...there." She pointed to a small patio a hundred yards away. "That's where the tremor will arrive."

"Yes. That's the least I can do."

"All right then. I've got to find Parker."

"Nice working with you, quantum sister."

Kim nodded. "We'll see each other again, have no doubt."

T'sai blew Joe a kiss. "I'd love to see you later, handsome, but it's not in the cards."

"Thanks, T'sai," Joe said. "I mean it."

"Look below in the castle basement first, Kim, above the sub-basement," T'sai said. "Parker's got a safe-room there where he might be holed up. But take Joe with you, esper powers or not. Tammelou's no pushover."

CHAPTER 38

In such a place as this would miracles happen? Never
could I have guessed this.
The *kami* do work in mysterious ways.

Yoshima Mitsu, the Luminous One

Zone of Concealment

"**A**ll of you!" Daiyu shouted as she crossed her forearms in front
of her chest. "Estansa will be occupied with the separation
barrier. Concentrate only on her thralls!"

The four Maghi sorcerers split up, each one going after Daiyu and
her companions. One sped toward her, tall and thin beneath his flaring
robe, red eyes flashing within the dark oval of his cowl. He reached
out a skeletal hand. A flash of light emanated from his fingertips. The
ground beneath Daiyu cracked and heaved upward.

Daiyu spread her arms and floated up above the fissure that had
opened below her feet. She landed a few feet away and brought the
palms of her hands together in a loud clap.

The attacking Maghi's head snapped back as Daiyu's magic struck
him like a fist, his hood falling from his cadaver-like face. He is ravaged,
Daiyu noted. He and the others have been taken from Aizenev. The
sorcerer stumbled for a moment, whirled and leaped toward Daiyu in
a flying one-legged kick.

Daiyu blocked the kick with her crossed wrists. The Maghi landed
clumsily on both feet at her side. Daiyu stiffened the fingers of her
right hand and rammed a knife-like thrust into the Maghi's neck. As
the sorcerer cried out and dropped to one knee, Daiyu uttered a quick
incantation and stepped back.

The sorcerer fell flat to the ground, his body withering and turning
to ash until only the robe was left.

David Amamoto crouched in a defensive stance, keeping his eyes
on the onrushing Maghi. This one had dropped his hood, a sneer
twisting the features on his emaciated face. Evidently, he thought David
wouldn't be much of a problem.

"Come on!" Amamoto shouted. He didn't go through two years of war to be beaten by this freak!

With a flick of the Maghi's bony wrist, four small glowing spheres appeared floating in the space between Amamoto and the Maghi. Those spheres quickly became long, gleaming knives, spinning in the air and hurtling straight toward Amamoto.

Amamoto pivoted under and around the first two knives, the sharp blades barely missing him. Without thinking, he held up the jade tiger he still clutched in his hand. The third and fourth blades swerved to either side of David, clattering behind him against the black barrier Milaar had erected.

His attacker stood shocked, staring at the figurine. David shook off his own surprise and threw the figurine as hard as he could at the Maghi. The tiger struck the sorcerer in the chest and burst into green fire. The Maghi screamed, his robe lighting up like a tinderbox. Flailing like a windblown paper doll, the sorcerer fell in flames to the ground.

Jaraal would get his fight after all, it seemed. Grinning, his hackles raised, he charged his attacker. The Maghi, a woman, drew a glowing symbol in the air before her. At her shouted command, the symbol shot forward and enveloped Jaraal like a lasso.

Jaraal stopped as if he'd hit a wall. Growling and spitting, he struggled to break the invisible bonds holding him, straining, pushing. The sorceress approached and slashed a hand downward in a cutting motion.

The shackling energy began to squeeze, crushing Jaraal's body, pressing into him. Jaraal gasped, his breath cut off. No, he thought. Not force.

He shut out the pain and brought another of his powers to bear. Quickly, he metamorphosed, his warrior's body shrinking, falling into itself, until he became Hideo, his cat persona. Smaller by far, Hideo wriggled out from the clothes he wore as Jaraal and slipped beneath and through the binding spell.

Hissing, his fur standing on end, Hideo leapt at the surprised sorceress. His claws whipped at the woman as he slammed against her chest. Her throat ripped open, the woman fell gurgling to the ground.

Zaronelli easily avoided the magic energy shot at him by his Maghi attacker. Though his wounded side cried out in pain, Zaronelli moved swiftly, forming a tethering spell to grasp hold of two of the knives David's attacker had conjured. Picking them up from the ground, Zaronelli whirled, one arm outstretched and directed the knives at the Maghi.

The sorcerer tried to avoid the blades but the speed which Zaronelli magically threw them was too great. His neck and heart pierced, the Maghi was dead before he hit the ground.

Zaronelli turned toward the lamia Milaar, who focused on keeping the separation barrier intact. "There was a time, Estansa," Zaronelli said, "when you could maintain more than one spell at a time. Like your minions here, you too have been diminished."

"Orcus take you, Zaronelli!" Milaar hissed, her features showing the strain of her spell casting. "I am still stronger than you."

"But not both of us."

Zaronelli turned as Daiyu came to his side.

"And you, Daiyu of the East! You should have died long ago!" Milaar turned away from the barrier and flung an arm toward Daiyu. A rippling stream of red light blazed toward the sorceress from Milaar's hand.

NO! Zaronelli thought. I couldn't help her once before. I can now.

Zaronelli stepped in front of Daiyu, throwing his hands up. The red light cast by Milaar erupted like an exploding star. Daiyu positioned herself beside him, raising her hands to add her power to his. Both propelled their magical energy at the lamia.

Milaar screamed, flying off her feet into the wall behind her. She slid to the floor, shrieking.

The black barrier dissolved.

Amanozako and her army surged forward unerringly toward Milaar.

⸻

"We've done it," Daiyu said, turning to Zaronelli.

"Yes," Zaronelli said, his face deathly pale. "I...am glad." His eyelids fluttered and he fell forward.

"No!" Daiyu caught him before he hit the ground. "Amedio!" Blood gushed from a wound on Zaronelli's side. As she lay him down, Daiyu realized some of Milaar's deadly magic had gotten through Zaronelli's defense, reopening his injury.

He had taken the death blow meant for her.

"No, no, Amedio." Not like this. Not for me!

"Ah, Daiyu," Zaronelli whispered. "At last my long sleep is over. I am sorry. I wish… I wish…"

She held Zaronelli's lifeless body, sobbing. *Another life gone because of me!*

The soft touch of a hand on her shoulder turned her face up and around. Lazo Sibulovich towered above her. He leaned over and gently pulled her to her feet. She fell against him, crying and shaking.

"Over here," Lazo said softly. He led Daiyu to where Estansa Milaar lay against the wall, groaning. Another woman stood with her back to the lamia, a corona of blue light surrounding her. Daiyu gasped, pulling away from Lazo.

"Lazo," Daiyu said, as if noticing him for the first time. "And you are his wife, yes?"

"I'm Jenny, yes. Daiyu, I presume?"

Daiyu bowed her head. "I am at your mercy, noble Archive. Do what you will with me."

"Archive?" Milaar rasped, coming fully awake. "She of the Void? What madness is this? That cannot be."

"Oh," Lazo said with a smirk. "It be, all right."

"Hello, Estansa," Jenny said sweetly. "Eat any good cigarettes lately?"

"You!" Milaar gaped. "How…?"

"Close your eyes, everyone," Jenny said. "And cover your ears. Now!"

A whirling dizziness struck Daiyu as a sudden breeze kicked up. A roaring, like a great wave crashing to shore, sounded all around her. A brilliant flash of light surrounded the monstros. Amanozako and her army began to break apart. Their bodies wavered in and out of sight as if being pulled in many directions at once.

She saw Amanozako gazing reverently at Jenny. The goddess' expression radiated surprise and…joy. She and the monstros dematerialized in a blinding lambent explosion.

Again, strong hands grasped Daiyu, this time those of Jaraal. He supported her as her trembling legs threatened to give out beneath her.

"You sent the monstros away in order for them to return to their correct times and places, Noble One?" Jaraal asked.

"Yes. I directed a displacement tremor to arrive here. I've that ability now, to rein in the Spirit Winds, to get the cosmic house in order. At least for a while." For a moment, a rapt expression overcame Jenny's features. For a moment. Then, "I've already gotten some, shall we say, instructions on certain matters but I've still got a lot to learn."

"And I?" Jaraal asked.

"You're an exception, Jaraal," Lazo said. "I'm afraid you've got more work to do in our world."

"But." Jenny smiled. "It's been arranged, Jaraal, for your family to join you here for the duration of your stay."

Jaraal's cat eyes widened in surprise. "Noble Archive. You have my gratitude," he said with a bow.

Milaar fell to her knees, groveling pitifully. "Forgive me, Numinous Lady," she wailed. "I was bespelled."

"Yes, bespelled by your own evil and lust for power." Jenny stabbed Milaar with an angry glare. "You have a different fate awaiting you, Grand Mistress. One that won't be so quick and easy as death."

Milaar opened her mouth to scream. And disappeared.

Jenny turned to Daiyu. "And you," Jenny said her eyes hard.

Daiyu stiffened. Ah, so the great powers, through the Archive, would punish her for her negligence and weakness. "Indeed, Noble Archive. Do with me what you will. I am undeserving of serving the Radiant Way."

"Nonsense! You're not going anywhere, Daiyu," Jenny said, a smile lighting up her face. "I'm sorry for your losses but what happened to Lydia, Lenora, and Amedio wasn't your fault. They gave their lives willingly to save all of you."

"Could you not have saved Amedio?" Daiyu asked bitterly, instantly regretting her question.

"In this case, no." Jenny's expression saddened. "It has to be this way, I'm afraid, but you can't let their deaths be in vain. They certainly wouldn't want that, and I don't think you would either. You have more work to do, Daiyu. We all do." She glanced at Lazo as if for confirmation.

Lazo shrugged. "She's the Archive. Knows all. Sees all."

Daiyu placed her hands against her chest, the tears flowing again but this time for a different reason.

CHAPTER 39

We have to erase this history of the Jade Court. It has to be done to ensure the sequence of future events plays out correctly. The future has to be secure.

Shioko Yoshima as the Glorious Ko

Castle DeGroot

Center Point, West Virginia

Kim

Third Iteration

"**Y**ou know the safe-room's this way because of Ken's memories too?" Joe asked, pulling his firearm from its shoulder holster. He and Kim had entered Castle DeGroot through the front entrance, heading to the rear of a large library room.

"Yes. Right before T'sai transported us here, I got a strong visual from Ken's mind."

"Better than a GPS, huh?"

"Right. This way." Kim walked to a set of drapes drawn across a large recess in one wall. Pulling aside the drapes, she pressed a single button inset on the wall. A partition slid aside, revealing an elevator.

Kim gasped. She put a hand out to steady herself against the wall. Dizzy. The bilocation. My powers are waning.

"Kim."

"I'm okay." She pushed the button again and the elevator doors opened. With Joe right behind her, she stepped inside the lift.

Zone of Concealment

Kim

Second Iteration

Up ahead, a lone building seemed to have escaped the destruction of its neighbors. Though damaged, the several-story structure stood mostly intact. A copy of some kind of modern apartment building, Kim thought. That's where it looked like the Damara/Omori chimera had taken Wayne. At least that's where Hiroshi indicated they should go. He stood apart from Kim and ArcNight, his attention focused on the building.

Why didn't the chimera kill Wayne outright? Kim wondered.

"I'm going to circle around to the back of the building," ArcNight said. "Better to go at it from two sides. Besides, me being farther away might allow you to contact Brewster." He pulled a small gun from his service belt. "Mini flare gun," he said. "It holds two charges. Use it to protect yourself or to signal me when you've found Brewster."

"Okay, thanks. Be careful."

ArcNight headed away, his cape billowing behind him. Kim watched him for a moment then once more followed a waiting Hiroshi. As they got closer to the building, a large shape shambled out of the doorway.

The hominid she'd seen earlier. The apelike creature trilled like a bird, picked up a stone lintel as if weighed nothing and threw it at Hiroshi. The Ōkami dodged and lunged toward the hominid. The wolf stopped and quickly backed up as a second hominid lumbered out of the building to join the first.

No time for this! Kim called up a psi-stun but her esper energy fizzled and faded. Oh, Hell, she thought, fighting off a sudden wooziness. It's the bilocation. It's weakening me again. Has to be. She gripped the flare gun, thankful ArcNight had given it to her.

Hiroshi barked at Kim as it pranced close to the two hominids then away, drawing the creatures from the building entrance. It was plain what the Ōkami meant. Go after Wayne, Kim reasoned. I'll hold the fort here. Picking up her pace, she ran into the building.

Kim

Third Iteration

The elevator doors opened directly into the safe-room.

"Look out!" Kim cried. A very large man fired a pistol point-blank into the lift. Kim barely formed a psi-bubble, just strong enough to repel the bullets. Tammelou!

Joe raised his Beretta as Kim dropped the bubble but Tammelou lunged forward into the elevator. He slammed Joe into the back wall of the lift, knocking Joe's gun from his hand. "Get out!" Joe cried. "Get Parker!"

Kim stepped out of the elevator just as Joe kicked the button panel. The elevator doors closed. Kim stumbled into the safe-room, falling to her knees. Get up, Yoshima! she thought. Shake it off!

She stood just as something hard and terribly sharp tore into her thigh. She fell against the elevator, a crossbow bolt imbedded in her leg. Pain lanced through her, adding to the weakness of her superpositioned nature.

Across the room, a wheelchair-bound skeleton of a man cackled triumphantly, holding a crossbow. "Kim Yoshima!" Parker howled. "At last!"

Joe knew he was outmatched. Tammelou was bigger, stronger. The Samoan crushed Joe against the back of the elevator, his left hand around Joe's throat. He slowly pushed his gun hand, which Joe held by the wrist, down toward Joe's head.

But the big man had been injured. A bandage lay against the side of his head and his left forearm was encased in a cast, hooking around his thumb. Which didn't stop him from choking Joe but if Joe could reinjure that arm…

The elevator shuddered to a stop, the doors opening.

Gritting his teeth, Joe hooked one foot behind the Samoan's calf and shoved himself away from the wall. He knocked an off-balance Tammelou through the open lift doors and the curtain shielding the elevator into the library.

Tammelou crashed to his back, his hold on Joe's throat loosening. Joe reared up and punched the Samoan, not in the face, but in his forearm cast. Once… Twice. Tammelou roared in pain, bringing his legs up to knee Joe in the back.

Joe fell off Tammelou but grabbed the Samoan's gun hand. He rammed his elbow down into Tammelou's throat. Choking and gagging, Tammelou let go of the gun. Joe scooped it up and scrambled to his feet.

"Freeze, motherfucker!" Joe cried, pointing the weapon at Tammelou. His own throat throbbed, his back aching, but he held the gun steadily pointed at the Samoan's head.

"Damn you," Tammelou croaked, getting to his knees. "You can kill me but never the Eminent Lord. Never."

"Don't do it!" Joe ordered. Joe had been out of the military for several years. But in his deployment in Afghanistan, he'd learned there were some actions that needed to be taken in order to survive. "I've killed better men than you."

Tammelou bellowed like a wounded animal and leaped at Joe.

Kim

Second Iteration

Kim bit back a scream and leaned against a wall of the tower's first floor. Her leg…

Something's happened, she thought, grimacing at the pain shooting through her thigh. My other iteration has been hurt.

Blocking off the pain as best she could, she sent out her esper sight. ArcNight was right. Distancing himself from Kim allowed Kim to pick up Wayne's mental essence. Faint, but it was there, leading to one of the upper floors.

She limped up a set of stairs, listening for any sound. She had to hope her esper powers would be strong enough to face off against the chimera. If not, the flare gun would have to do. Here! A second-floor hallway; the trail led through here.

As she made her way quietly down the hall, the sounds of voices reached her from one of the rooms to her right. Chanting? Raising the flare gun, she glanced into a room. The wooden door had been torn off its hinges, scattered in pieces inside the room. Furniture lay tumbled against the walls, the middle of the room cleared away. The Omori/Damara chimera stood, her back to the door, facing a set of sliding glass doors that opened onto a balcony. At the chimera's feet lay a large…cocoon?

No. Like Hiroshi, Brewster had been entwined with the monstrous webbing. The bundle of spider silk jerked, Brewster struggling. He was still alive! The chimera did indeed chant as if performing some kind of ritual. Kim started, noticing long strands of white hair hanging from the chimera's head where none had been before.

Kim's eyes flicked to a corner of the room. A mangled, bloody body lay there. It looked to have been partially devoured. Judging by the clothes it wore, it had been Estansa Milaar.

The chimera whirled. "Yomitsu! You still live." Three voices vied for

Kim's attention, each one underlying the other, like echoes. Damara. Omori. And now Milaar. "Was it you who sent us the lamia to consume? If so, we thank you. With her magic and this umana to employ as a sacrifice, we can summon Orcus ourselves."

"Kim!" Wayne cried, part of his face breaking through the webbing. "Get out of here!"

"Not on your life!" Kim pointed the flare gun. "Get away from him, Omori or whoever you are, or I'll shoot."

The chimera chortled. "You will not. You can't risk harming your precious Wayne Brewster."

"Do it, Kim!" Wayne shouted. "Shoot it!"

Kim moved into the room, her thigh throbbing, sweat forming on her forehead. She licked her lips.

"And your famous mental powers aren't what they once were, are they?" the chimera crooned.

It was true. Kim couldn't form any kind of mental weapon. She struggled to stay focused. At that moment, her thoughts freed, her mind opening.

Kim! It's Jenny. Listen to me. This is what's going to happen.

A heartbeat later, a very surprised Kim pointed the flare gun to her left and fired a charge through the open balcony doors.

CHAPTER 40

In the comics, you heroes can talk and talk while battling
your enemies and never miss a punch but
that doesn't work here.

Kim Yoshima

Zone of Concealment

ArcNight dropped to the second-floor balcony, his cape fanning out behind him like raptor's wings. He released his one-handed hold on his tether-rope, the other hand still grasping the komainu statue. He placed the statue down on the balcony and raced through the open glass doors.

Kim Yoshima stood with her back to a wall, the flare gun he'd given her raised. A monster out of some insane nightmare faced her from across the room. The other Wayne Brewster lay on the floor, trapped in thick coils of what could only be the creature's spiderwebbing.

"ArcNight!" Yoshima cried. "Help me!" The beast roared. It swung its ugly head back and forth between Yoshima and ArcNight, momentarily perplexed at the sight of this masked interloper. Before the beast could act, ArcNight leaped upward toward the creature in a flying drop-kick, hitting it squarely in its chitinous chest. Screeching in surprise, the beast stumbled backwards through the doorway and into the hall.

As the creature started back into the room, ArcNight rolled to his feet and picked up a long board that used to be part of the door. He broke it across the face of the creature, once more knocking the monster back into the corridor.

"Let's go!" he yelled to Yoshima. "I'll carry Brewster."

"No!" He glanced at her in surprise. Yoshima looked shaken but there was a determined set to her jaw. "What...?"

"We have to stop it here!" she cried. "The displacement tremor I told you about is coming here. Just keep it occupied for another couple of minutes!" And then she darted out onto the balcony.

"Do it!" Brewster shouted from the floor. "She's got an idea!"

Quickly, ArcNight ran over to his fallen double and, pulling a small laser cutter from his belt, severed the web holding Brewster captive.

"Thanks!" Brewster said as ArcNight helped him to his feet. "I thought you and Kim were dead."

"Kim saved us."

The screeching of the chimera almost broke ArcNight's eardrums as it reentered the room. "Go help Kim," he ordered Brewster. "I'll hold it off! Go!"

As Brewster ran after Yoshima, ArcNight scrambled among four grasping arms and delivered a series of quick, hard punches to the creature's body. Though it was huge and strong and protected by its hard shell, the chimera could still feel pain and hesitated at this new onslaught. Taking advantage of the thing's indecision, ArcNight pulled a small capsule from his service belt and broke it in the chimera's face. A cloud of gas shot up the creature's slash-of-a-nose. The monster yowled like a banshee and doubled over, one set of arms clawing at its face while the other set groped for its opponent.

Swinging its head wildly, it released a string of webbing from its mouth, but ArcNight ducked under the gooey shot and, getting behind the chimera, leaped up on the creature's back. Wrapping his powerful arms around the chimera's neck, ArcNight applied pressure, hoping its physiology was even a little like a human's so he could at least weaken it.

Two clawed hands grabbed him and tore him away, dispelling that notion. The chimera flung ArcNight across the room into the opposite wall. He fell to the floor, dazed, but protected by his suit's armor. He got to his feet as the chimera clenched four clawed hands at its side. Its eyes burned, aglow.

It's going to create another explosion, ArcNight thought. The stone! He'd forgotten the gemstone the karura had given him. He pulled it from his pouch and threw it at the chimera. It exploded into fiery light. The chimera shrieked and stumbled back.

"Damara! Omori! Milaar!"

The creature swiveled its head to the left. Kim Yoshima stood at the balcony doors with Brewster by her side. She held the komainu sculpture in her arms. "Here's the one you really want," she said. Stepping forward, she knelt and placed the statue on the floor. "You didn't kill it with those cowardly explosions of yours. It's still alive."

The chimera stared at the lion-dog, then bent down, putting its monstrous hands upon the statue. ArcNight remembered what he'd been told of the spider-demon, how it had been supposedly killed by Jackson Yamaguchi's magical guardian, the shapeshifting being who could alternate forms between a statue and the giant living komainu creature.

"Now," Kim whispered.

The komainu rippled, changing. It grew into its giant living lion-dog form in an instant. One huge paw slashed at the surprised chimera, knocking the Omori/Damara/Milaar hybrid creature to the floor. The komainu backed away as the air in the room thickened, feeling sharp and tingling as if charged.

Kim and Brewster motioned to ArcNight to move back with them also. ArcNight had felt this sensation before.

"The displacement tremor aftershock!" Kim cried over a sudden roaring. "This tower is its nexus point!"

The chimera roared, struggling to rise. Abruptly a blazing ring of light enveloped it. The chimera vanished, sucked into the Void.

I can go back, ArcNight thought, the realization shocking him. He looked at Yoshima.

"Yes!" she said. "Jenny's arranged one final trip."

"It's been an honor!" ArcNight shouted. "I won't forget any of you!" He stepped into the light.

"**Y**ou too, Wayne."

Brewster frowned as he and Kim stood against a cosmic wind, buffeted once more by elemental forces. "What are you talking about?"

"The Spirit Winds take everyone where they're meant to be, remember? Jenny's shutting the tremors down, at least she's making them much fewer and far, far between, more stable. This'll be the last one for a very long time. You can make this journey. I know it's what you've wanted. The choice is yours."

There it was. The decision he'd been putting off for far too long, denying it since Odawara.

"Kim, I..."

Kim threw her arms around him. He returned the embrace, hard. "It's okay," she said. "Take this for luck." She gave him the Sanctuary Elder's paper kirin. Trell. "Now go. Tell Shioko and Jackson I love them. And give all the bad guys Hell." She smiled. "Ebon Warrior."

She pulled back. Brewster raised a hand in farewell and let the Spirit Winds take him away.

Kim

Second Iteration

The light vanished, the wind ceased. Kim stood alone with the komainu, once more in its statue configuration.

Damn, she thought. There's got to be an easier way to save the world. She thought she might cry but instead started to giggle. Especially one that pays!

"Kim!" Daiyu rushed into the room. "Jenny transported me here."

"It worked, Daiyu," Kim said, wiping sudden tears from her eyes. "Jenny's newfound power." A sudden vibration shot through the floor.

"We must leave," Daiyu said. "This pocket of reality is collapsing. The Mystic Realm and a Sanctuary Elder are helping Jenny to restabilize this section of the multiverse."

Kim staggered. Goddess, she was tired!

"Kim, Jenny explained what you've done. You must reintegrate yourself quickly!"

"I... I think I need a little help..."

Daiyu caught her just before she fell.

Kim

Third Iteration

Parker, in his desiccated state, fumbled with the crossbow, trying to load another bolt. His bony hands fluttered like bird wings. Drool dripped from his blubbering mouth. "Damn your primitive weapon, T'sai!" he croaked.

Blood ran down Kim's leg from the bolt's wound. She grit her teeth against the pain and recoiled at the hideous sight of Parker. "Parker, you son-of-a-bitch."

"I'll kill you!" Parker shrieked. "Even if I die, I'll take you with me."

Not if I can help it. I won't let this happen! Kim concentrated her failing esper energy. Playing a last, desperate hunch, she sent a thin beam of thought straight at Parker's warped mind. It penetrated the madman's mental barriers, returning Kim to a neural landscape at once familiar and devastatingly different.

Flames consumed what had been the vast wheat field of Parker's neural landscape. The bodies of water dotting the countryside boiled and bubbled. The once-blue sky had turned blood red. Kim and Omori stood on a hillock, surrounded by encroaching fire. The warlord held his arms out at his sides, as if holding back the scorching heat. "Yomitsu!" he cried. "You can't defeat me. You can't win."

"I don't intend to defeat you." Kim looked to the smoke-filled horizon, seeing who she hoped to see. A shadow there moved, getting closer.

I know who you are, Kim thought-sent. You were never the reincarnation of Omori. Omori invaded your mind when you were a child, taking over your body and imprisoning you here in your own subconscious.

It's true! It's true! The shadow cried.

Kim reached out. Go. I've set you free.

The smoke became a man, old, naked, his eyes lit up with hate. He faced Omori.

"Who are you?" the warlord asked, jerking in surprise.

"You know who I am. I'm Jeffrey Parker, the essence of the man you took over."

Omori's mouth dropped, his eyes widened. "Impossible! You are subsumed. Parker is me, reborn."

"No. I've always been here, trapped, smothered, locked away. But now I'm free and I'll stop you!"

"You stop me? You are weak and pliant. You have no power over me. You..."

Omori screamed, his eyes bulging, as Jeffrey Parker struck him down.

The thing that had been Jeffrey Parker leaned back in his wheelchair, blood coursing from the gash in his neck. He held a bloody cross-bow bolt in one claw-like hand.

"Parker," Joe said as he exited the elevator. "He's slit his own throat."

"No." Kim stood up from the corpse, her legs unsteady. "It was the real Parker, finally regaining control of his mind and body. Just enough to end Omori's reign of terror for good."

"Damn."

"Tammelou?"

"Dead."

Kim leaned against Joe, suddenly weak. More than weak. Completely spent.

"Okay," Joe said. "Let's get you to a hospital."

"Joe," she murmured. "I… I think it's finally over."

Her knees buckled and she dropped into Joe's arms.

CHAPTER 41

The continuum's been restored (except, perhaps, in another time-line, a rogue reality not taken, so to speak), everyone involved seems to be back in the spacetime coordinates where they really belong, and all's right with the multiverse.

Sanctuary Elder (T'sai)

Odawara, Japan

The Veiled Years

Jade Court Era

C.E. 1542

The Gardens of Beneficent Unity

Jackson Yamaguchi stood at the base of the outdoor shrine dedicated to the sun goddess Amaterasu. It was a warm sunny day, one befitting the welcoming return of old friends. He wore what was considered casual clothing for a member of the Jade Court. A haori short jacket over a simple brown cotton kimono, his feet shod in tabi socks and zori sandals. His long dreadlocks were pulled back and tied at the nape of his neck.

To his right stretched rows of violets. To his left, sunflowers. Bees, butterflies, and numerous other pollinators flitted from blossom to blossom. A grove of pear trees lay below in this part of the gardens. Stone pathways wound to and from the grassy dune the shrine sat atop.

I never thought I'd see this again.

Though it had been three months since he'd returned to Odawara, there were times when he still didn't quite believe it. A few instances he'd woken up in the middle of the night, confused, forgetting where he was until Aimi calmed and reassured him, allowing him to return to a peaceful, if astonished, sleep.

Most people didn't get a second chance at life. Jackson had gotten three.

I hope I prove deserving of them, he thought for the thousandth time.

Then he remembered his son Rinji's joy upon seeing him for the first time after Jackson had been gone so long. After thinking his father might never return.

All right, he thought with a smile. That had definitely been worth it!

"A yen for your thoughts," a soft voice said at his side.

Jackson smiled at Shioko, the Glorious Ko, his friend and fellow adventurer in time and space. As usual, she looked every inch as glorious as her title implied. Her kimono was of a floral design, red and white in color. A kanzashi ornament in the form of a flower adorned her long hair. Her dark eyes sparkled.

"You're certain the displacement tremor will arrive here on time?" he asked. Needlessly, he knew, but he admitted to a certain nervousness about the event.

"For the twentieth time, yes." Shioko smirked. "You know I'm able to sense the tremors like Kim and Mitsu. My esper powers aren't nearly as strong as theirs but they're there."

"You ever wonder why you possess those abilities too?"

Shioko's beautiful features clouded over for a moment. "Sometimes. I… I have an idea or two."

Yoshima Mitsu was your mother, Jackson thought. Not just someone who cared for you. You inherited those powers from her. He wouldn't reveal that to Shioko yet although he suspected Izanami knew the truth of it as well. He'd wait to talk to Shioko about it later.

"See?" Shioko pointed to the top of the dune. A bright whirling dervish of a light had appeared, accompanied by a low rumble. "Right on time!"

Brewster ached in every part of his body.

But, somehow, he felt…good. Except for the large wet thing running up and down his face.

He opened his eyes to see Hiroshi the Ōkami standing over him, licking him profusely. "Hey, boy," Brewster said softly, grabbing the huge wolf's head and gently shaking it. "Glad you could join me."

He turned his head to the side. A carpet of close-cropped grass lay beneath him and Hiroshi. A tall, red maple shaded them from a cloudless, bright, sunny sky. A cool breeze washed over Brewster. He raised himself to a sitting position and took a deep breath. The air smelled so fresh and clean.

Trell, the kirin, grazed a short distance away. He shot Brewster a look. We are home, the kirin's thoughts conveyed.

Brewster sat on a rounded, grassy dune overlooking a section of beautifully landscaped gardens. The acreage stretched away on both sides of him. Directly in front, in the distance, a huge castle, a fortress out of some fantastic dream, basked in the sun.

Brewster knew that castle. Odawara-Jo. He had traveled back to feudal Japan, to the Kanto Plain region where he'd lived an adventure as the Ebon Warrior. An adventure he'd never been able to forget. He stood up, shakily, a little disoriented as his head spun. He placed a hand on Hiroshi's strong, supportive back.

And remembered.

Kim. He hoped she had understood. Somehow, he knew she had and would be fine. How his life changed after first meeting her that day in Lazo Sibulovich's Old Books and Research Haven! He'd miss her, but he knew he'd made the right decision. Both of them had. Hiroshi head-bumped his hip. No, the three of them.

Hiroshi suddenly stiffened and looked down the dune's sloping surface. Brewster followed his alert gaze.

A group of people had appeared below, walking the stone path that led to where he and the Ōkami stood. He turned and saw the hokora shrine behind him, incense burning within, despite the force of the displacement tremor. This grassy dune was a sacred spot.

The group stopped below, as if waiting. Brewster and Hiroshi walked down to meet them. As they got closer, Brewster began to recognize them. He smiled.

"Brewster-san!" Hiroshi Yoshida, the Ōkami's namesake, no longer wearing slave clothes but, instead, looking very formal, like a dignitary, came forward to meet him. He stopped, bowing. "You have returned!" Brewster realized, to his surprise, he understood every word spoken. He'd learned some Japanese from Kim and Shioko but not this much.

"Hiroshi-san," Brewster said, as if in a dream. He laughed and pointed to the Ōkami. "Hiroshi," he said. "Meet Hiroshi."

Hiroshi Yoshida held his hand out to the Ōkami, who sniffed and nuzzled it. "I am honored you would name this noble beast after me, Brewster-san." He then raised his arms and embraced Brewster. A young woman walked to Hiroshi's side, garbed royally, like a princess. She too bowed. "Brewster-san," she said. "It is an honor to have you back with us." She took hold of his hand and smiled.

"Midori-san," Brewster said, not knowing what else to do. He felt numb with amazement. He hugged her, too.

And almost fell over when Jackson Yamaguchi, dressed in Japanese garb, walked up to him. "Mr. Brewster," he said. "Long time."

Wayne laughed and pulled Jackson to him. "So this is where you ended up!"

"One of the places. It's a long, long story. Really long!" He smiled. "I have a wife and son here. They're anxious to meet you."

"A wife and son…"

"We welcome you home, great warrior." Another young woman stepped forward, familiar, but different. She wore the clothes of an ordinary citizen, but she radiated the confidence and strength of a warrior. She stood in front of Brewster and said in English, "About freaking time you showed up, Mr. Tame Wayne. The Ebon Warrior has a lot of work to do. Welcome to the Veiled Years of the Jade Court. Don't let the name fool you. We're constantly involved with mysteries and dangers of all sorts." With that, she broke into a brilliant smile and wrapped her arms around him.

Brewster felt in a daze. "Shioko. Am I dreaming?"

Shioko Yoshima, the Glorious Ko, pulled back. "If you are, then we're all having the same dream. I guess the Spirit Winds know what they're doing after all."

Brewster nodded. "About that. We have a lot to talk about."

"Including the kirin over there, I imagine." Her face darkened for a moment. "Kim?"

"She's fine. She sends her love."

"I'm glad." Shioko looked away, then back. "I'm sure you and your sidekick here are tired and hungry."

"Another understatement."

Shioko knelt and rubbed the Ōkami's head. Hiroshi looked very happy. "Let's go. Among many other things, I've got someone I want you to meet also. Her name's Izanami."

A woman stood with several horses and a single palanquin and its bearers a short distance away. Even from this far, Brewster knew this was Izanami and sensed the energy surrounding her. The energy of a Warrior of the Light.

Well, Wayne Brewster thought, reveling in the sight of the friends and comrades he thought he'd never see again. I've a hunch this life is going to be very interesting.

Ambient-Milieu

Kutumba Coulibaly stood on a rocky shelf extending over a wide valley. The Valley of Tranquil Empowerment, he had been told, one of the many levels of the ambient-milieu. The majestic, snow-capped peaks bordering both sides of the valley were called the Tiger Eye Mountains.

And, on the valley floor, the River Tentai flowed through lush green-wood and meadowland. Groves of rainbow-hued flowers called hinta blossoms shone in the sun's amber light. Towering yan trees vaulted skyward.

The residents of this tranquil, spiritual realm were the karura, strange bird-like beings dressed in a kind of armor, golden wings sprouting from their backs. They served Seiryuu, the Guardian Dragon of the East. Never had Kutumba imagined such beings! Even his farseeing had never intuited anything like them or this place.

"I wish my friend Daiyu were here to see all this," a voice at his side said.

Kutumba turned to his newfound comrade, Lorenzo Portero. Though he and Lorenzo hailed from different parts of the world and different time periods, here, in this magical place, they could understand each other perfectly no matter what language they spoke. "And I, my master."

Appearing in front of them, the Sanctuary Elder glimmered like a giant firefly. "You boys ready to start?" the voice intoned.

"Yes!" Kutumba and Lorenzo replied enthusiastically.

"Good. You'll be staying in the, uh, guest house on the other side of the valley. Really nice digs. Great view. You know, location, location, location."

Lorenzo leaned in close to Kutumba. "Do you find the Elder's choice of words rather…interesting?"

Kutumba smiled. "That is one way of putting it, yes."

The Elder continued. "You'll have everything you need there."

"Including coffee?" Lorenzo asked hopefully.

"Absolutely! The good stuff, not decaf or instant or that flavored crap. And now, how about you meet the third member of your team. Her incredible experiences will help lend the book much of its value, its power, and its conviction, as she takes on the part of Yira."

"Wonderful," Lorenzo said.

"Thank you, noble Elder," Kutumba said.

"The karura Renta'Mur will escort you to the house shortly. If you need anything, just call. I'm in the book." With that the spectral being vanished.

"I bid you greetings, noble sirs."

Kutumba and Lorenzo turned around. A Japanese woman stood before them. Beautiful, ageless, dressed in a blue kimono and obi. Her dark hair tumbled down her back. Her fathomless eyes shone.

"I am Yoshima Mitsu and am honored to be working with two such talented and wondrous individuals," she said.

"And we you," Kutumba replied, awestruck.

"Wondrous indeed," Lorenzo whispered.

"So!" Yoshima Mitsu softly clapped her hands. "Shall we begin?"

CHAPTER 42

When people say, "There's a reason for that," or "It was meant to be,"
they haven't read Jenny's book. Which would make
a helluva Guillermo del Toro movie.

Kim Yoshima

The Void

I'm whole again.

Kim's reintegration of her multiple, simultaneous, bilocated, super-positioned selves had been successful. Although she was certain a'Kasha and/or Jenny had helped her with that.

Her leg wound had healed too. Dr. Daiyu had fixed that. Magically, of course.

Kim had convinced Daiyu and Antonio Calabria to accompany her back to Pittsburgh for a little R&R. Goddess knew they all needed it! They had agreed, neither having been to the U.S. before. Some diversion would, hopefully, help with the healing process of their losses. She hoped she could get them to talk to Mara Gellini

Now, dressed in regular jeans, sneakers and T-shirt, Kim tried to prepare herself for what she knew would be a tough goodbye. She stood in the Void library chamber she'd been in before with a'Kasha. Like then, the whole setting was dreamlike, fantastic, otherworldly.

"Kim," Lazo said, walking out from between two of the bookstacks, completely ruining Kim's image. "I've been thinkin'."

"Alert the media."

"Ha! Seriously, you realized Yoshima Mitsu was your ancestor, your first incarnation. But she died young, she didn't have any children, right? How can she be an ancestor of yours?"

Kim tapped her lip in thought. For some reason, she really hadn't thought of that. "Well, we really don't know if Mitsu had children or not. I suspect the shirabyoshi community frowned on their members getting pregnant, although I'm sure some did."

"Yet they had attendants, like Shioko, their 'little sisters'."

"Sure, that was part of their hierarchy." Kim glanced sharply at Lazo, his lips pursed, his arms folded across his broad chest. One of the floating light spheres hovered nearby. "Are you implying...?"

"Shioko is Mitsu's daughter. That would explain the ancestral connection."

"Oh, I don't know, Laz. That's a little bit of a stretch, don't you think?"

"Not necessarily. Mitsu gives birth, the father being a client of hers, and hides the existence of her daughter until Shioko's older and can become part of the shirabyoshi community. This way Mitsu can keep an eye on her, blah, blah."

"Maybe, maybe. But why didn't Mitsu tell me this? I've spoken to her in the ambient-milieu. She never mentioned it."

"Well, maybe because she's you and you're her and that means…"

"I'm Shioko's mother, five hundred times removed, which really complicates things! Except…" Kim held up a finger. "I don't think Mitsu's having any children soon. Or did. Or ever will. Well, you know. Explain that."

"She must have. Remember, she was with Izanami who wasn't exactly without certain ways of doin' certain things."

"You're so articulate." She looked at her old and dear friend and, noticing a slight twitch of his lips, began to laugh. Lazo joined in.

"Aren't you glad I'm around to sort this shit out for you?" he gasped between guffaws.

"What would I do without you? You'll make a great assistant archivist." At those words, the present slammed back into Kim. She sobered quickly and threw her arms around her friend's neck. He, in turn, enfolded Kim in a huge bear hug.

"I'm going to miss you, Laz," she said. "You and Jenny have been my friends and support for so long."

"And now you've got new friends to help you with that." The big man gently held Kim at arms' length. "I'm gonna miss you too, but, again, this isn't for forever and I figure Jenny and me will be in touch with you from time to time. In some form or another. We'll be back when our assignment in the Void's over."

"I know. It's going to be tough explaining your, uh, absence, though." Both Jenny and Lazo's parents were dead. Jenny had a brother with whom she was estranged and Lazo had no surviving siblings. Funny, he'd been the policeman involved in dangerous situations but had always been the survivor. But they both had a lot of friends and working colleagues. What would Kim tell them?

"Yeah, about that." Jenny appeared, her body surrounded by a shimmering aura of blue light. "That's all been taken care of, Kim. As the new Void, there are certain things I can arrange. No one will miss us. Trust me. No explanations will be necessary."

"You look good in shiny blue, girl," Kim said. She held out her arms. "Can I...?"

"You bet." Jenny and Kim hugged. Kim felt a tingle, like a mild electrical charge, emanating from Jenny.

"Take care, Kim," Jenny said, placing a hand on Kim's cheek. "Like Lazo said, you haven't seen the last of us. We'll be back."

"The multiverse is in good hands with you two." Tears sprang to Kim's eyes as Jenny took Lazo's hands in hers. The same blue aura flickered around Lazo's beefy form. They turned, looked one last time at Kim, and then simply weren't there anymore.

Kim reappeared back in Venice, blinking in the bright sunlight on St. Mark's Square. Despite the tears running down her face, she smiled.

Pittsburgh, PA

C.E. 2012

"Hey, look, Aunt Kim! Can we stop here just for a minute?"

Kim Yoshima smiled. Now that Ken and Marjorie had lifted their embargo on Kim being with her nephew, her and Bobby's relationship basically picked up where it left off. "Okay, Bobby," she agreed. "But just for a minute. Your mom and dad are expecting us for supper."

The sidewalk newsstand included a comic book section which Bobby ran to like a heat-seeking missile. Kim looked on, keeping her nephew in sight. If Bobby only knew his aunt bought a couple of those yesterday herself, she thought. I had to see if ArcNight made it back.

She watched a few other kids buy some comic books, shelling out several dollars for each. I remember when they were a dime, Kim thought. Who would have thought they were real? Real in another reality, that is.

The equilibrium, the anomaly, the Balance, entropy, was restored when Jenny took over. She closed her eyes, thinking of the great sacrifice Jenny and Lazo had made. Her friends were the real super heroes. The sad part was only a few would know what they did. She smiled as an idea struck her. It would make a good comic book adventure!

She noticed Bobby standing to one side of the newsstand, looking thoughtfully at three comic books he'd bought.

"What do you have there, kiddo?" Kim asked as she joined him. She ruffled her nephew's hair upon seeing the title of the topmost comic.

It's him, she thought. ArcNight. It's his book, his life, all done up in primary colors every month for the world to see.

And another…

FireDragon, Kim thought. They've brought him back. So he survived Orcus' attack. Good!

"What's this last one?" Kim asked.

Bobby held the cover up. "It's a new one," he said. "Forensic Detective."

Kim smiled.

Dartham City

Wayne Brewster, aka ArcNight, the Dark Avenger, stood on the building rooftop. He looked out over his city, glowing like an old friend in the night. The rushing blare of traffic, the sounds of pedestrians even at this late hour, the thousands of lights that glimmered like stars. It felt good to be home again.

Everything's back the way it was, he thought in wonder. The meta-physical loose ends have been rewoven and all's right with the worlds. He chuckled to himself. We'll have some stories to swap at the next Meta-Heroes' meeting, that's for certain.

He turned his intent gaze to an apartment building across from and below the parapet on which he stood. The middle apartment, seventh floor.

Her double. The alternate Kim Yoshima in this world who Brewster met. Whom I've read about in the arts section of the newspaper. She was a poet, a writer. He watched the apartment balcony, the lights from within indicating she was home for the evening.

He sighed. I can't get involved. There's no way. I would break my own cardinal rule. My life is too taken up with my work and my mission. It wouldn't be fair to either of us.

But heroes get lonely too.

Making his decision, ArcNight swung off the parapet and melted into the night.

EPILOGUE

Shuugouteki Compound - Spirit Winds, Inc.

Somewhere outside of Pittsburgh

Session Transcript #12, August 2012
Patient Kim Yoshima

Mara Gellini, Counselor

"**W**ell! Let's get back to you, Kim, shall we? It's been a couple of months since I last saw you. That was when you were recuperating at the Spirit Winds clinic after the Void affair. How are you feeling?"

"Good. Better. It was tough after Wayne and Jenny and Lazo left, but with you and Joe and Daiyu helping me, things are finally coming together."

"I suspect volunteering at the Fukushima Daiichi Reactor cleanup was cathartic."

"Was it ever! Talk about putting things in perspective. I'm glad David Amamoto and his wife Lu were there with me."

"I understand he's going to Lordsburg, New Mexico to see where the internment camp was located where his grandparents had been held."

"Right. He's always wanted to do that but was too angry and conflicted. Now he feels the time is right."

"Good for him. What about your esper abilities?"

"They're still there but greatly reduced, mainly relegated to some telepathy and telekinesis. All the other stuff, the psi-stuns and esper-sight, and bubbles, and Spirit Wind sensing, don't work anymore, which is fine with me. I don't feel like a super hero anymore. I don't need or want to. After Odawara, when I thought I'd lost those abilities completely, I felt I'd become addicted to them, that I needed them. I realize now the role I had to assume in this crazy cosmic adventure wasn't over then. Now it is. Finally."

"I sense you're at peace."

"Yes, that's it. It's a great feeling. Especially now Lazo and Jenny are back. Jenny's writing a book about her stint as the keeper of the Akashic Records, you know. It'll be categorized as fiction though."

"Good idea. The world isn't ready for that information."

"But, well, I've been thinking…"

"What?"

"I've been thinking of starting my own agency. I still feel I have some work to do, some good I can contribute."

"Ah, interesting. And healthy. What kind of agency?"

"Private investigation. One that takes on different, unusual cases I can use my telepathic abilities to help with."

"Like the X-Files."

"Yeah, I suppose, but I'll be working for myself."

"The Kim Yoshima Detective Agency?"

"No, I have another idea for a name. And I'll have a staff. A very special one."

***

Pittsburgh, PA

C.E. 2018

Old Books and Research Haven

"**W**elcome to the Book Haven," Jenny Sibulovich said with a smile. "What can I help with you today?"

The woman who'd approached the main Book Haven counter blinked in surprise. Mrs. Sibulovich had the most startling eyes. Mostly blue but gold motes were visible, floating and whirling softly.

My god, is she an alien too? The woman hid her discomfort by hurriedly checking her cell phone notes. "I have an appointment with, uh, Kim Yoshima."

"Of course," Jenny said, then turned around. "Lazo, honey, can you escort the lady to Kim's and Daiyu's offices, please?"

"Sure," a deep male voice answered. A very large but jovial-looking man emerged from an office behind the counter. "Hi," he said. "I'm Lazo. This way, please."

He had the same kind of eyes as his wife. "Tha…thank you."

He led her down a wide, carpeted hallway, its walls adorned with framed photographs and artwork. They passed a couple of what signs above the doors referred to as, "reading rooms" until Mr. Sibulovich stopped in front of an office door at the end of the hallway.

The plaque to the side of the door read:

The Luminous Detective/Psychic Consultation Agency

Kim Yoshima and Daiyu of the East
We Work in Ways to Solve the Mysterious

He opened the door, entered the office, and held the door for her. Upon entering, two black kittens darted past her and ran out into the hallway. An adult cat, white with gray paw, ear, and tail points, lay curled up asleep on one of the cushioned waiting room chairs.

"That's Alara," Mr. Sibulovich said, indicating the snoozing feline. "One of our library cats. They've got the run of the place. One moment." He knocked on a second door.

"I**ncoming," Joe reported over the desk intercom from his security office.

Kim looked at her laptop calendar. "Yes," she said to Joe through the intercom. "That's my two o'clock."

"Kim." Daiyu stuck her head out of her adjoining office. "I am going to order some sushi from Devi's. Do you want anything? You have not eaten lunch yet either."

"Hmmm, I am hungry, now that you mention it. Can you order me some black bean chicken, please?"

"I will. Oh, by the way, I heard from Antonio earlier. He sends his regards."

"How's the monster-hunting business?"

"Well, as we thought, there are still real monsters out there, many of them human. They're keeping Antonio and his staff busy." She ducked back into her office.

Kim stood up and briefly checked her look in the large mirror hanging over her bookcase. Not bad, she thought. Despite being forty-nine years old and having gone through more age-inducing experiences than any five people, she was still in pretty good shape. She'd been keeping up with her aikido, Tai Chi, meditation, and regular counseling sessions with Mara Gellini. Her relationship with Joe Martin was stronger than ever, as were those with her brother and sister-in-law.

She and Daiyu had succeeded at their specialized investigation business beyond any of their expectations. Life was good. And definitely not boring.

She wore a pair of jeans and a silk shirt, her gray hair cut short again. Her nephew Bobby, now majoring in forensic sciences at West Virginia University, had suggested Kim dye her hair purple or green like a lot of women had been doing these days. Kim preferred the natural (or unnatural) look. She'd be turning fifty next year, after all, and needed to maintain some dignity. Plus, Joe had given her a look upon hearing Bobby's suggestion. It implied Kim could do what she wanted but since he and Kim had been involved for several years now, he felt he had some say in the matter.

She decided to give Joe this one.

Speaking of Bobby, Kim remembered tomorrow was the day she'd have to tell him about her materializing in his dorm room—her future but his present. How Bobby and his girlfriend Marlene would save her life.

No pressure there, Kim thought, though Bobby was used to the numinous, spectral, magical world of her aunt. Especially since he'd assisted her on a couple of her recent investigations. As a result, he'd decided to go into forensics as a career.

She sat back down, glancing at her black cat Hideo, aka Jaraal, cleaning himself atop a wall shelf placed there just for him. And for the komainu statue sitting next to him, the one with the chipped ear. Hideo paused long enough in his bathing to cast Kim an enigmatic feline eye. His head darted to his left. A rapping sounded on Kim's office door.

"Come in," Kim said.

"Excuse me, Kim," Lazo said, opening the door. "Someone here for an appointment."

"Thanks, Laz. Send her in, will you?"

Kim stood up and shook the woman's hand. "Please have a seat, Ms. Taccario. Would you like some coffee or tea?"

"No…no, thank you." Katherine Taccario was an attractive thirty-something, dressed in a crisp green business suit and high heels. She kept her small purse in her lap, giving Kim a tentative smile. Most of Kim's first-time clients always seemed nervous at their initial visit. Or foolish.

"Now," Kim said. "What can I do for you?"

Ms. Taccario fidgeted for a second. "Um. I understand you investigate, uh, unusual cases? Ones other agencies won't take?"

"Yes, although unusual is a relative term."

A nervous laugh. "Well, this may sound rather mundane, but someone's been following me."

Kim contacted Joe. "Anything on surveillance out there, Joe. Any lurkers?"

"No," Joe replied with just a slight pause. Kim knew he was thinking of the bat-creature persona of the djinn he'd picked up on-camera a million years ago. She, in turn, remembered the attack on the book

haven by the shadow-tracker and the attempt on her life here by the serpent-like nagas. Old memories died hard. Especially in the place they'd been made, no matter how much time had passed. "Nothing, Kim. All clear."

"Thanks." Kim arched an inquisitive eyebrow at Ms. Taccario. "Have you gone to the police about this?"

"No, uh, you see, I think this...person following me is an, um, an extraterrestrial. I know that sounds ridiculous..."

"Ah." Kim glanced at Hideo, who suddenly stopped his bath and became all-ears. His mate, Alara, and their kittens darted through a cat door in Kim's office door, sat down on the carpet, and stared intently. The komainu statue looked to have shifted ever so slightly in Kim's direction. Daiyu walked out of her office, a slight smile on her lips, lunch evidently forgotten.

"Not ridiculous at all," Kim said, a familiar excitement and anticipation growing. "In fact, I think we can help you with that. Please, tell me more."